This is a work of fiction. Names, characters, businesses, places, events and incidents are either the products of the author's imagination or used in a fictitious manner. Any resemblance to actual persons, living or dead, or actual events is purely coincidental …

I0672040

Enjoy ∎

Part I

The City

The Preferred

The young watched the 130mm barrel come to a stop, hovering perpendicular to the front end of the tank's body. A handcuffed man stood under the shadow of the barrel taking muffled breaths through a potato sack that had been shoved over his head.

Two muscular City Guardsmen stood on either side of the captive. Their uniforms owned crisp gray lines; the medals on their chests sparkled under the lone floodlight fifty feet above.

The five figures stood in the middle of the city's lush green track field. A huge red and gold flag for the coming Phoenix Cycle hung at the south end of the field. The flag was flanked by the two crescent-shaped stands where the formally suited Phoenix Cycler boys and the lavishly dressed Phoenix Cycler girls sat.

"To the potato lovers of Ireland, and the dress-wearing Celts, your mothers and fathers did not earn their place in this city! And neither have you!" Line roared through an old-fashioned wired microphone. His finger pointed over the crowd as the lights illuminating him reflected on his sunglasses, and the tailored suit that covered his black and gold-lined priest's garb. All eyes turned to the man standing in the center row of the center booth on the north end of the concrete stands.

"But nonetheless, even after today's riot, inspired by that Irish sense of entitlement, The General has invited you here today! We have invited only the best from every corner of New San Francisco. No matter how pathetic their roots may be. Whether you come from a well-to-do family or find shelter in an orphanage in Edingburg, you were invited because you are the best! Whether you went to the best prep schools or received an education in Hell's kitchen, you were invited for being the best! Whether you were born with a copper spoon in your mouth or with no spoon at all, we have been observing you. We have been watching you grow and mature to this very day, and no matter where you started, you are here now because you *became* the very best of the 30,000 members of your Phoenix Cycler generation! And we want to be sure that it is YOU, the BEST, who shall RISE!"

The crowd applauded, loving the idea of themselves.

"And now here we are! Mere days away from making the climactic choice that could determine the value of your life! If and when you choose to apply in the coming days you will not only be choosing to pursue YOUR OWN rise, but to also be raising our greater unity! YOU are being given something, that for most of you, will be your once in a lifetime chance to join the Inner Circle, the one uniting force that has ensured that this city! Our city! Continues to rage against this all but extinguished planet! Where you come from will be forgotten! The sins of your fathers and mothers, washed away from your lineage. And for you Irish, your red hair will be turned to gold!"

Every wrist in the stadium beeped. Every boy and girl glanced down at the face of their watch. "00:10" then ":09" then ":08." Everyone turned their heads to the west. There it was. Right on time, as always. The nightly storm. A wall of blackness had lurched up into the sky, swallowing the setting sun.

The hairs on Steve's neck stood up, urging him to get the hell out of there. Instead he grabbed Leslie's hand, who sat quietly quivering next to him, instinctively pressing her bow into her head for comfort. Steve knew her shaking wasn't coming from Line's yelling, the storm, or even the tank pointing at them. Her quivers never came from the barrel of a gun, no, the ragging agony she held within her was the very same thing that pushed him back into the sheets when the sun finally rose—are we going to lose each other?

Leslie's mind pushed the feeling away for at least another moment. "It'll be all right," she whispered. Her brown eyes guided him to the dozens of mortar tubes pointing upward and outward on the vibrant green field and then to the perfect line of churning ash that approached the stands.

"Unity can only be achieved and be maintained when it is the STRONG who come together and fly under one flag! We, like no other in the world, have created a unity that has never broken, has never FLINCHED! When the rest of the world saw THAT—" Line's long arm pointed at the coming avalanche of black— "They all fell to pieces!"

The earth began to quake as the wall rose over them. Someone screamed. The mortars on the field fired as one at the roiling sky.

The blackness spilled over the stadium, then slid over the perimeter of the frizzing wall of static that had encapsulated the field. No Phoenix Cycler had seen—only heard rumors from past Cycle Pref parties—this blackness that was sliding over and them whispering their deaths. The Phoenix Cycle flag began to flutter as free elements squeezed through the static seal.

"This world used to allow weakness. It could afford pity on a scale that even allowed the weak to poison the strong. A world that allowed the mindless, the ambitionless a say in a world they only leached off! But no longer. The world decided to give us nothing more. So we followed in step and built the mighty walls that now protect our city from weakness."

Line looked around the stands. Even through his sunglasses, the cyclers could see the fire beaming from his eyes. "Every other city, every country, on every continent in the world refused to accept that the strong could no longer hold the weight of the weak! That is why—excluding you redheads—your parents sacrificed everything in order to earn their ticket here!"

Snare drums began to rattle. The Phoenix marching band had formed in three rows at the east end of the track to face the tank. It was still turned, its barrel pointing away from them. Behind them stood a golden goblet taller than a man and carved in stone. Each band member wore a red jacket with golden stitching, true to the Phoenix Cycle color palette.

One of City Guardsman standing beside the bagged man threw a long rope up and over the tank's long barrel. He knotted the rope around the barrel with quick precision and then began fastening a noose around the bagged man's neck.

Leslie pressed her face into Steve's arm. "Why do they have to do this now?" she whimpered. Steve looked down at her layered brown hair. She wasn't a real "Berger." Her parents didn't come in on a boat from Old

Edinburgh, Scotland. But she found a way to care about the like all the same. Steve lowered his head onto hers, strands of his crimson lock intertwined with her brunette.

"Our founding fathers executed the plan that promised to bring us upward!" Line shouted. "And to keep to that plan we must execute the people who threaten to hold us down!"

With a mechanical whine from the tank its barrel crept upward, tightening the rope around the bagged man's neck. His feet began to balance on his toes.

"This is one of the ringleaders of today's act of terrorism!" Line thundered. "An instigator of a needless riot that led to pointless loss of life! Now, terrorist, make your final plea."

A guardsman held a microphone up to the bag. The snare drums stopped beating.

A thick Irish accent came through the loose fibers of the bag. "Is dat you, Line? Is dat the bloke from the morning radio makin' all dat fuss? Ya sound like ya got a bigga bug oop ya ass in person. Didn't think it possible."

A few chuckles trickled through the stands.

The bagged man unbuttoned the top of his brown wool shirt. "Ya know, it's funny. How one o' ya demons from the deepest part of hell be lifting ME up!" he said, gesturing toward the tank. "Makes me wonder what direction up is anyma."

His bagged face panned across the crowds of children. "Don't listen to 'em, lads! Ya still young. Ya haven't been hypnatized yet! They aren't our leadas! The Inner Circle's our occupiahs! Yah, they're uniting us, but they're uniting us against ourselves! So do as they say and unite, lads! But not unda them! Join the IRA. Don't let 'em tell ya what way is oop!"

"Well, allow us to show you," Line said. He twirled his hand. The tank's barrel rose higher, and the man's feet began to dangle in the air.

Leslie clutched Steve's arm as the man grunted and choked in the only bubble of truly breathable air in the city. The guardsmen stuck a pair of wires leading from a speaker to the hanging man's chest. The beats of his heart pumped into the ears of every spectator.

The beats slowed, then palpitated before ceasing altogether. The guardsman removed the wires. The tank and man were left alone in the middle of the beautiful green field, bathed in the glare of the single floodlight, an image that everyone in the stands would hold onto forever. Steve looked up at the storm pounding at the static bubble above them, still doing its damnedest to punch through the veil and drown them all in ash. His entire life this storm had come in to bombard this city. But he could never tell if it came to wipe out the "weakness" of his own people or the fiery hatred that spat from Line's mouth. Maybe both.

Line began again, speaking more slowly. "There is only one evil: that which seeks to end our city. Our survival is our paradise; our hell will come with our demise. It will come on the day we are too weak to hold back the storm. And so we REFUSE to be buried." Line pointed up to the storm. "Every day we must grow taller because every day the ash piles higher. And so if a man comes to stop our rise, then we will use his very body to elevate us to the next day. We do not have the luxury of pity. We do not have the time for delicacy of debate. We can not afford to lose our focus because this storm never will."

The furrows on Line's forehead smoothed. He leaned back from the microphone. "There can be more to life than survival. There can be an actual life. For many. We have passed the days where death knocks and enters into our homes every night. Through our unity and iron will we have carved out an existence that allows us to attain our full capacities. So we have invited you here today to give you a taste of just that. We have put the clothes on your back for this one night, to help you understand what could be, what you could experience for the rest of your lives if you just work for it. Tonight you are doing more than being thankful to breathe in clean air—allow yourselves to breathe in life!"

The stadium lights dimmed, and an electronic beat began to grow. It came from a man standing in front of a soundboard under the flapping Phoenix Cycle flag.

The spectators in the stands stirred uneasily at the jarring change of tone. Ten men and women holding up red and gold–ringed batons sprinted out from behind the DJ booth and down each side of the stadium. Batons twirled upward and fireworks exploded into concussions of red trailing golden flakes. One of the male baton twirlers scrambled up the tank and began to slowly turn, gesturing at each section of the stands with a five-foot-long red baton. He was the only one wearing a military uniform and a helmet. He crouched on top of the tank's turret and the beats of the DJ grew louder and more intense. The man pointed his baton at the large goblet sculpture at the other end of the field.

"Are you ready!" Line shouted into the microphone. The lights shut off, and only the storm swirling above them was visible.

The man on the tank pulled a trigger on his baton. A rocket with a swirling gold tail fired out and exploded over the goblet. The rim of the goblet burst into flame, showering the stadium in light. Steve felt the heat press into his face. The music roared louder.

People in the crowd cheered. The baton wielders beckoned them down to the field. The stadium lights reignited with their full force and pulsed to the beat of the music. Trickles, then floods of Phoenix Cyclers began climbing down from the stands.

"Enjoy this night!" Line shouted. "For those who choose to take the Inner Circle's test, this is only the beginning! If you choose otherwise, then savor your one single night when you can truly be human!"

My ... Diary?
Journal Entry #3

I guess I should make something clear to you. I know this diary isn't personal, and I'd hate to ruin your reading experience, you lying piece of shit.

With the passage of time people come and people go. That I can deal with; it's the people that never came at all who continue to pack the growing bags beneath my eyes.

Part of me is sorry. Another enraged. I have so many years left that it seems like I'll never run out of them. But somehow, on that single day, I lost an entire lifetime. And no matter what I do, I can never get it back.

I just want you to know. I blame myself for not stopping you. For not putting you in this cage instead the other way round. But at this point it really doesn't matter who enchains whom. It doesn't matter that you're the master now and I'm the slave. We're both miserable and nothing we do to each other can ever change that. This fight we're having, this hatred for you that still keeps me warm at night, it's all just a distraction from the fact that we both failed to sculpt this world into something resembling the beautiful.

For now I think it's best I tell our story. Perhaps once I tell it to ourselves, we will finally receive from our actions what our soul really wanted: transcendence. Don't scoff; allow me this final ember of hope.

This next part is the only truth I've found from what we've done to each other and to our world. It is important to remember it always.

I am not made of one, I am made of many.

Each and every person is made up of many smaller people. Everyone has a saint. Everyone has a lover. Everyone has a sinner. Everyone has a monster.

What defines us is not what people we have within us, but which people we develop most and how great those people become.

The Preferred, Part 2

Steve and Leslie were one of the few still sitting in the stands. On the field below, the dancing mob continued to grow as it was fed by their fellow chosen Phoenix Cyclers.

"Why did you insist on coming to this?" Leslie asked, looking up at Steve with glassy eyes. "Are you thinking of changing your mind? Are you thinking of applying?"

Steve looked at her carefully before answering. She had never looked so beautiful. A platoon of stylists and tailors had spent hours before the event to make sure that all of the chosen looked stunning. Leslie's long brown hair had been brushed and curled into a style fit for a royal portrait. Her blue silk dress wrapped her body with precision.

Steve gripped her hand. "That is the one thing you never have to worry about. We've been through too much to just let go of one another now. Without you, who would I be? Having a bunch of medals on my chest wouldn't legitimize me. But having you around my arm does." Steve smiled with a wink.

"You don't need medals or me for that," Leslie said. She looked down at her dress, quietly smiling. "Tell me? Why am I here in this dress tonight? You know I don't need these things."

Steve hesitated. Reluctantly, he pointed at the dead man hanging from the tank barrel. "Him."

"What?"

"Aside from him, I'm the only one who made it out of the protest. That so-called terrorist act that Line just shat on."

"You went! You said you wouldn't! What if you—"

"Shhh, honey. You knew exactly where I'd be. You know now more than ever that we have to be heard. Things just keep getting worse."

"Well, I didn't want to know. How did you even …" Leslie shuddered, remembering the haze of nights Steve had come back home late, bringing with him another stray Irishman from the street. "He's part of the cause," he'd always say. His eyes locked onto hers. "He's a good man, the only bad part is he hasn't a roof over his head. Kleiner's finding him one, should only be a night or two until he gets him one."

"Everyone else died?" Leslie asked.

"I organized all the cyclers I could from my end. Irish strays, even natives came out. We figured we'd finally had enough people to make a dent." He looked out over the mob of dancing people. "Before we marched Haadin gave a speech. It was good. So good it could inspire the whole city to wake the hell up. So me and Conor—" his eyes drifted to the dangling body— "we taped the speech with a recorder. People need to hear it before the application process begins, so they can hear what those bastards are killing us for saying."

"Could anyone identify you?"

Steve needed a moment to click into how her question was even relevant. But her big glassy eyes and brown hair reminded him. She was in love with him, not the movement; as much as she supported the concept of it all, without Steve her involvement with the IRA would have never stretched further than listening to the news headlines of what they'd done next.

"Not sure. They haven't yet." Steve squeezed her hand. "Best not to worry unless they start looking. And now I've got to get that tape."

Leslie's eyes widened. "No! You're going to get yourself killed!"

"I'm sorry, but I have to see whether he has it. Otherwise … all of that was for nothing."

Steve's knee was bobbing vigorously against the bleacher. Leslie put her hand on his thigh to soothe his nervous tick.

"I can't do that to them. I pushed many of them into that shit. Stopping now would just be." Steve struggled to breathe. "Stopping now would be like me killing them. I didn't shoot them, but I told them to line up in front of the firing squad!"

"Leslie!" A short and frontally built girl was waving to them from the field. "Get down here, girl! You can't waste this night with him!"

Leslie put on a pleasant face in order to smile back at her and wave. "Honey. I really want to feel for you right now, I do." Leslie didn't stop looking at the girl 30 feet away smiling at her. "But you brought us to a party where nearly everyone wants to apply and fight IRA members in order to get a badge or promotion. And so unless you want to be strung up on that tank barrel too, I really suggest you kiss me and start acting civil." Leslie stood up, her eyes fixed on Steve, still trying to beat down the wall of decision he had built around himself. She held out her hand and they walked down to the field together.

"We're coming, Bridget," Leslie said. Bridget was wearing her own rented dress, a little black number that complimented her large bust, and golden flowers were woven into her blond hair. She grabbed Leslie's arm and sucked the couple into the mosh pit.

"We gotta take a pic next to that tank!"

I'm not going near that thing!" Leslie shouted over the music. She yanked her wrist free and looked at Steve. He nodded his head to follow her friend.

Leslie grudgingly extended her hand back to Bridget, whose short body had already been nearly walled off by the jungle of grinding bodies. With a smile, Bridget grabbed Leslie's hand and dragged her along in her wake.

There was an unmarked but palpable no man's land surrounding the tank. Bridget twisted the face of her watch, stretching it out from the band it was connected to by a thin metal coil. She tossed the watch face into the air, and the gyro inside felt the sudden drop and pulsed an electric frequency into the coil, stiffening it and holding the watch face two feet above Bridget's wrist.

Bridget wrapped her free arm around Leslie and posed for their picture. "Smile! We need a good pic for this!" Leslie fastened a smile onto her face as Steve walked steadily into the empty grass around the tank, staring up at Conor's dangling body.

Bridget snapped her index finger and the watch head took their photo. Then she flicked her wrist to the side and the watch dropped down and spun around her wrist until it tightened. "Soo cute! That's getting posted!"

"Don't," Leslie said.

"But we *need* a good pic! You know I'm applying for the test! I need as many likes as I can get! Please!"

Leslie shook her head.

Bridget smirked. She looked down at the photo, studying it. "We look hot. Like really, really hot." She glanced up at Leslie and observed the perfect symmetry of her friend's face. Then she tapped her watch, instantly posting the photo for the world to see.

"Bridget!"

"What? Everyone here's posting hundreds of pics from tonight. All of them racking up mad juice. And I could use the boost before App day. You know Inner Circle boys read the feeds from events like this! You'll just be in one! I know you're foo-fooing the test, but come on! God!" Bridget looked down at the pic and smiled. "I mean honestly, you are like the hottest chica ever. You'd definitely pass the application phase if you took it."

"Just shut up," Leslie said with a strained smile. Bridget smiled back and started to dance, flaunting her lack of remorse to the beat pulsing through them.

Steve looked up at Conor's body, which was constantly changing colors as it reflected the strobes and all other forms of lights pulsing and spinning over the field. Steve's right hand began to shake, and he tightened it into a fist. With a steady expression, he scanned the crowd surrounding him. No one seemed to be looking at him too closely.

He looked back up and saw a faint arrow drawn underneath the button Connor had unfastened while he spoke. It pointed up to his head. Steve stared at the bag. A green four-leaf clover was painted on it. Above the clover read KLEINER'S KEEP; below was the tagline YOUR MOM'S FAVORITE POTATO BAR.

Steve stared until he noticed something else—a flat piece of black twine. The tape! He'd somehow hid it in the potato bag!

He took one last uneasy look at the crowd, then took a few steps closer to Conor. His mind was churning, trying to find a way to get that potato sack off Conor's head. He jumped, reaching up for the bag. The floodlight lamp filled his eyes, blinding him.

Too high. Stupid. How was that ever going to work? Conor's head was a good 12 feet off the ground. Steve looked back down, blinking at spots swirling in his eyes. When he looked up he saw that dozens of cyclers had stopped to stare at him. He felt a jolt of panic but he kept his face remained still. Then he had a thought and smiled. He ran over and grabbed the arm of the biggest man in crowd.

"Come on, Hank!" Steve shouted. Hank didn't budge. Steve pushed him as best he could to the tank barrel. "Bend down." Hank looked around at the crowd that was slowly beginning to point its full attention toward them.

"Dude, come on!" Steve pointed up to the bag. "Let's get it!" Hank looked up at the bag. Now he understood. A smirk grew on his face.

"Boost me up, man! It'll be epic!" Hank obliged and jolted Steve up to a sitting position on his shoulders. Hank walked toward Conor, and Steve reached out for the bag, smiling wildly for the crowd. Some began to cheer. Not because they loved the idea of messing with a dead body, but that someone was finally willing to poke fun at the spectacle that had left them in a state of joyous distress. The kind of joy where the outside senses are driven into a furor but your mind doubts your every action and your soul cries no matter your choice.

Steve grabbed the potato sack and lifted it up by the base, making sure to keep the tape from tumbling out. Conor's long red hair draped over his bulging eyes. The crowd went silent. Life was cheap in Edingburg, and they were accustomed to waking up and seeing corpses in the streets. But those deaths were always caused by the aggression of the elements, not from the fervor of their fellow men. The IRA had been making a huge push recently and the Inner Circle was definitely pushing back. No one was sure how to align themselves. All they knew was that staying in between didn't seem to be working out.

Hank took a couple of steps back and turned around. Steve held up the potato bag for the crowd to see and began to jolt it up and down. Then he shouted the motto they'd all grown up on: "The Best Shall Rise!"

The crowd roared, accepting the reaffirmation of the Inner Circle's motto as their conformation, the choice they were all being forced to soon voluntarily make.

From his position on the north stands, Line smiled. He signaled at a City Guardsman to take off the bead his scope had on Steve's head. "Boy's with us. Good choice, kid."

Walls

Journal Entry #138

I was about 16 when the walls started going up, both around me and the entire city as well. It was getting worse, more dangerous every day. But the danger didn't come from outside of the walls; it came from within.

Before then it was simple. Survive the night, breathe between gusts, stay together, and wait for sunrise.

To this day I wonder why the walls went up. I guess the answer lies right beside me, but I still wonder. There was nothing out there that could attack us. Everything was long dead. The walls didn't even come up in the beginning, when we were most vulnerable. They went up after years of pushing, drudgery, and warped hope. They came when we'd finally made a world no longer buried by ash. They came when the decision between life and death was no longer a daily contemplation.

They went up when we had lives that were no longer shackled to the whims of the unrelenting elements. The walls went up when we could live for more, when we finally had to face the full capacity of ourselves. As it turns out, some had more capacity than others. The walls allowed some to flourish and allowed the others to rot. It was the time of decision. It was time to define ourselves as something they called "civil."

That's when the walls went up. Right after we heard that word, the ash found itself back into our lungs.

Tape and Tubes

Steve turned on the camera lights on his work cufflink and pointed them at a man-sized blinking red tube numbered 869. "Crap," he said, looking around the mess of corroded tubes that he'd had to struggle past just to get to number 869.

He had accepted his morning gig from the online list that the city and business owners posted to meet their daily needs. Given that Steve had no scalable skills or social standing, he generally had to accept the worst sorts of manual work. But he'd gained a fair number of five-star ratings and unlocked a better clearance level, one that enabled him to bid on the better jobs that involved more touchy cargo.

He'd chosen a gig in the Tenderloin District. That way he could pass one of their many old electronic "junk" shops with an excuse if he was stopped by the City Guard. Outsiders weren't welcome in the Tenderloin—Tube Town, as people called it, a neighborhood of cracked streets, shattered windows, and crumbling brick buildings where junkies pissed their lives away in the virtual "reality"–making tubes—but sifting through their trash he'd found what he needed to make the cassette playable again.

Steve began unhooking Tube 869 from the dozens of wires that attached it to the wall and the surrounding tubes. He held his breath as he disconnected the green sewage pipe running from the tube, then worked as quickly as he could to seal off the ooze coming from the inside of each end.

He charged the magnet of his basic contractor clamp, watching the meter bars grow and turn green. He stuck the now-magnetized rectangular slab situated on the bottom of the contractor clamp into a slot on the front of the crusty metal tube. The clamp beeped when it'd made a solid seal. Two pistons holding what looked like a black rolling pin grew out the bottom of the slab and touched the ground. Steve yanked at the handle and began banging the beat-up tube down the dark hallway.

After about 20 minutes of cursing, maneuvering, and shoving other tubes out of the way, Steve made it out into the smog. He strapped a bandana around his face, banged the tube down three steps, and lined it up against the heavy dumpsite for the building next to the steps. The he took a long roll of orange tape and wound it around the tube to secure it closed for its coming trip to the dump. He took a picture with his contractor cuff, activating a few RFID chips in the area. A checkmark popped up on the screen and just like that, Steve was $20 richer.

He sat on the stoop of the front stairs and took the tape out of his pocket, scrutinizing every inch of the new plastic casing. It was a pure ivory white. His pinky gently picked at the cassette wheels; they seemed to be turning smoothly. Spot of good luck finding such a good old cassette. Now he just needed a cassette player and a loudspeaker.

"Are you really gonna settle for working this crap all day?" a voice boomed.

Steve shoved the cassette into his pocket. He looked up to see an enormous guardsman standing in front of him. The guard was taking his time sliding out a thick rolled cigarette from the front pocket of his standard-issue gray uniform, which camouflaged him in the ash-filled fog that was busy choking every cubic inch of air, as it always did around this time of day. The two brown rings clipped on either side of his shoulder indicated he worked under "Silent Knights INC." The company always advertised that it specialized in keeping city streets quiet and under control. It had recently won the Inner Circle's contract to "ensure the security of ongoing operations being held within the Edingburg zip code."

A second guardsman approached in a darker officer's uniform that had three brown rings on each shoulder. The officer shouted a muffled yell through an old gas mask that pressed against his entire face. The name CRAUSE was stitched into his uniform. "Do you insist on having a death wish, Private Heintz? How zee hell did you even get through basic training! Put your breather on! It's not even ten A.M.! The ash from the storm hasn't settled yet!"

Private Heintz smiled at Steve and brought the fat cigarette to his thick lips. His nostrils flared while taking in the scent of one of the few luxuries the people of Edingburg ever saw. Then he nodded at the dumpsite.

"I earned these cigs after I snapped that Tuber in half. Prick was going off about how our computer took some of his EBT credits. Bunch of crap. *His* EBT?"

Heintz walked up to Steve's special delivery and ripped off the biohazard tape.

"Hey—" Steve said.

"Not talking to you, trash boy!" Heintz said. "You been paid, right? Shut it." The guard twisted the handle to the tube and broke the airtight seal. His nostrils flared. "Pffft, still fresh. It's roses in there." He pulled on the tube, toppling it back down to the sidewalk, then ripped open the door. A body fell out of the tube, kicking up a cloud of ash as it landed.

"Got all your stuff *given* to you by the City," Heintz growled. "How could we take something you never earned for your own damn self to begin with?" He looked up at Steve. "Our system did take a big percentage of his EBT though. But we didn't take any of it from no Tuber. Took it from the Inner Circle. Not that they give a shit. At least we're earning it. Without us taking a percent, who'd help you good-for-nothing losers get your handouts to begin with? Not me."

"Well, you could just do your job without taking people's lunch money," Steve said. "Your boss gives you a salary."

Heintz smiled. "Lunch money? What is this, kindergarten?" He pointed at Steve's Phoenix Cycle tattoo with his cigarette. "You'll graduate soon enough. Then you won't have Mommy taking care of her cute little boy any more. Christ, if only that were true. Inner Circle talks all this smack about not putting up with you Irish bastards, but here you little shits are. But if Tubers need a mommy, then I'll be the daddy." He kicked the corpse with his boot. "And give you spoiled little snots a spanking. But I'll be damned if I don't get paid what my spankings are worth. Hell, without me these around the slumlords owning these crap buildings couldn't collect on their rent."

"Hallo!" Crause smacked Heintz with his open hand. "Are you

listenin' to me, Private?" Steve's eyes glanced down at the guardsmen's hips. They'd come armed with pistols and regulation axes. He resolved not to say anything else. He'd seen a man get chopped up by the guards once and didn't want to repeat the experience personally.

"Smoke break, sir?" Heintz asked, holding out another cigarette to the officer. Heintz lit a match, which reflected in the impassive glass lenses of the officer's mask. The lit match burned lower and closer toward Heintz's fingertips, urging an answer.

Crause pushed his breathing mask up off his face and let his fingers comb his golden blonde hair. "Well, if we're going to be make breathin' this filth worth it," he said. He took the cigarette, and Heintz lit it.

They looked down at the corpse as they smoked. Steve sat silently on the stoop, hoping they would forget about him.

"Well, you gonna do it or what, kid?" Heintz asked.

"Do what?" Crause asked, taking a drag of his cigarette.

"Is he gonna apply for the Guard and get his? My money's on he's too big a bitch. He'll never earn his killing license. These redheads are all too yellow. He's just gonna sit on ass and take EBT handouts like the rest of them. You hear that, kid? You deserve living in this shit! I don't because I'm a man who's got a pair."

Crause smirked at Steve, who looked down and saw that his hands had tightened to fists. "Ohhh," the officer exhaled, his exclamation ending on a high pitch. "He's got a little spunk. Perhaps we should open an investigation."

Stepping casually over the body, Crause looked Steve up and down. "Disheveled reddish hair, ripped jacket, decent weight," he said with mock precision, pointing his cigarette at different parts of Steve as he went. "A little taller, freckles, light skin, scraped up knees and pants, generally dirty and—" Crause leaned in closer— "*such* a pretty face. That smooth jaw line and those hazel puppy dog eyes of yours make you a perfect applicant!" The officer took another drag from his cigarette and smirked. "For an Inner Circle girl."

Private Heintz's laughed hysterically, then broke into a coughing fit.

"Oh, that's why you're the officer, sir. You always know exactly where someone belongs."

"I'm not sure this is where this one belongs," Crause said. "Sitting on a stoop in the worst part of town with the ash still clouding the way. Unusual to find such a committed—" the officer looked at the tube that Steve had wrapped up and Heinz ripped open— "trash boy." Crause pointed to a lamppost. "The electricity is clearly still on. So why would someone who bothered to venture into Tube Town just sit on a stoop and not in one of those magnificent personal tubes inside?"

"He's just here to steal shit," Heinz said, glaring down at Steve. "You know, from the citizens who actually contribute!"

"Are you sure?" Crause's arms widened, gesturing to the buildings that even in the smog were clearly nowhere near up to code. "Steal what? The signs? Everything here is garbage."

"Should we get back?" Heintz asked, nodding to the intersection where a team of guardsmen was setting up a long shining-white table that stretched across the street. The table floated over magnetic plates that were installed under the concrete. A 12-wheeled gunmetal gray armored personnel carrier was parked next to the table. The turret on top wielded a .50-caliber machine gun. The name PUSSY PATROL LLC had been assigned to the vehicle via elegantly painted red cursive letters on its side. Underneath was a caricature of a seated fat man surrounded by food with the lower half and forearms of a woman in an apron serving him even more food. Next to the fat man's whining face was comic book bubble with the words IT'S STILL NOT FAIR!

Heintz put his hand on the handle of the ax at his waist. "Let's put his ass in a tube first."

"No, Heintz," Crause said. "You know perfectly well that getting into one of those lovely little virtual reality tubes is a completely voluntary process."

"Yeah, yeah. But he's such a little bitch. He'll do it eventually. Let's just get him off the street."

"No. Respect the process. We don't like Tubers, but what they do to themselves is their business, and it helps keep us *in* business. Without Tubers, our Edingburg contract wouldn't be worth half as much as it is. Our pay would be shit!"

"Exactly! More Tubers means more money!"

As the two guards began squabbling over the legality and merit of shoving Steve in a tube, he watched the square box on the side of the troop carrier jolt left and right along a metal rod. A wide piece of paper slid out from under the mechanism. Printed on it were the large red words MOST WANTED. The block continued zipping left and right as it printed the rest of its message on the paper. Then Steve's eyes widened to perfect circles.

It was printing a picture of him.

"Goddammit! He's just sitting there," Heintz said. "No one's around! Let's just shove him in a tube!"

"Exactly, Private! He's just sitting there. We can't do anything about that! We could lose our license to operate if we break regulations! Nor should we. We want *him* to do the work! That's the whole point! When people are too busy being pissed off at themselves or at each other for being shitheads they don't have the energy to blame us!"

"Yeah, but—"

"Heintz, you thick fuck!" Crause barked. "You just aren't getting the point. We're done here. Go set up the rest of the EBT station; it's almost ten."

The two began to turn away from Steve and toward the wanted poster with Steve's face.

"So that's it?" Steve asked. "The big one swings his stick around and you yap a bunch of business theory?"

The guardsmen slowly turned back toward him. Heintz's brown skin went red. The officer's blue eyes had gone ice cold.

"Oh, kid," Crause said. "It seems you just assaulted a licensed and contracted officer with a deadly weapon. You saw that—right, Heintz?"

Crause drew his pistol and cocked back the slide, chambering a round. He pointed the barrel at Steve's head.

Light footsteps pattered up the dark hallway of the building behind Steve. A little girl with blond pigtails sat down beside him. She brushed at her dirty white dress and bounced her orange teddy bear in her lap, apparently oblivious to the guns pointed at her.

"Little girl," Steve said, "you should go back inside."

The girl held up her teddy bear to Crause. She began spelling out the name stitched on his uniform: "Cr-ow-ss."

Crause grunted, then holstered his gun. He accepted the outstretched teddy bear and kneeled down to her height, exposing to Steve the now finished wanted poster of himself.

"Sir, what the hel—"

Crause raised a finger to Heintz. "Little girl. Thank you so much for sharing your bear. It reminds me of when I was a youngster. I had a coin that my mother gave me. It was a silver dollar, so quite something to hold on to. It meant so much to me, and even more after she left. I remember just staring at it—" Crause looked over the bear— "for hours. Turning it around." His hands began gently turn the bear over in circles.

Steve watched the box that printed the poster of him flick its green light back on. He did his best not to react as it began spraying a red X over his face. A blade lowered out of the box and cut the top of the poster from the vehicle's side. Then it began to print a new poster.

"But then a day came when I got hungry," Crause said to the little girl. "Quite hungry, and I was on my own, you know. So I gave my silver dollar to a baker for some bread. She asked me why I was crying as I held the large loaf in my hands. I explained to her what that coin meant to me and, well, she gave me back the coin and let me on my way. I felt much relief."

Crause smiled. He fingers ran through the soft fuzz of the plush bear in his hands. "But the baker began to tell others about me and soon every kid on the block knew about my silver dollar. One day five kids came to claim my silver dollar as their own. As you might imagine I fought back with everything I had. Broke my arm, my nose, near everything. They won. And they took it.

"But that's not what hurt most. What hurt most was the taunting afterward. The kids laughed at me. They laughed at the story the baker had been telling everyone. They used the meaning the coin had to me to hurt me. Many years later I applied, got placed in a corporation, climbed to the necessary rank to leave corporate, and started my own little business. With my new killing license, I've killed three of those five kids from that day. I didn't need to, but also I very much did, because they'd stolen my innocence on the day they took my coin, when they crushed me for holding on to the last thing I held dear." Crause's voice turned cheerful. "But they helped me to grow stronger than anything I could have ever been. Now I'm a successful sub-contractor with a full convoy and level three killing license issued by the City Guard. So whether those punks deserved death or not is of no consequence, because all that mattered, to me at least, was that I demonstrate to them the fruits of their labors."

Crause gave the bear back the little girl. "So perhaps you will find the same luck and rise above this place as well." He winked. "If you grow pretty enough, you too could become a woman of the Inner Circle some day."

Coughing echoed through the intersection. A man was bent over and dressed in the rags of what used to be decent clothes. "Give me my EBT!" he shouted. "I ran out! This is a bunch of bull!" He lurched over to the guards' table, grabbing its edge to keep it from falling. A disc rose up from a hole that opened in the street pavement, and a foot-long metal string uncoiled from the disc and began to spin. A video of a blue-outlined woman appeared.

"Citizen, welcome to the EBT station. Please follow the prompts and your EBT will be distributed to you for your immediate spending use."

Two poles rose up from each end of the white table. A long hologram flickered on between the poles.

"This station is brought to you by the Department of Smoke and is intended to give citizens who do not produce anything of value a handout. If you have achieved something of notable worth, please refrain from using this service. If, however, you have achieved nothing with your life, then you have come to the right place."

"Yeah, yeah, yeah," said the gray figure. His knees slumped as he held the end of the table and coughed.

The video of the woman continued in its upbeat and professional tone. "The General and the Inner Circle, while they can not relate, acknowledge your woes of being a failure. That's why we have dedicated this EBT program to the Tenderloin District, where people of your stigma can congregate and continue your chosen existence until you die."

The man pushed himself up against the table. His gray hand fluttered through a series of popups on the hologram.

"What!" he shouted. "Only 20 EBT! That's a lie!" He grabbed his chest and fell forward onto the table, slicing through the hologram. The image frizzed in white sparks around the man and flashed red all the way to the poles.

"Goddammit!" Heintz shouted. He marched over, yanked the man off the table, and dragged him to a sitting position against one of the huge wheels of the City Guard's personnel carrier.

As the man panted, Steve heard the wheeze. The wheeze that meant the ash had finally broken into the lining of the man's lungs. Once in there was no getting it out. The man had maybe a week until he asphyxiated.

Steve looked down at the girl. She rocked forward and back as she watched the wheezing man. "I breathe good," she whispered.

"Hey, sir!" Heintz shouted, pointing his ax at the wanted poster. "It totally looks like this piece of crap!"

Crause strolled over to the wheezing man. He leaned down to get a better look at him, pushing greasy hair out of the man's face with his pistol. "Now how could such a pathetic creature ever earn a place on the most wanted list, I wonder?"

Heintz grabbed the man by his hair and yanked him up. "You one of those pussies who bitched for more free shit at the protest?" Heintz looked over at Crause. "Bet you this one threw a tantrum and assaulted an officer or something."

Crause holstered his gun and wrinkled his nose. "It smells. It smells like a rabid dog." He grabbed the man's face with his gloved hand, the genuine leather squeaking as his fingers clenched. "I guess that makes us the dog catchers. Well, off to the pound for you. Load up and let's roll to processing!"

"But sir," said a gas-masked guardsman. "It's nearly ten A.M. Who's going to keep the generator here going?"

Crause scowled. "You really want to stay here and wait on those Tubers? Screw their EBT. Attach the generator to the back of the van and let's move! We've got a high-profile catch and I intend to cash that bitch in! Grand Pa-Pa needs himself a new .50-cal."

Steve did his best not to stare at the original poster of his face, which had folded over itself. A gust of wind pushed it back, partially revealing his face. Steve looked at Crause, then involuntarily glanced back at the poster. A cat had come and sat on the exposed part of the poster.

"Gonna spade and neuter this one," Heintz laughed. He threw the man over his shoulder and climbed into the back of the vehicle. The other brown-clad guards followed suit.

"You'd better be sure he sees a doctor!" Steve shouted.

Crause slowly turned back to the stoop. "Come here, kid," he said, beckoning Steve over with the fingers of his black glove. When Steve didn't move, Crause drew his pistol and dangled it at his side. The officer's eyebrow rose, indicating his final request. Steve stood up and walked over to Crause.

"On your knees, kid," Crause said, amused. Steve felt his face grow hot. He shook his head. Crause rolled his eyes, then smashed his pistol against Steve's temple. Steve fell to the ground, and Crause stood over him. "Do yourself a favor and go step into one of those tubes, kid."

Crause strolled back over to the personnel carrier. As Steve rolled onto his shoulder to watch him go, the officer looked back with a smirk. Then Crause crouched down next to the cat, which was still sitting on the wanted poster with Steve's face. The officer and the cat stared at one another, neither moving.

"We bagging this mutt or what!" Heintz shouted from inside the vehicle. Crause stood up and winked at Steve, then pointed at him with a shooting gesture. He climbed into the personnel carrier and it rumbled away.

Steve exhaled. He closed his eyes and felt the slightest breeze pushing through the fog. His eyes suddenly shot open and he grabbed at his pocket. The cassette was still there. He held up the cassette to make sure it was okay. A beam of light that had finally crept through the haze shone through the cassette's toothed holes. He stood up, hobbled over to the stoop, and showed the lightly trembling girl the cassette.

"Don't be sad, little girl. When this gets played, everything is going to get better. People will realize what the General is truly afraid of and they will finally understand what they're doing to themselves around here and to the people they love."

The girl looked up at him. She took something from the pocket of her dress and handed it to him. It was a button of some kind.

"What's this for?" Steve asked. The girl pointed at her ear and then returned her attention to the teddy bear in her lap.

"Thanks," Steve said, putting the button in his pocket along with the cassette. "So do you have a name?"

"Yeah! I had it before I was born, because of before. But now I am here! So we have to wait for before to end, so I can have it next!"

"Huh?"

The girl responded with a sweet smile and giggle.

"Sure," Steve said. "Anyway, don't worry about what they said. You don't have to be like them to be happy. All you'd do is hurt other people. There's never been a person in the world who had a happy life by making others miserable. There are plenty of good people out there. You just have to go find them. And together you can make a great life."

The girl played with her orange bear. "Yeah. Good people. Like your girlfriend."

"Sure," Steve said again. He turned and walked into the middle of the intersection. The video of the woman popped back on. "Citizen, welcome to the EBT station. Please follow—"

Steve whipped out a metal wand. He slid back its long handle and the wand began to crackle. Steve tapped the floating disc with the wand and the video of the woman cut out. The disc wobbled and zipped away.

Steve picked up the end of the fallen poster. He looked at his X'd out face and smiled at the little girl. "There's always someone looking out for us. Even when we feel most alone, we aren't. No matter how bad we feel, the reality is never as dark as we think." The little girl smiled back.

"Oh, just shut up!" said a voice in Steve's pocket. "Now put me in your ear, wherever *that* may be, given your severe birth defect of having a butt for a head."

Steve took out the button and stared at it.

"No, it's not her talking, butthead."

Steve whirled around. "Who is this! Where are you!"

"Good friggin' lord, butthead! No need to yell. The mic works fine!"

Steve put the button in his ear. "Are you watching me? Are you with us? Say the secret word."

"Say the secret word," the voice mimicked. "And Butthead will let you in his secret club! Nope. No secret word for you. We've got stuff to do! Got the tape?"

"Who is—"

"I'm the guardian angel who saved your butt! So quit fartin' on me and show a little appreciation! That APC would've printed out a hundred copies of your smiling face if I hadn't hacked it. So unless you're in the mood for getting neutered, I did you a solid."

"Well. Okay. Cool. Thanks so much I'm really relieved to see there's more of us out there and—"

"AND I just put on that whole show with that Tuber guy and his EBT and slapped his face over yours!"

"What?" Steve asked. "You framed him! You just got that guy

killed!"

"He was half-dead already. Scratch that—three-quarters dead. Nine-tenths, even. You know how much hacking that took, Steve? I had to prep for months to do that. Not even gonna mention the signal boosters I had to put in every decent hiding spot to be sure that printer would get the signal through the smog. Gah!"

"How do you know my name?"

"Oh, man." The voice seemed disgruntled. "That actually is your name, huh? I was hoping that was dated intel. That is like … the crappiest name ever. STEVE! I don't trust it. Sounds like a name someone thought of on the spot … during a lie. Because they're a liar."

"Um."

"Okay! Down to brass tax, butthead. We need to get that little cassette hooked up to the biggest horn we can get. Gonna rally our cause. The voice paused. "Sorry about all the stuff that went down, by the way."

Steve looked down. "I can't believe they did that. All those people."

"Whoa!" the voice said, taken aback. "Nope. Get outta here with that. We all got problems, kid, and I'm not being paid by the hour to listen to yours. What with your abandonment issues, having freckles, and boohoo orphan story."

Steve paused, he didn't even want to know how this guy knew all these things about him any more. Not that it was hard—the guy probably read his status updates when he was a kid and onnected the dots. "What do I do next?"

"Boom, there we go," the voice said. "That's why you're the butthead who made it out of that protest alive! Just go to Kleiner's for now. He'll keep you safe for a little bit. Who knows if guards are still looking around for you or what."

The face of Steve's watch glowed. It was almost ten o'clock. Power outages were frequent around this time. The other districts around the city were waking up and beginning to flip switches, and they had priority over this place.

"You should really go home, little girl," Steve said. "It's going to get a little hectic around here soon and I don't want you to get caught up in it."

The girl jumped up and ran into the black opening of the building that Steve had dragged the tube out of. His eyes widened. "Don't go in there!" He ran in after her.

"Hey! Go to work!" the voice in his ear shouted.

"Shut up!" Steve shouted back. He stopped in the hallway, giving his eyes a moment to adjust to the darkness before he navigated the jumble of tubes strewn everywhere. On the wall a torn poster of a shoe was labeled YOU STAND WHERE YOUR FEET BROUGHT YOU. Steve looked down at his feet, which stood in front of a warren of thick electrical cables running from tube to tube and into the walls. The hum of hardworking CPUs increased as he walked deeper into the building. Aside from the glowing buttons on the tubes, the room was pure black. The humming enveloped him.

"Little girl, you need to get out of here!" Steve shouted. "This is not a place you want to be! It isn't safe!"

He finally found her banging on a fallen tube. "I told him I breathe good! I told him!"

Steve weaved between the jumbles of tubes, many piled or leaning on each other. He glanced at his watch. 9:59.

"Little girl, stop! Just get out of here, go home!"

The girl collapsed, her thin legs a tangle on the sticky floor. She hugged her bear. "I'm trying!" she cried.

Electrical shorts fired out from multiple tubes. The girl screamed. Steve grabbed her as the room turned to total black. The humming stopped, and Steve's ears rang in its absence.

Red lights crept on. "Mama!" the girl cried. The corroded tube that the girl had banged on began to open.

"Shut it!" a woman shouted from inside the tube. Steve backed up, keeping hold of the girl. The door to the tube opened fully and a stringy woman sat up. Her hair had gone feral. Her eyes moved in ticks. They clicked onto Steve holding the little girl.

"I have three more hours! Three more hours, you son of a bitch! I spent my EBT!"

Other tube doors began creaking open.

"Mama!" the girl pleaded.

The woman's eyes clicked to her girl. Her tone changed. "Oh, hey baby. It's okay, go outside. You breathe good dear, don't worry."

Arms and legs began slithering out from the tubes. Steve scrambled for the hallway with the girl in his arms.

"Hey, that's my daughter! You have no right! She's mine! And it's my EBT!"

Steve tripped over something and turned as he fell to protect the girl. As he got to his knees he locked eyes with a wraith of a man lying in his tube.

"Turn it back on," he wheezed, his bony finger pointing to the power switch.

More figures poured out of the tubes. Steve pushed through hands grabbing at him and his pockets. At they followed him outside, the nearly silent street exploded into shrieks of garbled nonsense and staggering, ranting creatures.

"The EBT station's broke!" a woman shrieked. "And there's no generator!" The crowd began to rage at the news. Steve picked up the girl and ran across the intersection. A handful of Tubers staggered after them.

Steve came up to the bent lamppost just south of the intersection and turned around.

"Spare us some EBT," a Tuber said.

"Yeah, EBT," said another. The girl pressed into Steve's legs.

"I—I don't have EBT," Steve said.

"You FUCKING have it!" another Tuber bellowed, his yellowed teeth chomping out the words. "That girl alone gets you 30 EBT a month! You've got it! I see it!" He pointed a bony finger at Steve's jacket.

The Tubers crept toward him. Broken bottles, nails, and razor blades glinted in their gripped hands. The girl buried her face into the bear, sobbing.

"Okay!" Steve said. He unzipped his jacket. "I've got 50 in here."

"Fifty!" a Tuber screeched.

"A month straight of tube time!" cried another. "Enough time for me to become Grandmaster of the Empire of Steel." His eyes unfocused. "Grandmaster," he murmured.

Steve threw his jacket in the middle of the pack. They jumped it, razor blades and bottles slashing. Steve hurried the girl past the lamppost and away from the melee. Anything after the flickering lamppost was a dead zone. And the Tubers never dared nor had reason to ever cross beyond it.

Steve bent over gasping, his lungs wheezing with the morning ash. Steve hated Tubers. Nearly everyone did. Not solely because they were prone to violence. The Tubers' world was confined to their own few blocks of Tube Town. Leaving the zone felt to them more like going through withdrawals than breaking out.

No, the true horror of the Tubers was more like the hell of someday having to look into a mirror one day and see just how much you've aged with so little to show for it to your younger self.

Nearly everyone in Edingburg knew that they'd eventually end up a Tuber, that they'd essentially be sealed into their own caskets. And the worst part of it was knowing it'd be you packing yourself into it. You knew you'd eventually "try it out," knowing full well that you were there for far more than just a taste.

For many, life in Edingburg was horrid; there was no delusion about it. The General made sure everyone in Edinburg was equal in that regard. He also made sure you knew that if you were still living there after you turned 21, it was your own damn fault. What's worse is all the other zip codes in the city seemed to agree. You never saw anyone from a decent part of town strolling into here, unless they themselves were looking for a taste on the tubes.

"Oi! Steve!" said the voice in Steve's earpiece. "Did you die? Please don't be dead. That would be so not chill. Did I mention how much I've had to do for you? You owe me."

"Yeah, I'm alive."

"Okay, great! Happy for ya. So get a move on! Go to Kleiner's! Just kick back! Have a drink on him!"

"What about the little girl? She—"

"Oh you mean the one you just had to go and gallantly save! AKA, jeopardize the mission with your little girl heroics because abandonment issues baggage! You really just projected your problems didn't you! Way to go, my little basic Freud boy!"

"Do you seriously not care about her!"

"Whoa, now. Don't you go and try to make *me* look like the butthead. I've got her covered *way* better than you do."

An enormous outline of a figure appeared in the distance. Steve's eyes widened at the sight of a herculean Samoan. He was easily seven feet tall. The man's bulging arms and shaved head were heavily tattooed, but his face it was somehow calming. Serene even.

"Don't look at him like that," the voice said. "I know you're doing it. Everyone does it. But he *really* doesn't like it. He's sensitive."

The little girl walked up to the man with her arms outstretched and tears in her eyes. "Mommy couldn't see me," she said. The man bent down, picked her up, and gently swayed her back and forth. A tear glimmered between his shut eyelids as he did so. The man turned around and began walking away.

"I'll see you someday, Steve!" the little girl said. "I think you're nice." The enormous man disappeared into the ash, the little girl safe in his arms.

"Go get drunk at Kleiner's!" screeched the voice in his ear. "Or I'll have the big guy carry you there! GO GO GO!"

Day Break Radio
Broadcast #7205
Choosing Your Future

It's ten A.M. You're listening to Day Break. I'm your confidant, Line, here to keep YOU informed to make sure YOU are ready for the coming storm.

Please excuse our mandatory broadcast from any interruption we may be causing you. For the next few moments I will be informing you of essential updates around the city.

Let's begin.

An enormous terrorist attack is reportedly underway in Sector #6 today. Hundreds of City Guardsmen have been deployed to the sector in an effort to quell suspected IRA members. The IRA has become far more violent in recent weeks and is affiliates with the Irish-Scot sense of entitlement. Members of the IRA were reportedly well armed and carrying propaganda designed to maim public morale.

Please, please be sure to SPEAK up against suspicious activity and call the Department of Smoke hotline if you see ANY of the wanted and likely redheaded fugitives. It's more important now than ever.

Now to the Phoenix Cyclers. Your days of decision are near. Don't let the IRA cloud your judgment in the coming days. They are cowards who didn't have the courage to apply for admission into the City Guard or the Department of Ladyhood. Instead, let their self-loathing help you see the true colors of your situation.

Finding your way to the Inner Circle without applying is far harder than applying. While we encourage you to become an industry titan of a corporation or trending star on social media, there can only be a handful that make it to the highest rungs in that way. So it's advisable to seize this once in a lifetime opportunity, because no matter how intense or bloody it may become. YOU WILL RISE! And fast ...

Ladies. Tomorrow is YOUR special day. Don't forget that this is the best chance that you will ever be *given* to reach the rungs of the Inner Circle. How can you expect to trend online without your certificate of ladyhood? It's up to you to choose your future. What's it going to be? What does your destiny have in store for you? Is it greatness? Tomorrow you will decide exactly that, ladies. Best of luck to all of you. That is all for this broadcast. I'll see you all tomorrow at daybreak.

Have a nice morning, New San Francisco, and keep on pursuing HAPPINESS.

Sundown

The room was 78% steam, 18% starch, and 1% ash. Even at one percent you couldn't get that tar taste out of your mouth.

Kleiner banged on the bar top. "Oi!"

Steve was staring deep into the folds of the cassette tape. Aside from his bobbing leg, he had sat frozen on his barstool the entire day.

"Oi!" Kleiner barked. "You in er out!"

Steve responded with a blank stare and a faint "Uh."

"You crazy, boy? The sun's settin' and I fer one won't be having any more o' dat ash blowin' into me bar!"

Steve looked through the open iron door. The sky had already turned that ominous purple shade that made a man want to run and jump into whatever hole would fit him. How had he lose track of the time? He'd never gotten caught at sundown. Steve looked back down at the cassette.

"I'll do a howler," he murmured, shoving the cassette into his pants pocket.

"Right then," Kleiner said. He dipped around the bar and over to the thick iron door, grabbing the handles of the door's large crank lock. "Last call!"

Steve scanned the room. There must have been 20 other people sitting along the bar or seated at the tables. None of them budged.

"Right then," Kleiner said again. He swung the heavy iron door shut and turned the handles of the lock, pushing steel beams into the thick concrete walls and sealing the room from the outside world.

Kleiner hadn't even taken his hands off the handles when a distinct woosh banged against the door. The lights above the bar swung and flickered.

Kleiner stroked his scraggly red beard. "Oi, that was a close one." His face lit up. "Best we get to drinkin' lest it spoil the mood!"

The men cheered. Steve was shocked by the sudden liveliness of the room. Men in the corner started singing and strumming their instruments. Older women in green uniforms traipsed between the rows of tables, serving Kleiner's famous "spirited potatoes" that had steeped in an orange liquid inside the glass cylinders that lined the bar's back wall, each one of cylinder rising all the way to the ceiling.

Stitched together Irish and Scottish flags hung from the rafters, and pictures the outside of a church at Knock, a photo of a thatched house with ROBERT BURNS written in sharpie on the frame, and drawings of potatoes decorated the walls. This was the last true place left demonstrating Scots-Irish culture in the city with blatant pride.

"You all right, boy?" Kleiner asked.

"Yeah," Steve said, though he felt like he might fall off his stool and sink through the floor. He hadn't heard from Leslie today, which is what he'd told her to do given the circumstance, but the necessary distance between them so close to application day made it wearing nonetheless.

"Ah, no he's not!" Ryan interjected from his stool at the end of the bar. "He's dating a Phoenix girl!"

"Well o' course he is! And a fine one at that." Kleiner grabbed a drink from a passing waitress. "On the house, boy. Fer foinding such ah good one."

Steve accepted his drink. The cup was made of a potato that'd been cut in half and then partially hollowed out. The orange alcohol floated in the scooped out portion and saturated the potato flesh.

"Don't be all in tha dumps, lad. I'm shur she won't apply fer the event."

"I'm not worried about her," Steve mumbled. "Just that it's still happening."

"Oh yeah she will!" Ryan said. "Have you seen his girlfriend! She's a total shoe-in."

"Now that's enough from ya!" Kleiner said.

"Oh, I haven't even started!" Ryan jumped up from his stool and began humping the boy next to him.

"Piss off!" Yoden said, shoving him away. "Girls that pretty aren't going to settle for anybody who's not in the guard or Inner Circle."

"Why should they!" Ryan said. "Girls know what they want. Why should they settle for scraps? Steve's not even gonna be able to earn a killing license if he doesn't apply. Might as well cut off what manhood he's got altogether at that point!"

Steve drank his potato. The liquid hit his lips sweet and smooth, then burned him with a fiery afterbite.

Kleiner shook his head. "Not all girls have to go an' be like that. Steve's a fine lad. And I see no attraction in the whole roight to killin' thing. Who's tha bloke who went ta thinkin' he had the right to be givin' out such a putrid license anywho. A real arse. That's who."

"Well if he wants to earn his balls," Ryan shot back. "He can still join the City Guard. He's a Phoenix just like me and Yoden here. So we can all get our licenses and get a real man's jobs later."

"Well thaz his choice den, ain' it? Not everyone gotta go buying into all that Department o' Smoke crap."

"You got a problem with the Department of Smoke, potato man? I'll have you know that's exactly where I'm going to be applying for transfer once I make a high enough rank to transfer from the guard to the Inner Circle!"

Kleiner glared at Ryan. Both men looked rather formidable in their own right, Kleiner with his meathook arms and Ryan with his slender yet muscular body.

"Now don't go spoutin' off! You go and do what makes ye happy. All I be sayin' is Steve here's gotta choice, just like all dem other boys—and girls, for that matter."

"Believe it or not, some people got dreams!" Ryan said. "And some even got the balls to make them happen! The Department of Smoke's right! The Scots-Irish aren't appreciating what's been given to us. This is the only city in the world that's kept its shit together. They know what they're doing, so fall in line!"

"I'll be applying too," Yoden said.

"About damn time for you to come around!" Ryan said. "When'd you decide that?"

"Tuber, bro. Saw him walkin' all tall yesterday. Still kinda with it too. He was braggin' storms about how he was a grandmaster of some game to a girl. She wasn't even feelin' it. And she was like a five at best. You get tops of something around here and you're still nothin'."

"Dude, no one gives a shit about what the Tubers do outside of other Tubers," Ryan said.

"Well, what the hell else we gonna do around here to get ahead?" Yoden asked.

"You can start a bar, boy." Kleiner smiled. "Or somethin' of the like! Nuthin' wrong with bein' a business owna. Improves tha community. Darn near anyone can start a business nowadays. The one thing I be liking in this city here is tha free market. Might be a bit slimy when you be gettin' into a big corporation like Capsule, but the rest of it's alright. Heck, if more people stuck with sumthin' round here fer more than a month instead of all trying to make it big with them online trendin' mess or applying fer killin' licenses or ladies goin' an' embarrassing themselves applyin', Edingburg wouldn't be half bad by now."

"Ha!" Ryan yelled. "Peeling potatoes in some shithole bar isn't a dream. Fuck that. No one's livestreaming you mopping the damn floors. The application day the city gives us is the one real thing that's saving our people's ass! It gives a real opportunity for the good get out of this crap!"

"Lay off him, bro," Yoden said. "Kleiner's doin' all right with the bar."

"Sure am." Kleiner gleamed. Thinkin' of expandin' into tha next space next door soon. Gonna have Steve here in charge of it all." Kleiner winked at Steve.

"What is your obsession with Steve anyway?" Ryan asked. "Why you always helpin' him out?"

"Well fer starters he don't go spoutin' off a bunch o' nonsense every day. Second, there's nothin' wrong with givin' good opportunities to good lads. Steve's always had it together ever since he got outta that blasted orphanage."

"Whatever. Doubling the size of a shit bar only makes it twice as shitty." Ryan looked up at the ceiling, his eyes gleaming, his fingertips white from his grip on the bar top. "In a couple days everyone's gonna be hearin' about the shit I pull during basic. I've been gettin' ready for bootcamp for a long time. I can do 100 pushups, 200 crunches, and run ten miles in an hour flat."

Something buzzed in Ryan's pocket, and he pulled out a silver cylinder. "The new 8Q," he announced. "Best way to watch the news." He clicked the top and bottom of the cylinder with his thumb and index finger. Two long rods flicked out at the ends and stretched upward 90 degrees, forming a U shape. A holographic screen appeared within the U, and the cylinder flashed and glowed to the podcast's colors.

"Firecracker!" the podcast announced. "Stormside." On the screen a flaming stick exploded. Stats blew out from the virtual explosion. "Find out what was goin' down seconds before the storm!"

"Now thaz enough," Kleiner said. "Put that away. We're havin' ourselves a growler. None o' dat stuff. That's just more propaganda from tha bastads that went an' made our dialect synonymous with bein' dull!"

Ryan waved him off, and the podcast continued.

"Miss Iggy was just a few interactions short of 50,000 on her comment to Jerry Strongbow. It went, 'Tired of your shit. I'm not letting a has-been boy hold me back! #girlsownboys #strongerthanstrongbow.' Isn't she cutthroat? Wouldn't mess with that one. No way.

"This comment just went up while Strongbow's feed is barely squeaking into the hundreds of interactions this week! I think we're seeing the last of him. Say goodbye to that penthouse, Strongbow. No way is the Inner Circle gonna keep footing that bill. Meanwhile Miss Iggy is DOMINATING the feeds. If she keeps this up expect to see her getting a bid from the highest circles the Inner Circle has to offer. TRULY inspiring. Now the fast feed."

Other trending subjects began popping up, all toting how many likes and comments they'd gotten. Then a picture of last night's Phoenix Cycle preference party came up.

"Oh shit," Ryan said. Steve looked over. It was the photo of Leslie with her friend Bridget, though they'd cropped Bridget out.

"That's what we got," the podcast concluded. "Weather that storm and we will be back with ya in the A.M.! This is Firecracker. If it's cracking and popping, you'll hear it here."

Ryan looked up with a smile. "In a week all Iggy's gonna be commentin' on is me. Fuck Strongbow." He fluttered his hand through the hologram, which fluttered like a sail in the wind. "It'll be my name in every person's hand real soon. If Steve's girlfriend doesn't overshadow me, that is."

Steve began considering Ryan's murder, killing license or no.

The room quaked, the lights flickered. "Air pressure be gettin' real low out there," Kleiner said.

A wooden rivet was sucked through the wall. Air from inside the bar rushed out with a loud whistle. Yoden clasped his ears. "It's like we're in a damn kettle!"

An enormous gust punched down onto the building, and people fell to the floor. Multiple wooden rivets popped from the walls from the sudden reversing of air pressure. Black soot gushed into the room. There were screams as people grabbed for handkerchiefs to cover their mouths and noses.

A siren went off and fans activated. Small tornadoes of the ash swirled upward through the twirling fans. Kleiner held up a spear gun with a big green square at the end and fired. The flat square thudded into the loose group of rivets, and the goop on the square patched the leak shut.

Kleiner flicked a switch and the siren and fans shut off. He snapped at the fiddle band and the music resumed.

Yoden shook his head at his still swaying potato on the bar. "Sick of this shit, bro. Need to get me a cush life in the Inner Circle."

"Nine seconds flat," Kleiner said. "Thaz a record, lad. We're getting it figured out." He put his spear gun back under the bar. "Things get better with time. Soon the storm won't come vistin' us ever again. I can feel it."

"It must be as sick of comin' here every night and lookin' at these waitresses as I am," Yoden said.

"Well, hey," Ryan said. "You'd get a real girl if you gave them what they want. So screw 'em and be through with 'em. That's the way it's supposed to be and they know it. You ever see a girlfriend treatin' her guy right nowadays? No, because she wants out. Heck, my last girlfriend called me a cheater every day. That was her way of beatin' on me."

Yoden puffed out his cheeks. "Well, I bet you were."

"Hell no I wasn't. Never even thought like that. Was like pussy Steve over there. But hell, if you're gonna get blamed for being bad no matter what, might as well cash in on the fun parts." Ryan took a drink from his potato.

"Hey now," Kleiner said. "Plenty o' good women don't go spouting a boonch of hate like all your firecrackers an' posters an' all tell 'em to. There's a whole world o' people who don't be needin' none of that."

"Yeah? And who's that? The Dirties? The ones who bitched out on their application day but still haven't tube'd up? Yeah, great group. My dad was one of those for the first 12 years of my life. Woulda done everyone a lot of good if he just tubed out sooner. I told you, I don't want some mediocre life. Yea, I could go get a decent job on the other side of town, but my life would basically turn into one big snooze alarm lifestyle. Wake up, go to work, drink a beer in my quaint little apartment, and root for other people on the TV who are making shit happen. No. No way. I'd rather tube out."

"You pocket any bullets from the munitions factory?" Yoden

asked. "Need to practice my shootin' before application day."

Ryan's eyes narrowed. "Where'd you get a gun?"

"Come on, man. We grew up together. I wanna place in basic and push up my rank quick like you. Lend me some bullets."

"Neighbor or not, it's fifty-fifty shot you're going to be on the opposing company or worse, get looped into mine. I don't want the competition. Kleiner, a drink!"

Kleiner set down a pair potatoes and dropped in his signature clovers. "Good luck to ye both, lads. No matter what. An' don't forget there's a life after application day."

Ryan stood and raised his potato. "To the Phoenix Cycle! The best shall rise!"

The music played louder as the night went on, the patrons desperate to tune out the ominous howling that roared just outside the door. It finally died down an hour before sunrise. The musicians fell silent and the patrons stopped drinking. They'd found positions in chairs or on the ground that would allow them to grab an hour's sleep before the day began. Steve remained on his stool, his leg still thrumming. He had taken out the cassette tape and carefully unwrapped the piece of paper around it.

"Best put that away," Kleiner murmured. "We don't be needin' anyone seein' dat. Tranquilized or no."

Steve put the cassette back in his pocket. "Tranquilized?"

Kleiner glanced around the bar to see if anything still stirred. "Put some doses a somethin' strong in the spirits soon as ya stayed for tha growler, except fer yours o' course." Kleiner flicked Ryan's ear, whose face was pressed against the counter. "This whole lot should be out good fer a few, but I don't like testin' me luck, so let's make it quick. How'd it all go?"

"It wasn't what we were expecting."

Kleiner leaned in. "Did they really do it?"

"They certainly did it. Almost everyone showed up, actually. Hundreds of IRA members. Couldn't believe it."

"Really!" Kleiner looked around the room, then lowered his voice. "Well come on den, what happened? Were they taken seriously? Tha whole town's been talking whispers about it. All I be seein's is that terrorist attack blinking on the bulletins round town. But you knows that could mean everything or nuttin'."

"Yeah, it means something this time," Steve said. "The General himself even showed up."

Kleiner started wiping down the bar. "You don' say. Who'd a thought we'd all get this far. Thaz amazin'. They gotta address us now. Maybe they'll put off yer bloody application day for you cyclers while it all gets mulled over."

"That's not going to happen."

Kleiner glanced up from his wiping. "The General didn't jus' jail 'em all, did he? That'd never go over, it's too big. All Edingburg's going to find out about dis sooner 'r later."

Steve shook his head, tears welling from his eyes, unable to shake the feeling that the only real contribution he'd ever made in his life resulted in the deaths of hundreds of his friends. Kleiner bent over the bar and grabbed his shoulder.

"Keep it together, lad," he hissed. "Now what happen'd over there?"

"The General … he burned them. Burned them all!"

Kleiner snapped up straight. "Sweet Florian, it can't be so. You sure, boy?"

"I saw the smoke after I left with the tape … the smell … he burned them!" Steve felt like he was going to throw up. Telling a fellow brother of the IRA about it all hit him in a whole new way. His guilt was beginning to turn evolve into total revulsion of his own existence.

One of the passed-out band member's instruments slid off his leg and the clang echoed through the room. Steve gripped the counter in a futile attempt to steady himself. People began to groan and sit up. Kleiner glanced over at the red light on top of the door.

"What do we do?" Steve sniffled.

"We stick to da plan, lad. This was step one. We 'Open the Gates.' That's what them young kin went protestin' fer. To show to tha world there's a problem with how things are roonin' around here. That the IRA ain't jus' some roudy boonch but a group o' proactive lads comin' together fer us all."

"But they died! That wasn't part of it!"

Kleiner placed his hand on Steve's arm. "Perhaps the problems round here are even bigger than we thought, lad." He grabbed the bottom of his apron and wiped a tear from his face. "Sittin' here mopin' is only gonna bury them deeper, lad. Step two: 'Rally.' We need people comin' together fer this all."

"But that's exactly what we did! And look what happened!"

The light above the door flicked from red to green.

"We can't change wha' happen, lad. And we can't be goin' an' changin' our minds now because they went an' proved themselves the monstas we been claimin' they is all along. Best be goin', boy. Lay low and keep dat tape safe. Me bar's bound to get turned to bits by the guard fer dis. I'll get on tha horn. Our people gotta at least know tha basics."

Steve stood up and turned to leave. Then he took the earpiece out of his pocket and held it up. "This weirdo told me to come here. He rants all the time and calls me names."

"What'd he call ya?"

"Butthead."

"Ah, must be Ramfert talkin'. He's taxin' but it's best you be listenin' to him anyways. He'll get you out alright."

Kleiner walked around the bar and grabbed the latch to the metal door. "I can't be stressin' enoof how important dat tape is fer us, an' fer them lads. We be needin' a voice o' our own or else the General will just keep speakin' fer us. Good luck lad, be strong. I'm sure Ramfert's got somethin' planned fer ya."

Day Break Radio

Broadcast #7206

Present Day

It's ten A.M. You're listening to Day Break. I'm your confidant, Line, here to keep YOU informed to make sure YOU are ready for the coming storm.

Please excuse our mandatory broadcast from any interruption we may be causing you. For the next few moments I will be informing you of essential updates around the city.

Let's begin.

Today's the day, ladies. Today you choose ... Will you choose to reach out? Will you REACH out your hand to see if it will be grasped? Or will you keep your hand by your side and walk away from the biggest opportunity you will ever be offered? The choice is yours.

Orange has just released its new mobile device, the Orange 8Q. They're offering it for free to anyone who is willing to agree to the terms and conditions. Just check the box and it's yours.

New features focus on giving users more opportunities to gain bonus points by completing minitasks throughout their day. They can then apply these points to their online profile and their game of choice in the cloud. It also includes a retina scanner to identify YOU as its rightful owner, thereby keeping your personal information safe. You can get the device at any Orange store or order it off the Department of Smoke's public website where they are offering FREE shipping for the next 14 days to anyone who agrees to additional terms and conditions.

Lastly, there is a controlled burn taking place at the New San Francisco golf course. The Masks of the Inner Circle, at the General's request, have decided to make the course a desertscape. The water savings will be donated to orphanages around New San Francisco. The fire is being fueled by excess grass trimmings and the IRA terrorists who stormed the course late yesterday. Hey, looks like those freeloaders finally contributed to something! Ha, ha.

Johnny McHenry, the mayor of Edingburg, has given no comment, but his staff made a statement.

"Mayor McHenry has always stood with the people of Edingburg. However, taking opportunities that were not given by the Inner Circle is unlawful and endangers the public at large. We would like to remind the people of Edingburg of how lucky we all are to be a city with choices. So in order to keep such a privilege we must be responsible and own the choices that we all have made. Therefore we are in full support of the dutiful actions the City Guard made in defense of Edingburg and its freedom to choose at the IRA's unwarranted protest."

That's all the news today. A stunningly heartfelt interview with Colonel Strongbow and Miss Iggy about how they felt on their application day is next.

Again, good luck today, young ladies!

Have a nice morning, Edingburg, and keep on choosing your dreams.

Sunrise

"All right, let's do this," the voice in Steve's earpiece buzzed.

"I'm going with Leslie to her application day."

"What! NO! Steve, I am going to friggin' bend you over and spank your face! That is NOT what we are doing today."

Steve glanced up slightly, seeing Leslie's sandals and toes walking toward him. Steve took out the earpiece. "Hey, you listen to me, Romeo!" the voice raged. Steve shoved the earpiece into his pocket.

Leslie sat down beside him on his ash-coated porch. Her beauty was a stark contrast to his shack of a home behind them, which seemed to be held together by nothing more than a patchwork of scrap metal and plywood. Her hair flowed elegantly down her shoulders and framed her perfect cheekbones and full red lips.

"The whole city is talking about the protest," she said, putting her hand on Steve's knee to quiet its relentless trembling. "Are you okay, honey? They aren't after you, are they?"

"Not any more, it seems," he whispered. Her eyes widened at "any more." He gestured to her dress and makeup—no one ever got done up, as makeup was almost impossible to smuggle into Edingburg.

"Honey, it's not what you think," she said. "I don't want to look bad when I have to stand up there."

Steve just looked back at her, and her eyes flared. "You need to stop comparing me to your mother. I'm not the one who left you here when you were a baby. I dressed up because tens of thousands of people are going to be looking at me—don't you care about that even a little bit?

It's embarrassing. The lady at the preference party last night gave me a bunch of makeup. I sold most of it, see." She took out $200 and stood up. "For the house. Now come on, let's put it in the safe." Steve got up and entered his home by bending over and pulling up the tracked garage door.

Inside was the only livable room of his house, his garage. He'd modified it slightly by adding a fireplace. A bright floral couch stood in the middle of the room facing the fireplace.

They entered and Steve closed his front door. The barred window in the rear let light cascade onto an artfully fractured mirror that refracted the light, causing it to bounce and beam small streaks of light throughout the room.

"Okay, I'm sorry. I saw you trending on the Firecracker thing, and I—"

"I didn't even post that!" Leslie snapped.

"I know, it's just—"

"Honey, not now. There's too much going on today for me to be patient. I get it, but I'm the one having to get up there today, not you." Her hands came up to her face. She was doing her best not to tear up. Her fingers quivered millimeters away from her skin, not daring to smear the mask they'd just painted on her.

Steve put an arm around her shoulders and rocked her quietly. It made sense. He'd probably be having his own share of breakdowns come his day. Coming to a decision even before your application day didn't really make it any easier. It was like choosing whether you wanted someone to push you off a cliff or to jump off yourself.

Leslie went to the couch, lifted the right seat cushion and reached into a small hole. She brought up a jar full of cash. Steve walked up from behind and held her. "We're almost there," he said. "Soon we'll have enough to build us a real bedroom."

She smiled and dropped the rolled-up $200 into the jar. Steve squeezed her slightly and kissed her cheek; her makeup shined in a beam of the mirror's refracted light. They sat down on the left seat cushion. Steve tossed a bead into the fireplace, sparking the logs in the fireplace into ignition. Warmth.

"How long until applications start today?" asked Steve.

"Not long," she said, frowning into the firelight.

"Wait, where's your family then? Are they meeting us there?"

"I asked them not to come. I don't want them to see me out there. I just told them I'd be back later. I don't want them worrying. They've got enough going on. My dad's pawnshop is always super busy around application day."

"Well, isn't everyone going to see the applications process today?" Steve asked.

"Yes, but right before there's sort of a secret movement of girls that show up to his shop super early to pawn their stuff just before applications. There's so many he opens up before the smog burns off."

"Well, why does he open up to them! Doesn't he hate application day? I remember him saying it was the most disgusting thing a girl could do. Heck, we met at a protest against application day. That's how we met, back when protests were … not so dangerous."

Steve looked into the fire. He did his best not to drop his face into a frown like Leslie's. The hell that just happened to him and his friends, it happened. For now, he needed to push it down and be strong for her, because she wasn't dead yet. They still had a future. For better or worse, his friends did not.

Steve forced a smile. "That protest where we met was amazing. Remember your dad? He'd climbed to the top of a streetlight and hung upside down from it by his knees. To this day I have no idea how that bar didn't snap under his weight, he's so big! And …"

Steve couldn't help but genuinely laugh. "He hung upside down and just kept screaming. 'You wanna see some titties, you Inner Circle pervs! Well I got a pair of 'em right here!" And, upside down he let his shirt fall from over his head. And thousands of people just cheered him on. So I ran over to see him and I saw you standing right under him. With that same little pink bow in your hair."

Leslie pressed her bow to her head with a slight smirk. She rarely ever took it off. It had become one of those things. A connection to something not only to her youth, but to her innocence. She'd only remove it when going to bed with him.

She smiled. "And do you remember what I was doing standing under him?"

"Trying to catch him! Just in case he fell!"

"Hey I had some help," she said. "You started holding your arms out just like me."

"Well, there was no way you were going to catch him by

yourself."

Leslie gripped his thigh and smiled for a moment at the crackling fire. "He opens up the shop early because he said they'll stand out there all the same. Getting sick in the smog. 'Once they've decided,' he says, 'they've decided. Nothing's going to stop them. So might as well just let them in from the elements."

"Well, what if they don't get accepted?" Steve asked.

Leslie leaned away from Steve and into the couch. "Getting accepted or having a plan isn't everything. It's way more than just some rational decision that gets made in a day. Miss Rand says it's the culmination of a lifetime. The culmination of your identity. How you see the world, your life, yourself. She says today isn't about making a decision because somewhere, inside of you, it was made a long time ago. In fact it's not even up to us what we do. Our inner self makes the real choice, not us. And so our only conscious part in it is simply revealing to the city what is within us. Not deciding it. It's about seizing destiny, not making a decision."

Steve blinked. "Wait. Why are you talking like *them*?"

"Steve, I'm not talking like anyone. I'm just trying to help you understand that maybe for you and you boys your day is some complex math equation that you need to figure out, but it's not the same for us girls."

"Wait. What are you saying?" Steve leaned away from her and fell halfway off the seat cushion and almost into the little hole with the jar of cash.

Leslie looked at him. Seeing him in pain was one of her greatest griefs. Ever since that day she met him, seeing him with his arms outstretched right next to her, looking up at her dangling dad, she knew he'd be there for her. Ready to catch her if she ever fell, even if it squished him. Just like her father would do for her. But what she would never tell him was the part that she loved most about that memory: the white collared shirt he was wearing that day, tucked into blue shorts. It was essentially the uniform of the unwanted. The children of orphanages. To teach them discipline, the children had to keep their white shirts spotless at all times or else they'd threaten to "kick them to the curb," not that they actually could until they were 15. But there he was, freshly escaped from the orphan's compound, dirt covering absolutely every inch of him. They quickly found him and brought him back in, of course, but she became attached to the idea of the only thing he'd ever done as a "free man" was to futilely stand next her to help catch her dangling dad.

Until he reached 15, she'd come over to the orphanage nearly every day after school to play with him through the fence surrounding the orphanage compound. When he finally got out, he latched onto her immediately. She loved feeling so wanted; with it, she felt she could do anything. He was the only friend she'd ever kept. It seemed as though nearly everyone else in the city saw caring as weakness that must be gotten rid of.

Leslie reached out and brought him back to her. "I'm saying you'd better treat me to a nice dinner when all this is over." She reached over him, got the jar, took out $3 dollars, opened up an app on her watch, and waved the micro RFID chips in each dollar over the watch. The RFID's vibrated a frequency when activated and dyed an orange square into the dollars, showing they'd been used. She crumpled the dollars and threw them into the fire. Her phone beeped and flashed a check mark. "Done, there'll be super noodles delivered and waiting when all this is over. I got our favorite kind."

Steve laughed. "You spoil me."

Leslie's phone flashed again.

"That photo of me and Brittany is still trending. If we keep it up a bit longer we could maybe even qualify for a better loan to fix the house."

"I don't like all that. It's all self-made propaganda."

"Oh Stevey, just play the game a little bit. It's just some photos and blurbs. Everyone knows it's BS anyway because if I can keep our account trending just a bit longer we could make the garage into our home."

"This is our house."

"Exactly, a house. And so far you and my dad have done a great job with finding something for us, but we're barely able to keep the payments up, let alone with paying my dad back for what he fronted us. Inner Circle banks are still giving out zero-interest loans and even gifting some of the money to people who trend online. So let me just do this. If we're going to get ahead on this house it's going to need a lady's touch to make it into a home. If you hate the Inner Circle so much, then at least enjoy taking their money."

"Fine," Steve said. "You take their money and I'll use it to build a home shaped like a giant middle finger. Point it right at the Inner Circle's banks."

"Sounds fun," Leslie said. "Now aren't you forgetting something?" She stood up with her chin facing upward, peering around in imitation of a lost person. "There's a city of boys out there professing their love to their girls today … where could my boy be?"

Steve smiled, took her hand, and fell to one knee. He took out the cassette from his pocket and unwrapped the sheet of paper protecting it. He unwrinkled the paper and read the from the note inside.

"To my darling: Before I understood just how alone I was, you were there. Our talks between the bars became my world. I like to think you did it because you knew that under all the filth and grime there was a me beneath it. You let the *me* come out for a moment or two a day in a place where I couldn't be. Because of you, I've never felt like a lonely stray but like an *us*. Since that day it's always been us, and I always want to keep it that way. I never want there to be a fence between us again.

"So Leslie, will you continue to love not only me but the *us* we have created … or at least be able to deal with me now that we're on the same side of the fence?"

Leslie smiled, her eyes tearing. "I will always love you, Steve."

Life was hard in Edingburg—people starved, the nights were cold, and the homes provided little insulation from the storms. But so long as Steve had her, he could endure. His knees wobbled as he stood. He hadn't slept since the night before the protest, but the idea of keeping her beside him kept him going.

A foghorn blew and filled the city with a low shaking vibration. The kind that shakes your bones just to see if they will crack. It was time. Applications were about to begin. They walked outside.

Steve looked back at the shack behind them. Most of the second floor had blown away, and the remainder was nothing more than varying degrees of rot. The door to the garage, which made up half of the first floor, could barely close due to how badly it had been warped by the ash storms. The $200 she had made would help, a bit.

He looked out across the dirt to the row of other ash-coated two-story shacks lining the opposite side of the road. Smoke plumed upward from the ammunition factory at the corner. Its steam whistle blew, cutting the day short for the event. Crowds of men shuffled out of the factory, heading toward the Great Gate.

Steve trudged over to Leslie and they joined the crowds of men pouring out onto the street. He glanced at the large red stickers on the front doors of the houses that had been vacated since the protest.

Steve and Leslie walked to the end of the street where the stream of people fed into the river of bodies on Lincoln Way. Tens of thousands of ripped and mangled shoes trod the cracked concrete, all footsteps heading toward the event. Steve grasped Leslie's hand to prevent losing her to the crowd.

The walk through Edingburg and the other zip codes was long. He passed hives of privately owned miniature magnetic power plants, the main industry aside from handyman work. New tributaries of men filed out of every building they passed, except for when the road passed the edge of Tube Town. Not a soul was leaving that place.

They passed under a poster hanging in the middle of an intersection. It showed a man and woman falling from a bright cloud into a dark abyss. At the bottom of the poster it said FAILURE: YOUR COST FOR FREEDOM.

For nearly half of the procession, the Great Greenhouse loomed over the left of Lincoln Way. Aside from the artificial calories and carbs they pumped into the veins of Tube Town, the Greenhouse was practically the sole food source for New San Francisco—leafy greens and hydroponic meats for the nicer parts of town, like the Inner Circle; potatoes for Edingburg. The windows were still blackened with ash; the cleaners must have already left for the ceremony.

Whispers shot through the crowds of men. "Have you heard?"

"Have ya heard about the golf course?"

"I heard one of 'em was locked oop and shipped ta Alcatraz."

"Alcatraz! Ain't nobody been sent there in decades!"

"Why the hell hasn't Johnny said nothin'? He's the mayor, for God's sake."

Steve did his best to block out the gossip and the growing unrest around him. For the moment, he only cared about the girl whose hand he was holding.

Steve's feet hit untracked and clean concrete. Slowly the quiet shuffled walk of feet turned loud. Protest signs and Irish flags began to emerge from the crowd as they began to walk into the nicer and less

Scots-Irish parts of town. The buildings were from the old times, but they'd all been pretty well restored, almost like the apocalypse never happened. A large group of women and dots of men stood like rocks in the stream of people. A large banner hung over them saying SUPPORT OUR SISTERS.

A gangly little pigtailed girl reached out and tugged on Leslie's wrist. Steve looked down at the girl, who gave him a huge smile.

"Hi, mister! I'm happy you're okay! Is this your girlfriend? She's so pretty!"

Steve stared at the somewhat less little girl. She was still wearing a white and blue dress, but if it was the same one it had grown along with her. "Little girl, did you—"

Her green eyes gleamed. "I had a growth spurt!"

"You're like … a foot taller."

"And you're a foot shorter!"

Leslie, meanwhile, was talking to an old woman. "We hope you are the one choosing the outcome of your own life today, my dear," the old woman said. "I sure didn't. I let a man dictate mine and so here I am. An orphan caretaker. The drudgery, it's never ending. But this little girl —" she put her hand on the little girl's shoulder— "won't be making the same mistake I made. She will have a real life, with real men."

"I hope to see you again!" the little girl said to Leslie. "Steve is the bestest, and he really likes you!"

"Sir, will you be a gentleman and support your girlfriend's decision on this big day?" the old woman asked.

"I'm sure he will," another old woman butted in. She winked at Leslie. "And if he doesn't, then she'll surely know that she *must* decide for herself then."

"You're so pretty," the little girl said to Leslie. "I'll be looking for you guys up there!"

The old woman leaned in and quickly took a selfie with Leslie and posted it.

Steve pulled Leslie away from the women, and she turned and frowned at him.

The posters on the buildings grew in number as they walked toward the stadium. Irish arms began reaching out toward the posters, ripping them off as they went. Nonetheless, the walls got to the point that they were completely plastered over with layers on layers of posters, with new ones glued over posters from years or even decades past. One showed a tearful woman with an exhausted holding a bundle of dirty clothes in a dark room. Next to her a pretty woman smiling as she stood under a rare clear blue day. The words SECOND CHANCES ran along the bottom, with the Department of Smoke's insignia stamped in the corner.

Another poster from the Department of Smoke showed three young women smiling and pointing upward. ONE LIFE, ONE CHOICE. CHOOSE TO GET THE MOST OUT OF IT!

An old poster lay on the street, ground into the pavement by endless feet. Steve recognized it immediately. The Department of Smoke had posted it everywhere during the great famine ten years ago, which they claimed was caused by the mass Scotts-Irish immigration. It showed a contented red-haired man with closed eyes, his chest puffed out with the rising sun behind and ash clouds surrounding him. BREATHE FREEDOM IN, it said. The Inner Circle loosened its regulations during that terrible time, allowing people in the city union to catch up on the wall building project in the ash-choked early hours after the nightly storm. Soon after there were less people to feed and the famine ended.

Three tall red banners stood in a line on the street. THE PHOENIX CYCLE was printed on the top of them in beautiful gold lettering with the Phoenix symbol underneath it. They had almost reached the stadium, and Steve felt like he was going to throw up. Leslie's wristwatch beeped, automatically posting her status.

A towering bronze statue of a woman stood at the entrance to the stadium. Her raised arms held two plates at shoulder height. A soldier stood on a dais in front of the statue.

"Spectators to the right!" he shouted into a megaphone. "Women from the Phoenix Cycle to the left! Family members and loved ones may join to the left or may separate here!"

Leslie's watch flashed 30 LIKES. Steve glanced up at the statue and noticed a small orange teddy bear sitting atop one of the plates.

They walked until they met up with a short line of other applicants. Some of the girls had their entire families with them, others friends or lovers, and some were completely alone.

50 LIKES, Leslie's watch flashed.

When Steve and Leslie made it to the front of the line, the guard didn't bother looking up from his clipboard.

"Name?"

"Leslie Putain."

The guard checked her off. "Are you carrying anything with you?"

"Just my wrist camera. Is that—"

"That's fine. Post whatever you want."

The guard's eyes traveled off the clipboard and glanced at Steve's beaten shoes. "Are you with the man next to you?" he asked, still looking down.

"Yes," Leslie replied.

"Hand, sir," the guard said, his voice mechanical. Steve held out his hand, and the guard fastened a thick metal band around his wrist. Steve stared at the wristband like it was going to bite him. A Phoenix symbol was engraved into the dark metal, and the grooves lines were filled with a brilliant red stone.

"There is a blade in the band," the guard recited while thumbing through papers on his clipboard. "The blade has been treated with a chemical that prevents clotting and a stimulant that sharply increases your heart rate. If you attempt to run onto the podium, the stage, or any forbidden area, the blade will open your radial artery and you will bleed to death."

The guard flipped another page on his clipboard and continued with the procedure. "If you avoid causing a disturbance, a guard will deactivate your band as you exit the stadium. You get to keep it for as long as you wish as a warm reminder of this iconic day. Arm, ma'am."

Leslie raised her right arm, revealing the Phoenix Cycle tattoo on her bicep. The guard glanced up. He finally looked at her. His eyes lit up as he gawked at her from head to toe. He looked back down at the clipboard with a smile.

"Verified. Please move forward single file."

Leslie went first. Steve followed right behind her, the band heavy on his wrist. They came to a second guard who stood with his back to a massive limestone wall. The guard handed Leslie a ticket with the number 3 on it.

"Go to the area displaying your group number," he said. "When your number is called, you will make your way to Section One, where you will wait for your turn on the podium. No one else can join you on the podium." The guard glared at her. "Do you understand?"

Leslie nodded, and Steve followed after her toward the pearl-white limestone wall, the pebbles under his feet crunching with each step into his mind. He watched in woe as Leslie's hair fluttered in the breeze.

The wall was only brought to the stadium for this ceremony. Normally it was locked into the exterior of the main gate that encircled the Inner City. The wall resembled an upside-down wedding cake, with each layer jutting out six feet farther than the layer beneath it. At 50 feet up the wall widened out evenly like a parking cone.

As Leslie and Steve followed the wall's perimeter, a slight hum filled the air. Steve grabbed her hand and brought her to him. He gazed into her coffee-brown eyes, which looked back at him sadly. The hum had grown into a coordinated chorus of voices. Never had such soothing sounds entered his ears; their tone ravaged his mind. So much of him was sure about what was going to happen next, but the other part of him knew, perfectly well, that the opposite was true.

High Noon

Steve and Leslie walked single file through the narrow pitch-black passageway. The chorus of voices grew louder as they stepped out into the blinding light of the enormous stadium. Thousands of footsteps filled the stadium as people found their sections.

Steve and Leslie walked into the standing-room only section numbered 3. From across the large open field that separated the people from their betters, the Boys Chorus sang their hymns. Steve studied the fine furniture and gold embellishments in the levels above the choir, but then his eyes inevitably fell to the podium looming in the middle of the field.

The podium was shaped like a bullet casing, cylindrical with a flat top. The limestone walls had been carved away into intricate statues of devils grabbing for angels. The podium was encircled by six enormous magnifying glasses spaced a hundred yards apart, each connected to a tall granite slab to hold it in place. Two of the magnifying glasses faced the Inner Circle's section, two faced the Phoenix Cycle's section, and two faced the huge crowds.

The two large lenses facing the crowd had an alignment of successively smaller lenses; each lens piggybacking off the image created by the lens before it. The lines of lenses stretched deep into the enormous crowd, their alignment resembling a telescope whose casing had been removed, the lenses remaining in their respective places.

The hymns faded; the event was about to begin. Steve searched for Leslie's hand, and their bracelets clanked together.

A single godlike thump quaked the ground. The crowds made one combined flinch. A long hooked wire rose from a hole in the top of the podium and began to spin, creating the whirling shape of a light bulb. The image of a man began to flicker inside the whirling bulb. The man's image was choppy, as if Steve were looking at him through a propeller. Steve had heard of this man before; he went by Aizen.

Aizen's arms spread open. "Welcome, potential applicants of the Phoenix Cycle!"

Everyone from the Inner Circle clapped, as did most of the crowd of onlookers. In the stands holding the Phoenix Cycle girls and their loved ones, the reaction was much more mixed.

"Every year a cycle ends and another cycle begins. For the young women of the Republic, their 21st cycle comes with a once in a lifetime opportunity. An opportunity that, should they choose to accept, will change their lives.

"Every woman who is part of the Phoenix Cycle must appear here today, but understand that applying for the chance to become part of the Inner Circle is a choice they will make completely on their own. Make no mistake—no harm will befall those who refuse. Nothing but their own feelings will push them over one side of the line or the other. But be forewarned, no matter what decision you make, it will be final. So if you choose not to apply, know that you have forfeited your best opportunity to enter into the Inner Circle. Know that you will almost certainly continue to live your life exactly as you've known it, until your final breath.

"However," Aizen emphasized, "if you choose to apply and are accepted then you will never leave the Inner Circle. This is a one-way ticket to greatness. Know that you will never see your brothers; you will never see your mother or father. You will never have a family or raise one of your own. Everything, everyone you now know will cease to exist.

"But if you do choose to apply you will have a life unlike anything you have ever known. One without starvation, sickness, or the unrelenting clouds of ash. Instead you will live a life of luxury. You will leave your bare homes and enter into a palace. You will never again work a 15-hour shift. Your hands will never again be stained by soot; your hair will always be flowing, your rags replaced with royal dresses. You will always be beautiful. You will never have fear when a man approaches you for you will always let him in. And when you get dirty, you will bathe in milk.

"This used to be an impossible prize to give. In a rage, God sent a mountain of rock to obliterate us. It covered our world in darkness. Mother Nature damned us all. Those who survived faced oblivion. They had nothing. Nothing but fiery hope and a desire that proved even stronger than the rock that had come to exterminate us all. These few came together from around the world! United! They rebuilt on this peninsula! A place detached from the rest of the dying world that had proven unwilling to carry onward. It is through their will that we all stand. And through the General's leadership, each one of you has the opportunity to stand taller. To rise from the ashes and reach for glory."

The Inner Circle's stands erupted in applause.

"Before the process begins," Aizen continued, "the women of the Inner Circle have prepared a performance so that you potential applicants can better understand their lives."

Aizen's image began to flicker, then vanished completely as the spinning line that had cocooned him slowed and retracted into the podium. Steve looked over at Leslie. She was leaning forward in anticipation with her wrist raised.

A single angelic voice rose from the silence. It came from a blue ball that was rising above the great wall. Thousands of little flashes and clicks lit out from the stands.

A slice of granite spanning from the bottom to the top of the wall detached itself. It was shaped like a needle with its point holding up the fragile blue ball, threatening to pop it at any moment. Goosebumps rose on Steve's skin like a rash.

The ground boomed again, not once but repeatedly this time, creating a distinctive beat. The granite needlepoint started to descend onto the field. Electronic sounds began to build and complement the beautiful voice. The crowd cheered as the sounds melded together in a terrifyingly beautiful and powerful song.

The needlepoint came down and rested its tip into a slit on the podium. The blue ball sat motionless on top of the podium surface. It was made of glass and filled with a thick blue fog; the faint silhouette of a woman gleamed through it.

Ohhhhh, I started with nothing, she sang.

Started with nothing

Started with nothing

I awoke in the ash

Among the dust

Rose with the dying sunnnnnn

I slaved all day

I cried all night

Knew nothing but pain

And then this day caaaaaammmmme

A line of stunningly beautiful women appeared from the opening in the wall, marching confidently across the narrow granite needle in six-inch heels. The crowd erupted. Each woman was dressed in a long piece of twined royal red silk that emphasized their every feature that the men of Edingburg could only dream of having. The women stopped just before the podium, where the blue ball sang.

I remember the pain

Remember the pressure

Remember the heartbreak

Remember the fear

The line of women spun, and the end piece of their robes unraveled and floated down to the floor of the bridge. A thin line of spikes on the edges of the bridge speared the silk, trapping it.

It held me back

My soul failed to breathe

I could barely stand

Knees wobbling

The women halted mid-spin, half facing the bullpen to Steve's right, the others facing the stands to his left.

The angelic voice paused and then reached an epic climax:

And then I let gooooo!

The women stepped off the edge of the needle. People in the crowd shrieked as the women plummeted toward the ground, their robes unraveling from their bodies. The unraveling slowed their fall, allowing them to land gracefully. The singing silhouette of the woman held her note. The women kneeled motionless, eyes closed, arms outstretched, their now-naked bodies silhouetted behind the streams of silk, the emblem of the Phoenix Cycle etched in their fibers.

The voice faded away, and the electronic beat stilled. A nervous bead of sweat ran down Steve's back. The electronic music slowly began to build up once more. Thunderous applause rang out from the stands.

Golden sparks shot all around the stadium. The beat abruptly stopped at its crescendo. An enormous white flash banged into the stadium, flooding every eye with blinding light.

And look where I am noooowww!

The percussion boomed again. As the crowd's vision returned, they saw hundreds of women armed with unfathomable beauty saturating the entire field in perfect lines. They danced in flawless coordination with one another, following the mood of the beat like it was their own. They all dressed in royal red two-pieces of silk and composite. Men in the crowd bellowed testosterone-filled roars.

I got what I want

I gave what they need

I didn't have a thing

Now I have everything

The needle bridge began to rise, leaving the singing blue ball behind on the raised podium. The lines of silk detached from the bridge row by row as it rose. Ten six-foot wide discs rose from the ground. Long metal poles slowly pushed the discs upward. One by one, the women threw themselves onto the rising poles and held onto them with their slim thighs.

It took a lot to rise

To hear my family cry

To explain to all

As to why

Without the refuge

Of a lie

The poles rose higher and higher until every pole was covered with women. Those at the top were nearly 60 feet in the air, all still holding on with nothing but their legs. The bass bumped as the voice on the podium sang.

I had no help

I was by myself

I had to ...

To face myself

To hate myself

I had to do it all

For myself

I dared to stand alone

Live a life that some condone

To leave my home

... And then I entered ...

And now I KNOOOW!

The only love I need is of my-selllllllllllllllf!

Steve plugged his ears as the beat imploded in on itself, tearing and ripping down everything that the long buildup had created.

The blue ball splintered, lines of cracks growing over the orb like vines. The voice screamed even louder, and the thin lining of glass exploded from the stress of the vibration. A percussion blast shot out in a flat horizontal wave, carrying clouded shards of blue. Like a waterfall the women-clad poles spilled back into the ground. Steve looked through the magnifying glass to get a quick look at the mysterious singing girl as everything shattered to pieces, but the podium was empty. The field had emptied as well, and only the woman's voice still echoing through the stadium and the dumbstruck crowd gave any indication that the spectacle had ever even happened.

Then the Inner Circle in the stands across the field stood and clapped. Steve looked around his section; the Phoenix Cycler nominees looked enraptured, their companions defeated. He touched Leslie's arm and she slowly turned to look back at him with a blank stare. The crowd cheered.

"Number three," shouted a guard in the front of their section.

Steve's heart beat wildly. What happened to sections one and two?

The nominees in their section looked around at each other, uncertain. Leslie's head was down. Steve watched as her feet began to move forward. Steve reached out and touched her fingers, but she slipped away and walked down the steps that led to the field.

"Please join the line forming in section one," the guard instructed her. More young women began trickling down the stands. Steve watched as girl after girl walked down those same front steps, forcing him to relive Leslie's exit over and over again.

A few painful minutes passed as the women lined up for the coming event. Then another quaking boom, even stronger than the others, shook the earth. A long pole rose inside the General's unoccupied booth and began to spin, casting the outline of Aizen's body.

A young girl slowly rose up from inside the podium. It was Leslie. She stood alone under the visual scrutiny of the entire city, her image plastered onto every magnifying lens.

Aizen spoke to Leslie with unrelenting rigidity, his voice shaking the stadium.

"To the city, do you declare that you are 21 years of age and were born during the Phoenix Cycle?"

Leslie's voice whimpered through the speakers.

"Louder!" Aizen commanded.

"Yes."

"The decision you are about to make is yours and yours alone. Do you understand this?"

"Yes."

Aizen paused, allowing anticipation to bloom.

"Do you wish to apply?"

All of the Republic leaned forward, curiosity burning.

Leslie's voice whispered through the speakers. "Yes."

Steve's heart tore.

A large projection filled the smooth sloping wall above the Inner Circle's booths. Green bars flicked longer and shorter in quick spasms.

"This device will measure your honesty. Now, state your reason for this decision."

"I want to live the life of the women in the Inner Circle."

The bars flicked larger and smaller, but remained green and docile.

"Continue," Aizen said.

Leslie looked up, her eyes bright with tears. "I don't want to live in a garage any more! I don't want to always be covered in dirt! I want the jewels, the beautiful clothes! I want a life filled with color and excitement!"

"What about your family? Your loved ones?"

Leslie's head dropped back down. "I love them. I want what's best for them … We always said we could make it, but it would just be too hard for them to support me. I'm a burden!"

The bars surged and sprung all the way across the wall, turning red hot toward her last statement. A buzzer rang through the speakers. The podium shook hard as if it had been kicked. Leslie fell to her knees.

"Liar! Liar!" the crowd chanted.

Aizen's eyes were glowing red. "If you lie again, your application will be revoked. Now answer the question truthfully."

Leslie sobbed on the floor of the podium. Her worst fear had come. Until that buzzer rang, she'd told herself the same thing each morning, but could never tell if it was really true or just something she used to mask her from her real self.

"I care about them, I do. They're great people and they've always been there for me and I appreciate everything they've done. But I refuse …" Leslie lightly punched the floor with her fist. "I refuse to be in debt to them. I do not owe my family or anyone anything. It was their decision to treat me as well as they did, and I love them for it, but I refuse to let them hold me back. I should put myself first! I am free to choose my own life, no matter who it might hurt!"

The bars on the projection turned back to green, and Aizen gave a satisfied smile. "Rise."

Leslie got up, facing Aizen. The crowd stood at attention—the most illustrious and infamous moment of the event was here. Aizen spoke with cold fire. "Prove to the Inner Circle that you are willing and able to fulfill your duties."

Leslie took a breath, and her left hand slowly slid down the front of her dress, unfastening the buttons. She pressed her right hand against her chest for a moment. Then her dress slid down past her thighs.

With trembling confidence she stood completely naked under the scrutiny of every man in the known world. The podium began to turn, and every angle of her body was gaped at and judged through the magnifying lenses that encircled her. The podium finally stopped when she had made a full rotation, and all had taken their fill.

The projection of the lie detector had been replaced with a voting panel. A gold bar slowly crept up the projection, and with it, a gangway extended toward the podium. Leslie's naked body trembled as the bar inched higher and higher with every favorable vote from the Inner Circle onlookers.

Steve looked down at his feet. He watched one of his tears fall and darken the concrete. Had he been betrayed? Or did he lose a love he never truly had?

The gold line reached its summit with the sound of an enormous lock unlatching. Leslie took a quivering step onto the gangway, then walked naked and alone into the Inner Circle. Her discarded watch, amplified by the microphones on the podium, pinged frantically as it notified the city of the cascade of likes their profile was receiving. The gangway retracted, locking her into that world forever.

Steve thought of his mother, her face as she lowered him onto the ground beside the statue outside the stadium. She kissed his forehead and she said she would love him forever. Then she stood and turned away, never to return to the squalid streets of Edingburg.

He looked down at the guard standing at attention by a magnetic warning sign next to the exit of his section. The guard looked back, and a little smirk slowly budded onto his face.

Steve touched the cassette in his pocket. He still believed in

Haadin's teachings, but his methods, they were too much: "For every strike they deal upon you they grow weaker, not from exhaustion but from their own hatred, the hatred of themselves."

But that was nonsense. That guard's smirk wouldn't disappear if he let the man beat him. It'd probably grow into a full-blown smile.

Steve glared at the guard in a rage; the guard's smirk held. It may have even gotten a little bigger.

Steve was done with unconditional benevolence. He was done with tackling injustice by letting evil men do their worst to him, like he was some wisdom-revealing rag doll.

Beating him didn't make them feel bad. Protests only excited them, like a pack of wolves finding a lost calf. Allowing these monsters of a child's nightmare to do as they please didn't cure them of their black hearts—it provoked them. By quenching their thirst their desires grew even darker. Steve fumed as these thoughts turned to truths inside his mind.

Steve's hand became a fist as he hurled himself over his section. He came down on the guard's face with incredible force, shattering the man's jaw. Sparks flared in Steve's vision as something struck the back of his head. Steve turned and grabbed the second guard's nightstick. As they wrestled for it Steve kicked him in the chest, knocking him back onto the railing. The guard grabbed Steve and flung him past the magnetic warning sign. The band on Steve's wrist activated, slicing open his artery. The guard lunged forward, cracking his nightstick across Steve's forehead, and he collapsed to the grass.

The guard who had been smirking at him stood over him, holding his jaw. Steve's vision blurred, but he could see the shine of the guard's bloodied teeth. Another set of combat boots appeared, but these had golden plates at their toe. A man in a gas mask kneeled down to Steve's level. "I'll dispose of him," he said to the other guards in a deep muffled voice. His gloved hands reached into Steve's clothing and took the cassette. The masked man was so close, Steve could hear his earpiece.

"Did you get him?"

"Yes," the guard said.

"Does he have the cassette?"

"Yes, Mom."

"Thank goodness. Bring Steve back to us, dear."

From under the guard's sleeve's a cold spray shot out and froze Steve's bleeding wrist.

Part II

The IRA

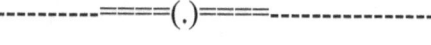

Know Your City!

Discover the History of this Great City, via Line's Broadcasts!

-Uncover the foundation that created our empire.

-Understand the Scots-Irish sins and the General's good heart.

This is a poster they would hang in school when I was a child. It showed our place in the world and what we could become.

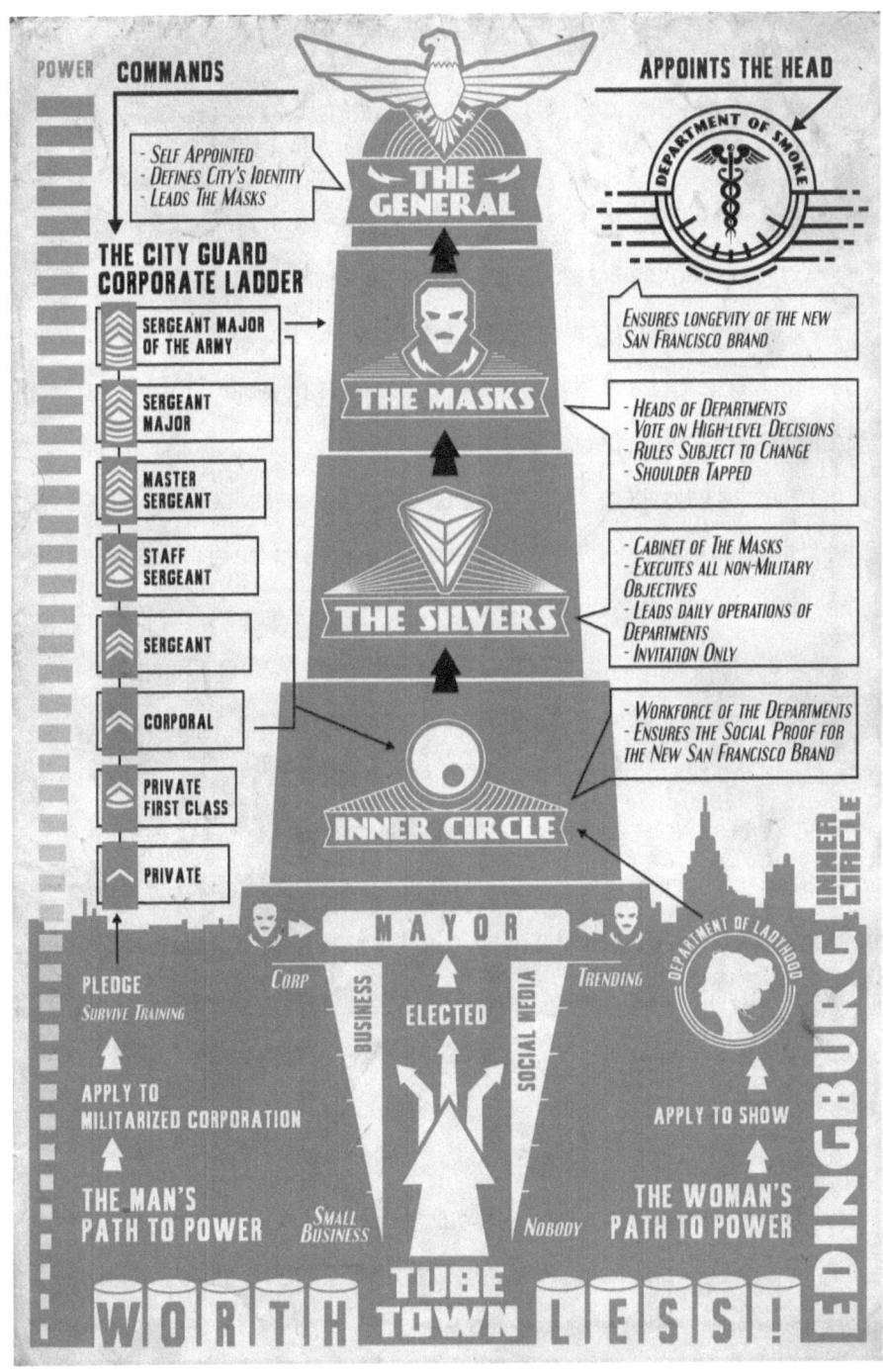

Day Break Radio

Broadcast #5

Mr. Mayor and His Grand Plan

Good morning, New San Francisco. This is your confidant Line here. Thank you for taking the time to listen to this mandatory broadcast.

We are coming to you live from the steps of the Capitol. Our new mayor, Mr. Johnny McHenry, has been in office for 100 days now and will be divulging his grand plan to restore peace and order to the city. He has pledged to his "children," as he calls them, that the needs of the poorest of our city will and must be met. He also understood this must be done even with the slimmest budget this city has had since its reestablishment.

We will be turning our microphone over to Mr. McHenry now, who is shaking the hands of some of the thousands of citizens who have come from every part of the city to hear his speech. Even members of the Inner Circle have come out for this pivotal address that shall determine the future of this city. He is approaching the podium with the newly rehabilitated ivory Capitol building behind him. Some still find his wearing a mask over his face at all times a highly strange and even worrying tactic. However, even masked, his folksy charm and message shined through to the voters. So if you ask me it's not what he looks like that matters. It's what he says right now. Here he is.

Mornin'

The hundred days went pretty quick, didn't it? Well, let's get to it. It's no secret this city's got problems. First bein' food, second bein' shelter, third bein' healthy in general. It's a tall order to be fixin' all that, given the storms and everythin' else we got goin' on 'round here. And to fix it, we gotta admit to some of our own sins. Not everyone's pullin' their weight. Not everyone's puttin' in as much as their takin' out. Now don't get antsy; I know we all got problems and things are tougher than ever round here. And as I promised, with me leading this administration we are finally gettin' Edingburg the resources it needs, because nobody in the world needs more help than Edingburg. As we all know, near all our best children been cherry picked from us by the City Guard an' the Inner Circle. And it just isn't fair. So I went up to 'em 'n' got them to listen for once. So I told them. Come on over from them big walls of theirs, roll up their sleeves, and help. Us. Out.

So Ms. Rand, would you please wheel that beautiful contraption out here we've been developin' so they all can see it?

It appears the beautiful Miss Rand is coming onto the stage now. Attached to her luxurious motorized wheelchair is what looks to be a … tube of some sort. Mr. McHenry is now plugging wires into the tube. More lights on the tube are sparkling on. A nice low hum is coming from the device. Mr. Johnny McHenry has grabbed the mic from off the podium. A demonstration, perhaps? Let's see where this goes!

All right, what we have here is what the boys and girls in marketing call Capsule. This puppy is going to revolutionize our city. It'll end the hunger and free y'all of pains of the day. It'll take away the horror of the night and give you breath of fresh air. It'll save this city from utter collapse by massively reducing the waste of our precious resources.

How? By doin' exactly what I promised. By givin' you a new world! A virtual one. One where even the most horrific storms can't wake you up. When you're in one of these, the pains of the outside world won't be worrying you any. Inside here, all your needs, food, water, shelter, sanitation, and even clean air will be met at a fraction of the cost it cost y'all now. Capsule is the microverse of the future.

Now let's take a tour of her!

Mr. McHenry is pressing a few passcodes into an LED screen now, unlocking the door. Okay, the door is slowly rising open now. A thick fog is drifting out of the tube now. My pamphlet here tells me that the fog is actually a kind of soap, keeping the inhabitant in a clean and infection-free space that can even catch any outside debris that may float in from the storm. And here she is! Oh, wow. The beautiful Miss Flannery is standing inside the new Capsule. Her eyes are closed. It seems rest and relaxation are the only thing that happens for many in these tubes. A few strings and chords are cascading around her hips and body. There seems to be a respirator slash feeding tube resting over her nose and mouth. Mr. McHenry is now gently removing the chords. Careful, Mayor, I know about a hundred City Guardsmen who will be very unhappy if you misplace a single strand of her fiery red hair.

Her eyes are opening. She is rubbing her right eye vigorously, probably from her long nap. But she is smiling, happy to see Mr. McHenry. He is escorting her out of the tube. He's about to speak.

Miss Flannery, how was your stay in Capsule?

Flannery: It was wonderful actually. I feel great! There's a whole other world in there! With fresh air. Blue skies. And even a city!

A city, huh?

Flannery: Yes! It's just like Edingburg, but it's beautiful. It's everything the city could be! There's no broken windows or debris or those dreadful camps of the homeless.

Yes ma'am. The creators of the program have already built the NEW New San Francisco. Everything this city could become has been designed and computer-generated.

Flannery: *It was wonderful. Lonely though.*

Lonely, huh?

Flannery: *Yes, I was the only one there for a whole week.*

Well I'd wager that won't be for long because we are about to roll out the first 10,000 Capsules this year! So that all you boys can keep Miss Flannery company!

Also, did y'all hear that! She was livin' there, inside the Capsule, a whole dang week straight! Now this isn't going to be the norm, of course, Capsule is meant to be used like a regular home where you can relax, sleep, and play and then go out and tackle the day. But the week straight just proves how resilient this machine really is. And it says right here on this screen that she only ate and breathed about $20 worth of food and clean air for the week! Compare that to the $60 a day it takes now to even survive round here right now and you start seein' the real potential we got here!

But how can we get you everyday people one? How are hard workin', honest people gonna get themselves this thing that looks about ready to blast off to Mars! Well, that's why I got the Inner Circle involved. They have agreed to finance and subsidize this brand new job-creating industry. It'll work just like buying a home. Where you lease to own. And after only ten years of payments, this spaceship yours!

This will greatly enable everyone in the city by greatly reducing their expenses and ergo make the budget we currently have, more than ample to maintain our current welfare programs for those most in need. It's even possible for the disabled to find work within these tubes. By creating a virtual utopia, we've laid the first bricks to making it a reality!

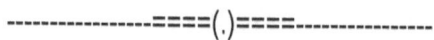

Day Break Radio

Broadcast #72

The Great Franchisement

Gooood morning, New San Francisco.

We have received word from the General's great embarkment! He and 3,000 of our best boys have landed on the beaches of Edinburgh, Scotland! With olive branch in fist he has shaken the hand of their prime minister. Turns out they've done pretty well for themselves! Nearly a million inhabitants. Can you believe it! Almost half of them Irish! I guess redheads and kilts just go together huh.

Their prime minister, Fergus Brown, had this to say in regards to our interest in bringing the Capsule program to their city.

Firstly, Oid just like to say it be givin' us real comfort knowin' thar be people livin' somewhere's on yer side of tha world. Haven't seen a boat come from the west in ages. It also humbles me ta know that you've been goin' through sum o' tha same mess we've been goin' through. In that way we have ourselves an understandin' and I believe me I feel fer ya. When them gusts o' wind come rippin' through yer homes so hard, yer not sure if it'll be takin' you or yer little ones with it. On that I gotta tall glass o' sympathy for ya.

With that said I understand the need fer distraction with yer Capsules idea. Admittedly we've been gettin' by on a pint or two a night, but we find it real interestin' the practicality of it all; given the cheap air and livin' conditions. Might just be what we need before winter hits us again.

If our people be wantin' something like yer Capsule and are willin' to barter for it in their own way, who are we to get in the way of it. This is a great opportunity fer our people to be gettin' to know one another. So come on ova! We'll have a pint with ya any time!

Well there you have it! The new Capsule franchise has opened its first remote branch. Capsule is already shipping over 500 Capsules as we speak and Ghost Fox is already setting up a specialized port and facilities for our coming establishment there. This is a great opportunity for our city and a great way to build relations. By trading and earning the best of what each city can provide, Capsule may be the world's first step to coming back together!

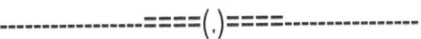

Day Break Radio
Broadcast #204
LA's Great Shepherd

Gooooood morning, New San Francisco! Thanks for taking the time for this mandatory broadcast. I'm your host, Line; let's begin.

Our boys are back! They have ended the siege of our Capsule colony in Old Los Angeles and they brought with them the final 500 blue bloods to our cause. The rest of them just didn't have the right stuff. And reports are saying that

LA is weeks away from total self-implosion. We are done there. We refuse to associate with the weak.

The Shepherd of the Final 500 had this to say:

Making it to New San Francisco was hell. But that's all we ever knew in LA. So now I feel we have finally made it! To a city of people with the right priorities! We have left a city of excuses. We have left a city of people with no gumption, no will to stand with pride!

For God's sake, the nuclear waste from 70 years ago still poisons our dirt! They still haven't cleaned it out! My generation that grew from that filth would rather wallow and commend each other's wounds instead of one another's achievements!

For three years I converted and housed our colony in LA. We grew to over a thousand. We built a wonderful compound with clean facilities, erected a greenhouse to perfect San Fran specs, and sold as many Capsules to LA as they could buy. By doing so we finally earned our ticket to your great city. But LA wouldn't let us go. They had become parasitic and depended far too much on our abilities to maintain their Capsules. So they made our compound into a prison. A place where our only joy was fixing what we had already sold them. In return for our slave labor they'd spit on us. Curse us for the machines they obsessively used day in and day out. Forcing us to keep them online in the very thing they damned us for.

Ruth Hinder, our colony's hero, found a way to send out a distress beacon to the General. Three days later your Guardsmen, Ghost Fox Corporation, appeared and ripped those demons apart, liberating us. We are forever grateful and are ready to continue to prove our worth to not only your city but to her values.

LA's Best Have Arrived!

That sobering message is from George Whitefield, the Lead Shepherd of our now dissolved LA colony. He will become the head of their labor union as they integrate into our city. Please welcome them with open arms. They earned it. They sold a lot of Capsules.

It is with a heavy heart that we remember the 500 who did not make it out of LA. It is important to remember that many of our colony's have experienced extreme prejudice towards our people and the businesses they grew under the Capsule franchise umbrella. And just like LA, Seattle, London, Edinburgh, Paris, Berlin, and countless towns along the way, we will protect our colonies wherever they stand. And so long as they've earned their ticket, we will bring them home to New San Francisco, no matter the distance.

The Capsule franchise is what keeps our city strong. It is the seed that allows us to grow colonies throughout the world. It keeps essential goods, trade, and high-quality personnel flowing into our city. So it is imperative we hold strong and protect our franchise because they are the ambassadors of our city and her values. So to the final cities still standing and listening, an attack on our Capsule colony's is an attack on New San Francisco herself. If you raid our colony's, hurt our people, or even spit on the Capsule logo, we will arrive at your door and we will knock it down.

If you have a problem with the Capsule's products or services. Then don't buy them. It's your CHOICE! No refunds!

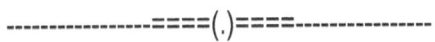

Day Break Radio

Broadcast #350

The Great Salvation

Good morning, New San Francisco. This is your confidant Line here. Thank you for taking the time to listen to this mandatory broadcast.

We've got one heck of a shipment of Eding...Eding...burg-ians? Well whatever you call those kilt-wearing boys. They're all sailing over here en masse! Turns out the city was ill prepared for winter and mass starvation is occurring. Not enough potatoes in the cupboard, I guess. Now normally we wouldn't let some beggars who lack personal responsibility come on over to our city and grovel for scraps, but the General has struck a deal with them that allows them to earn their lunch.

As you are well aware, given our increased security concerns, last year the General announced the construction of the Grand Wall around our city. But as of today we are already about a year behind on the project. Given nearly every city left in the world has gone dry of worthwhile inhabitants, it's become near impossible to find good help these days. So this Edingburg situation has come at a rather advantageous time, for both our peoples. We get our wall and they get to be part of a real city, with real values.

In return for giving them this great opportunity, their prime minister accepted the official apology given by Capsule to the people of Edinburgh on account of the food shipped to Edinburgh went bad well before the advertised expiration date. As a consolation Capsule will be giving them free food for the winter, here in New San Francisco. So all is square.

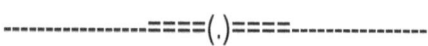

Day Break Radio

Broadcast #495

The Great Transfer of Property

Good morning, New San Francisco. This is your confidant Line here. Thank you for taking the time to listen to this mandatory broadcast.

We are nearly ten years into the implementation of Mr. Johnny McHenry's Capsule program. Meaning that in the coming weeks the lease-to-own program for the over 10,000 people who signed up for their very own Capsule in New San Francisco are about to finally become home owners!

But as always, there are a lot of gripers out there! So let's straighten a few things out before this great transition of property to the common man takes place.

First are the reports that parts in the Capsules are breaking apart more often now ... Well, of course they are! Your Capsules are nearly ten years old! People are gossiping that the Capsule's parts were designed to only last as long as the ten-year contracts, which is total garbage. Ten years is a long time and people have been using the Capsules far more than anyone planned for. Remember, Capsules are supposed to be a place to sleep and unwind in for a couple hours. If it breaks apart because you can't get your butt out of it, then that's your choice, isn't it? You're about to be homeowners; it's time to start taking some responsibility. Complaints won't fix your Capsule. You will.

Next big gripe is location. People are complaining that older buildings and warehouse districts are essentially becoming trailer parks for Capsulites. If a Capsulite wants to move out of their apartment to stay within their means, then I'd call that responsible budgeting, wouldn't you? It's their choice to move, and I stand behind their right to live anywhere they can afford! So no, don't expect a bill regulating where people can live or dictating how the warehouse owners should handle this new use of their space. Yes, the reports on the living conditions of some of the warehouses are pretty nasty, but if a Capsulite really hates it then they can just move, can't they?

Last big gripe is about the feeding tubes and some of the vendors providing the nutrients. This one I don't get because the big payout from the class action lawsuit last year should have put this one to bed. Don't get me wrong, I completely agree that those vendors should have regulated their food products more strictly. And it's inexcusable that the nutrients being sold from the vendors for the better part of a decade should have discovered and fixed the addictive properties found in their products. And the courts agreed with you too. That's why they gave everyone harmed by those vendors a big subsidy in power for their Capsule for the foreseeable future. Also as a courtesy, the vendors involved handed out their products free for the next 12 months as an apology to the harmed parties. Heck, put all that together and you basically live for free! Yes, the vendors messed up, but it was the Capsulites' CHOICE to take the nutrients after that. I remember they even had the word ADDICTIVE written in bold over half the packaging. No excuse for missing that.

Well that's all for today. Again, congratulations to those ten of thousands who are soon to become homeowners in the coming year. Take pride in seizing your piece of the American dream.

We salute you.

Augmented

"Is he alive?" the voice in the earpiece asked.

"Is who alive?"

"You know perfectly well who! Quit screwing around, we need to know!"

"There are tons of people who are either alive or not alive! Be more specific!" Ramfort threw up his arms as if someone was around to see him.

A frustrated pause hung over the line.

"… Here's Mom."

"About time," Ramfort said.

"How's Steve, dear?" a woman's voice in the earpiece asked.

Ramfort swung his gaze at the bed that stood at the end of the concrete garage. An IV bag fastened to the garage door was slowly trickling fresh blood into Steve's veins.

"He's stable."

"Good."

Ramfort stood up and kicked the embers in the crumbling fireplace with his commandeered City Guardsman's boot. The room reignited with twinkling light and hummed with flickering pops.

"Where are you?"

Ramfort circled around the floral sofa. It sat like a tacky tropical island in the middle of the drab room.

"Steve's place. Did you get anything from—" Ramfort flung out his fingers in a mystical gesture— "Johnny?"

"Yes, we've gotten his version of what happened at the burning."

Ramfort paced over to the end of the room and bent down to peer through a hole in the bent and rusted garage door. A half-dozen guardsmen stood at the edge of the property. They had anchored two long poles into the ground and slipped another bar horizontally on top of them. A crowd had gathered, most of them men. Due to the Phoenix Girls' application process, young women had become quite scarce around the block, and the excess testosterone was piling up.

A teenager was suddenly pushed forward from the crowd. "Show these boys that my son can bring rise in the world just as well as they have!" a man yelled, presumably the kid's father. A guard waved the teen over with his handgun.

"And what, pray tell, does Johnny think he saw?" Ramfort asked.

"We've only compiled the ending of the memory so far. It will have to do. His memory of the event has been uploaded to the headset."

Ramfort snapped his head over to a table that was hugging the near corner of the room. A small orange light on the mobile receiver station holding the headset fluttered and sparked green.

"No! No way I'm plugging in, especially into one of his memories!"

"It's important you experience it for yourself. Aside from Steve,

Johnny is the most important person to our movement. You must be able to understand him."

"Can't you just tell me?"

"Please watch it, dear. I realize the machine's effects, but this is of utmost importance."

Ramfort's shoulders slumped. "Crap."

The metal garage door roared, echoing the crack of a gunshot outside. Shouts. Ramfort ran over to the door and hunched down to peer through the bullet hole. The teenager outside was frantically doing pull-ups on the freestanding bar as the crowd cheered and counted along.

"One! Two! Three! Four!"

The man's voice came back onto the line. "What's going on, what was that noise?"

"I was talking to Mom," Ramfort hissed.

"What. Was. That. Noise."

"Gunfire."

"Gunfire! Have you been compromised?"

Ramfort grinned. "Yeah."

Immediately there was a commotion on the other side of the line. Ramfort stood up straight and stretched his arms, allowing them to take some of the weight off his long spine.

"Fifteen! Sixteen! Seventeen!" the crowd outside chanted.

"Proceed to point bravo, I will call Kl—"

"They're everywhere!" Ramfort shouted, lines of sarcastic horror etched into his thin face. "They're coming through the walls!"

"Get out of there!"

"Oh no! They got me! They got meeee!" Ramfort shuffled backward and fell onto Steve's sagging couch. His gangly legs flew upward. "Ugh! I'm … down."

"Twenty-seven! Twenty-eight! Twenty-nine!" the crowd chanted outside the garage door.

"No! I'm coming to get you. Don't die on me. I can't lose you!"

"What?" Ramfort gasped. "Why not?"

Ramfort snapped out of his act and sat up perfectly straight on the slouching couch. His head cricked to the side. The flames from the fireplace danced in front of him.

"You can't lose *me*?" Ramfort asked.

A confused fuzz floated over the other end of the transmission.

"… What?" An angry fist crashed down onto an unfortunate table somewhere on the other end of the line. "Are you kidding me?! You shithead."

"Language!" Ramfort barked. "And it wasn't my fault. I was having some flashback recall thing from the headset. I'm telling you I shouldn't put that thing on any more—"

"That wasn't a fucking flashback, you little piece of—"

"Stop cursing," Ramfort said, rolling his eyes, "or I'll tell Mom."

The voice fell silent.

"Forty-five! Forty-six!"

"Man, that kid can go," Ramfort got up from the couch to peer through the bullet hole again.

"What kid?" the voice asked. "You mind telling me what's actually going on over there?"

"There's a crowd of people cheering this kid on as he does pull-ups. It's weird."

"It's a tradition they hold every year after the women's application. They're competing to see who's the strongest on the block before the 21-year-olds apply for the City Guard. Keeps the rah-rah up for their applications and makes the winners feel more confident before they apply."

"Fifty-seven! Fifty-eight …" The boys arms were shaking wildly, and his face was bright red. "Fifty-nine!"

The boy went for another. His body shook so wildly the bar quaked. Then he bellowed with such ferocity it seemed as if a beast had been awoken.

"Sixty!"

The boy dropped to the ground, and the guard gave him an affection thump on the chest with his gun. "This kid's got fire in 'em! Way to go, Yoden!"

"There's no real correlation to pull-ups, getting promoted, or getting into a reputable mercenary group," the voice said, "but you can see why it would comfort them."

"How does the City Guard work, anyway?" Ramfort asked. "It's like an army made up of smaller armies."

"Essentially yes. The City Guard is a heavily regulated for-profit industry. The Inner Circle sets the basic rules of how the companies are to be structured, how they get new recruits, and how people can be promoted within the company.

"Everyone who joins the guard has to initially work for what people call 'corporate.' It's almost like a regular army, but it's structured like a for-profit business. The money comes from 'contracts' the Inner Circle gives out publicly. The companies then compete to fulfill the contracts. The company that completes the contract gets paid—a lot.

"There's only two main corporations now. The others got eliminated one way or another. So right now they are the only ones that can meet the Inner Circle's 'training' requirements needed in order to receive new recruits each cycle.

"Once a recruit gets to a high enough rank, they are seen as competent. From there they are allowed to switch from whom they work for. They may also join the Inner Circle or start their own little mercenary business. Most new businesses do security or patrols for parts of the city —basically any contracts that corporate doesn't want to deal with."

Ramfort straightened up and walked over to the headset sitting on the table. "Did you find out where all those guns came from? Edingburg's been going bananas every since the girls shook their fannies on application day. Some kind of Santa apparently dropped off 20 crates of guns and ammo right into the middle of—" Ramfort looked at the scribbled words on his hands— "Old Hate Park during the show. When Edingburg got back. They all saw it. Been hearing gunfire every 15 minutes since. Can't believe these guards are still having their little pull-upalooza during all this. Wonder how much they're getting paid to do that little stunt."

"No, we're in the dark on those guns too. Our source is being difficult," the voice said, "It's not the method we were wanting, but the city is definitely paying attention to Edingburg now. We can use this to work for us. Now watch Johnny's episode on the headset." The transmission ended with a click.

Ramfort blew out his cheeks, then lifted the headset out of its charging station. He walked back over to the couch and sat down. The flames from the fireplace reflected on the strained lines in face.

"I'd rather be doing pull-ups," he murmured.

He put on the headset and flicked a switch on its side. A metallic box covered his left eye. The pinchers inside it slowly inserted themselves into the whites of Ramfort's eye, and a small light on the box blinked green as the device activated. Ramfort's other eye stared blankly into the fireplace as he left his own consciousness and fell into the mayor's memories.

The Burned

The General swooned happily in his chair as he inhaled the smells of the campfire. He turned and looked over at the mayor of Edingburg. "Would you like a drink?"

Hearing no response, the General opened his bag and pulled out a bottle of wine. "Ah, this will do nicely, a 2009 Cab!" He held out the bottle and a servant immediately ran up to retrieve it.

The General smirked at the mayor. "You know, I'm actually really glad you made it through all this. It's impressive. And I've been so busy lately, I haven't been able to just sit and chat with the mayor of my favorite borough in the city. I have to admit, you've done a hell of a job for the most part, for the past—what is it now? Twenty-five years? Five elections? The poor bastards in Edingburg really seem to love you. And you did it all wearing that gimmicky mask I made all you little mayors wear the whole damn time. The masks were supposed to make it to where they couldn't identify with you and so wouldn't really get into it. How did you spin it again? You said it showed that it's not about you but the people? That anyone can help Edingburg? You're one for theatrics, aren't ya? And that stupid voice you put on made you stand out all the same. But they like it. Truly incredible. But the red and the freckled never were the brightest bunch, were they?"

The servant returned with a freshly poured glass of wine on a silver platter. "Two glasses," the General said. The servant bowed and ran back to fetch a second glass.

The General turned back to the mayor. "So, Johnny! This girl, is she something special to you? Never saw her in the limelight during your campaigns."

Johnny didn't respond. He didn't even have the basic manners to look at the General. All his focus was channeled straight in front of him. He took in every twinkling flare as the flames blacked the corpse of the young woman. Johnny watched the girl's golden locks slowly burn into oblivion.

He was broken from his trance by a metal ping. The General had flicked open a lighter and was lighting another cigar. He took a long drag from the cigar and examined the brass bird etched on his lighter as he sat comfortably in his wooden chair.

Rays from the sun continued to trickle over the horizon, coloring the western sky in a purplish orange. The bloodstained grass fairway flickered behind the General's campfire. Johnny sat in a small collapsible metal chair, rope binding his wrists and ankles.

The servant returned; two glasses now stood on top of the sparkling silver tray. The General bit into his cigar and stood. He took hold of the glasses and the servant bowed and scampered away.

The General walked over to Johnny, one glass outstretched. "Bah, of course!" He set the wineglasses on the arms of his wooden chair and untied Johnny's arm. The mayor continued to gaze into the fire, hypnotized as the young girl's blackened corpse popped and sent ashes up into the air.

"So let me guess. She was the girl next door. You grew up watching her from your bedroom window … Occasionally, you could muster the strength to 'run into' her when you were taking out the trash."

The General's voice had become a singsong as he wove his story. "But when she brought other boys home, time seemed to come halt whilst you laid sleepless in your bed. And when you finally rose again, the only sensation you got from your morning stew was from its steam fumigating your face. And when the boy left her you were first in line to offer a shoulder. You became her friend. You were 'nice.' But somehow, someway, you bridged that friendship gap, didn't you? How neat.

"And she was amazing, wasn't she? Oh, she wasn't *perfect*, but her imperfections made her all the more real. Which is exactly what you wanted. She had become more than an image in the window. She was yours."

The knot around Johnny's wrist slipped loose. His arm dropped and hung motionless, unaroused by its regained freedom.

The General drew a metal rod from his bag, extended it, and walked over to the fire, the burnt grass crunching beneath his feet. The flames danced on the lenses of his sunglasses.

"Someone cared; you were actually worth something. Your actions had meaning. She made you feel like a real man."

The General began to stoke the fire with the rod. "She gave you virtue." The metal rod glided over the burning girl's hand. It slid beneath her fingertips and slowly began to elevate her hand upward.

"Stop!" Johnny shouted.

The General twisted on his heels and stared, his face devoid of expression. The fire stilled. Johnny shook uncontrollably as his eyes sunk into the tar pits of the General's sunglasses.

The General stabbed the rod into the charcoals of the fire and lunged at Johnny, whipping out a pistol from his jacket and shoving it into Johnny's face.

"So the mayor of Edingburg can speak!" The general grabbed Johnny's shoulder and shook him violently. "You want me to stop?! You want this to be over?!"

The General slapped the pistol into Johnny's hand. "Then end it!" he said, grabbing Johnny's hand and forearm and jamming the gun into his own chest.

Johnny swooned in his chair, disoriented by the General's suicidal behavior. "I have virtue," he said, his voice dull and mechanical. "Edingburg will rise with virtue as well."

The General scowled. "You? Virtuous? You restrain yourself from doing what you lust for, and that somehow makes you virtuous!"

Johnny looked up into the black-clouded sky. "I follow nature's river."

The General snorted. "I don't remember the last time water came from those clouds."

"The world began as fire," Johnny said. "It will end as fire. It's okay. I will go with nature. I will not lose my way to passion."

"All right, that's enough." The General backhanded Johnny, knocking him out of his meditative state. "The only fire you need to worry about is the spark from this bullet's firing pin. Not a slave to passion? Nature *is* passion! Nature doesn't think! It does not reflect, it does not question what it does. It only does what it feels, what comes naturally."

The General tightened his hold on Johnny's forearm. "Now do it! Listen to what you want and do it! Follow that river, let it run with blood!" He cocked back the hammer and pressed the gun tighter against his chest.

"No, I am not you," Johnny mumbled.

"You think being passive will stop me?" You think cute little words comin' from that horseshit accent you spew at those boyos will stop me?" The General pointed at the fire behind him. "They thought that too!"

Johnny began to hyperventilate as his finger slowly crept onto the trigger.

"I killed the love of your life," the General hissed. "I killed everyone you ever knew! I have taken everything—everything—away from you!" His voice was throaty with passion as he lowered himself to Johnny's eye level. "… And I loved it."

Johnny tried to push out the thoughts, but couldn't help acknowledging the capabilities of the gun in his hand.

"You feel that?" the General barked. "That urge secreting from your loins?!" He drove his fist into Johnny's crotch, then pulled Johnny back up by the hair. "You feel it, don't you? That burning desire to kill me? You feel it infecting you with every pump of your heart." The General inhaled deeply as he listened to the crackles of the fire. "It's arousing isn't it?"

"You've destroyed everything that should have been," Johnny said, his voice cracking.

The General smiled, one hand on Steve's shoulder, the other still pointing the gun at his chest. "Yes. So you know what you have to do, because you and I both know that I'm never going to stop."

"You poisoned our roots," Johnny said. "There's nothing left for you to destroy or for me to save." He shook his head free of the General's grip. "You've ruined our home and I will not build you another one to burn!" He swung the gun around, pressed it under his chin, and pulled the trigger.

A flash shot out from the barrel. A casing flung out from the chamber and pinged against the General's sunglasses.

Johnny looked at the General, wide eyed, in total shock.

The General glared back. "God, you are stupid." He straightened up, grunting as he did so. "You really think you could do that?" he asked, grabbing the quivering gun out from under Johnny's chin. He pointed the gun at Johnny's chest and fired three times. Johnny winced with every shot, his will to live slowly rising to stable levels. The General shook his head.

"Idiot."

The General turned on his heel and walked back to the fire. He grabbed the metal poker and drew it out of the fire. He looked up into the distance and waited for the last ray of light to trickle away. Then he strolled back over to Johnny with the rod and stood over him, the tip of the poker glowing red hot in the darkness.

"You know that what you've done can't be reversed. All you can do now is live with that guilt."

The General looked down on Johnny, his face expressionless, the lenses of his sunglasses devoid of reflection. A snarl split the General's lips, revealing rows of gritted teeth. His knee cocked up and he shot his boot into Johnny's chest, sending him flying backward onto the burnt grass. The General spun the rod, its glowing tip sending off gelatinous drops of molten metal. "No, that's your job," he said, pressing the rod to Johnny's chest.

Johnny let out a feeble scream.

The General pushed his boot into Johnny's throat, muffling Johnny's screams to gurgles.

The General spoke with a controlled rage: "I used to like you. You were useful. It's why I've put up with Edingburg having legitimate fucking elections. It worked, because you were the only fucker I couldn't corrupt, and the people saw that. You gave them hope, which was good because it shut them up. And whenever real hope would spring up—through some movement, some rebellion, some guns getting smuggled into Edingburg—you'd tell me. You'd betray the people you're supposed to represent with some half-cooked belief that fighting me was the wrong way. A peaceful rise is the only way to elevate ourselves or some other horseshit."

The General pressed down harder Johnny's throat. "The real reason you'd tell me, and the real reason why you're so damn useful, is that you inspire them just enough to feel like something's going their way, but when they actually start doing something that might matter, you suddenly don't have the balls to carry out the job."

He lifted his boot off Johnny's throat and pressed it against his seared chest. "You are every bit as responsible for this city as I am. And 25 years in we are still far from retirement … partner. So to help you pull yourself together, I'm granting you admittance … to Alcatraz Prison. You are going to be beaten, starved, frozen—and with any luck, fucked!"

The General leaned in. "And it's going to happen every day. Until you start to fight and kill. Until you finally see that liberty only exists if it means you have the freedom to express your will unto others." Wind began to whip across the bloodstained fairway. "You will remain enchained until the day comes that you begin behaving like God himself. Until then, you'll be taking a leave of absence as mayor of Edingburg." The General raised his middle finger toward the coming storm that was shooting above the horizon.

"When that day comes, when you become a man who walks as the Almighty, I will see you again, and you will set us free."

The memory cut out and the transmission ended.

Checklist

When Ramfort's consciousness returned, he found he was bent over, inches above the still unconscious Steve. The red light from the headset glowed on Steve's closed eyelids. Ramfort's bare eyeball widened as it became aware of what it was staring at.

Ramfort's threw himself backward, tearing off the headset. He stumbled backward and collapsed onto the couch.

The fire popped, and Ramfort jumped. He rubbed his eyes, trying to wipe out the hell that'd been jammed into them.

"Did you watch it?" the voice in Ramfort's earpiece asked.

"Yeah … What was the point of that?"

"For now, it's to know what you're dealing with. If we're going to take him out, then we need to know how he works."

"And I take it Johnny was the only survivor of the protest?"

"Aside from Steve, who was ordered to leave early to deliver the tape, yes. It appears the General didn't want to be killing the famous mayor of Edingburg just yet."

"I don't trust him," Ramfort muttered.

"Johnny's been feeding us information, moving people, and getting our guys out of fixes for decades. He's the only man who's done a single thing for Edingburg since the General took over and he's lost everything in the process. He's pure."

"Pure? You been drinking stupid juice? You heard the General—when shit hits the fan he wimps out and reports everyone! Only reason we're still here is that buttface didn't pick up on what the important stuff was. Now you want to let him in on the big stuff!" Ramfort pulled off the headset and dropped it onto the couch cushion next to him.

Steve stirred in his bed. He tried blinking through the gunk clotting his eyes and made out a plastic tube that traveled down to his arm. He glanced up to see the blood bag hanging over him.

He reached down to his pants, feeling for the cassette. He wasn't wearing any pants. A shadow fell over him. A gold-toed boot cocked up onto his bed. It was the guard who'd dragged him out of the stadium. "You've got one hell of a right cross," the guard said.

"You … you're …" Steve groaned.

The guard pointed at the blood bag. "I'm the guy who got you this. Along with a cocktail of other vitamins and—" he coughed— "steroids. Good thing you finally friggin' woke up. Ran outta IV bags. Anyway, the authorities call me Ramfort. Your name isn't actually Steve, is it? Well?"

No answer. Ramfort flicked the blood bag. "Is this thing working?"

Steve continued to stare, still groggy.

"Helllllooooo, who are yoooouuuu? Did I save Steve or some mooooroooon who just punches peopllllleee?"

Steve nodded.

"What does 'nod' mean? Are you Steve or a moron? Both?"

Steve swallowed and cleared his throat. "Steve."

Ramfort's face crumpled in disgust. "Really! I'd hoped they got the wrong name! Your name sucks!" Ramfort spun and began to pace the room. "Such a basic, uncreative … NAME!" Ramfort paced circles around the floral couch. "Did you even *try* to have a better name?"

Steve blinked, alarmed by the guard's mood swings. What was he doing here? What weird company did he work for? Was this psychotic going to torture him?

Ramfort stomped back to the bed and leaned forward, bringing his face inches away from Steve's. He turned his eye far to the right, exposing a line of three black dots. Even through the haze in Steve's mind, he recognized it immediately. He'd never actually seen this man before—no one had; he was an urban legend of the IRA resistance.

"It's you!" Steve gasped.

"Most likely! Now, where is everyone? I feel like I've been hallucinating this whole time, but I could have sworn there was thing called the IRA."

Steve pulled the IV needle from his vein and swung his legs over the edge of the bed.

Ramfort raised an eyebrow. "Awake for 30 seconds and you're already being a moron." He grabbed Steve's rubbery legs and dropped them back onto the bed, then reinserted the IV needle into Steve's wrist. "You may be pissing blue with all the steroids I got in ya, but you still need a minute before you start moving around."

"What … what happened?"

"You were busier punching guardsmen than delivering cassettes, that's what happened. You basically got yourself killed, but I, the hero, saved you in the nick of time. But you, playing the role of the lazy drama queen, had to go to sleep for a couple of days. So I had to find a way to wake you up, and seeing as I'm no white knight and you'd make for a very ugly princess, the traditional smooching tactic wasn't going to get us anywhere."

Steve groaned. "How long have I been out?"

"A couple of days, so guess what? We are now days behind schedule."

Steve looked up at Ramfort blankly. "What schedule?"

"Believe it or not, we planned a bit more than just that protest!"

"Where's Leslie?"

Ramfort took a step back. "You don't remember?"

Ramfort spun in place, looking around as if Steve had dropped the rest of his memory somewhere. Ramfort looked back at Steve and scrunched his nose. "Don't punch me."

Steve looked at him, confused. The cheers and shouts from outside had faded away, and the fireplace crackled in the still the room.

"She applied."

Steve shut his eyes. The unwanted memories flooding back into him. "I'm alone," he said. "She left me too." He stared up at the long shadowed crack on his ceiling. A moment slunk by. Tears trailed down his face, and a dulled pain pumped through his heart. He thought he'd really had one. A person who found him to be worthwhile enough to keep around. A person who would say they loved him and then wouldn't turn to leave him, like some kind of sick joke. The pain felt inescapable. Even if he were to cease to exist at this very moment, leaving only a hole of where his existence had been; his failure of never finding a person who found *him* worthwhile enough to *not* abandon would still find a way to appear beside him and keep him company in the void.

Ramfort nervously bobbed his head. "I realize you've got a … situation, but I need to know, who do we have left? Who can I contact? Is there even an IRA still around, or did they all just kinda die?"

Steve didn't budge; he'd become a potato. Ramfort looked at his watch, then laid down on the floor, his head next to the foot of the bed, his feet by the headboard. "Everyone's selfish," he said. "Including you, ya little brat. It's how we're wired. All anyone wants is power. It's the basis of everything and every relationship. You're just pissy cuz your girlfriend kinda changed the power dynamic a bit."

The house began to vibrate, the walls sizzling as if it had been thrown into a frying pan. A sudden series of explosion shook the garage. Ramfort jumped up. Long sprays of distant gunfire echoed through the peephole in the garage door.

"That one was real." Ramfort said.

The voice buzzed in Ramfort's ear. "Transponder is flooded with dispatch contracts. Chatter's saying Edingburg is going into full revolt. I guess word is officially out about what happened at the protest." A deep wailing sound grew and shook the air.

"They're liquidating Edingburg! They're gonna block off this whole zip code!" Ramfort said. He jumped up and started throwing his equipment into his rucksack. "Stupid siren!" He threw a City Guardsman's jacket at Steve. "Powwow over! Put it on!"

Steve slowly began trying to rise back out of bed. "Good," Steve moaned. "Edingburg's alone anyway. Now that they're putting up a fence, they're just being more honest about it."

"We need to be ready to move! That siren is every subcontracting mercenary's wet dream! That horn is basically declaring open season on us until the barriers get put up around Edingburg! Those guards could knock down this door right now! No warrant necessary! No paperwork required to put a bullet in both our heads!"

Ramfort ran over to the garage door and shot a quick peek through the bullet hole. Crowds of people were scattering while the guardsmen hurriedly broke down the pull-up bar. The boss was pointing everywhere to secure the area. His finger finally pointed straight at Steve's house. In a few moments they'd be coming.

"Crap!" Ramfort shot over to the fireplace and scooped items off the mantle. "Uhhhh story time! We need a cover story! We're undercover operatives and we got info on some revolutionary dude somewhere and we gotta bust down his door before he flushes all his IRA contraband down the toilet or moves it elsewhere, because you know this siren is giving him a shock. With this ID—" Ramfort held up an ID badge— "and that story that boss man will be licking his lips for getting a ransom like that." He looked over at Steve, who had reached into his nightstand by his bed and was now cleaning and cocking a small pistol.

Steve began watching the blood from the IV tube flow into him; it was poison, another kind of sick joke. No one had ever tried to help him. Just kept leaving him without a care. Now, when he no longer cared, someone went to the trouble of finding some AB-negative blood to stick into him.

"How about a different story. How about, when they get to the front door, I greet them with a bullet to the head?"

Ramfort charged over to the bed and slammed his fist into the Steve's chest.

"We-don't-have-time-for your-teenage-testosterone-problems-Steve!"

"Get off!" Steve shouted.

Ramfort slapped him. "We're telling them my story! We can't hold them all off with a pistol!"

Steve's leg shot out. Ramfort doubled over and sunk to the ground.

"There is no we, you story telling coward! Only me and Edingburg!" Steve pointed up to the wail of the siren. "Get out of *my house*!" Steve shouted.

He got a long burn in his stomach from his last two words—*my* and *house*. Those were words of his now distant past. If the cosmos would not let him have an "our home" then he'd make sure it was "his city."

Ramfort spoke from the floor: "Steve, if they come knocking on your crappy garage door and we're still here, then they're going to see all this stuff and any story I tell them will look like bullshit!"

"No stories!" Steve groaned. He checked the pistol's magazine for bullets. Plenty. "You think any of those bullets flying around out there come with stories?! Words are over with. Edingburg has finally awoken!"

Ramfort held up the recorder to the side of the bed. "This little thing right here is going to be the inspiration and direction for everyone in Edingburg. The bullets being shot outside is NOT an awakening kid. It's the Edingburg's final death throes. We lost way too many of our top people at the protest and so I've been having one hell of a time trying to coordinate anything out there because we don't have any central leadership right now. You wanna kill stuff? So do I! Sounds like a dream, babe! But this Edingburg rebellion of yours is doomed if it's only made up of pissed off teenagers clutching their little pistols! Especially yours. What is that? 3-D printed? Damn thing will melt before you get half way through your clip."

Steve attempted rising up from his bed again. The siren wailed. Ramfort kicked a leg of the bed. It snapped, making the bed drop diagonally. Steve slid down the mattress. The two men glared at one another. Ramfort began to sing:

We'll find you a new boo!

There's plenty of good women willing to skiddely do,

with you,

no matter what they say or or who they screw!

Man, it's just that one girl who went and ducked you!

And when we do!

You'll be able to do more than punch

and say boohoo!

"Shut up!" Steve yelled. He rolled himself off the side of the bed and fell to the floor. The world spun as he grabbed for the nightstand. The siren was so powerful it seemed to be shaking gravity itself.

"He's up!" Ramfort shouted. He grabbed Steve by the elbow and hoisted him to his feet.

Ramfort batted his eyes. "Hi, Steve. You don't look too good. Need a hug? Let's go get you a hug."

"Without her, I don't know who the hell I am any more," Steve murmured. "I've lost everything but these stupid concrete walls that I can't even afford. I've got nothing but my ideals now! And they're not taking that away too! Now get the fuck out of my way! Let me answer the door. I'll give those killers for profit a welcome they deserve."

"Ohhh, there's still something to lose, my little drama queen. You'd lose your life and everything you've ever been. Maybe what you've been didn't turn out all that great. But if you went'n let those buttheads put you down you'd be all gone." Ramfort pointed to the ceiling. "But not the problems you created. You've got issues, kid, but some of those issues of yours are aggravating some really crappy people out there. Far more than the two you might get at your front steps right now. Keep on livin' and punchin', and you'll get the biggest prize of all. Getting to defy this madness of an existence." Ramfort gestured to the general crappiness of Steve's home. "And doesn't that just feel great?"

Steve's eyes went blank, processing. These guards and everything they represented just ruined his entire life. And now this guy he just met wants him to go up to them and play nice while everyone else in Edingburg got to shoot at them? Bullshit.

The printed pistol shook under Steve's strengthening grip. The handle of the hard-starch pistol snapped under his hand's pressure. Steve looked down at his ruined killing machine.

Ramfort clapped his hands. "So that's it then for your stupid plan! Let's try mine now." Ramfort picked up his rucksack and flung it onto the partially collapsed bed. Then he started collecting the rest of his gear. "Now that you're done bein' stupid, we can go. So put that friggin' jacket on! We've only got a minute or so until they show up." Ramfort threw a canteen onto the bed. "And drink this. You haven't drank anything through your face hole in days."

Steve bent down and picked up the canteen with a shaking hand. He was stuck doing Ramfort's plan now whether he like it or not. He drank almost everything in the canteen. It wasn't until he finished that he noticed a strange taste. "What's in this?"

"A combo of drugs with names that end mostly in -oid and -ine." Ramfort smiled. "Feeling awake yet?"

Steve suddenly felt a bit more than awake. His body felt like it'd explode if it didn't start moving. He started getting dressed. "Where's my pants? I can't go out there without any pants."

"I don't have another pair. But don't worry; they won't even notice."

"What do you mean they won't notice!"

"Too much going on right now, Steve." Ramfort kept packing. "Nobody's got time to worry about pants."

"Whatever, I hid my other pair in the couch," Steve said. He picked up the cushion and reached into the hole—nothing. He picked up the other cushion. He looked around his feet. "What the—" He looked at the fireplace. His pants and the remnants of $200 were smoldering in the fire.

"What the hell!"

Ramfort waved his free hand around sarcastically while the other continued packing, "You wanted to settle down in your little house with your little chica. What's the point of that? Gaining the power of owning a crappy little house amidst your crappy little life?"

"It's not about power! It's about having a real life!"

"Pffft, life is real whether it's fake or not. You wanted the power of stability. Look where that got ya. Don't even have a pair of pants to your name. So lets gun for another sort of power instead. In fact, let's go for the opposite. The convoy's here," Ramfort said, looking through the hole in the garage door. "You ready?"

Steve finished lacing his shoes and mulled over his sorry pair of boxers. His mind buzzed for an excuse for his lack of pants. "I traded my pants in exchange for some information."

"I'll be sure to mention something like that." Ramfort grabbed the handle at the bottom of the garage door. "Just let me do the talking; you're really coming off as a nutter right now." Light flooded over the cracked concrete and rose up the walls as the garage door rose with a coarse rattle.

Prisoner 594-AZ

Location: Alcatraz Prison

"Wake up!"

Johnny's head rolled to the side as he hovered along the edge of consciousness. He was still strapped to the folding metal chair that the General had tied him to.

"Wake up!" the intercom barked again.

Johnny jolted in his chair as bright light poured onto his face. He looked up, wincing at an aging incandescent bulb floating over him.

"Pay attention!" an impossibly deep voice shouted through the intercom.

The room took form as Johnny's chest convulsed with a fit of coughs. A cube made up of nine televisions stood a few feet in front of him. The old cathode ray sets were sloppily stacked atop one another on top of a thin wooden table.

"What's your name?" the intercom asked.

Johnny slumped forward in the chair; if his chest hadn't been restrained by the ropes, he'd have easily fallen off. "What … what's going on?"

An electric shock fired through the metal chair. Johnny went stiff; his back arched as his eyes bulged with the pain.

"Name!" the intercom demanded.

Johnny looked to his left at the silhouette of a man behind a fogged glass window that stretched across the top of the entire wall.

"Johnny … My name is Johnny McHenry."

"Where are you from, Johnny?"

"Edingburg. I was the mayor for five damn terms!"

"Why were you sent here?"

"Treason."

The chair zapped on and Johnny convulsed again.

"Don't you bullshit me with things I already know! Everyone's here's a traitor!"

"I … I publicly supported the IRA at the protest yesterday at the Inner Circle's golf course."

"Why did you attend?"

"Someone needed to back Haadin. Someone the people knew and trusted."

"Who sent you here?" the voice demanded.

"The General sent me. Why the fuck don't you know that? You fucking work for him, don't you?! He's the only man who could approve my fucking admittance to this place!"

The televisions flickered to life. Lines of code filled some televisions while databases booted onto others. Then, one by one, the screens turned to static until all nine televisions crackled as one fizzing wave that tore at Johnny's mind.

Then the nine televisions snapped on as one. Together they displayed a single image. It was live video of Johnny, sitting in his small metallic chair. He looked around for a camera.

"Good lord," the intercom crackled. It was a woman this time. "If you would please stop zapping him? Now, Johnny. What do you see on the screens?"

Johnny looked back through the frosted glass—the man still stood alone on the other side.

"Who are you?" Johnny asked.

"Answer the question!" the man barked. Electricity flowed through the chair again.

"Enough zapping or I'll put you in time out!" the woman snapped.

"Alright! Fuck!" Johnny panted. "I see myself."

"Good, but what do you look like?" the woman asked.

Johnny looked at the beaten and bound man on the screens. He felt he understood the point she was trying to make.

"I look like a prisoner."

"That's right, you are a prisoner," the woman said with a rather curious hint of concern. "But you are not *our* prisoner. The supply boats come and dock. They deliver prisoners and supplies to our bolted doors and then stand on the outside of our blast-proof walls to proclaim their delivery … and then they leave. The security is so tight that no common deliveryman has the clearance to enter. So once we took the interior walls, there was no one to notify the world outside. We now control every inch inside these walls and so have implemented new protocol. So please, for our own records, state your age, weight, descent, hair color, eye color."

Johnny looked at the televisions and answered. "Brown hair, blue eyes, Irish, around 190 pounds, 43 years old."

His face on the televisions was replaced by flowing lines of code.

"This may sound like a bit of a silly question, but how are you feeling?"

"Who are you?" Johnny shouted. "I've heard your voice before!"

"I am concerned for you, Johnny. Why did the General send you here?"

"I— I was part of the protest. I revealed my part in the movement. I helped lead it. I figured if a man of my position showed up, it'd go differently."

"Why did you go?" the woman asked, her voice staticky in the intercom. "Why now? With so many years past, why now? Why this movement?"

Johnny looked down. He didn't care to know what was going on any more, or what was going to become of him for that matter. His only fear was that if he looked up, he would see her again, burning in the fog of the crackling fizz of the television screens. His love for her had never been a portrait that a French romantic would paint on canvass. To him, it had always been more than that. More of a relationship that involved a justified pedestal. He had never known, let alone loved, a woman of such a high caliber as her. The General enjoyed pointing out her quirks and her great waste line to him, but the General had always missed the point about her. The one, inescapable, irreplaceable draw—her essence. The sun itself seemed to beam out of her and the only person that seemed completely incapable of feeling the warmth, was the General.

"Why now, Johnny? With rebellions rising nearly every cycle. Why risk your career, your freedom, your life, for this movement?"

He said nothing.

"I understand your pain," the woman continued. "I know how it feels to lose the one you love most. Loss is … what I know best. It's why I'm speaking to you today in this manner. Loss is exactly why I have pushed this so far. But do you know why I'm here, Johnny?"

Johnny looked up at the speaker.

"Because I am still in love," the woman said. "My love has driven me further, falling deeper with every moment. It's pushed me to stage a rebellion against a man who calls himself nothing other than the General. So much has been planned, calculated, reinforced, and sacrificed. And now, over 28 years later here we are. Everything I have planned is finally coming to the surface."

Johnny was frozen. If what she was saying was true, more than 28 years without detection, she must really be something. Every little uprising he'd been made aware of had only been a few months old at most. This also meant she was the head of the rebellion. Not Haadin.

"If you really loved her, then I hope to see you push at least as hard as I have."

Johnny sunk down into his battered metallic chair.

"There, there. No matter how much we try, we can't change what's happened. All we can do is the best we can for ourselves and our children."

The static flowed over Johnny, cocooning him in a fizzing blanket of sound.

"I have no children," Johnny said. He took a long breath. "My only children were the people of this city. Now after the protest, most of the good ones are gone. What's left over there aren't human. Many are just monsters who live for selfish fulfillment. There is no justice, courage, modesty, or shred of wisdom. That died with her! He killed her! Right in front of me!"

"Johnny, there is a young man who is going through something much like what you endured. His name is Steve. He needs our help. He is with another one of our boys. They need to know where the supplies are."

Johnny shook his head. "Just let it go. There's nothing left to save over there. I helped raise hundreds of those wonderful boys and girls at the protest with my private shelters. Those were the only ones in the whole damn city that grew up with any form of compassion. The rest are wild dogs."

"Johnny, this is important. Everything has gone dark since the protest. Edingburg is getting liquidated by contractors and Silvers. We've even lost Haadin. We need to be sure about where the supplies have gone. Someone may have panicked and moved them without the message coming back to us."

"If you'd please, I am tired and would like to be put into my cell now."

Fists beat into the frosted glass window. A moment later, a flood of volts flooded Johnny's nervous system.

"You think you're the only one left!" the man shouted through the intercom. "You think this all came together solely because of you! Fuck you! You're giving us that intel!"

Johnny slumped forward, panting and coughing. "Kleiner," he wheezed after a moment. "He owns that potato bar in the Dog Patch. Near 22nd and 3rd streets."

"Ah, Kleiner," the woman said. "An old friend. I assumed as much, but you can never be too sure this far out. Thank you, Johnny."

The man behind the glass picked up a phone.

Load Up

Ramfort marched toward the squad of soldiers. Steve followed closely behind him. The scream of the siren and the sun's UV rays made it feel like his skin was sizzling.

Three ten-wheeled black personnel carriers pulled up to the edge of Steve's dead yard. The rear door of the front vehicle dropped, and guardsmen in riot gear marched out.

"Load up!" an officer shouted. "Get this crap in the convoy now!"

"It's okay, it'll be okay," Steve murmured to himself.

The officer glared at Ramfort and Steve as they approached his convoy. He drew his sidearm and aimed it at Ramfort's forehead. "Halt!"

Ramfort clipped his heels together and saluted. "It's at Kleiner's," his earpiece buzzed. "You need to get there quick."

Ramfort slowly withdrew his salute. "Special Agent Victor Lustig, sir." He bent over, took off his shoe, and pulled out an identification badge from under his sock. He held the badge up to the officer.

The officer held up the badge in his black leather glove. Steve looked at the agent's nametag: CRAUSE. It was him again.

"A mountain of contraband is likely to be at a bar on 20th and Tennessee," Ramfort said. "Is your convoy heading in that direction, sir?"

"Have you reported zis?" Crause said, affecting a German accent.

"No sir. This siren going off is screwing up my plans. Comms are too busy with containment instead of contraband. But I've got a big enough haul to pay 100 times what any containment contract might give you."

Crause looked up from the badge. He gazed over the neighborhood. Many of Steve's neighbors were already standing at attention in front of their homes, ready for the coming processing.

"You're in luck, Mr. Lustig. Zis address lies within the sector we're soon to be ripping apart. I've just accepted a gig that deploys my unit about a mile from your destination. Give me a nice tip on what you get from your contraband reward and you may trolley a ride with us, then hoof it the rest of the vay."

Crause looked at Steve. "You are familiar?" His eyes darted up and down Steve's body. "Why the hell aren't you wearing any pants?"

"Well, I—"

Ramfort shoved his hand into Steve's face. "He's a priority informant. Found us some pretty heavy IRA contraband. I traded him my jacket for some info. As you can see, his wardrobe is a bit … limited."

The guards chuckled as Crause smiled. "Well then, you'll be leaving him here; the information has been given. And I'm not dealing with your red tape situation by bringing a foreign civilian into another sector we're currently liquefying."

"Yes, sir. The ride will be most advantageous, sir. But this siren has got to have them jumpy. So they'll be looking for undercovers. If I go in with him I have a better shot at—"

"I do not take my orders from some special agent with a hunch!" Crause threw Ramfort's badge back at him. "Your badge got you a ride, zat's it!"

Ramfort snapped straight and saluted again.

Crause turned his attention to his crew of men breaking down the pull-up bars. "Let's move! How long's it take to load up a few bars!"

Guardsmen hurried back and forth. Steve, who was struggling to not hyperventilate, was spun around as guardsman holding a large pole slammed into him. Steve stumbled, and Ramfort grabbed his shoulder. Steve thought he saw Ramfort wink just before he punched Steve in the throat. They fell to the ground and started wrestling. Ramfort grabbed Steve's hand and shoved a grenade into it. When Steve saw what he was holding his eyes went wide. He kicked and thrashed, flailing the grenade about as he did so.

"Grenade!" Crause shouted. He pulled his gun back out.

Guardsmen fell behind their riot shields. Ramfort wriggled back up on top of Steve and started raining punches down on his face. He snatched the grenade out of Steve's hand and rolled Steve over, pressed a knee into his back, and cuffed him with a zip tie. Ramfort looked over the confiscated grenade then held it out to Crause like a ripened apple.

"That piece of shit went right for you, sir!" Heintz roared from the turret atop the vehicle. He climbed out of the turret and jumped to the ground. "It's that freeloading kid from Tube Town! I told you we shoulda shoved this piece of shit in a tube!"

"These boys have been getting bolder since the protest," Crause said to Ramfort. He looked at Ramfort's grenade as if it was poisonous. "The info zis sack of shit gave you is garbage. All he wanted was to get up close to an officer. He's jealous of successful business owners in my industry."

Ramfort smiled. "The safe house exists, sir. I've been hearing whispers about it for months. This kid's just feeling a little guilty after ratting them out for a jacket."

Crause plucked the grenade from Ramfort's hand. All eyes fell on him as he rolled the grenade around his fingers. The siren's constant screaming returned to their consciousness. Then Crause holstered his pistol and the siren came to a lull.

"It's strange how …" Crause shifted his eyes to Steve, whose exhales were creating small puffs of dry and particalized ash. "We found this man stumbling about the streets. At first we thought he was a drunk. We checked his pockets for ID and found that he was … far from home. Very strange, considering liquidation had just begun. So strange, in fact, that we detained him for questioning."

Ramfort smiled, and the guardsmen chuckled at the faked police report that was about to be filed.

"He kept going on about some kind of safe house of the IRA. But whilst putting him in the APC, masked figures biked from around the corner. He shouted for their assistance. It was then that the biked men took one look at our unit and began to cycle away quite hastily."

Crause turned and opened his free hand. "Naturally, we gave chase?" He was answered with a unanimous nod.

"We eventually boxed them into zis … bar … where we found—" Crause pointed— "you, Mr. Lustig. You were already inside the bar, but your cover, it had been blown. So I had to order an assault on the bar in a heroic attempt to save your life. There was fierce resistance, however … forcing us to take more lethal measures."

Crause raised the grenade. "And this! Which zis kid hid … so well. We couldn't be there all day searching, of course. We were in the middle of liquidation and we had contractual obligations! So we took him out of the APC to point out where the contraband was hidden. That's when this malfunctioned and—" Crause shook the grenade; its pin jingled— "Detonated."

The guards beat their riot shields with their rubber-covered axes.

"So, unfortunately for the investigation—" Crause looked down at Steve— "there are no survivors to give any critical feedback of our performance. The report is closed and we all get paid."

Steve exhaled, and a puff of ash rose from the asphalt by his mouth. Ramfort yanked him to his feet and threw him into the APC. The guardsmen piled in after them. The back door rose from its hinges and sealed shut.

The convoy began to rumble through the streets. Ramfort's foot continued to ensure that Steve's face remain acquainted with the floor. A corded walkie-talkie on the vehicle's wall beeped, and Crause answered. "Yes sir," he said. He hung up and addressed the convoy: "Seems we have a bit of a detour, gentlemen! Before we head to our objective, we must now do a bit of babysitting at the town center for the liquidation process."

The men started grumbling. A few minutes later, the convoy stopped, and a light above the back door of the vehicle flashed green.

"Form up!" Crause said. The guards snapped up and faced the rear door in two lines. "Look strong, gentlemen! We've got over four thousand people out there to process! And I don't have to remind you that there's kids out there that are considering interviewing for my fine business after they get through basic! So show 'em what we got!" He glanced down at Ramfort's boot, which was still smooching Steve's face. "What they can become!"

The door fell open. The guardsmen jumped over Steve to fill a gap in a rapidly forming wall of armed mercenaries who were charging out of the other colored APCs and forming human passageways for citizens to file through so they could be processed in an organized manner. Ramfort removed his foot from Steve's face and threw him out of the vehicle.

Crause waved off his men with his gloved hand. "My men will be fine on their own. Someone was tipped off you being here, boy." He glared at Steve. "Looks like I'll have to be processing your testimony after all." He glared at Ramfort. "No matter. A few tweaks here and there and our little story will still be quite plausible." He looked at Steve. "I don't let down those who've proven so enthusiastic to kill me. Mr.

Lustig, if you have any interest in collecting on your own little reward today, I trust you'll play along."

Crause walked through the perimeter and gateways with Ramfort following behind with an iron grip on Steve's arm. The guards parted as they went along. Sounds of scuffling feet and the crunching of dead grass filled the air like a thunderstorm. Citizens shuffled through the maze of guards.

An enormous curved white balloon floated 30 feet over the park. The projectors encircling the balloon displayed trending social media photo uploads of the event. Photos of people posing with shield-bearing guards behind them seemed to be the most popular.

Crause, Ramfort, and Steve approached a processing desk in the middle of McKinley Square. The desk sat at the end of a corridor made by guards holding their riot shields in front of them. All wearing the regulated uniform, but with different company logos on their shoulders and shields. A well-manicured 50-year-old woman sat at a plain plywood desk, bare except for a nameplate with the name MS. RAND etched into its silver finish and a stack of paper folders.

Steve had no idea what to make of it. He'd never been through liquidation before.

Rand glanced up from her papers at Officer Crause. "Purpose?"

"Priority informant, ma'am." His leathered hand wafted over to Steve.

"Who is the procuring cause for this citizen's testimony?"

Ramfort began to open his mouth. "I—"

Crause's glove rose higher and covered Ramfort's face. "I am, ma'am."

"Noted." Rand dotted a form. Ramfort glared at Crause as if he'd never been so offended.

Rand took off her glasses and looked over at Steve. The ballpoint pen wriggled in her hand. "Please … divulge."

Steve looked down at her hand and saw her sliver-lined black tattoo. It started just beneath her pinky and continued all the way up into her sleeve. His eyes widened. The silver lining meant that she'd obtained a seat of power within the Inner Circle.

Rand tilted her head and sniffed. "Well?"

Steve eyes darted around the walls of soldiers, terrified to be in the presence of a Silver.

Ramfort kicked Steve in the boot. "This fine woman asked you a question! Answer the lady!"

"Oh, I wouldn't call me fine," Rand said. She floated upward from her desk. There was nothing but a metal plate beneath her legless hips. "The 'being fine' part of my life is over."

Ramfort saluted, his face expressionless. "Apologies, ma'am."

"Apologies?" Rand's nose shot upward. "You think I'm some kinda charity case?" she roared. "Is there something wrong with my form of chastity! I'm twice the woman you are!"

Ramfort's eyebrow rose.

"Yes, ma'am," Crause hollered.

Rand's pupils darted between the punch-drunk Steve and the nonplussed Ramfort. "One of you better start telling me why you're both wasting my time!"

"Informant has claimed that a cinema on Portal Street is stashing a sizable weapons cache," Ramfort said.

How old is this boy?" Rand asked.

Ramfort tore open Steve's jacket, revealing the Phoenix Cycle emblem tattooed on his chest.

Rand looked at Steve, surprised. "Your cycle is about to mature. If you're about to apply you can't get any points for this." Her nose wrinkled as she tried to figure out his angle. "This won't get you in good with the commanders. No bribery! You will earn your starting rank and specialization with your own hands!"

"He's not applying," Ramfort interjected. "His girlfriend is a Phoenix too; she just applied at her cycle the other day." Ramfort pushed Steve and scoffed, "Apparently he's not okay with her choice."

Rand glared at Steve as she floated closer to him, swaying slightly on the magnetic waves that held her up. "You think applying makes her a slut? Hmm?"

Steve couldn't muster an answer.

"I keep this thing running!" Her hand gestured to the organized chaos around her. "Do you think *you* have such a capacity! Such a dedication! If you aren't even mustering the gumption to apply then I can't think of a single thing that our city needs you for!" Her legless body floated back to her desk as she pointed at the wall of guards. "Those are real men, men worth being with, and I should—"

"You're all a bunch a black-hatted, baby-bashing swine is what you is!"

Steve looked up. He knew that voice anywhere. Outside of the perimeter of guards raged a stout but huge red-bearded man. It was Kleiner.

The wall of soldiers behind Rand parted for an officer. He walked up to Rand and whispered in her ear.

Her eyes lit up. "A moment," she said to Crause. Once again her legless body floated away from the desk. The wall of guards parted with a flick of her hands and she drifted over to Kleiner. A small bot on treads followed under her, the plate atop its body projecting the magnetic waves that held her up.

At Rand's order, guards strung Kleiner to two metal poles in the middle of a circular podium that hovered in front of a stone wall. Guards shifted and formed new walls with their shields, redirecting civilian traffic around the scene. Kleiner tugged at the ropes that held him.

"You're only making things worse!" a woman shouted from the crowd.

"Oh shove it, Melinda! I know it's you who went'n blabbed! Hope that new steam Tuber'n contraption or what have ya keeps ya warm at sundown!"

"Hey!" a man standing next to Melinda shouted. "Don't go pointing the finger now that you're up there! You got yourself up there!"

"Harold, you's the stupidest man that'd ever crawled outta a woman!" Kleiner shouted back. "Only a man with a head as dense as yers could a thought this a good idea."

"Hey now. You—"

"Hey ya self! Now ye start talking when I is all strung up! Bet you went and put Melinda up to it, ya wimpy little shit! An' jus' what is tha matter with *all* you!" Kleiner added, now addressing the entire crowd. "Tryin' to trend pics of a man bein' strung up like some pig to slaughter! I'm not bloody content for ya feeds! I'm a man!"

"*They*," Rand drawled, "have made the right choices and have their own responsibilities to attend to. *Your* inability to act civilly is no longer their concern. It's people like *you* that got them into this mess in the first place!"

"Wha!" Kleiner's head jerked around to see Rand coming up behind him. "Some retired harlot on a floatin' slab has sumthin' to say about civility!"

"I'd be more careful with your tone if I were you, mister—" Rand looked down at her clipboard— "Claymore?"

"It's Kleiner, ya floatin' wench! What I have to go'n hold ma tongue fer? What happen to free speech an all dat! I know I heard this city claimin' ta have it somewheres!"

"Mr. Kleiner, you have been accused of harboring heavy weaponry for terrorist activities. Your own actions have condemned you. Please cease your search for a scapegoat."

"Oh, so you go stringin' everyone up who gets accused, then! Guess I shoulda went'n pointed a finger at you before you pointed at me if that's all it takes!"

"*We* are the protectors of this city. *We* ensure that it continues to run and that people like *you* don't slow them down with your parasitic actions and impulses!"

"Me, ruinin' the city! Bollocks! It's you lot who're goin' an makin' us blow up our own town! I run a plenty fine establishment meself. One o' the few left that's got any Irish pride left in it!"

"Terrorist groups like yours are destroying the sanctity of this city and I won't have it!" Rand snapped. "So long as I'm here, your cell's raids and false stories of victimhood shall never be able to loot from those who choose to do great work! I won't have it!"

"Greatness!" Kleiner roared. "You're the one pushin' us to do build your bloody great works, ya floatin' witch! If you've made one thing clear by choppin' up the city inta ghettos and palaces it's that we ain't you! We ain't you! But here you is, comin' inta our Edingburg and processin' us like cattle!"

"We do this to maintain the peace and help the innocent find refuge until we clean out the area " Rand said.

"Peace!" Kleiner scoffed. "Not until the foreign oppressive presence of the Inner Circle has removed itself from our town there won't an ounce o' your peace! Not until Edingburg can be handlin' her own affairs and be able to be determin' her own destinies without you lot boostin' inta ah homes and tellin' us how ta live and feel 'bout ourselves we can't be havin' any of that peace you're spoutin' about!"

A number of individuals in the waves of people filing around the processing area had stopped to listen.

Rand looked down at her clipboard. "Your people have always had representation with Mr. McHenry, your mayor. And you *have* been left alone. And what happened? Hmm?" She floated around Kleiner in half-circles. "Your whole city fell apart. *You* came to us!" She patted her clipboard to the beat of her orders. "If you would just behave, you could rid this town of its squalor. So if you don't like it around here then BEHAVE!"

"Came to you! That's rich you scheming Inner Circle lot made it to where we had to come here!"

"Enough of your Irish conspiracy theories! You just have no capacity for self-reflection! I needn't remind you that it is *your* people blowing up Edingburg right now. *We* are the ones risking life and limb to save it!"

"It's your bloody group that be goin' an' makin' such atrocities certain! You're all a booncha schemin' devils, you are! Trying to make more devils, so you don't go gettin' outnumbered!"

The stone wall behind Kleiner began to move. Hundreds of small columns pushed out. Rand's eyes lit up at the sight of the face that was beginning to materialize from among the moving columns.

"He's here!" she shouted. The ground boomed. The waves of people passing by froze and watched the face in the wall.

The wall began to speak, and the columns moved with its voice. "Sacrifice," it growled, "and pain are the only paths to pleasure and beauty. Engorge your tastes and fantasies. Sacrifice everything to your pleasures. Sacrifice your homes, and your lives. Sacrifice it all, so that the best can succeed in gathering a few roses among the thorns of this sad world." The columns retracted and the face receded into the stone wall.

"Absolutely beautiful," Rand said, wiping a tear from beneath her glasses. "Even in the darkest times the General sees the poetry. Now let us do our best!" The walls of different guardsmen companies held up their axes and rapped a single unified beat against their logoed shields. The crowd slowly began to flow back into the rhythm of their processing. Desks for identification, place of residence, union verification, and "tattle booths" were planted all around Rand. She breathed in the scent of perfect order.

"This is absolute cobble squat!" Kleiner shouted.

"That is quite enough from you Mr. Claymore."

"Ohhh, this'll just be the beginnin'! You won't be gettin' a inch from me!"

Crause strolled up to the floating platform. "Miss Rand, a moment?"

Rand floated toward him. Crause spoke in a low tone, turning and pointing at Steve and Ramfort as he did so. Rand looked at Steve and smiled.

"Very good!" Rand spun toward Kleiner. "Seems we won't be needing even an inch from you anyway. My personal guards will be taking you to Officer Crause's convoy. Officer Crause has already found the location of your IRAs contraband."

The guards unhooked Kleiner and began to cuff him. "Allow me!" Rand said. She strapped a pair of her own ivory cuffs onto Kleiner.

"It's obvious why you didn't apply in your day," she said. "It's because there's nothing in you but noise. Noise that will only be heard by those who lack the gumption to define themselves."

The guards escorted Kleiner toward Crause's caravan. Steve ducked, worried that Kleiner would see him and think that he was the one who turned him in.

"Let's go, Steve!" Ramfort shouted, pushing Steve forward.

Kleiner looked back at them with wide eyes. "What in bloody name!"

The guards shoved Kleiner forward, then threw him into the last vehicle of Crause's convoy. Ramfort dragged Steve into the middle vehicle. Guards piled in after them, and the back hatches of the three APCs latched shut. The wheels began to turn, spinning them toward Kleiner's bar.

Steve had been tied to a bar at the end of the vehicle, far from the rear hatch door. He glared at Ramfort's innocent face. Soldiers lined each long wall, facing one another with their gear stowed in the middle of the walkway. Small squares of light coming through windows flickered on their faces as APC's engine roared, drowning out the screams of the siren.

"So what route are we taking?" Ramfort shouted.

"We're on 20th now," Crause said. "Straight shot to Tennessee!"

"Good." Ramfort leaned back and closed his eyes.

"Just passed Texas!" a guard shouted, looking out a window.

Ramfort leaned forward. "What!" He picked at his ear. "Texas! We're moving so fast every kid with a walkie-talkie's gonna know something's up! Slow down!"

Crause brought up the grenade, turning it on the tips of his fingers. "So, what brought you to wanting to blow me up? I don't remember doing anything to you?" He reached over and brushed Steve's chin with a finger. "Or did I?"

Steve didn't dare speak. Crause was leaning in so close that Steve felt that the officer could already hear the lie he was forming in the back of his throat.

"His girlfriend applied," Ramfort said.

The guards sitting nearby erupted with laughter, and Crause grinned.

"Which one was she?" said Heinz.

"You're not going to know who!" said another guard. "There were way too many girls applying this year to remember every—"

"He was dating Leslie," Ramfort said.

"Leslie!" the guards shouted in unison.

"Well, that explains the grenade!" Heintz laughed.

"Take a page from his book, gentlemen," Crause said. "He's a romantic! Wants to be with the same girl day after day! Talking to her even when he'd rather be out! Putting up with her menstrual cycles, only to be dumped when the Phoenix Cycle came!" Crause grinned down the long cabin. A coy snicker rose among the men.

"Leslie, now that was a particularly scrumptious one," Crause continued. "You're a smooth talker, aren't you? Come on, give us a line."

Steve dropped his head, and Crause pushed it back up with the grenade.

"Just one little line."

"I …" Steve murmured.

"What?"

Steve looked and stared at the gray sky through the window. "I will never leave you."

"Oh." Crause put away the grenade. He adjusted his gloves, then rubbed his forehead. He looked back at Steve. "Do I say that before or after I get acquainted with her?"

Heintz and the other guardsmen burst into laughter.

"Why'd you want a girlfriend, boy?" Crause shouted over the roaring engine. "You had your whole life ahead of you. You could have lived! You could have gone and only done things you can do when you join the guard. I've been part of the liberation of fifteen colonies. All over the world. Fifteen. I've done, incredible things. That's how I obtained a high enough rank to branch out from corporate and start my own subcontracting business. But you pissed your potential away on some girl who doesn't even give a damn about you." He leaned back in his seat, and the medals on his lapel jingled as the vehicle bounced along the rutted street. "Oh, well."

"Yeah, and why be with a chick for 30 years when you can get the best of her in 30 minutes!" Heintz said. "Shit, if you just wanted to bang you coulda applied and in a year jumped ship from corporate and into the Inner Circle."

"Well that's not gonna happen for me either. Doing a lifer," Ramfort said.

"Ahhh. A true blue blood," Crause said. "Perhaps you'll earn for yourself a high enough level killing license to start a business and get some real contracts."

"Yep," said leaning back. "Damn old Inner Circle farts only letting me have a Level 3 killing license. Can only kill three people a year without being sent in for review! And the paperwork is so deep it's barely worth killing one!"

"On that note we agree," Crause said, tightening his gloved hand. "But my little outfit is starting to finally obtain the fruits of its scale. The Inner Circle is beginning to identify my company as true professionals. It's nothing like being allowed to self regulate like the corporations, but our personal judgment calls stand up as enough justification for most," Crause looked over at Steve, "KIAs. Our paperwork is minimal."

"Some of the best in the biz!" Heintz shouted.

Crause stood up, holding the side of the wall to keep his balance. He grabbed the wall walkie-talkie.

"Alright, Alpha, Bravo, and Charlie vehicles. A terrorist on board has given us a present: a now less than safe house that's holding some pretty nice contraband. So we'll be paying them a little visit. Bravo and

Charlie teams, you're on crowd control, so keep those rubbers on your axes. No guns. I don't want the paperwork. Also, no lethal explosives in zee handles! Tear gas and flash bang inserts only!"

Crause turned and looked down the APC's long cabin. "Alpha team, you're on me. We're going in. No rubbers for us."

The guardsmen in the vehicle cheered and banged their long-handled axes against the floor. "Doin' it raw!" Heintz shouted.

They began ripping off the rubber coverings on their ax blades, exposing the sharp steel. Some unscrewed the standard handles on their axes and replaced them with handles with an explosive charge in the butt. Other guardsmen began unlocking compartments and grabbing assault rifles.

Heintz removed the rubber from his ax, disconnected the handle, and slid his fingers through four holes in the metal part of the blade. He held the handless ax like brass knuckles. It had a large blade on one end and a spike on the other. His wide eyes were bright with exultation. He inhaled deeply, puffing out his enormous chest. "Yeaaaahhh," he exhaled. Then he started hyperventilating as if he was about to hold his breath under water.

He tapped the spike. "See that? This spike's got gunpowder in it. It shoots out a couple inches when you hit it into stuff. I think that's pretty inspiring, don't you?" Heintz was bouncing in his seat. "You see it? Huh?" He kept tapping the spike. "See it?" Steve glanced up at the spike. It jerked down toward Steve's knee. He lunged back and slammed himself into the wall before the spike could shoot through his kneecap.

Heintz roared with laughter and threw himself upon the guard next to him. "Not the spike! Mommy says spike is bad!"

Ramfort smiled at Steve. "You flinched."

The convoy stopped. "This is it," Crause said, peering out a window. He shifted over to another window, then another window on the opposite side of the cabin. "Where the hell?"

Crause marched over to Steve and grabbed him by the collar. "Where is it! Where's the bar?!" Crause peered into Steve's face, then threw him back into the wall.

Crause glared at Ramfort. "This kid got the better of you!"

"Couldn't have," Ramfort said as he stood up. "Been hearing chatter about this place on nearly every block!"

"Then it was all lies!"

"No, it's just a different type of place. Bar's gotta be slang for something else!" Ramfort looked out the window at the dilapidated two- and three-story buildings surrounding the convoy. He spied a small alleyway between two of the buildings.

Crause snatched an ax from a guard and brought the blade up to Ramfort's throat. "You are part of the lies, Mr. Lustig. You are no agent. That grenade scene from before was just for show, was it not?"

"I saved your life!" Ramfort said. "I can—"

Crause slammed Ramfort's head against a window, splintering the glass. "Who do you work for!"

"The General!"

"Lies! You two are working together! Tell me why else you'd be so apprehensive about us getting here so fast! Are you with Capsule? Which corporation, huh! Don't think I won't skin a corporate snake! No one comes into my fucking unit and fucks with my company!"

"You were attracting attention driving that fast!" Ramfort said.

"We're an armed convoy; we attract attention at any pace! No! You wanted to buy time for this bullshit going on out here!" Crause pulled the grenade from his pocket and held it out to Heintz. "Get two shields and stack zem!"

Heintz grabbed his shield and the guard's next to him. He placed one shield over the other and took the grenade as he marched past Heintz the grenade, his face of smiling teeth as Steve thrashed at his restraints.

Heintz used the shields to press Steve into the corner, effectively shoving him into a triangle-shaped blast room. With his free hand he held up the grenade and wriggled it playfully.

"If you don't talk in five seconds, Mr. Lustig," Crause said, "Heintz is going to take out zat pin and share the rest of it with your little companion."

"If you touch him you interfere with my investigation!" Ramfort said, his Adam's apple bobbing against the ax blade. "The General's investigation!"

"Cut the shit!" Crause shouted. "Three seconds!" Steve was frantically banging his head against Heintz's shields, trying to escape the death trap he'd been pinned into.

"If you pull that damn pin, I'll make sure your head's popped off as settlement for his!"

"One second!"

"I'm working a contract for the Alcatraz LLC. They've been having some issues with their prisoners! This contraband is somehow involved! They need it as leverage to get him to talk! Check my ID again! Clear it with headquarters directly! Bet I've got a higher damn clearance than you working at Alcatraz! I never set foot on this damn peninsula unless I'm getting some nookie from the Inner Circle, so excuse me for not wanting to bounce up and down on your shitty streets!"

Ramfort fished out his badge and held it up. Heintz looked over his shoulder at Crause for his orders.

Crause grabbed the badge. "No one has been sent to Alcatraz for longer than this boy has been alive. So why put you on such a detail?"

"Good question!" Ramfort yelled. "But it's questions like that that stopped you from getting the good contracts, huh! Curiosity killed the contract!"

Crause lowered the ax. "Watch it," Crause whispered. He walked over to the mic to verify Ramfort's license.

Ramfort stood perfectly still. His face was neutral, his breathing steady, but his hand twitched ever so slightly. A blade slid from his sleeve. He took a step toward Crause, who was reporting the code on the badge. Ramfort inched another step. The blade grew in Ramfort's hand.

Crause looked up at Ramfort. "My apologies, Mr. Lustig. It appears you are who you say you are."

Ramfort's sleeve swallowed the knife, and Crause waved off Heintz. The guard squatted to look Steve in the eyes.

"You'd better start saying one of your lucky Irish prayers, kid. Because if anything happens out there …" Heintz straightened up. "I can do a lot worse things to your Irish-loving ass than play hot potato."

A whisper flowed through Ramfort's earpiece: "Get ready."

"Officer Crause," Ramfort said, pulling himself to attention, "I foresee no reason for any prob—"

A shockwave thrust through the cabin. Crause's feet sheared off the metal floor. The vehicle jolted back. Loose equipment ricochet off the walls as Heintz rolled over Steve and slammed into a wall.

"Rocket!" a guard shouted.

"Get off!" Crause bellowed. He was trapped under a guard who had been impaled by a loose ax. He reached for the swinging walkie-talkie. "Alpha, move up, damn it!"

"Can't," the driver shouted through the intercom. "Engine's blown out! We're fried, sir!"

"Charlie, watch our rear!"

"We're boxed in back here, sir!" came the reply.

"Shit!" Crause rapped the walkie-talkie against the dead guard's helmet, stretching the cord to its ripping point. "Someone get this dead lump off me!" Two guardsmen pulled off the corpse, exposing Crause's mangled leg.

"All units fall out!" Crause shouted into the walkie-talkie. "Look alive and kill 'em all!"

As the guardsmen scrambled for their weapons, Crause staggered to his feet, leaning on his uninjured leg. He pointed at Steve. "Cut him loose!"

Heintz cut Steve's arms free from the bar, leaving his arms still tied together. Crause hopped over to Steve and drew his gun. "You're my new crutch, boy!"

The guards lined up inside the cabin. "Who are we?!" Crause shouted.

"The guard!" his men roared.

"Who fucks with us?!"

"No one!"

"Drop it!"

The back door of the APC fell open. Toxic yellow light filled the cabin. Dust and the screams from the siren poured in. The men charged outside and into the fray, and Steve's eardrums were hit by a hammer as the turret gun began to fire.

Crause pulled Steve out of the APC and onto the cracked pavement. A bullet snapped past Steve's head. Crause jerked Steve to the side of the vehicle.

The guardsmen had made a wall with their shields, facing a wall of rubble and garbage about 25 yards away. People wearing red colors shot at the guards from behind their makeshift rampart. A large machine gun began firing at the guards.

"Focus fire on that that machine gun!" Crause shouted. "Obtain fire superiority in three … two … one … NOW!"

As one, the guards unholstered short machine gun pistols from their legs and unleashed a hail of fire from behind their shields at the red-clad figures.

A rocket spun toward Steve like a crazed bee and exploded in the sky. The concussion blew Crause back onto his injured leg. "Gah!" he shouted, grabbing onto Steve to keep from falling.

Gunfire thundered above them. "Get out of the open, you stupid shit!" Heintz roared. He was in the turret, gripping the gun with both handles. He unleashed another spray of bullets, and several red figures hunched and fell.

"You see dat, kid?" Heintz pointed at the falling figures. "That's on you!"

Return fire snapped through the air and pinged against the APC. Steve ducked and broke to run but Crause held him back with a strong hand. "Vat, lose your nerve?" the officer asked with a smile. "You should've blown me up when you had zee chance, kid!"

Crause fired three times at the rampart. "Hey, at least you know none of them's your girlfriend!"

Enraged, Steve shoved his shoulder into Crause with all his might. Both men fell to the ground, and Crause's injured femur gave way with a loud pop. He screamed and fired his pistol as Steve struggled to get up, his arms still tied behind his back. He started to lurch away when

Crause coldly ordered him to stop. Steve turned to see the officer's pistol leveled at his head.

The two froze in place, two figurines in a freshly shaken snow globe filled with dust, the siren wailing its carol.

"I've had enough of you," Crause said. He spat blood next to his injured leg sprawled out in front of him.

There was another blast, and Steve staggered back as ash sprinkled over his face. A glowing heat pressed into him, then fell away.

He opened his eyes, shocked to still be alive. The APC had exploded. Ramfort was standing rather casually next to the mangled vehicle. He eyebrows wiggled at Steve as if to say, "Well?"

Steve looked down at Crause, who was looking over his shoulder at the blazing APC. Steve swung his leg, connecting with Crause's gun at the same instant that it fired. The bullet sent searing heat up Steve's arm, and he fell backward to the ground. His vision filled with the stinking haze of the dying brown sky. Shouts and gunfire served as the only reminder that he was still here on this earth.

Ramfort's head peered into Steve's vision. "Back on the ground, are ya?" he asked, hoisting Steve up. "You're fine! What doesn't kill you —"

A rocket exploded into a building. The two shielded their heads as debris rolled down like an avalanche. Ramfort, hunched over, pushed Steve through a narrow alleyway between two buildings.

The siren came to a lull. Steve looked behind to see whether Crause was watching, but the debris cloud was swallowing up the outlines of the red brick buildings and churning it all to a cloud of gray.

Potato Famine

Ramfort hurried Steve through block after block of back alleyway. The wind pushed through the cracks between the buildings, bringing particles of ash and dust to clump into piles along the building's edges. Though the siren had stopped wailing, its echo still rang in Steve's ears.

They came to the end of a back alley. Steve slumped to the ground, panting and holding his arm.

"So dramatic," Ramfort said. "You'll be fine. We'll just rub a potato on it when we get to Kleiner's."

"What the heck was ..." Steve pointed down the alley with his uninjured arm. "Was that? Who attacked us?"

Ramfort took a rag from his pocket and tied above Steve's wound. Then edged to the corner of the alleyway and peered down the street.

"Attacked *us*?" Ramfort repeated. He turned down the street, beckoning Steve to follow. "You're as stupid as the lead that went through your arm. They saved us. They're IRA."

Steve stood up, wiping away the dust that had clotted his eyelashes. "The movement's nonviolent. We don't fight."

"Well! Look at you on your high horse. I remember dragging a certain gentleman out of the stadium after he'd punched a buttload of guardsman in the face."

"That was ... fighting isn't killing!"

"One must fight before one can kill. Those people who just saved us are a special branch. They've been doing ops for me for years now.

They're the strong ones. And now they've got guns thanks to Santa's ammo dump at the park!"

Ramfort reached in his pocket and flicked the pin of the grenade onto Steve's lap.

"Heintz left the grenade in his back pocket. I saw it and took it thinking you'd want it as a memento. I was trying to get it all back, but, well. All I got was that. So, you know …" His fists came together and spread out. "Buoohmm."

"You're a psycho."

"Oh, don't act like you didn't want to pull that pin."

"Shut up! I'm not killing anyone! I told you before I …" Steve cringed at the pain in his arm. Whatever stimulant Ramfort had given him was wearing off. "I've got my principles. And why the hell did you tell that officer I was an IRA informant! Why not your partner!"

Ramfort pressed a finger against his nostril and snorted out a jet of dirt. "Partner? You have to be part of the City Guard at some point to become an undercover operative. As soon as they saw your Phoenix Cycle tattoo they'd have shot us both. Idiot."

"Well … you suggested it!"

"And why'd you listen to me? You met me like an hour ago!"

"You were the one talking into my earpiece," Steve said. "We worked together for—"

"I prefer the term voice in your head." Ramfort stopped. "Okay there she is." Kleiner's pub stood quietly across the street.

Ramfort crept forward, then slowly extended his foot into the intersection. He tapped the asphalt with his toe, then jerked his leg back like he'd been burned. "Yeah, just gotta … cross this wide open space and we'll have ourselves a pint."

Steve edged to the corner and peered around the building down the street. "No one's here. Let's go for it."

Steve turned and began jogging across the lonely road. Rocks crunched under his feet. Yellow fog clouded the growing space between him and Ramfort. Ramfort made no move, staring at Steve like he was a nut for so gallantly running across the street.

The pub's huge metal door was ajar. "Strange," Steve said. He pushed his uninjured shoulder into the door and grunted. The door reluctantly swung open. Everything inside was black. He reached over the bar and turned the dial. The lights flicked on one by one.

Cracked and off-center pictures of personified potatoes hung on the walls. Hundreds of circular wooden rivets spanned the walls and ceiling. Along the back of the bar, five long glass tubes filled with potatoes and blue liquid began to bubble. Tables and barstools had been knocked over and were strewn about the room. Steve leaned over the bar again. All the cabinets hung open. Potatoes and glass shards littered the walk space. Steve reached under the bar top and felt around until his fingers found the handle. He pulled out the spear gun and propped the butt of the gun on his leg. He grunted, trying to pull back the long slide with his one good arm. The metal bow vibrated under the pressure. When it clicked to, he turned around and examined the empty bar. Then he crept over to the metal door that led into the kitchen. He tapped the door with the spear gun. "Anyone here?" he asked as if he was scared of being answered. "It's me, Steve."

Nothing.

Steve pushed the door open and stuck his head into the kitchen. He saw only blackness. "Hello?"

"Steve?" came a voice from behind him.

Steve whirled around, accidentally discharging the spear gun, launching a harpoon into the ceiling. Standing in front of him was the little blonde girl in the white and blue dress. But somehow she was much older now, and looking back at him from almost eye level. Unable to refrain from dropping his eyes, he saw that her body had grown into the classic ideal of a beautiful woman: tall and thin, yet standing with an unconfident posture.

She stared straight at him, not acknowledging the butt of the harpoon quivering between them. Her large green eyes seemed to be analyzing every part of him with a natural understanding.

"I'm Melody."

Steve tried to bring back an image of the little girl holding a teddy bear. All that was left of it was how her forearms had nervously curled around one another and pointed down her waist.

"I'm Steve."

Her eyes flickered away from his. "Yes." She reached up and pulled the harpoon from the ceiling. Her stance bounced up slightly, her shoulders shyly turned from Steve's direct stance toward her, as if she'd become ashamed. She then flowed around him, quietly relieving him of the spear gun and setting it back beneath the bar.

She looked back up at him suddenly, her eyes widened as if to withhold a guilt filling inside them.

"You're the little girl with the bear, and those growth spurts. How did you … what are you?"

Her eyes flickered down. "I'm not a what. What I am could change. It's who I am that doesn't." She glanced up at him. "I'm sorry about what happened with Leslie. I was so scared I'd lose you when you started fighting the guards and that band … slicing you open." She shuddered. "I couldn't lose you."

"Can't lose me?"

"I have to protect you. I should have been there for you."

"You're talking like you're a guardian angel," Steve said.

She cringed. Then she pulled a bright white first-aid kit out from under the bar and took out a roll of bandages. Timidly she walked up to Steve and began wrapping his injured arm.

"Angels come from a wonderful time," she said. "But we cannot find any in this place, because the people here no longer reach for them."

"So you're religious?"

"I don't know."

Steve watched the top of her golden hair while she bandaged his arm. Her movements were quick yet done with a peculiar care—sure, yet timid. Steve hadn't a clue what the heck was going on with this girl. Was he going crazy? Holy crap, he had a bullet in his arm! The shining pain began to increase tremendously as his adrenaline and the drugged canteen from Ramfort wore off.

She finished with the bandages and looked up at him with her green eyes. "I wonder what he thinks of me," she said out loud. "Hmmm, no. He just thinks I'm … off still. So I guess what matters more is what he thinks of Leslie."

Steve stared at her, his jaw muscle slowly beginning to bite down as the pain in his arm continued to rise. He bit back a tear. "I think she's a bitch."

Melody stared back at him. "I wonder why," she said again, almost to herself. "Maybe because she lied. But you had to know. I only saw her for only a moment and it was obvious. She was all done up. Yes, she lied, but it was really you who had to push yourself to believe it."

"And you bring this up why? Trying to see how you can manipulate me too?"

"Because I want to understand you. How you let it get to the point to where you could be completely destroyed by it." She looked down and frowned at his cut wrist from the blood band.

"Wanna know so bad? Because I didn't want it to end. I barely made it out of the orphanage until she started showing up. She was my rock. Or at least the reason for me to become the rock. So if I lost her, I'd lose me." he looked down at his bandaged arm and then his cut one.

"I find you very attractive," she said.

"What?"

"You don't need to latch on to something else in order to make yourself beautiful."

"Beautiful? Really? Because that's my priority."

"In here." she pointed at his chest. "Your girlfriend and your ... mother left because there was something wrong with them inside. Not because there was something ugly inside of you."

"Knock it off, you two. Five seconds in and you're already all over each other!" Ramfort shouted from the front door.

Melody turned and quietly shuffled back behind the bar.

Ramfort peered around the empty bar. "I don't see any tanks or guardsmen in here. So that's a plus."

"Yes," Melody said.

"Is this place compromised at all?" Ramfort asked.

"No." Melody said. "But the guards came and dragged Kleiner out." Her palms gripped the bar top. Steve watched her knuckles turn white. "He had the key."

"Well, he should be around somewhere," Ramfort said. "He was in one of the convoys with us!"

"Oh!" Melody said. Her cheeks went red.

"Relax, ya hot little potato," Ramfort said. "You blew up my vehicle, not his."

Melody slumped, embarrassed.

"That was you?" Steve asked. "You did that?"

Melody wrinkled her nose. With her head down she pulled out a grenade launcher from under the bar.

"No way."

"Yeah, she's not that basic Leslie chick you were making kissy faces with," Ramfort said. "Got her hands on some of the good guns that just appeared like magic at the park the other day."

"I'm sorry!" Melody said. "I saw you get out of the car so I did it! I'm so sorry!"

"Who are you?" Steve asked. "How did you—"

"Grow?" Ramfort interrupted. "Milk, Steve. It's a wonderful thing. Now where's Kleiner? With your constant drama, this is getting impossible. We've got a schedule. A very behind schedule."

A clamor of footsteps blew through the door. Six men and a woman burst into the room. "Ramfort!" shouted one of the men, "Tom's not lookin' too good!"

Ramfort looked down at a bloodied man who had been strapped to a door. His body was a carnival of red bandanas wrapped around his many wounds.

"We need to get down there!" the woman shouted.

"Would love to, Carrie!" Ramfort said, "but we don't have the key!"

"What?!" one of the men said as they set down Tom and his jury-rigged stretcher. "Well what the hell! Tom's goin' to be dyin' on us pretty soon!"

"No he won't be doin' any of the like."

Everyone turned to turned to the door.

"Kleiner!" Melody cried. She ran to him and hugged his belly.

"Nice to see ya too, bug," Kleiner said. He pulled off a metal stick that was hanging from his neck. He looked around, and his eyes fell on Ramfort, who was casually gathering up the battered potato cups on the bar.

"You!"

Ramfort turned and smiled with childlike joy. "Kleiner!" He rounded the bar, hands outstretched for the coming hug.

Kleiner grabbed Ramfort by the head. "You best explain why you twos was next to that floatin' wench's desk."

Ramfort sighed and leaned into Kleiner's outstretched palm. "Yeah, that was awkward, but the thing is we totally didn't rat. I was posing as an undercover to get us here." He held up his fake badge.

"Bollocks," Kleiner said. "IDs never get verified, specially when the Inner Circle goes'n cross references 'em."

"Well, the floaty lady didn't really have the chance to check it. You kinda made a spectacle of yourself out there before she had a chance to. But it fooled the City Guard."

"It's true," Steve said. His face had gone white. "Kleiner, I'm sorry. I don't know what's going …" He wobbled and leaned against the bar. "I don't know what's going on."

Kleiner frowned. "You're a lucky one, Ramfert. Lucky I trust me Stevie here ta death." He looked at Steve, whose head was rolling as he fought to avoid passing out. "Let's get you fixed up, lad. I'll have ya a nice hot stew in no time."

Kleiner held up a metal rod and pinged it with his finger. The rod started vibrating with a steadily increasing intensity. Kleiner let the rod go, and it hung in the air. Its vibrations grew stronger without Kleiner's hand to dampen them. Soon the rod turned to a blur.

The frequency hit its peak, and the entire floor of the bar jolted down a few inches. Potatoes rolled off the bar. Melody helped Steve to a chair and held him steady. Ramfort bowed down, balancing himself with his arms stretched out.

The floor crept lower, descending into the earth. Ramfort looked up at the spinning wooden fans on the receding ceiling. The walls of the bar were replaced by four walls of earth shot through with potato roots.

The floor jolted as it ended its descent. Ramfort looked back up. The spinning fans above him had turned into a blurred brown specks. Before them stood an enormous blast door.

Little Cricket

"Here we go!"

The needle wobbled through the grooves of a spinning vinyl record. An old song hummed from the brass megaphone and into the stained and peeling jail cells that lined one side of the long two-story hallway.

Johnny stirred in his chair as he heard the thwap of a wooden bat, then the bounce of a ball against concrete. He slowly raised his head from his chest and blinked through blurred eyes. Rows of rusted metal bars confined him inside three stained and cracked concrete walls. Everything, including his body, was coated in dust. A tarnished bunk bed stood next to him. The shadow of a ball rolled past his cell.

"Jolly good, Gordon!" said an aged voice. "I do believe that's 8,032 for four."

"Jes, very gratifying, Franz!"

The shadow of a man appeared, headed in the same direction as the ball.

"Two carrots mo' and you'll have the record, Gordon!"

The shadow of the man walked back across Johnny's cell, holding the ball. The man passed Johnny's cell; the echoing clop following his footsteps halted.

"Well, come on now, pitch it! The rock's record isn't going to defeat itself ... Franz, what are you doing?"

The tip of a visor glided over from the corner bars of Johnny's jail cell. The man was wearing a helmet. Johnny sat quietly as the old cricket player stared at him, his smile shining through the bars.

"Gordon … I do believe we have company," the old man exclaimed.

"Oh, fantastic!"

The second man came over and peered into Johnny's cell. He wielded a wooden oar, one meant for rowing boats. Johnny's eyes bounced between the two men. They were both quite old. Gordon was far shorter and notably broader than Franz, who was rather tall and lanky. The shorter old man had a large bald head and a well-trimmed beard that complimented the still-strong lines of his face.

"We've boiled a kettle for yah!" Gordon said with a grin. "We took the liberty of choosing the tea. You seem to be the embodiment of an Earl Grey man, yes?"

Johnny didn't have a clue what they were talking about. What was a kettle? Who the hell was Earl and why was he gray? But the strangest bit was probably their voices. He had never heard an accent like theirs. Those who chose to defy the Inner Circle affected Irish accents, and the guards who opposed them often did their best to sound German. The elite Silvers and Golds of the Inner Circle had their own diction. He heard hints of it in these two old men, but he'd never heard of anyone in the Inner Circle being sent to prison, certainly not this prison.

The two men continued to smile kindly at him through the bars.

"Right, well," Gordon said. "We'll fetch the tea." The two men started walking off.

"Wait! Please, get me out of here!"

Franz turned to Gordon as he flicked his visor up. After a moment they looked back at Johnny.

"We aren't ... supposed to let you out," Gordon admitted.

"Please," Johnny pleaded, spittle shooting from his split lips. "I've been in this chair, I— I don't even know for how long. I've been tied down ever since the General strapped me into it."

Franz and Gordon took a step back.

"Please!" Johnny implored, his eyes filling with tears. "I'm the mayor of Edingburg!"

Franz removed his helmet and glanced at Gordon. Franz had a rather thin and pointed face. His hair assisted in the emphasis of such a feature by being slicked back in careful rows.

"Well, I guess we can get you out of that chair ..." Gordon said.

The two looked in opposite directions, checking either side of the long hall, then looked back to one another for a confirmation of clear coasts. Franz wedged the oar into a long slit next to the doorway and slid it down. Mechanisms clanked and churned, then echoed through the long hallway.

"Quietly," Gordon hissed.

"What would you have me do?" Franz whispered.

Gordon grasped the door handle. He looked at Johnny with second thoughts riddled across his face.

"What was your name again, lad?"

"Johnny."

"John … you're not a nutter are ya, John?"

"I— I don't think so, no."

"You won't be going away for the moment, will you?"

"No?"

Gordon smiled, reassured. "Works for me." He pulled the door open and the two men shuffled into the cell. Gordon bent down and began untying Johnny's wrists.

Franz stopped in front of Johnny and looked down at him. "I understand you're quite the romantic!" he said.

"Franz! That is incredibly rude!" Gordon scolded.

"What? No! Of course that's not my intention! I just know it's on his mind, and I, for one, am not a fan of unacknowledged elephants!" Franz tapped the wall with his oar. "Johnny," he said, seeming to choose his words carefully, "Mum's briefed us on what you've said and seen. It's absolutely dreadful. I'm sad to hear how it ended for your girl. It must be incredibly saddening for you losing whom you love most … and feeling a tad responsible for it, far worse. It … was *your* fault, wasn't it?" Franz flung up his free hand. "Bah, let's not worry about that quite yet. But you'll be glad to hear she—"

"There it is," Gordon said.

Johnny's newly freed leg shot into Franz's shin. Franz spun back, then hobbled a few steps while using the oar as a cane.

Johnny lunged out of his chair, grabbing it by metal seat and hurling it at Franz's face. Franz easily deflected the chair with his oar, then neatly wedged the oar between Johnny's ankles, tripping him as he charged.

Franz walked around the crazed man's prone body and kicked the oar up to his hand. After a moment's reflection, he swung the oar over his head and administered an unholy spank upon Johnny's behind.

"You must learn to remain in control," Franz instructed. "Anger inevitably creates conflict, and conflict rips the mind to pieces. And the pieces have a way of getting away from you."

"Earl Grey," Gordon said, picking himself up from the floor with a groan. "Jes, that'll be perfect for you."

"Indeed," Franz said.

The two old men helped Johnny up and threw his arms over their shoulders. Johnny was exhausted; he hadn't eaten or been able to stretch his legs in days. The old men guided him down the long hallway, shuffling their feet under his weight, Franz using the oar as a cane. They brought him to a pure white aluminum door. LIBRARY, read the placard above the doorway.

The library was a single large room with surprisingly high ceilings for a jail. Tall mahogany bookcases stood between the barred windows. A fireplace flickered in the corner of the room. It was jagged and of an awkward build given its mismatched bricks, but it burned wholesomely nonetheless. Franz and Gordon brought Johnny to the middle of the room, where two classical armchairs, a mahogany side table, and a plush chaise lounge rested on a large rug. They laid Johnny onto the chaise, and the mayor's head drooped off the chaise toward the chairs. Johnny's back cracked and popped as his spine slunk down into the cushioning.

Gordon retrieved the kettle next to the fireplace and poured three cups of tea. He held out a cup to Johnny, who didn't move. He'd become an absentee operator of his own body, leaving his eyes to stare into the flames of the fireplace. Gordon sighed and placed the teacup and saucer atop Johnny's stomach. They rattled softly as they rode his inhales and exhales.

Franz and Gordon sat on their forest green armchairs facing Johnny. They watched him closely, sipping their tea between concerned grunts and faint head shakes. Franz's oar stood quietly in the corner, leaning against the fireplace mantle.

"Sooooo," Franz began.

"Just give him a minute, Franz," Gordon said.

Franz rubbed the paint decorating his teacup. The fire crackled, and Johnny flinched each time a pocket of sap popped in the burning wood. Johnny rolled his head in the other direction and quietly watched the shadows of the fire on the opposite wall.

Franz's knee began to bob as the fire cracked. He glanced at Gordon, who calmly drank his tea, letting the fire get all the say. A huge pop came from the fire, and Franz clanged his cup on its saucer.

"So what happened then!" he blurted out.

"Franz, you are by far the worst co-host I have ever worked with," Gordon said.

"Excuse me, my good man, but I am trying to open a civil dialog here!"

"You are being far too pushy," Gordon murmured, trying not to alarm the man-child with the argument between the adults. "You need to show more temperance, Franz. Proper moderation before self-interest, and being mindful of the needs of others is a virtue worth having."

The two old men looked back at Johnny. The teacup on Johnny's stomach toppled onto the floor. He continued to stare into the shadows.

"Oh by the gods, can we just get on with it!" Franz shouted, rising from his seat and spilling his own tea in the process.

"Franz, he doesn't even know who we are!" Gordon hissed.

"Well, then let's tell him!"

Franz gripped Johnny's chin and turned it toward him. "John … John. The General imprisoned us here way back during the great coup. That way he'd be the only voice in New San Francisco."

"You were his political opponents?" Johnny wheezed.

"Not quite," Franz said, letting go of Johnny's chin.

"We are philosophers, Johnny," Gordon said. "All of us here are. The city had just begun. It was young and the people who had come were all displaced from round the world, scared and far too young."

"The beast saw his chance," Franz said. "Getting rid of the few folks like us would allow him to develop not just the bones of the city but the soul solely by himself."

"He got it while it was young," Gordon said. "He took a few of our ideas and other pieces of the past and slung them together into something rather …"

"Warped," Franz moaned.

Johnny winced at the bright light from the fire. "From the beginning? If you are philosophers, then how—"

"Look, I'm sorry, Johnny, but Franz is right," Gordon said. "We just don't have much time. We have already made moves that can't be taken back. Before the General, everything was fine."

"From out of nowhere this man just appeared," Franz said, "lit a match, and set our reality ablaze. We need to know who that man is, Johnny. We need to understand the man who strapped you down and tried to make you his prisoner. The same man who has imprisoned us for all these years. We need to know who he is, so we can beat him."

Johnny shuddered. The very idea of challenging the General again seemed like trying to seize molten rock with a pair of already burned and raw hands.

"Johnny!" Franz urged. "That protest you helped lead. All those people. It will be for nothing if we can't get a better idea of what's going on … up here." He poked Johnny's forehead. "It's very important you tell us what's going on, Johnny, otherwise the movement will continue to fail."

"I was the mayor of Edingburg. You know how little that means! I was nothing more than a reluctant puppet trying to make its own strings. It's the leaders of the Inner Circle and the City Guard who really worked with the General. They're the ones who know things, who had control. At the meetings of the high council, I'd sit at the other end of the table hiding behind my fucking mask." Johnny gripped his hair. "I was just a fucking figurehead. The General made the leaders of each sector. All we had to do was be popular enough to sell the lie that we were actually elected. I was the only one who actually won the votes, but that didn't end up making me any better than the others. If anything it gave the few good people of my city false hopes, stopped them from truly rising up like they should have. I've got nothing, okay! I don't know shit about the General and the people in my sector still don't even know who I am even after five damn terms. I'm not worth shit to the IRA. Nothing. No one. My good intentions only lead to the erosion of the possibility of real change."

Franz and Gordon looked at one another. "Johnny," Franz said, "you've been sent to Alcatraz. Not one other person has been sent to Alcatraz since the coup. You're certainly worth more than even you may be aware. If anything, the one thing that you've lacked until now was … nothing."

"This—" Gordon gestured to the walls— "is the last stop. Nowhere to go from here. So now you may stop worrying about losing something at every turn, and instead focus on what there is to gain."

Franz picked up his oar. "So you can either do that or you can play cricket with us … for the better part of forever." He smiled, spun the oar in his hand, and set it back down. Then he rejoined Gordon in the chairs facing Johnny, their sales pitch finished.

The fire went still.

Johnny cleared his throat. "What, what do you want me to tell you?"

"Let's begin with the end," Gordon said. "What did the General say was the reason for sending you here?"

Johnny looked at the two seated men for the first time. "He said he wants me to act like God."

Franz and Gordon exchanged a glance. "Well, that doesn't sound particularly perverse," Gordon said.

"Not exactly," Johnny said.

Haadin, Part 2

The wave of energy continued to surge through the protestors. Hollers of insurrection spewed from the crowd, a treble that shook the earth. A faint rumble drifted into Haadin's ears.

Lines of black dots zoomed over the hilltops. They slid down the hills from every side, printing the dotted spots of grass with fine lines. As the dots neared, the sound of rumbling turned into an enraged growl. The shapeless dots formed into shadowed black boxes: it was a pack of City Guard jeeps.

The crowd reared back in fear of being trampled. The jeeps halted and encircled the crowd, guardsmen training their machine guns from their top-mounted turrets. Soldiers jumped out and cocked their weapons at the crowd of young men and women. They wore blue emblems over their standard-issue grey uniforms.

"Do not give in, my brothers!" Haadin called out. "Come what may, we will not quietly submit to this injustice any longer!"

Silence fell; neither side budged. Only the fluttering of white bandanas tied to the young men and women proved that time still passed.

Then a blithe tune hummed from above. The crowd turned to the lone noise. The top of a green hat came into view from the crest of the hill. It was the General dragging a wheeled golf caddy bag behind him. The crowd gasped.

"Remain pure!" Haadin shouted. "Let them burn in their own flame!"

"Burn?" the General answered. "It's not me who's going to burn. At least not today."

A guard set down a large wooden chair decorated with a cross; a thousand eyes watched as the General strolled over and sat down. The chair was pure white, the product of fine craftsmanship. The General reached into his front pocket and out a cylindrical casing. The metal grooves ground against one another as he unscrewed the top. He glanced up through his pitch-black aviator sunglasses. "Why would I be the one who burns?" He rested the now-open casing on the arm of the pure white chair and stared at Haadin.

"Next to air and water, brotherhood is the greatest necessity of life!" Haadin proclaimed.

The General stood and began fiddling with his golf bag.

"God has given us the ability to love," Haadin continued, "the ability to connect. But you have systematically tried to rip that gift away from God's rightful children! To rob them of such a gift is to rob us of our very humanity!"

The General withdrew a golf club from his bag and took a few practice strokes. He spoke in a calm, collected tone: "You seem to not understand, my simple and fainthearted friend, that what fools call humaneness is nothing but a weakness born of their own fear and egoism." He dropped a dimpled white ball to brown grass. "This purported law of nature you're trying to impose upon humanity is rooted from nothing but pathetic, chimerical virtue. Virtues such as yours enslave only weak men who wish to hide in a fantasy."

The General smiled. "You should be thanking me. With lines of code, I gave your kind a virtual salvation. A place where you would be free to jack each other off to such things. But out here—" the General raised his arms— "this world. This salvation. Is mine. Unless, of course, you want to try and take it from me." He centered himself over the golf ball. "Which is your right." He wound up; the crowd fell silent during his backswing. The club hurled itself down and with a quick ping, the ball flew into the sun.

The General kept his club raised, watching the trajectory of his shot. "Keep an open mind, develop yourselves, and have a pair. If you'd done that, you wouldn't be trespassing on my lawn, because you'd own it."

"Our insistence on humanity is not the product of weakness!" Haadin shouted. "We care for our fellow man because we understand him!"

The guards raised their guns, most aimed at Haadin as their center point. The General waved them down.

"It is fundamental to remember that we are all human, not beasts!" Haadin shouted. "It is our ability to understand our fellow man that separates us from the herd! An animal can only understand itself. Its being and existence is all it knows! And so all it believes in comes from and is for itself. Whereas we!" Haadin stretched his arms out low toward the crowd of young men and women. "We understand each other! We know our brother's joys. We are aware of his hopes. We feel his hardships! Our consciousness not of ourselves but of each other is our most beautiful gift; to smother its potential with selfish vice is the greatest waste a man can do. God himself would weep from such disappointment of his own children! To waste this gift from God is to waste our humanity!"

The General plopped himself down onto the white chair. The ash trees behind them rustled in alternating tones of green. Wind whispered between their branches.

"We will not squander this ability we have been given," Haadin said, calmer now. "No, we will use it to its greatest potential. To do this we have taken our first step: we have pledged ourselves to the welfare of our fellow man."

A guard jogged around the perimeter of Humvees with a metal box. A belt of bullets jangled from the box's opening.

"To make this first step," Haadin said, addressing his people now, "to come here today, has taken strength! It takes little to help oneself; even the simplest of creatures can meet their own needs. Forwarding the welfare of mankind, however, is a truly trying test. Our minds, bodies, and souls must now all work in sync. Marching forward for humanity is not the action of a weak man! It is, however, very simple to turn your back on your brothers!"

The guard hoisted the bullet box up to a turret gunner. A line of bullets rolled out of the box onto the thick armored plating of the jeep's roof.

"Feeding a Tuber who is starving in the streets when you barely have enough for yourself is not the work of a weak man!" Haadin shouted. He stood with his legs apart, his fists on his hips, and his chest outthrust. "Building a sturdy shelter for the elderly to keep them warm on the coldest of winter nights while you prepare for your own hardships is not the work of a weak man! Standing for the rights of people who have been denied their basic humanity when it is easy to walk past and plug into a world that only exists between the cracks of a circuit board is not the work of a weak man!"

The gunner on the jeep ripped the breech bolt back, trapping the bolt behind the trigger sear. The gun's firing spring flexed in hopeful anticipation.

A breeze puffed through the trees. The pure white bandanas worn by the young men and women of the crowd fluttered in the sun's rays. The General's hands came together in three isolated claps.

"God. Understanding," he mimicked. "You think the bastard gave us this ability so we could help—" the General pointed at an extremely short man in the crowd— "him?" A laugh bellowed up from his bowels.

"We all come from the same source," Haadin answered. "We are all the products of God! All of us are rays of light born from the same sun! So by pledging ourselves to one another, we are evolving mankind as a whole. The sun will grow stronger, and we will all shine brighter!"

"Now that's a cute analogy. Misguided, but very cute." The General leaned forward in his chair. "Why does my ability to understand another man mean that I actually have to give a shit about him? God does not want us to help one another." He shook his head shook, the falling sun shining on his sunglasses. "God's pragmatic; he understands the value of information. So, being given the ability to understand my competitors, well, that gives a beast like me quite the edge."

"The Bible—"

The General cut him short with a brutal punch to his golf bag, which clattered violently to the ground. He leapt from his chair, brandishing the cylindrical case. "What the hell do you know about what God wants? You self-righteous little bastards who know nothing of God spew these complicated, drawn-out crocks of shit about whatever the hell you think God wants from us!"

The General gazed over the crowd, his sunglasses reflecting and warping the faces of hundreds of young men and women.

"What I know of God is from what I see! Not from some ink scribbled on parchment, guided by unwarranted interpretation, but from the world God has created with his own hand!"

The General thrust his hand upward. "Nature is not blotched by the ink of man. It is pure! Nature is our only true guide. All we must do is follow only its example and leave the interpreting to him. Look at nature for what it is. Each part of nature works, fundamentally, for itself. Each part is selfish and operating without compassion. All wanting to rip the other down, just to pull itself up. And it is in the ripping and pulling, raising and lowering that something beautiful is created. A superorganism. A whole that when seen in full is beautiful. It is from that collective, that unification of beasts and bastards, that creates the divine. To stray from that beacon is to stray from the path of God himself."

The General unscrewed the top of the casing and abruptly turned it over. The crowd winced. A cigar slithered out from the hole. The General held it up for all to see. He inspected the trimmed cigar for a moment and then bit it with his teeth.

"You've all come together and have lost yourselves to the crowd, believing that compassion will make you stronger, more human. Absurd. Allow me to show you what happens when you stray from nature. From God itself."

The General slung an arm behind his back and withdrew an ink-black Beretta; the number 606824 was etched into its side. He pointed it at Haadin. The General tilted his head and aligned his sights. Then he looked up, as if he had almost forgotten to mention something. "Have you ever read Le Bon?"

Haadin glanced at his rally flag in his hand. The General fired, and Haadin dropped to the ground with a bullet lodged in his aorta.

The crowd froze. The situation became painfully clear to every young man and woman: they were now stuck between a cooling carcass and a heated gun.

The guardsmen held their positions with barrels pointed, and ears cocked. All listening for the order to pull the trigger.

The groan of mechanical parts began to rumble, shaking the ground. Strained eyes darted around the crowd. A long stripe rose over the hill of the driving range just behind the General's back. What followed was a 68-ton Abrams battle tank. As it breached the horizon, its 17-foot-long barrel grabbed for the sun. Then the tank's front began to descend, and in one fluid motion its body twisted to the right while the head of the tank turned leftward toward the crowd.

The boomed down onto the golf course. The mouth of the barrel looked blackly over the General's right shoulder.

"Your turn," the General announced to the youths what was to happen next as if he were an usher for a theme park ride. Guns clicked as their safeties were switched off.

A single scream shot out from the crowd, then panic erupted. Picket signs sunk into a whirlpool of now scurrying bodies. Waves of people clamored for the center of the crowd in a desperate attempt to find refuge behind a wall of others. Hundreds were screaming now as they trampled each other, pushing fallen bodies deeper into their future graves.

The General basked in the scene. Such a disintegration of man was to be cherished. For in this single moment, he controlled every emotion, hope, and even belief in their lives. It was at this moment that they were finally being true to what they were.

The tank fired, and a wet cloud of red plumed upward. The guards joined in with machine gun fire, chopping up those who dashed toward the edges of the perimeter.

One man in the crowd, however, did not run. Through a metal mask he stared into the blinding light from the sun, a drunken spectator of spots and sparks. He stood in oblivion as bullets snapped past, women screamed, clods of earth and flesh rained down. He watched a particularly beautiful girl screaming at a seemingly impossible pitch as the world erupted around her. Even disoriented, he recognized his lover in an instant. He ripped off his mask and ran toward her.

The tank fired again, and the pressure wave threw Johnny away from the girl and down into the mud. The girl continued to scream, her golden locks stained with red.

"Helena!" Johnny cried out. Like a puppet, she swung her head toward Johnny, her eyes wide like a wind-up doll's.

Johnny struggled to stand as people blindly knocked into him. Helena's arms stretched out for Johnny's embrace. He ran toward her, wanting only to cover her from a falling world. He was only an arm's length away when her chest exploded from a .50-caliber slug.

Her body fell into his arms, and they collapsed together to the ground. The world covered Johnny in a blanket of red while bullets screamed around him.

The general marinated in pride, sitting giddily in his white chair. He'd given them all a great gift, a perfect gift. The stream of smoke from his cigar quietly rose into the sun. This was a good day. Today he'd gone so far down the path that he'd finally caught up to God himself.

Tea Party

"Hmm," Franz murmured.

"Jes, quite," Gordon answered.

Johnny turned his head from the ceiling and looked at the two old men sitting erect in their chairs.

Franz leaned forward. "You said he brought you here so you'd start acting like … God?"

Johnny nodded. Gordon frowned and stirred his tea. The fire burned steadily.

"Johnny," Gordon said, "you must understand something. There are so many things that can be taken from us in this life. But what you should realize is that this life only lasts so long."

"It wasn't her time," Johnny said. "She shouldn't have been there. I'm the one who brought her into this. Without me she would have never been involved. She deserved so much more than what I did to her; she deserved to live in this world no matter how short life may be."

Franz and Gordon fiddled with their teacups, primly looking away as the grown man on the chaise quietly wept in front of them.

"Johnny, not to be insensitive, but she was always going to die," Gordon said. "There's no changing it. What really matters is what she didn't lose herself. She died a good person. She fought for what she felt was right for herself and for her people. In the end, being a good person and finding truth, that's all anyone can hope to do."

A moment passed. Johnny kneaded his temples. His breath quickened. "Shut," he panted, "shut up! Who *are* you people?" Johnny sat up and glared at Gordon. "Huh?! Who are you?!" Gordon gave no reaction. "You're … you're just some guy, aren't you! Some old man who rotted away in a cell with nothing else to do but find an excuse as to why you're here. Because you can't deal with THAT HE WON!"

Johnny fell back down onto the chaise, grinding his teeth. Then something escaped from him, and the lines on his face deepened another fraction. A face worn by a lifetime of endless effort met with constant failure.

He turned away from the old men and the fire. His stared a barred window facing the brown ocean. "Twenty-five years later and here I am. Sitting with the losing end. The only real difference between us and him is that he sits over there—" he pointed toward the city— "and we sit—" he fluttered hand to indicate the totality of their surroundings— "here, where old men lie to themselves."

Johnny watched their shadows flicker along with the fire along the opposite wall. He could feel them staring at his back.

"All the things you say … all the things you think you believe … it's all just meaningless shit, because it's all just distract you from the fact that you have no power over your own lives. You either believe in something to help get what you want or to deal with the fact that you can't have it. Virtue is no more real than the shadows you cast on this wall."

Franz rubbed the cracked leather upholstery on the armrests of his chair. Gordon stirred his tea. The fire popped.

"I'm taking it that where one's convictions sit is based upon how much power one has," Gordon said, "and one's belief of one thing or the other thing is dependent entirely on one's position, yes? Johnny, every feeling of power is simply an illusion. *That* is what's no more real than the shadows on the wall. It's something that flickers onto the screen one day and vanishes the next. Whatever you may believe you have, it can be taken from you, Johnny—or leave on its own accord. You may be able to hold onto it for a while, but you will never come close to actually owning it. Eventually we lose everything we've never had."

Gordon peered around at the sparse selection of books on the shelves, at the stained bare walls. "It does not matter how much you have or what you try to do in order to keep something, what matters is what you do knowing that someday you will have to let it all go. There is, however, one thing that we can truly lose, but it cannot be taken away. It can only be given away. I almost lost it a hundred times whilst I rotted in my cell. Do you know what that is, Johnny?"

Silent tears bled down Johnny's face.

"It is ourselves, Johnny. Our character. It is the only thing we truly possess, the only thing we can actually control. And if you give that away, then you really will have nothing. You really have lost. That is why the General sent you here. He wants you to lose the only thing any of us really have: the power over yourself. To trick you into parting with yourself he's trying to convince you—and the rest of the city—to let the appetitive part of our soul that lusts for things and power to take over. When it is in control it misguides our spirit into toppling the noble part of our soul that speaks the truth of what is rational and good. And if you let this happen, it will overturn not only your life but also everyone else's. You'll become nothing more than a vessel that may be boarded for someone else's bidding." Gordon inhaled the warmth of the tea. "And the only plus to such a thing is that they will do the lying for you."

Gordon looked up from his tea. "When that happens one is reduced to nothing more than a shadow on the wall. A shadow that can be used to fool the world into thinking that what you are and what you stand for is something more than two-dimensional. Something people may someday throw their hopes and dreams into."

"And that's what you became," Franz said. "A shadow of what you once were."

"But there's a silver lining here," Gordon said. "We believe you've finally hit rock bottom, my boy."

"And that's wonderful," Franz said. "All those wrong assumptions you've had. All those illusions that you've built up of how you could stop the General with half-measures have finally been knocked down. So now that those illusions have fallen, now that you've been zapped by your mistakes, you're finally ready to move forward— and remember the truth. And it's finding the truth that is most virtuous."

The library door opened with a creak. A man in a white winter trench coat stood in the threshold. His metered steps beat into the concrete as he walked to the center of the room. His face looked at is if it had been chiseled from bedrock and glacier ice. Even with the fire and his thick white trench coat it seemed no warmth could comfort him. He looked at Johnny's head poking up from the top of the chaise and took some sort of remote from his trench coat.

"No, don't!" Gordon shouted, rising from his chair.

"That's enough," the man said.

Johnny pushed himself off the chaise, his exhausted body wobbling underneath him. His eyes fixed on the button in the man's hand. The man pressed it.

Nothing happened. Johnny stared at the man for an answer, and then an electric shock fired through his body. He convulsed, falling against one of the bookcases and upending the shelves on his way down. Literature rained on Johnny as he plummeted through each shelf of books.

The man walked over, his foot stopping next to the sporadically twitching fingers of Johnny's hand. The man bent down and pulled Johnny up to the surface of the pile of books.

"How-did-you-get-out?!" he asked, shaking Johnny with every word. Johnny glanced over at Franz and Gordon for help, but they were not there.

The man looked around the library and grimaced at the sight of the teacups. "I'm putting you where you can't play tea party any more."

Subterranean Jungle

Kleiner pressed an elevator button, and a potato-filled column of dirt began to push the floor of his bar back up to ground level as they turned down the tunnel.

Steve was all but blacked out. Ramfort had him by the one arm wrapped around his shoulders and was dragging him through the tunnel that led to the entrance of the bunker.

"Ramfort! Hurry yourself up!" Carrie yelled. She was pressing down on Tom's stomach as she jogged alongside the two men holding the stretcher. The rest of the group was much farther down the tunnel.

Ramfort kept dragging Steve along.

"Would you hurry up?!" Carrie barked.

"Well," Ramfort huffed, "maybe if I weren't the only one moving Steve's dying ass from heeeerreee to waaaaayyyy over theyaa! I'd get there a little quicker!"

"Stop bein' a wee wimp and hurry it up! Everyone's a hurtin'!"

Ramfort pointed down the tunnel. "The kid's not even registered yet! That door isn't opening until everyone's registered, ya dolt! So maybe you could give me a hand?!"

Carrie's eyes widened. She ran back to Ramfort and Steve.

"Never mind," Kleiner said. "Won't be a problem. Go back to Tom."

The rest of the group made it to the entrance. The enormous blast door opened. They ran into the bunker, Carrie sprinting after them.

Ramfort's mouth fell open into an O. His eyes darted around the tunnel, taking in all the touch, light, and heat sensors and iris recognition cameras.

"What!" he shouted. "He's registered?!"

"Yes, lad," Kleiner said. He took Steve from Ramfort and slung him over his shoulder.

"How!"

"It was part of tha' plan, lad."

"Hey! Don't 'lad' me, ya overgrown leprechaun! I'm not another minion! What's going on here! Why's Steve registered?!"

"You musta been in diapas when this bit was marked off fer happenin', Ramfert. So I guess ya don't remember me briefin' ya. An' nobody's a minion in this here movement. Minions are thoughtless wolves and thazz a big parta what we're foiting against, aren't we? We need ta be havin' good lads who got enoof sense in 'em to know an' act when somethin' wrong's afoot."

Ramfort stopped and stood bewildered while Kleiner walked through the blast doors into a room that had been hollowed out from the rock. The wounded lay connected to a slew of puffy white IV bags that hung over mountains of medical machinery.

A water droplet tapped Kleiner's head. He looked up. Above the room was a hanging jungle. In the middle hung a long thick rod of glowing rocks. Glowing vines and vivid leaves reached for the rod from every angle.

"That's new," Kleiner muttered. He heard a jingling and looked down to a bloodhound trotting toward him. The dog hopped up, pressing its legs against Kleiner's chest and trying to lick his face. "Down, Sniffer. Ain't be the time."

Kleiner laid Steve on a shining metal gurney and wheeled him between two other men injured during the battle. He hurriedly placed a few wired anodes on Steve's chest. The machines flashed yellow, and Kleiner let out a huge sigh of relief. "There ya go, Steve. Not all bad, then."

A figure stood over one of the gurneys. Lines of wires connected the figure to the medical machines. As it moved its arms over the injured man the machines flickered, pumps either slowing or speeding up.

"What's all that up there, then?" Kleiner asked, pointing to the ceiling.

The figure continued waving its hands over the man. "The gates have been opened. We proceed to step two."

"That's stage two, huh?" Kleiner asked, still looking up at the ceiling.

"No, it is the backup for step two," the figure said.

Ramfort barged into the bunker. He'd had a moment to collect himself and more than enough time to gauge just how pissed off he was about not being informed of Steve's clearance. "KLEINER!" he shouted.

Kleiner turned from Steve to find Ramfort in midair flying toward him. His boot plunged into Kleiner's sponge of a stomach. Kleiner grabbed Ramfort's leg as the boot sunk into him, then shoved him backward, sending Ramfort sprawling to the floor.

"Come on, fat man," Ramfort said, lying flat on his back. "Stupid giant. McFatty. Fat boy!"

"There are people dying here!" Carrie shouted. "What the hell is wrong with you two?!"

"You ask him!" Ramfort said. He sprang back to his feet and clawed for Kleiner's neck.

The figure turned and looked at Steve with its human eye while its mechanical eye jolted from left and right. It raised a pair arms covered in wiring over Steve. The arms started clicking as they honed in on one spot, then the clicking grew louder. The thing turned its head to see a red light flashing from the medical devices. It let down its arms and looked at Steve for a moment. It seemed as if it was muttering something just before it cut the wires connected to Steve's mind and pushed his gurney into the middle of the pen, where Ramfort and Kleiner were still fighting.

The gurney banged into Carrie. She turned. "Hey!" The figure was already walking over to the next wounded man and raising its arms.

Carrie looked down at Steve, then up at the big red light. Her eyes widened. "Knock it off!" she shouted, kicking Kleiner in the shin. Kleiner knelt down in pain, bringing both of them to her eye level. She pointed at the red light.

"Oh." Kleiner said. He wobbled over to Steve and looked at his wound. The veins around it bulged from the skin.

"Nikolai! What're you wheeling' him over her fo'! We've hoondreds of vials of antivenins stored away here."

Nikolai turned back, and its mechanical eye zoomed in on Steve's wound. "New strain. Too advanced. Our synthetics are antiquated."

"What's going on?" Ramfort asked.

"They used poisoned bullets on 'em," Kleiner said.

"You sure?" Carrie asked. "The rest of 'em don't have any signs of poisonin'!"

"Officer shot him with his pistol," Ramfort said. "He's gotta be in with someone in the Inner Circle to get those kind of rounds."

"Bastards get slimier the higher oop they get," Carrie said. "Nikolai! You can't just go leavin' him for dyin'!"

Suddenly the ground quaked behind Kleiner and Carrie. They turned to see an enormous Samoan looking right at them. The Samoan man was so massive he towered over even Kleiner. He wore nothing but a wife beater and jeans. A tattoo of a tiger stretched up his massive left arm.

He walked over to Steve, picked him up, and climbed up a vine that seemed to materialize from thin air.

Kleiner looked up, speechless.

"Ha!" Ramfort shouted. "Sucks not knowing what the heck just happened doesn't it!"

"Wha— who?"

Ramfort brushed and began walking toward the next room. "Why don't you ask the robutt. I'm gonna grab a ladder."

Kleiner and Carrie looked at Nikolai.

"Stage two," Nikolai said, waving his arms over a wounded man as he conducted his machines to bring the man to stable condition.

Carrie peered up into the misty jungle. "'Unleash the Titan.'"

Nikolai's mechanical eye snapped up and scanned the foliage. "Yes."

The Watching Tower

Johnny sat with his back propped up against a rusted iron grate. Growing piles of dust gathered along the edges of the room. Long horizontal streaks flowed through four narrow iron slits that followed the circular walls of the room. The streaks conjoined in the middle of the browning floor, creating a brilliant circle of light.

Johnny wasn't sure how many days he had sat here. Two? The only thing that gave him any reference to time was the circle of light, which crept around the corners of the room throughout the day and would quietly slip away through the slits at night.

Franz and Gordon tried their best to be accommodating. Ancient bags of ramen noodles and a kettle of hot water were slid through the slits three times a day. Nevertheless the packages lay in a growing pile, untouched. Johnny had become unaware of his weathering body. The only thing his mind was doing was playing the repeat button, of her death.

Keys jingled, and the door cranked opened. Sunlight cut a perfect rectangle onto the watchtower's floor. The man whom had grabbed him in the library walked in, still not bothering with an introduction. He unfolded the metal chair that Johnny had been strapped to and slapped it down into the middle of the circle of light.

The man looped around the chair and stood on top of it. He pushed up a circular piece of the ceiling and pulled down a long wire. Then he stepped off the chair and looked down at Johnny. Johnny's eyes darted between the man and the dangling wire. The tape in his head paused.

Johnny scrambled to his feet, filling the hollow tin space with cacophonous moans. "Come on," he wheezed. "I'll lose this fight too, but I'll be damned if I make it easy on you."

The man stared back at Johnny, utterly unalarmed. "Progress," he said. "You have a visitor." The man turned and left the room, leaving the door wide open.

Johnny stared at the open door with clenched fists. He wasn't sure what to do next; the open door was giving him more options than his mind was prepared to consider.

The man walked back in with a box, set it down on the chair, and connected the wire to the box. The box responded with a quick static click. Johnny glanced between the man and the box, keeping his fists up for whatever may come next.

"Don't punch the speaker," the man said. He turned and left, locking the door behind him.

The box clicked on. "Hello, Jonathan." It was Mom.

Johnny's knees buckled. He slid down the wall and he fell in a heap of relief. At least she didn't want to kill him.

"How are you?" Mom asked.

Johnny coughed up a clot of dirt. "I ... I'm alive."

"I hope you are, Jonathan."

Johnny didn't show it, but he was somewhat happy to hear that someone seemed to care about him, even if it was just a voice coming from a box.

"Johnny, I've been told that you left your cell and went to the ... library ... for tea. Who were you speaking with?"

Johnny pursed his lips, reluctant to give away the only kind people he'd met in this prison.

"It was Franz and Gordon, wasn't it, Jonathan?"

Johnny remained silent.

"I take that as a yes. Well, if you have to talk to anyone besides me, it's best you talk to them. They are inseparable, aren't they? Very kind gentlemen. They only want the best for you, Jonathan. What's best for the city. It's important you remember that."

Johnny suddenly regretted throwing his chair at Franz.

"Jonathan, I'm going to ask you something, and you must be honest."

"All right."

"Now before I ask the question, I want to make something perfectly clear: no particular answer will free you."

Johnny felt his heart plummet into his stomach.

"But any answer can free you from here."

"What do you mean?"

"No matter your answer, you will be allowed to do as you wish from here on out. You can stay with me ... Or if you would like to go back, we will make accommodations for you to be sent back to

Edingburg. You'll be given a new identity and you can live a completely new life if you wish."

"Impossible. I can't get away. I can't be free. It doesn't matter where I hide, he'll still get me."

"Jonathan," the box said, "if all goes to plan, the General will no longer be able to wield power over anyone."

"You've taken over a prison on a rock that's stranded in a dead bay," Johnny said. "It means nothing. The only thing your little coup has achieved is taking over something that's already been written off."

"Just because someone has written us off doesn't mean we should write ourselves off."

Johnny looked away from the speaker. She was insane, or at the very least delusional. "The General has walls, guards, guns. All I've seen here is old men with cricket bats."

"What the General has is strength and a capacity for violence. But those qualities are not power. Power is not like a gun. Power is not something he can store or pick up whenever he wants. No, his power is the ability to convince another man to pull the trigger—and under his own accord. And he has to convince them to do it every time.

"This prison wasn't for people who merely committed treason. Traitors were killed on the spot. No, people were imprisoned for a different reason. Something the General understood to be his real threat. And that's the ability to passionately counter his arguments, to make people question his justifications for his actions. To question his underlying sense of fulfillment or the very nature of happiness.

"You see, Jonathan, the General's real power does not come from the City Guard. His power comes from his ability to influence. To make others value what he values. He's influenced them to solely value the idea of success as the be all end all. He has freed them of an exact definition of it, but at the same time chained them to a select few choices that they can make to begin building 'their' dreams. His self-enabling choices are nothing more than poisonous tools. They provide ability to build, but degrade the user. And so with every brick the people lay to forge their legacy, it breaks away another piece of themselves. And when their insides have fully rotted away only the bricks remain and it is the General standing atop them. But even worse, if you refuse to use the tools he's provided, then you are seen as a failure. No matter the success you may forge on your own. Instead you are a failure and it is best for everyone if you simply, as you said, 'write yourself off.' That's why so many choose to apply, and why those who don't eventually crawl into their virtual coffins and wither away."

A long breath flowed through the speaker.

"This is not how it should be, Jonathan. So it is our duty to free New San Francisco from its choices. To liberate its people by giving them the freedom to become the best version of themselves, with their own hopes and dreams, so they can someday turn those individual thoughts into individual work and action that can better form and shape us all as a whole."

Johnny gazed at the city through the bars of the window. He'd known all this to be true—probably better than most. But he'd never heard it in words.

"What would I do with freedom, then?" Johnny asked. "By leaving this empty cell I'd only gain a hollow life in Edingburg. The only difference is that the walls here are more visible."

"So is that your answer, Jonathan?"

"Is what my answer?"

"To the question."

"You never asked—"

"Do you still think that all the beliefs and philosophies people hold are based purely on their own status and self-interest where … you sit, I believe you put it?"

Johnny went white; she must've heard the entire conversation he'd had with Franz and Gordon.

"If you can call that an answer," he said.

"Then please tell me, Jonathan."

"I've been thinking a lot about children lately. About how they are. They act no different from the people who put themselves in virtual tubes, or from how the women in the Inner Circle conduct themselves when they want something. Or the City Guardsmen, when they're angry.

"When children are hungry, they scream or chew on what's nearest them. Children seek out what is most basic and natural to them, things that preserve them, like food and comfort. Then when they grow older, turn to teenagers, they start to really recognize relationships. They start to understand other rational human beings. They start to care about them. But when they're finally starting to form a bond that's outside of themselves, it's all shattered. By applying they are dropped into a new world. The world that comes next, it forces isolation and disparages real lasting relationships from forming.

"So people regress to the children they were instead of evolving into the next stage. Children that are far more capable and far less innocent."

"And what would have happened?" Mom asked.

"They would have evolved and grown on a personal level ... so they would better understand and support those they love. It's in that stage when real virtue can be realized. True consciousness—sentience—can be gained.

"So my answer is yes. People's beliefs do have to do with where they sit; their beliefs are easily shifted according to their own needs. What they believe is simply a justification to get what they want—*if* they never evolve to the next step."

Johnny gripped at the bars in the window. "But if they do evolve, then maybe it doesn't have to be that way. Maybe we can evolve into something better, and even if I only fail in my attempts to lift people higher in this lifetime, at least I will not have willingly succeeded in pushing them lower."

"That is the answer I was hoping for, Jonathan. I understand you feel trapped, and I promise I'm doing everything I can to free you, dear. And I'm afraid you are right, Johnny: a ticket to Edingburg won't get you anywhere. But by joining me in our struggle, maybe you can finally be liberated. It will be a long road, but together I believe we will finally uncover the path that's been blanketed by years of ash."

Warmth filled Johnny's soul. He wasn't aware of it, but he was smiling for the first time in years.

"Will you join me, Jonathan?"

"Haadin is dead. Without him the movement may change into something else."

"It will change. But only its methods. Our movement will remain a nonpolitical one. We have no interest in taxes or petty social norms. It's about more than that. It's about the development of human beings. We believe that nothing can be improved until we improve ourselves."

"Good, that's what Haadin preached."

"It is, but you must remember that he was just the beginning of the movement. There is so much more to follow. We are adding to the base that Haadin founded. Our people have died because they were never given a shot at knowing what it is to live. Will you join us, Jonathan?"

"Yes."

"Good."

A slight breeze of salt air flowed through the room.

"Now before we begin, I want to make something absolutely clear. I need a promise, Johnny. A promise you must keep and tell no one of. Someday you will have to let me die … and you must bury me where I've fallen."

"What?"

"Can you do that for me, Johnny?"

"I don't—"

"Promise me."

"Okay. Yes … I promise."

"Good."

The static hummed softly for a moment.

"You are aware of phase one, correct?"

"Yes," Johnny said. "Open the Gates."

"Yes. Now we must Unleash the Titan."

"Yes."

"Call it woman's intuition, but I feel you will prove instrumental to the conclusion of this movement. I just hope it's the conclusion we've both dreamt of. Okay Jonathan, let's get started."

The door swung open. The man stood outside, waiting.

Nuts

Steve sat up to find a long pulsing light in the center of a tubular frost-filled jungle. The hanging light immersed him in a vibrating world of blue and white. He sat in pure white snow, but to the touch it reminded him more of a cool untouched blanket. His arm had healed. No hint of a bullet wound. However, the line of scar tissue on his wrist still remained.

An enormous figure stood with his back to him, and the silhouette of a woman ran silently around the pulsating pole. It was Melody. She approached him and dropped to her knees.

"What is this place?" Steve asked with a puff of steam coming from his mouth.

"Jombo grew it."

"Jombo?"

"The big man who takes care of me when I'm young."

A memory flashed through Steve's mind of the huge tattooed man picking up the much smaller Melody and cradling her in his arms. He looked over at the enormous man.

"Do you feel better?" she asked, her eyes glassy.

"I do." But he felt uneasy around her, unsure of whether her concern was good for him, no matter how sincere she seemed.

Melody smiled. "This is a wonderful place. None of the bad is here. We can rest." She lay down beside him, the snow crackling beneath her body as she looked up into the endless branches reaching toward a nonexistent canopy of white. "I'll explain to you the best I can. Yes, I've grown up over the past week, but—" she touched her temple with a finger— "I've experienced far more than that. Even now memories are flooding into me. Right now I remember sitting on top of a tall red column that's rising out from an even taller and redder mountain. A man is sitting beside me, holding my hand. Our feet dangling over the high edge. We're looking over an incredible world. Filled with red and brown mountains that look like a painter stroked them with his brush in layer after deepening layer of crimson. And below them, a valley of green with spots of yellow and purple flowers of all shapes." Her eyes widened. "He's turning to me." Her eyes shut. "He's kissing me. He's asking me to be his."

Melody rolled onto her elbow and looked into his eyes. "These memories are forever flowing into me, filling me more and more. Every day. Every moment. Every second that passes I learn something, discover something about a past I never knew I had, but had never lived myself."

"Um … so then why are you so focused on me? There's so much going on with you. Why am I even relevant?"

Melody touched her chest. "Because in this life. My life. All I've ever felt is you."

Steve was suddenly conscious of his face, and he willed it not to change expression.

"You ran after me," she continued. "You saved me from who I thought was my mother and a place I thought was my home. But I was wrong. I was wrong in the same way you were wrong about Leslie. We both held onto something because we thought it just had to hold onto us back. We didn't look at where we were or who they really were because we thought they still felt the light."

"The light?"

"Yes. When you ran in to save me. Why did you do it?"

"Well, I had to. The whole place was going to go up around you."

"But why did that matter?"

"Well. You could have died."

"Why would that matter?" Melody asked. "The guards knew that, but they drove off. Why did you bother while they didn't?"

"Because you just can't do that."

"Why not?"

"Because. You were a little girl."

"So?"

"So!" Steve sat up. The very idea of having to put something so basic into words felt almost insulting. "You had your whole life in front of you. There was so much that could have been lost by losing your life. You were still innocent, pure, not yet critically damaged. So there was still something in you. Life. You were alive. Still present. Still had hope. Still felt things without that underlying stint of pain attached to everything. You were like …" Steve paused.

"I was like you?" Melody rose to her knees and touched his forearm, guiding him back to rest in the snow. "You did it because you still believe in the beauty of being human. You still feel the warmth coming from the energy inside you, keeping you alive.

"That is why we held onto the cold ones around us. The ones who let us go so cheaply. We always felt the cold of their touch, but we thought that on the inside there was still warmth within them too. We told ourselves it was just the outside elements making them feel so dead. We didn't think any of this when we held them, but we felt it. We loved it because love is the most basic understanding and yet most powerful knowledge that can be held onto. Something so true and inherent that it bled into all other parts of our lives and being. But to them, to the ones frozen through, we were merely a furnace. And they left when our flame could warm them no more."

"Are you okay?"

Melody rolled away from him. She dug into the snow and brought up what looked to be a large pearl. "I am lucid, Steve. I know how nuts I seem to you. But is it what I'm actually saying that's crazy or is it the order to you I'm saying it in? If you knew me like I knew you, if we had spent more time together before I had to say all this, then maybe it wouldn't be. But sadly the order of things has all been jumbled, our development cut short or forgotten, so we can only do our best and let the quality of our message speak more powerfully than its unfortunate timing."

Steve sat back up and looked around him. He'd never been in such a clean, calm, and quietly magnificent place. It was hard to grasp that above the colorful fruit, the glossy leaves and vibrant flowers, that somehow above all this there was a churning wall of ash burying them deeper into this world.

"So what are you trying to do?" Steve asked. "Why are you here?"

"Because as nuts as I may be I have not turned on what energizes me, what warms me from within. And I think you've seen that it's the people above us whom have fallen into that kind of cold. I'm doing the only thing I can: Helping them find the light again. To feel the warmth that's already burning within them, so that they can finally relearn to love themselves. And if you'd like, I want to help you with that too, because even though you're getting colder, I know you still feel the warmth. That's why I'm part of the movement. And it's why I'm lying next to you."

"You are so …"

Melody sat up from the snow. She gazed at the blood band covering the scar on his wrist.

"Good. You not die."

Steve spun around to see the giant standing over him.

"Your spirit trained your DNA well," Jombo continued. "Your chromosomes follow your RNA with honor." He stroked a long furry leaf that began to glow as he stroked it.

Down below them, a dog started barking.

"You're making dog nervous," Jombo said as a ladder clanged on the wall beside them. "You need to make amends with the dog!"

"Don't do it!" Ramfort shouted up to them. "I want to see what he does!"

"Okay, okay," Steve said, worried the giant would break him in half. He climbed down the ladder. The dog jumped on him and licked his face as it whined with excitement. When it finally lost interest and hopped down, Steve looked over to see another huge man staring at him, this one with a mechanical eye.

"You're not dead," Nikolai said. "Aren't you glad?"

"Where am I?!"

"In an empty space."

Ramfort walked over and laid down with his arms crossed, and the dog hurried over and started licking his face.

"How's it hangin'?" Ramfort asked.

"Screw you!" Steve said. "You almost got me killed."

"That's true. And yet you followed me here, a complete stranger. Because you wanna really stick it to that ex-lady pal of yours by taking down that goshdarn Inner Circle. You'd get revenge and you'd be the top dog. Which sounds pretty sweet for a man in your position."

"Is that it then?" Nikolai asked. "Is that your purpose for being?"

"Bah!" Ramfort said. "Everyone's got the same purpose, it's just what they see it as that's different."

"That is true," Nikolai said.

"Yeah." Ramfort said. "Isn't that right, Steve?"

"It's not your reason, however." Nikolai said.

"Yeah it is, Crapbot! Everyone's little 'purpose' in life is just an excuse to grab more power."

"That's not true," Nikolai countered. "Obtaining or expressing forms of power is not the only meaning man can have. Ourselves, we have a low chance of survival. Many among us think the IRA cause hopeless. But they still here anyway, because they have made this revolution their purpose. People are not willing to sacrifice their lives merely for the sake of their 'excuses.' They are here because it is virtuous to them, which gives them reason to live."

"Whatever, Crapbot. They caught a case of the virtue because just being power hungry wasn't sexy enough. Too basic sounding. People are simple, Stevie Wonder. They've all got these brains that can do some complex stuff. So they go and overthink just how simple this is. They build over their actual point in life with these—" Ramfort stretched his arms wide on the floor, exciting the dog again— "elaborate purposes!"

Ramfort grabbed Sniffer and spoke to him. "These denial-made purposes eventually get so big and complex they need gears, buttons, levers, and every kind of wizzwow to operate their self-peddling, deceptively egocentric piece of junk that is their excuse for being such a dang power hungry basic bitch! In time people start to mistake their advanced doodads—" Ramfort nodded at Nikolai's robotic arms— "as part of their meaning. But the machine they've made is still just a tool they've glorified." He flexed his pelvis off the floor. "To help them get some!"

Ramfort jumped up. "And don't mind this overgrown toaster here. He's got identity issues. Now tell me why you followed me. Yeah, you've heard of me, but come on, you walked up to a convoy of guards with no pants on."

"Watch your mouth, child," Nikolai said.

"I wish you were." Ramfort poked Nikolai's metal arm. "At least that way instead of getting all this lip we could offer these kids—" Ramfort's arms widened— "toast!"

"We don't have bread," Nikolai responded dryly.

Ramfort's arms shot up. "Gah! Well isn't that just perfect!"

"It's not power we want," Steve said. "People crave an identity we always thought we'd grow into. A name that everyone will know. A presence so that whenever we enter a room, everyone will acknowledge us."

"Yeah, but you suck," Ramfort said.

"Exactly," Steve said. "We're all nobodies who grow up being told we're great, that we would take over everything because we had something spectacular and unstoppable inside us. But we're all the same special nobodies living in the same dump."

"Nobodies?" Nikolai asked. "Why call yourself that?"

"Because we're all nobodies looking up at somebodies all day. All being buried by the never-ending avalanche of updates and trends. All of us forced to breathe in the ideal that is *being famous*. They're the only people we hear about, all we see outside of this shit, the only people who seem to be making life happen, the only ones who are clearly as special as us. They inspire us but at the same time poison us with the idea because while we're convinced that we're just like them, we aren't living like them, so day by day we have to swallow a bit more of the idea that we might not actually be special."

Ramfort and Nikolai stared at one another. "Or," Ramfort said, wriggling his nose in contempt, "you could stop caring about what you see on a screen and make shit happen."

"That's what I'm trying to do!"

The ground quaked and banged. The dog yelped and scurried away, tail still wagging.

"We have to go now," Jombo said. "Time for you to sign up for City Guard."

"What! I'm not applying!" Steve protested. "No fucking way!"

"You must." Jombo grabbed Steve's arm and started pulling him toward the doorway.

"Quit being so grabby-grabby," Ramfort said.

Jombo dropped his hand, and Ramfort looked at Steve. "Look kid, we need a guy on the inside. Telling us where the boys are, where they're going, when they're fighting. We've got some shenanigans planned for the games and we can't pull 'em off if we got a thousand crazed teenagers with guns popping up out of nowhere and lighting up the whole damn block."

"What shenanigans?" Steve asked, rubbing his arms. He looked around at the strange walls, the alien devices, the cyborg, the huge Samoan, the jungle above. "What the hell is going on here?"

Ramfort looked at Steve, confused. He glanced around the bunker. "This is the revolution? We're going to beat the General and this stupid city. What else would it be?"

"What else could it be?!" Steve shouted. "What the hell is it?!"

"It's as he said, lad," Kleiner said, walking into the room. "It's the revolution, same as you know. Just a bit ... flashier."

Steve looked at Kleiner as if he were an imposter. "I've been coming to your ... bar," he said, nodding up to the ceiling somewhere up above, "ever since I could walk. I swept the floors. I cleaned out the back, until I was 14. Is this why you had me go work for the unions? To cover up making ... this from me?"

"No, lad, I assure ya. This has been here since before ya could crawl, let alone the walkin' 'n sweepin'."

Steve stood teary eyed, unable to know what to think.

"Lad, I assure ya. I'm the same ole coot ya thoughts I was. I jus' so happen ta have me a bunker beneath me bar. I wasn't jokin' about the IRA, lad. That's why I had ya go joinin' da union and made ya into a bit of a stranger. We got busy the past few years and supposin' we got caught, I didn't want ya all strung up next to me."

"You still had me doing stuff for you," Steve said. "The rally. The cassette."

"Not linkable to us and our happenin's. Figured you'd get jailed fer a bit if ya got caught, but nothin' like we'd be gettin'. General'd be havin' a real hard time findin' dem dots between the protest and what's happenin' with you and us. So we figured ya safe."

"Safe? You care about safety? Everyone died! Mary, Mitch, they've all been burned!" Tears began to stream down Steve's face. "And no one even cares it happened. The point was to show that the issues with the city can be addressed. That people who speak up can be heard, but no one even knows what the protest was really about."

"Word's spreadin', lad. Through the right channels. It's not just the people like you'n me we be needin'. It's people o' power too. Not everyone's impressed with the General, lad."

"You weren't even there! How can you spread the word, huh! Why were you the only one who didn't have to go?!"

"Look, lad, it's not fer me to be choosin'. I'm not the shot caller of this thing. Mum is. I fill the post she instructs fer me. Me job is to keep this bunker runnin,' and ta keep everyone togetha and movin'."

Kleiner put a hand on Steve's shoulder. "I'm feelin' just as sick with what happened, lad. Believe it. I looked after that whole lot fer years. They were my kin, they was. So I can't be losing meself now. They died fer that dream, so we gotta make sure we see it happenin'. What we do now be more important than eva."

Steve stood quietly for a moment, trying to push through the pain to think. "Who— who's Mom?"

"She's the leader of the rebellion, lad."

"Well, *where* is she?"

The others stole glances at one another.

"She is buried deep in Inner Circle," Nikolai said. "She only communicate to us through speakers."

Ramfort gave Nikolai a dirty look, then took out a cigarette and bit it. "I highly suggest—" he lit the cigarette— "you don't go gossiping about that to the wrong people. In fact, don't talk. Ever. Yes, that's probably for the best."

"Step two, lad," Kleiner said. "Rally. That's what's next. We need people comin' together fer what happened. Right now people who know be actin' on their own. Need them comin' togetha. To do that we need all the people of New San Francisco in the game. So we gotta have them hearin' what Haadin had to say. Make it known what happened. What's going on now. What's next. It's why I had ya deliverin' that cassette. Should be playin' soon."

Steve went white. He smacked his jacket pockets with a flurry of hands.

"Right here." Ramfort took the cassette out of his jacket.

Steve's face went from white to lava. A sick wave of guilt washed through his body.

"Don't worry, lad," Kleiner said. "We've had more than a sack of setbacks. Luckily we've got an even bigger sack o' backup plans. Speakin' o' which," he said to Ramfort, "when's ya brotha comin' ta visit?"

"Just got buzzed on that. They'll be here soon. That piece of crap Johnny finally made up his mind. He's with us. The douchebag's going to be walking all over this place talking all fancy about how he's totally not a douchebag and that we should all just get in a circle and kiss."

Kleiner scowled. "Now don't be sayin' all that. I know the situation's a bit roof fer yea but—"

"A bit … roof?!" Ramfort shouted. "He's why all this happened to me! And he's going to keep doing it! He's not with us! He has never been with us! Why the hell should we be singing kumbaya with that nutjob?!"

"Look lad, tha man's comin' round. Mom trusts him. You just need ta have a bit o' faith. He's been helpin' us whenever tha General wasn't 'round him. He's the best guy we got in there."

"What happened?" Steve asked.

Ramfort puffed out his cheeks, scrunched his face, and turned away.

"Johnny's the one who reinstituted Alcatraz …" Kleiner began, "but it was the General who went and threw Ramfort and his brother in there."

"I was a baby!" Ramfort shouted. "A cute little baby, with the rosy cheeks and the eyes full of wonder!" He pointed at his dull blue eye. "Now I got holes in my cornea. Thanks, Johnny! Great idea! Putting holes in my eyes! Can't wait to see you through them!"

Ramfort leaned in so close that Steve could see the small scarred holes dotted around Ramfort's eyes. The two stared at each other.

"It's time for Steve to apply," Nikolai said.

"Bot!" Ramfort shrieked. "I was having a moment!"

"You sad about some holes in your eyes? I remember when I had two eyes. That was good. Now's just fine too. Tomorrow even better." Nikolai's mechanical eye magnified toward Steve. "You apply now. We need you get mobile job detail so you can track the cycler's movements and pass them on to Ramfort."

Steve could feel a load of pressure coming onto him from all angles. He looked down at his arm, surprised again to see that there wasn't even a scar. "How long have I been—"

"You were out for 17 hours and 23 minutes," Nikolai said. "You were healed by minerals from the plants Jombo grows. Jombo is an arborist. He grow rare plants for the Inner Circle at top of glass greenhouse pyramid. He defected from General's post a week ago and started growing the farm above us." He pointed up at the jungle.

"What were the glowing rocks up there?" Steve asked.

"Special rocks to grow special things," Nikolai said.

"Rocks from the asteroid!" Steve exclaimed. "The one Aizen talks about!"

"I know no Aizen." Nikolai checked a gauge on his wrist. "Time to go apply. Take the sewer."

"What sewer?"

"I'll show you," Carrie said. She stood at the edge of the room and motioned for him to come.

Steve followed after her.

"Hey look, Steve found a new girlfriend," Ramfort said.

"Best shut yo mouth, Ramfart," Carrie said. "Still your fault Steve got shot."

"Bah, he's alive. You two go make out or whatever. Just don't let Melody see. Or do. Scandalous."

Carrie waved Ramfort off and motioned Steve into the hallway. "I don't blame ya bein' unsure 'bout all this. Some bad stuff's been going on lately."

"How long have you been doing stuff like this?" Steve asked.

"A good bit, but I guess it's gonna be a good bit longer before we be makin' things roite around here."

"How come I've never seen you around? You look my age."

Carrie crinkled her eyes. "Kleiner took me in way back. Had to hide me as I was what some might think of as an orphan. Guess he didn't feel right sending me to that brainwashin' hellhole of an orphanage. Damn monster factory, that place is." She tilted her head, amused. "But best not be studying me too close there, Steve. I'm in no mood for men to be looking too close."

They walked to an enormous door that was made of solid iron and was shaped like a hubcap. Carrie tugged on one of the door's giant lever and pulled it down. Pins clicked, joists groaned. The hatch swayed open, revealing a tunnel.

"Climb on in," Carrie said. "Take a left then go up the third tunnel. It's about a mile, so pace yourself."

Steve's legs were trembling. He looked at a smiling Carrie, who beckoned him in with a wave of an arm.

"Why do you do this?" he asked, partially to buy time to not be in a sewer.

"Me only methods o' gettin' on in dis world are foitin' or fuckin the men I hate. Foitin' 'em seems loads more appealin'."

Steve reluctantly climbed in. "Wait, how am I going to talk to Ramfort?"

"Oh, him? He'll find a way. Trust me, you'll be tired of hearing from 'im soon enough." She began to push the hatch closed. "Oh, and don't mess up those directions. You can only open that hatch from inside the third tunnel."

Steve watched the hatch shut, sealing him into the darkness.

Part III

The Fight

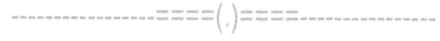

Do you like the idea of becoming powerful?

Great.

Then lets go over some fundamental on how.

They do work. Just not for me.

How This Really Began

Journal Entry #156

When it's someone close to you who dies, it always feels like murder, and you somehow took part in it. It's impossible to escape the fundamentals of such a guilt. Justified or not you pay for the sins you hold onto; and it will change you.

That guilt fractured my identity. It compartmentalized our lucidity. That's when the rift between here and now turned to chaos. When she died that day. When the savior of my world burned, we were born. Through her death, came our life.

And in my life I discovered the dance between power and lucidity. It's that little number that built our city and made the idea of "civility" into something far more savage.

It is from the insatiable pain of something that you can not control, comes an unending lust for power.

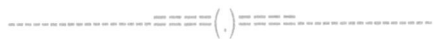

The Glory of Groove
Journal Entry # 159

Mom is love. The strained kind. The kind that burns when you get close to it, but freezes when you drift away. That's not her intention of course, she genuinely wanted to help me, but it's her fault all the same.

It's her fault because she awakened me. She made me aware of my misery so that I could address it and even transcend it. But lucidity of my misery hurt me, and brought me much distress. People get used to things. They "adapt" and habitualize anything and everything into the routine. A daily groove. It usually starts with brushing your teeth, to saying "Have a good one," when exiting the elevator. All of this is done to make it easier. Whatever pain you might feel inside, doesn't have to be felt if you aren't lucid enough to feel it.

And that's the first step to good dancing. Finding the groove. The groove that lets you move without sobriety of self. But remember, *your* groove will only give a good buzz if it syncs up well with other people's groove. And the best way to ensure a good dance party is for everyone to adopt a basic way of flowing. Once everyone's plugged in, you can get as close or as far from anyone on the dance floor as you'd like and you'll never feel too hot or too cold again. Just numb.

But everyone around you will be convinced that you feel, that you and your group are the way to be. So much so you and your party believe that they feel and feel it better. This is the first step to power.

Apply to the City Guard for more information.

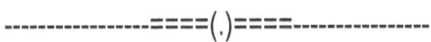

--------------------====(.)====---------------

Certainty

Journal Entry #452

Certainty is the most sought after luxury and the most soul-crushing hardship. For the established and the rich, certainty is their one true crown jewel. It gives to them a future that is not unlike their satisfying present. For the struggling, certainty is the iron-barred cage that keeps them in their place. Every soldered bar is a surety to the free and a reminder to the caged that the day after tomorrow will be just the same.

But no one prefers a cage, or at least, not when they're aware they are   in one. So that's the next trick to power and   lucidity. Putting people in cages for your own   gain, but never letting them worry about it. In fact, make them need it. Make the cage hell and they'll eventually break out. But make the world a terrifying place and the cage their own personal fantasy world, and they'll fight whoever dares try to rip them out of it.

Everyone likes having a guard dog who comes with its own leash.

Now back to my story …

Coin Flip

"Heads or tails?"

Steve stared at the medals on the colonel's well-pressed uniform. On his front jacket pocket, the words "Hell on Wheels" had been hemmed beneath his corporate logo.

"Heads or tails, kid?"

Steve glanced down at the coin balancing on the colonel's thumb. He'd applied. Against every fiber of his being, he applied. In that moment of replying "Yes" to the question "Are you applying?" he'd lost it all. His job, his neighborhood, his home, his identity, his life.

"Last time! Pick heads or tails, kid! Need I remind you that you are now a candidate for my corporation! So you are being held to the same standards as a guardsman as of NOW! And as of RIGHT NOW, you are NOT FOLLOWING THE ORDERS OF YOUR SUPERIOR!"

"Okay!" Steve shouted. "Sorry!"

"Okay? *Sorry?* No! Not fucking okay, you little shit! What the fuck is sorry! You trying to speak some Irish bull here! This isn't Edingburg! Look at me, you bastard!"

The colonel pointed to a long scar that stitched his throat together. "Do I look okay to you?"

Steve looked away to where the second colonel sat. He was fat and sweating on a foldable metal chair. His legs were propped up on a wooden table.

"Did I tell you to stop looking at me!"

Steve looked up and into Colonel Bradshaw's eyes for the first time. Bradshaw wore a flat-billed gray hat with a silver phoenix pinned to its front. His face was thin but with a strong jawline that was reinforced by high cheekbones. His hair was neatly combed into rows of gray.

"You know how I got this scar, kid?"

"No sir!"

"By having to yell … at you … STUPID LITTLE FUCKS ALL GODDAMN DAY! Now fucking pick a side of the coin, you fucked little shit!"

"Heads puts me on … what team again?"

"Jesus Christ, kid!" Bradshaw smacked Steve in the head. "You are the most retarded creature I have ever come across! From now on you will spread your asscheeks when I give you an order! Because if you're going to keep spewing a bunch of shit, I'd rather it be authentic!"

A vein bulged on Bradshaw's forehead. "These aren't teams! This isn't like tag where you play grab ass! If you get the coin flip right you're a pledge for my multimillion dollar corporation. You get it wrong, you're on Yorker's bullshit outfit. Now choose! And you'd better get it wrong, kid. Pray you get it wrong, because I swear to god you'll never make it past private."

"All right … tails."

Bradshaw looked back at Colonel Yorker. "Candidate claims tails." Colonel Yorker waved him off. He was too preoccupied with wheezing and frowning at the sunburn that was spreading over his pale and plump skin.

"WRITE it down, Yorker," Bradshaw roared. "How the hell has your board of directors not fired your ass! Ohhh, that's right! Nazi Daddy money!"

"Two days we've been doing this," Yorker groaned. "Thousands of applications. In zis unholy sun. Zis kid is applying so late. If I knew what time it was I'd swear he missed ze deadline. Zis coin method is supposed to speed arduous process. But here we are."

Bradshaw looked back at Steve. "My competition. Fucking Germans lost their edge." He grinned. "Little trust-fund shit from the Inner Circle is CEO of Ghost Fox now. It's perfect." Bradshaw shouted so Yorker could better hear: "Bet you didn't count on a rebellion play, huh, you fat bastard!"

"Silence your tongue," Yorker said, sounding bored. "Fucking Edingburg bastard child. Never learned how to speak to people. It's why the Inner Circle never distribute funds to you outside of works you do."

Bradshaw gave another toothy grin. "Subsidized piece of shit. You're no better than a Tuber. I'll see you in the newly freed Edingburg, you and I both know that shit's winner takes all. And I'm gonna take over that whole damn market."

"We out number you three to von. You're barely even corporation, small boy. Keep talking. We will spank you soon. Decommission all your fresh pledges."

"Uhhh," Steve said. "Wait, aren't we fighting the IRA in Edingburg?"

Yorker began laughing. Bradshaw's gaze spun and fired down on Steve. Bradshaw took his time leaning down to Steve's height. "You think I'm here to *fight* the IRA? You think I'm here to *fight* a half-dozen redheaded teenagers with so much testosterone pumping through their dick they can't even see straight! This is not about the quelling of an uprising! This is corporate warfare! Now lets see whether or not I need to fucking kill you!"

Bradshaw's thumb shot up. The coin flew and landed in his hand. Heads it was. Ghost Fox.

Steve slumped in relief. Bradshaw glanced over at Yorker, whose head was now resting flat on the table. Bradshaw looked back at Steve, his eyes shooting fire.

"You little shit. WHAT THE FUCK DID I TELL YOU! You had ONE order. ONE! I told you to get the coin toss WRONG!"

Steve looked at the coin in Colonel Bradshaw's hand. "But sir, I got—"

Bradshaw drew his pistol and pointed it at Steve's face. "SHUT UP!" He yelled so loud that the seams of his throat threatened to tear. "You are under my command now! You do one more thing out of line and I will shoot you in the head for insubordination!"

The colonel walked over to the table. He grabbed the handle of one of the two metal rods that were plugged into cigarette lighters that looked liked they'd been ripped out of an old car. He turned to Steve, brandishing the glowing red tip of the rod.

"You work for my corporation now. No matter what. If you try and switch sides in Edingburg, all Ghost Fox needs to do is look at your brand and they'll hack you apart. Desertion before you're eligible is death. One damn thing we all agree on."

Steve's eyes went wide. "Wha—"

Bradshaw rammed the molten-hot metal rod into Steve's throat. Steve fell to his knees, his windpipe smoldering. Bradshaw took out a spray tube and shot a gelatinous film over the circular brand on Steve's throat.

"Goddamn, kid, can't even take a little pain. You keep that shit covered until this revolt is over—or until you bitch out. NOW GO THROUGH THAT DOOR and get battle ready, you little shit, or I'll brand your ass too!"

Steve scrambled to stand and sprinted for the door, passing a nearly knocked out Colonel Yorker. Opening the door he looked back and saw Bradshaw pick up Yorker's papers. Bradshaw began writing something down.

Steve entered into the door and peered around the dark room. He was in a long, wide hallway that stretched to his left and his right.

"Stick or rock?" a voice asked from somewhere in front of him. There was an outline of a man standing behind a wooden table.

"Uh, what?" Steve wheezed, his throat flaring with pain.

"What?" the man mocked as he lit a fat cigarette. "You ask annoying shit all the time, don't you, pledge?"

"Uh," Steve said.

"Uhhhhhhh," the man parroted. He took a drag from his cigarette, the only real source of light in the room. "The time for 'what' and 'uhhhh' is over, pledge. This isn't a place for questions. Questions get you killed. In fact you'd be better cuttin' out thinking in general, because you don't know a damn thing."

The man pulled down a lever. A bulb frizzed on from above him, coughing down light onto the table. "Stick—" the man pointed his cigarette at the hollow handle of a City Guardsman's ax on the table — "Or rock?" His cigarette puffed a trail of smoke to the shining blade of the ax.

Steve walked up to the table. "For what?"

The frantic barking of a large dog roared from down the hallway. It was coming this way. Fast.

"Any more questions, pledge?"

Steve's eyes widened.

"Good," the man said. "You look like you're ready to learn something. Lesson one. This is a place of instincts. Any hesitation in what you do and you will die, but if you do what comes naturally, you will become one glorious bastard. Up to you, pledge. So, stick … or rock?"

Steve looked down at the table, then back up at the figure of the man. An orange light appeared on the center of his face as he took a long drag from his cigarette.

Steve grabbed the ax handle and cracked it into the shadowed man's skull from over the table. He grabbed the ax blade with his other hand and ran like hell down the hallway, away from the coming beast of a dog.

He sprinted down the dark hallway. Each step clanged and bounced off the metal walls. The barks chased after him. A pair of double doors was coming up. Steve grabbed the knob. Locked. Steve looked back. The dog was getting closer. Steve banged his shoulder into the door. It gave a little. He rammed it again. Again. Steve could see a pair of glowing eyes bounding toward him. He screamed and rammed the door so hard that his shoulder dislocated. He fell forward into the room. The ax blade and handle slid across the floor. He kicked the doors shut.

The doors banged. The dog was trying to get through, and Steve had broken the lock. He propped his feet up against the doors, his back still flat on the ground, as the dog raged and pummeled the other side. Steve could feel the heat from its breath every time it cracked open the doors.

The dog fell back for a moment. Steve spun and sat up, slamming his back into the doors. He noticed a pair of door handles on either side of his head. The ax handle! Frantically, he looked around. The ax handle had rolled a few feet away. He extended a foot, trying to reach the ax handle and drag it back without letting go of the door. The door slammed into the back of Steve's head so hard that Steve saw spots. Autonomously, his foot reached out and slid the handle toward him. Steve's arms shoved it through the door handles, pinning the doors shut.

Steve turned and took a few stumbling steps back, watching the doors jolt toward him and rear back. The barking stopped, and the dog's nails on the hallway floor skittered away. A cold sweat broke out over Steve's body. His shoulder felt like a dull blade was jammed into it.

Steve heard a ping behind him. He spun around. A man his age had picked up Steve's ax blade. "You took both, huh? Damn, wish I thought of that."

Steve raised his one good fist. "Who are you!"

"They said questions would get you killed, but don't worry, I'm a pledge like you."

Steve winced.

"You hurt?"

"Shoulder, for … the door."

"That's unfortunate, buddy. I ran and kicked mine open."

"Where are we?" Steve asked.

The guy walked into a little closet-sized space cut into the wall. "See that arrow?" Half of a glowing arrow pointed upward on the wall above the doorless closet. The man looked up at the ceiling inside the closet where there was a small oval hole. At the top of the hole was a glowing red button.

"We gotta press that button. Way too high to jump to. I can't get to it since I got my stick wedged in the other door. Listen."

Steve heard shallow breathing coming from the far side of the room.

"Mine didn't leave," the man said. "Been pacing out there for hours. Guess I was waiting on you to get to the next step. Seems we're in some kinda team-building exercise. Go check your door. You hear anything? If it's gone we can use your stick to hit the button."

Steve walked over to the door. Nothing.

"Pretty sure it left," Steve whispered.

"Perfect. Slowly take the stick off the door and throw it to me. Stay there just in case it comes back and I'll throw it to you. I'll do the reachin' and the jumpin' seeing as you got your shoulder broke and all."

Steve hesitated.

"Come on," the guy said. "I've been here for hours. This room doesn't get any better."

Steve grabbed the stick with his good arm and slowly slid it through the handles. He looked at the guy standing by the closet, then back up at the arrow. He paused. The arrow? That wasn't an arrow. It was a number one! Steve let out a long breath. This guy was trying to trick him. Only the guy who hit that button would advance to the next step.

"Come on, buddy," the man said. "Let's go!"

Steve looked at the expectant eyes and outstretched hand of his new "partner." His hand tensed around the end of the handle. Steve threw open the door and shouted. He banged the stick against the doorframe.

"What the fuck are you doing!" the man cried. Steve kept shouting. The dog howled in return, its claws frantically scrabbling over the metal floor.

"Give me that stick or I will beat you to fucking death, kid!"

"We can both go!" Steve shouted. "We can find a way!"

The man raised his ax blade and charged toward Steve. Steve swung his ax handle and cracked the guy in his kneecap. As he fell over the dog lunged though the door, pinning Steve into the pocket of space between the opened door and wall.

The man screamed as the dog tore into him. Steve ran past the carnage and into the closet. He jumped for the button. It was still too high, even with the ax handle. He circled around the beast as it ripped into the still-screaming man, picked up the blade, and screwed it into the handle as he ran back to the closet. He poked the ax through the oval-shaped hole and jumped for the button. When he landed, the dog was looking up at him, its face smeared with blood. The two stared at one another in the now silent room. The dog took a few steps toward him. Steve jumped with all the strength his legs could muster. The button clicked.

Double-sided iron bars shot up through the floor and a cap slid over the oval hole, sealing Steve into the closet.

Gears turned, and the closet jerked. Cylinders from an engine fired on. The closet tilted backward, detaching itself from the rest of the room. Sunlight poured in. Some kind of forklift was taking him away.

Steve watched the dog until the closet turned on its back, turning Steve with it. He looked up at the yellow clouds floating above the bars.

As the machine rolled Steve away he heard groans and cries for help. Steve remained silent. Minutes slowly ticked by, then accumulated into hours. He could feel his throat muscles squeezing, trying to wring out any moisture that might still be housed in his throat and mouth.

"You want some water, kid?" a voice asked.

"Yes," Steve croaked.

The opening of a huge hose slowly floated over his closet. "Here you go, kid."

The hose blasted on. A gust of salt water slammed into Steve's chest. The water rose and completely flooded the closet. Steve grabbed the bars, squeezing his face as far as he could wedge it between the gaps. The water covered all but a portion of his nose.

Steve's vision blackened, and calm overcame him. He could see her again. Leslie. Lying there. Beside him, looking out the window to the gates. The gates opened with a veil of light. Light so bright he went blind. Then the light went away, and so did she.

Steve opened his eyes and looked up at the wavy image of the sun. He turned in the water to face the bottom of the shadowy closet. He grabbed the ax, unscrewed the blade, and used the hollow handle as a snorkel.

The oval cover plugging the hole at the top of the closet popped off, draining half of the water. The bars above Steve slid away, and a pair of arms pulled Steve up.

"You're not dead, kid! Welcome to Hell on Wheels! We bring hell in a hurry!" a guardsman said as he heaved Steve to his feet. "Ha! Look at that shoulder! Don't worry kid, I'm a learned doctor." The guardsman spun Steve around, grabbed him by the back of the neck, and punched Steve's shoulder back into place. Steve screamed. The guardsman let go and walked over to another barred closet beside them, dragging the hose with him. "You want some water, kid?"

Steve fell to his knees inside the closet, sloshing the puddle of water. He didn't know whether to continue screaming or cry.

They were in the middle of Haight Park, surrounded by rows of other toppled closets. Thousands of them. Most of them with people sitting or standing on the edge of their own closet, all looking just as distraught as Steve felt. Muddy paths lay between the closets as guardsmen dragged and sprayed their hoses.

Steve stumbled over the edge of his closet and a guard pushed him back in. "Not yet, kid. Lucky for you, you came late. Only a minute left till showtime."

Steve considered asking what "showtime" meant, but lay in his bath of salt water instead.

I let another person die. I watched him get ripped apart. He forced it. It was me or him. He made it that way. It didn't have to be that way. Nothing had to be this way.

Steve opened his eyes and watched the yellowing clouds dissolve above him.

You were my life. Then you left. You didn't even look back. You couldn't even pretend that I still existed. That I ever existed. You've trashed my memories of you. Of us. What I thought we were. What I thought we had been doing. Apparently you were doing something else. Which means I was wrong. About everything I thought we'd shared together. When you left, you didn't just erase my future, you rewrote my past.

A fist drove into Steve's stomach. Steve lurched up. "Lie around on your own time! Show's starting!" a guardsman shouted. He pointed to a small stage that stood slightly above the rows of closets. A huge flag of the Phoenix Cycle hung behind it as a backdrop.

A trumpet played a short tune.

Colonel Bradshaw walked onto the stage. He waved a hand, silencing the trumpet. "This show's not going to be as flashy as the girls'! Instead of ladies wagging their goods, you get to see MY pretty face! And instead of some cutsie, trendy song full of horseshit, you get to listen to my CHARRRRMING voice! And you'd better listen because it's this ugly face and my voice that's going to keep you alive another day!

"First, let me make one thing clear as shit. There's no coming back from this. You are sitting here because you left another man in some hellhole to get ripped apart. You did that. I'll bet none of ya thought you could do something like that, huh? Well, you did. And you did it in about two minutes flat. And the only thing that separated you from getting the same was your instinct to live.

"Instinct is what drives you. Every part of you. When you're hungry, you eat! When you're dog-tired, you get some shut eye. When you see a girl, all dolled up and battin' her eyes at ya, you take what you can!"

The guardsman who'd punched Steve chuckled. A smirk was plastered on his face. The guard looked back at Steve and his smirk widened.

"But what happens when it's not so damn easy? What happens when you're hungry and you *can't* eat? What happens when your enemies start wearin' you down? What happens when that girl's laughing at you, pointing at your shriveled up piece of manhood?"

Bradshaw swung his finger up to his head. "You use this. You use your mind to get what your body orders you to take. When what you're wanting is hard to get, this hunk of mush figures it out for you. That's how it works, gentlemen. You acknowledge what the body wants and the mind will get it for you.

"Now if there's one thing I know that everybody wants in here, that's to live! To survive! To keep that heart pumpin'! Because if it stops, then it can't get any more of what it wants! And to keep it beating, you can't hesitate! So once the decision is made, GO! OR! DIE!

"I want you to look at the side of your box." Steve leaned over the side. His name had been branded into the top with a barcode beneath it.

"This is your coffin," Bradshaw said. "There are many like it, but this one is yours. Your coffin is your best friend. It is your life. Without you, your coffin is useless. Without your coffin, you are useless. You must react faster than your enemy who is trying to kill you. You must kill him before he kills you. You will …

"Your coffin is human, as human as you, because it is your life. The only difference is whether your coffin lies above or below the ground. Thus, you will learn it as a brother. You will learn its weaknesses, its strength, its parts, its soul. And in finding its soul, you will find yourself.

"So you will keep your coffin clean and ready, even as you are clean and ready. You will become part of each other. You will …

"Before GOD, you will swear this creed. You and your coffin are the defenders of your world. It is with your ability, and its reminder, that you will become the masters of your enemy. You will be the saviors of your own life. You will choose if you get into that coffin today, or tomorrow. So be it, until victory is yours and there remains no enemy!"

Colonel Bradshaw stood stiff. He breathed it all in, soaking in the glory of his students' new grasp of their situation. "Congratulations, you have been enlightened. That is all."

Paddle Shifter

The man at the back of the canoe glanced up from his front coat pocket. He and Johnny were rowing away from Alcatraz, bound for New San Francisco. But you couldn't really say that *they* were rowing as Johnny was the only one holding the oars.

Johnny huffed with each stroke. He'd been paddling for miles, and the viscosity of the liquid in the bay didn't help either. More and more of the stuff stuck to the oars as he pulled them toward the city.

Johnny contorted his face into a smile to shine at the man who'd been imprisoning him. It was hard to look sincere—given the seemingly very short staff at Alcatraz, chances were good that this man was likely the one who'd electrocuted him in his chair.

"So," Johnny asked, "what were you in for?"

The man kept rummaging through his pockets.

Johnny stopped rowing. "Must have been something worth talking about."

No reaction.

Johnny lifted the oars out of the water. "Well, these shoulders aren't gettin' any younger," he said, adopting the southern drawl he used with his constituents. "While I'm taking a rest, how about you help us pass the time and tell me a story. Maybe one about what the hell we're doing around here."

"You row the boat," the man droned, "I get us in, you lead the way, I watch our backs, and then when the time is right, we blow it all up."

"Well," Johnny said. I believe that's what they call a synopsis, not a story. You want to elaborate on just what the heck you just said?"

"The question is not *what* happens. The question is *when* does all that happen, and at this rate—" the man nodded at the immobile oars — "it looks like it's going to be a while."

Johnny whacked the man's chest with an oar. "You want me to lead the way? Lead where! I gave you a straight question. Now give me a straight answer! Like it or not, we're partners now."

"A straight question for a straight answer?" The man pushed away the oar. There was a line of sludge on his chest. "How about you answer me this, partner? Why didn't you shoot him? The General?"

Johnny stiffened. He was ready to fight again, but not answer questions.

"Why not just end it right then if you're so serious about finishing this?" the man asked. "The gun was cocked, ready to go."

"He gave me the gun, not the bullets."

"Good thing for you he didn't. I saw." The man tapped his head.

Johnny's eyes widened as he realized that his memories had been uploaded. Alcatraz had the machine to do it—he'd seen it in another wing of the lab that created Capsule—but he'd thought it'd be out of commission like the rest of their stuff by now. He felt naked, but had no idea which part of him was exposed.

The man looked him over. "That's what I thought. Straight questions? Straight answers? I don't think so."

Johnny shook his head.

The man watched Johnny. His lip twitched, then he took out a deck of cards from his jacket. He fanned the cards—they were made of thick bendable glass—and rattled them together with a pull of his thumb. "Here in my hands is the plan." He held up the deck. On the top side a holographic pattern of lights; on the back side a jack of spades. "The cards have already been shuffled, maybe even stacked, but I wouldn't know. This deck is everything that is going to happen, but I don't know the order, when each card will actually come into play or if it should be played at all. I just deal the cards I'm dealt and when I see the card, I do what it says. So when you ask what's going to happen next and how it's all going to play out, I have no idea because—" he kicked the oar back over to Johnny— "I haven't the faintest clue which card I'm about to deal or when or where it is to be placed."

The man brought the deck higher to catch the light. "The cards need the sun's rays to be seen, so all I do is hold it up and see how it looks and when I see it, well hopefully, everyone else will see it too."

Johnny picked up the oar. "And just what game are we playing?"

The man blinked forcefully. "A game like all the others," he said. "Beat the house and rein in something better. But—" he leaned in— "what makes this game special is we have no idea what winning looks like. This game doesn't require you to complete a particular objective in order to win. So that means high cards, low cards, they could all be the trump card in the end."

Johnny rubbed the scruff on his face. "But there is a trump card."

"You're missing the point. There's no rule except that in order to play there must be energy coming from a single source. One point." The man pointed to the sun. "Everything after that …" He held up the side of the deck with holographic patterns flowing out of the flat cards. He cut the deck, flipped the bottom half on top of the deck, and held it up to Johnny. The pattern on the top card looked like a small room surrounding a red ball.

The man removed a few cards from the middle of the deck and brought them to the top. The new top card showed a sound wave moving away from him. He shuffled again, showing triangles floating in a space. "Everything after that, every combination, every decision, every single part is interchangeable, alterable, and has the capacity to change the basis of everything that will have happened.

"All that matters is the combination of the cards we play and how the energy—" the man pointed at the sun— "hits it and evolves with it. He leaned back. "So even when the house does react—" he put down the deck on the canoe's bench between them— "by shaking up everything we've done—" he shook the orderly deck into a pile with many holographic images floating above it, some crossing over one another and interacting, changing— "what he does to us doesn't really matter because —" he pointed to a slanted card with its one-inch thick sides shining through another group of cards making a golden vibrating ring— "that might just be his undoing.

"Because so long as there's energy, so long as the cards intermingle and change the path, somewhere, somehow, in the billions of combination of cards there is the jackpot. So his only real chance at winning and survival is to harness the source."

The man reached into his pocket, brought out a black cube, and dropped it on the pile of cards. The floating holograms above the pile snapped to blackness.

"So our answer to his very likely to be impressive counter to us, we will answer with noise. Static. Random flickering chaos. And it's a reaction like that, that he just can't manipulate or anticipate. And even if he wins, it won't be over."

"But that's insane," Johnny said. "That's just irresponsible. How could a group of people even follow that kind of model?"

"The General is the grandmaster of his own kind of game. He's much like those Tubers I've been hearing about. But he's the master of manipulation. He manipulates things he can examine. Games with kings, queens, pawns—" the man waved his hand— "all laid neatly across a board. You give him that and he'll beat it." He made a fist. "Every time. But this game—" he pointed to the deck of cards on the bench— "is not so structured. It's not chained by rules that the General can use. So even if he were to take a card away—" the man removed a five of clubs from the deck, then flipped over the next card, showing an ace— "there's a chance that that very move will be his own undoing."

Johnny shook his head. "No. No. This is all insane. You're fighting the General's madness with insanity!"

The man leaned forward. "The General has created a world of black. A world where everyone is trapped on top of an infertile world, destined to die and join the black beneath their feet. But we—" the man removed the black cube and swirled the cards around with care— "we will make a world of color and dimension. Through combination and careful chaos we will construct a world where every person's true colors can shine their brightest and deepest on a landscape that transcends harmoniously into a single grand picture." The man stopped moving the cards, and Johnny looked down into a seemingly endless void of swirling beauty.

"So the first logical step is to free ourselves from any inherent value we would place on a particular card. Free ourselves of the mindset of whether a card is simply worth a lot or a little now; instead think of it as what it will become on the painting."

"So there's one deck?" Johnny asked.

"There are many, and they're all in play, but when we've finally won, there shall be only one deck."

"How many decks have you played?"

"Plenty, but that's unimportant. Because if not this deck, then we'll play the next deck, and if not that deck then the next." The man rubbed his jaw. "Somewhere, between the millions of millions of combinations between a deck and its sister decks, the jackpot lies." He put the deck of cards back in his jacket. "The only real question for the player is 'how lucky do you feel with the next hand,' so bet accordingly."

Johnny leaned back in the canoe. "Hold on. What about our steps? The steps we've all been sayin'?" He began to recite. "Step one: awaken the city. Step two—"

"It came up as a mission in the cards. 'Spread the basics,' it told me. Then it listed them. First time I think I've ever pulled a card like that, actually. This is one of the stranger decks I've dealt."

"How come the General hasn't found her by now? Mom? Nobody's ever ducked him for long."

The man glared. "The General isn't the only one who can build a wall to keep others out." He pointed to sky above Johnny's shoulder. We're here."

Johnny whirled around to see a giant black rectangle of iron not 15 feet away from him. It was a pier. It had no columns or even a hint of support between the edges of its dimensions; it simply jutted out from the shore. It rose at least 80 feet high and formed a perfect metal block over the bay. Johnny gazed upward; he could only see the crisp dark edge of the pier that met the cloudy purpling sky.

"What are we doin' now?" Johnny asked.

The man stood up. "We knock." The canoe rocked wildly.

"Hey! The hell are you doing! You're gonna tip the boat!"

The man responded by casually stepping over Johnny and continuing to walk forward until he reached the bow. The canoe was about two feet from the pier. The man reached inside his trench coat and brought out a stuffed orange bear that been tied up with rope. He tied the bear onto the lone bar that stuck out of the pier, brought out a toy green infantry helmet, and placed it snugly on the bear's head. Then he turned and walked back to his end of the canoe. He stood there for a moment, gazing into the purple sunset. "What do you think of the bear?"

A moment passed. Johnny blinked blindly in the sunlight.

"Okay," Johnny began, looking between the man and the stuffed bear tied to the pier. "What the hell is that about?! Who are you, kid? Gimme context. I can't work with some kinda mysterious card player."

The man at the back of the boat gave no response. "Remember, I was next to the General for years," Johnny said, "and while you clearly don't have a liking for him, he knows how to get shit done! So lesson one: tying teddy bears to militarized piers and asking my opinion on your decorating job isn't helping us do ... whatever the heck it is we're doing!"

Johnny threw his arms up and let them clap onto his thighs. "The hell is wrong with you! Were you in prison too long? Your mind go unhinged in there?"

"Prison?" the man asked. "Too long?" He looked toward Alcatraz. "That prison is my home." His hands clenched into fists. "And it's because of you I had to leave it again and again and again!"

The wind picked up, and the man breathed in the rising tide. He returned to searching the pockets of his trench coat. Quietly, Johnny grabbed an oar and began wriggling his fingerprints into the grains of the wooden paddle. The man began to whistling a mellow tune.

Johnny looked at the man with his back turned to him and then to the bear, and from the bear back to the whistling man, and then back to bear with the damn helmet on its head, then back to the man looking for god knows what in his trench coat pocket, then to the stupid fucking bear.

"Cut the shit! What the fuck is with this bear!" Johnny shouted. He stood up, wielding his oar. "Enough, kid! We're startin' this mission right the hell now!"

"You don't understand bear?" the man asked, looking up at the changing skies.

"No, goddamn it! Now tell me! What's this bear business all about!"

The man held out a device festooned with wires, resistors, small watch batteries, and a green chip all hanging beneath a big red button. The man petted the button gently with his thumb.

Johnny reared back, raising his arms to cover his face. "What the hell is that for?" he cried as he scurried backward.

"It's for Bear," the man said.

"Wha—" Johnny wheeled his head around to the bear and in that moment heard a faint click.

A wave of pressure plumed out from the bear, releasing the long laden fury beneath its stuffing. Johnny was instantly and completely enveloped in a sharp and dizzying fray of metal. He shrieked as fractalized iron bored into his face. A high-pitched buzz implanted itself into Johnny's ears. The muffled splash of falling rock crashed into the ocean surrounding him.

When Johnny opened his eyes, the man was standing over him. "Up." He grabbed an oar, unscrewed the top, and pulled out a metal spear inside it. Then he jammed the spear into the floor of the canoe before stepping into the freshly blown out hole in the pier. "It's time to move on."

Johnny crawled to the end of the sinking canoe and climbed into the pier's opening. Walls of humming pipes formed the room. The man reached behind one of the pipes and drew out a sheet of paper and an old cassette player with a headset.

"Here's how this is going to work," the man said. "I'm going to —"

Johnny kicked the man's shin, then grabbed him in a headlock as he doubled over.

"You little punk," Johnny growled. "Think you can fucking talk to me like that after you try and blow my face off. *I'm* going to tell you how this works."

The man groaned as he struggled to free himself.

"You're going to stop being a little brat and start bein' real pleasant real quick," Johnny said. "Now be a gentleman an' introduce yourself." Johnny tightened his hold on the man's throat. "Or I'm gonna kill you."

"Cottard," the man gasped. "I'm Cottard."

"Finally. Good. Now, please tell me—what am I doin' in this room?"

"Read," Cottard coughed. "Read it." He fluttered the sheet of paper that he'd grabbed from behind the pipes. There was a paw printed onto it.

"No more bullshit, kid!" Johnny flexed his bicep into Cottard's throat.

"Look!" Cottard wheezed. "It's a card!" Cottard hit the pipes three times with his hand.

Johnny looked, and the paper began to fill with words:

"Hello, Johnny."

The writing disappeared. New text came:

"Pleasure to be working with you again."

"Now …"

"You must keep the enemy off balance."

"Blind them from our true intent …"

"… So let them come."

"When you've knocked."

"Walk out the front door."

"—Deus X."

A list appeared:

"1. Clean yourself up."

"2. Listen to the tape."

"3. X marks the spot."

"4. Walk out the front door."

The paper went blank, then a postscript appeared:

"P.S. Be nice to your partner."

Johnny released his hold, and Cottard fell forward onto the floor.

"You can kill me, some guy you've never met," Cottard, staring down at the floor from his hands and knees. "But you couldn't shoot *him*? You had the opportunity. All you had to do was just pull the damn trigger." Cottard staggered to his knees. "If you had, I wouldn't be here and none of what's about to happen, none of it, would have to happen. You want to know who I really am? Huh! I'm the guy whose life you're ruining because you couldn't just do it."

"I couldn't ah shot him, kid," Johnny said. "The bullets were fakes. He was playin' mind games with me. Couldn't have stopped him anyhow."

"Just shut up." Cottard reached into his coat and brought out a first-aid kit. "You didn't even try. Now clean yourself up. You look like shit."

"So we're still on step one then," Johnny said. He opened the box and started wrapping gauze around the shrapnel wounds on his forehead. He put on the headset and pressed play.

"Hello John, It's me."

Johnny recognized Mom's soothing voice immediately. The tape continued.

"You are about to very actively fight the General and for that I am sorry. Until now you've only had a more passive role, but that clearly is not working if it has come this far. So I must do to you what he has done to us all. In order to free you, I must enchain you. But let me help you understand what his version of freedom has become.

"What the General has done is define freedom as an ability to choose. By simplifying the word he has robbed our children of freedom's real value: the ability to do something truly different, unexpected, new.

"Choices have been reduced to joining and living in institutions like the City Guard or the Inner Circle, that the General constructed for his own purposes. By creating an application process it forces an ultimatum on every boy and girl who come of age and chains him or her to a path that leads to a predetermined destination. By creating such a system the General has completely reengineered the definition of 'choice.' Now choices are nothing more than a justification of base desires. A justification that admits its selfishness and applauds the collateral damage such a desire would create when pursued.

"But the justification he provides comes with a price. The girls must make their choice publicly in the stadium. In that moment the entire city casts a lifelong judgment on them. In that moment any grain of innocence those girls could hope to have is destroyed and so subjects them to a lifelong decree of guilty for their actions.

"I remember when I applied."

Johnny cringed. A big part of him silently had hoped she was above applying for the Inner Circle.

"Yes, John. I did it. And I cannot lie to you just like I could not lie to the crowd. The truth is I wanted it. Everything. So I gave it all away.

"But haven't you noticed? The questions they ask the girls when they apply? They don't try to truly understand why you're applying. They just let the crowd infer. Infer that the girl on the stand is nothing more than a gold-digging whore. Nothing else. And from then on, when I was accepted and put into the Department of Ladyhood, that's exactly how they treat you. Like a whore who is willing to do anything, but that it's okay. Even if you're nothing of the sort they do their best to shape you into the bimbo they need you to become."

Johnny's head shook. Bullshit. Every woman in those circles, it seemed, appeared to have some sort of line they'd say to themselves. This was just hers.

"John. Listen to me. Even saying this so far from you, I can feel your resentment even now. You must understand before you judge. The institutions the General has created require such a hate-filled dynamic in order to exist because the fallout from the choices the young boys and girls are forced to make must alienate and separate everyone from one another. This forces hatred from the people of the applicants past, so the applicants have no choice but to cling to their new group identity in order to survive.

"The same is true for the men, who must destroy any sense of brotherhood by having to suppress their own people in order to get ahead. So if you have already applied and then stand up against the institutions the General has made, you would be held down by the very people you hope to liberate because your message would only fall on jaded ears."

Johnny scowled. "When all they see is hell and all they feel is pain, it's hard to blame them."

"I had a roommate in Alcatraz," Cottard said. "He couldn't take it, our life. He'd be screaming nearly every night. Cursing the world. Cursing the stars that looked to be floating so freely just outside our window. Cursed God for creating them. Cursed God himself. Until finally the sun rose back up, and then he'd cry. And he'd plead until he finally passed out on his wet pillow. Meanwhile I slept like a baby. And when the sun touched my face, I stretched and greeted the day.

"The situation doesn't matter. Two men can be in the exact same situation, yet live entirely different lives."

Cottard pointed to the ceiling. "It's time to wreak havoc."

Plan B

The floor thumped in a lonely room. A marble slab in the middle of the passageway softly popped up from its deck, the head of an oar propping it up. The paddle tilted from left to right; the mirror strapped to it helped gauge that the long dark room was clear. Cottard emerged from the opening and quickly found darkness in the corner. Johnny hoisted himself up and scrambled to the opposite corner. The closed door separating the two emitted a thin line of light through the crack at the bottom. The two men turned and stared at each other, adrenaline pouring into their systems. Johnny held his oar, his face expressionless, eyes scanning.

Large windows on the opposite wall revealed a magnificent view of the coastline. Radiance from the spotlights cascaded through the windows, illuminating a desk made of rich mahogany. A flag of the San Francisco Republic stood behind it. But what really caught their eyes was the massive Barrett .50-caliber sniper rifle posted on top of the desk.

Cottard floated over to the desk and looked down at the rifle through the night-vision scope covering his eyes. He flicked the scope up off his eyes to find Johnny pointing to the wall. A traveling spotlight from outside revealed three Xs chalked onto the wall.

"X marks the spot," Johnny said.

Cottard looked down at the rifle.

"Who put those Xs there?" Johnny asked. "And where'd the gun come from?"

"Got a guy on the inside," Cottard said. He took a breath, then spun the barrel of the Barrett rifle toward the Xs on the wall.

Johnny scurried away from the gun's line of sight and stood behind Cottard.

"Put that uniform on," Cottard instructed. Johnny glanced over at a coat rack in the corner. A spotless uniform hung from its arm. He looked back at Cottard.

"Do it! And finish that tape Mom sent," Cottard hissed.

Johnny propped his oar against the wall and started changing. Then he put on the headphones and pressed play while Cottard practiced moving the barrel quickly from X to X.

The tape played:

"People who refuse to apply have no pedestal to stand on either. They are not seen as innocents, but as weak and unambitious. The men are supposedly too scared to fight; couple that perception with the idea that they are 'damning' themselves to Edingburg, a place where they can never advance in life, find glory, or be able to leave a legacy.

"For the women, a warped sense of feminism does the trick whether they apply or not. Feminism was once supposed to allow all women choices—the chance to develop themselves into educated, able, confident leaders in any field or lifestyle of their choice. It was to enable them to do great and new things. Many people still think this to be true but now the movement is being used as a comparison, instead of a becoming. Feminism is now pushing for women's freedom to act in every sort of way that 'men' act. Sadly, they seem to focus on using the worst of men as their examples, allowing women to find solace in doing the lowest of actions instead of becoming the highest of beings. So if she does apply, she's a whore, but she knows what she wants. If she doesn't apply then she's a victim of anything she chooses, but is still a victim that should have known better.

"The General may not be able to guarantee who falls into what group or how they conduct themselves exactly, but that is not really important. So long as the right proportions of people fill each group, his institutions will be able to fulfill his agenda, while at the same time ensuring that there's too little collective energy in the population to jeopardize what only he has created.

"So it is up to us to destroy it and allow New San Francisco to become a city made of many, instead of a city forged by one. This is why I must ask you to do something. Quite active. John. You are standing in the General's office for his militarized pier."

Johnny's cheeks flushed. He slowly looked down to notice the uniform he was now wearing. In the dark he could make out the stars only meant for the General. His body shook like a wet dog.

"When Cottard shoots those Xs, the entire City Guard network will go into DEFCON. The Inner Circle's system will automatically make every contract in the city require that the General be secured before any other contract can be paid. An enormous reward also goes to the company that secures … you."

Johnny's legs buckled. He sat hunched over on the side of the General's mahogany desk.

"This will slow down the City Guard's liquidation of the ghettos. Giving our people more crucial time to get the right people in and the wounded out. When those X's are shot, all we need you to do is pick up that phone."

Johnny's eyes buzzed over to the red phone sitting on the desk.

"And tell whomever is on the line that your location is compromised and that you are going mobile. Tell them that you want all key personnel for the liquidation process of Edingburg to report to Edingburg City Hall until you can be sure their safety to operate is absolute. If the General can be reached by the IRA, so could anybody. Normally they'd ask tons of security questions for this, but given the circumstances we've created they will fall in line, afraid to disobey a direct order. Verified or no."

Johnny's neck steamed under the collar. His head shook.

"But why you? John, if I could, I'd ask anyone else. But it must be you. Because there is one passcode we can't get around. You are the only one who knows the passcode and security responses for the City Hall's panic room, where they will store all the VIPs. When they patch you into the automated network for validation, there's literally hundreds of security questions the computer could ask you in that moment. You're the only person we can count on getting all of that right under this sort of pressure.

"I hope you can do this for us, John. You'll be saving a lot of good people and helping bring back the beauty only you and I know lies beneath her."

The tape clicked to a stop.

"Shooting this thing's going to rile up every guardsman in this place," Cottard said. "Gonna have to split quick. What's your part in all this?"

Johnny put down the headset and brushed his commandeered suit down. "I—" He cleared the lump in his throat. "I'll be makin' one hell of an important call."

"Well, make it quick. I'm getting out of here soon as I shoot these Xs."

"Well, where the are you going to be running off to?"

"Where I've been instructed to go."

"What? How'm I gettin' outta here?"

"I imagine you'll find your own ride with that kind of outfit," Cottard said coolly as he brought his eye to scope. "Get over by the door. Their bullets won't penetrate the iron plate inside the wall. If anyone tries to run in, whack 'em with your paddle."

Johnny picked up the oar and crept over to the door. He felt sick.

Cottard looked through the scope. He practiced snapping the barrel to each X.

"Hmm, thought there would only be two X's," he muttered. "Ready?"

Johnny realized that he was chewing on his knuckle. He lowered his hand and nodded. "Let's just get it done."

Cottard took a long calming breath and peered through the sight. He pulled back the bolt, and a deep click filled the room. He exhaled, then pulled the trigger.

A sound wave rocketed out of the chamber. Pressure beat Johnny's eardrums.

A second shot fired. Cracked vines grew over the windows, cutting the glass like a splintering glacier. Cottard lined up for the final shot and fired dead center into the third X.

The wall exploded, the windows shattered, and the door was ripped off its hinges, falling onto Johnny. Cottard fell back behind the desk as iron shards fired toward him.

A thick haze of pulverized sheetrock filled the air. There was an angry shout from the other side of the newly expanded room, followed by the crackle of gunshots. The desk and the door that covered Johnny erupted with spouts of splinters thrown up by the barrage of machine gun fire. Johnny screamed as waves of bullets ricocheted off the door.

Then the room fell silent again. Cottard quietly drew himself back up to the .50-cal. He looked through the infrared scope and smiled at the guards creeping toward him. "I see you," he muttered. He pulled the trigger.

Click.

The gun had jammed. Cottard ripped the gun's bolt back and began frantically rubbing out the dust that had clogged the firing chamber.

Hearing the click, the guards charged blindly through the cloud of dust. They scuttled over a mound of debris that had been part of the shattered wall, tripping over mangled iron. Cottard furiously banged the gun against the desk, desperately trying to persuade the mechanism to push the bullet into the chamber.

Something kicked off the door on top of Johnny, and a guard fell over him. They stared at one another with unwelcome surprise. The guard grabbed for his rifle; Johnny went for his oar. They crossed weapons, and Johnny flipped the guard over with a twist of his oar. He jumped to his feet, then swung the oar down onto the guard's face.

Cottard yelled a warning, and Johnny spun around as a guard charged toward him, bayonet drawn. Johnny dodged the coming blade and pushed the guard forward, then clubbed him on the back of with his oar. The guard dropped his gun and drew a knife. Johnny brought up his oar to defend himself, and the guard stabbed him in the arm. Johnny popped the guard right between the eyes with the butt of his oar, then sent him backward to the ground with a kick to the guard's chest with the sole of his boot.

A faint "meow" keened through the cloud of soot as Johnny stood over the guard, his oar raised. He drove it down like a guillotine's blade, collapsing the guard's throat as his trachea gave way with a crunch. The guard's head creaked up, face contorted due to the lack of oxygen.

Johnny turned to see a third guard watching in horror at the grotesque scene. Then the man's face tightened, and he raised his rifle to Johnny's chest. He took one step closer, then another. The stock of the rifle was wooden—it was an AK-47, unlikely to jam even with all the airborne debris.

As if reading Johnny's mind, the guard smiled and patted his weapon. "The Russians got one thing right," he said. "Old reliable." He tightened his finger on the trigger, and another gunshot roared through the room.

The guard's eyes widened. He stumbled and fell forward onto the mass of gore that had been his chest. Cottard stood over the fallen guard, smoke from his rifle curling to join and swirl with the dust clouds in varying dimensions of gray.

Cottard slung the rifle on his back. "The hell was that?!" he asked. "A bomb? Damn thing could have got me killed!"

"The hell you looking at me for? Yell at your guy!"

Cottard stared at Johnny. Then he reached into a pocket of Johnny's uniform. "Another bomb, huh!"

Cottard held up a oblong metal object about the size of an egg. A blue X had been painted on its side. He turned it over, revealing a red button underneath a hinged square plastic cover.

"If you told the General anything about what we're doing, if you screw up my deck, I swear to god I will fuck you up."

"What, me? How could I have—"

"Did you?" Cottard smacked Johnny in the face and started roughly rummaging through his uniform. "Anyone else here! Anyone else listening in on our convo!"

"No," Johnny pleaded. "I swear!"

Cottard stepped back and held up the egg. He flicked open the plastic casing covering the red button. "This X had better have been made by our guy this time."

"How the hell would we even know?"

Cottard leaned in. "Because when I press this, we might very well blow up like this damn wall did."

"Then don't press it."

Cottard pressed the button. Johnny dropped to the floor. The room shook, and shouts from guards began filling the hallways.

"Hmm," Cottard said. He looked out the window. The nightly storm had begun engulfing the city and the sky. "Need to move." He turned and walked toward the wall that he had detonated, disappearing into the gray.

"That blew open the gates to the pier!" Cottard yelled. "I think you have your exit! I'll have them gun for me. Now make your call and get moving!"

Johnny grabbed the red phone. The debris clumps cracked and slid off the receiver as he brought it to his ear.

Johnny looked back down at the guard. Why did he kill him? What was he getting himself into? Why did she have to die?

"Sir, yes sir," said the red phone.

"I AM UNDER HEAVY FIRE! WE ARE OSCAR MIKE!"

A Short Stroll

Johnny stood shaking in a quiet dark opening that led to the open dock of the metal pier. He brushed at his uniform with his hands, took a breath, and walked out into the chaos.

Wind roared through the blasted opening. The huge doors of the pier had been blown off, reducing the long narrow pier to a wind tunnel.

Johnny's heart pounded as guards bolted around him carrying equipment and tools, frantic to re-secure their fortifications. A guard bumped into Johnny then ran off, giving no notice. Johnny quietly continued his casual stroll toward the gate. He was almost there; if he could pass through that gate the wind and dust of the storm would completely envelope him.

Guards milled around with jacks, wooden planks, shovels, anything that could possibly help them heave the massive doors back up onto their hinges.

"Halt!" an officer shouted. Johnny froze.

"Where are you going, Private!" The officer cocked his gun.

Johnny didn't budge. Could he talk his way out of this? No way. Maybe if he ran at an angle he could jump into the water before they shot him?

Johnny was still contemplating his chances when a car horn blared. A familiar black Lincoln Continental emerged from the storm and stopped where the blast doors had been. Johnny covered his face from the intense headlights. The rear suicide door opened; Gordon stuck his head out and beckoned Johnny in. Johnny gawked in disbelief, then stiffened his back. *Sell it*, he thought.

Johnny turned in place and glared at the officer. The officer's face had already gone white since the headlights had pulled up. He quickly holstered his weapon and saluted, not daring make eye contact with the silhouette of the General. Johnny turned back to the car and got in. When he shut the door, the storm's howling rage was immediately muffled to a whimper.

The driver turned around. It was Franz beaming at him. "So glad to see you're still with us, Johnny!"

"Jes, quite!" Gordon said.

Johnny glanced back and forth at the duo. "How … how did you know I'd be here?"

"Plan C," Franz said. "Mum thought something like this might happen."

"Good show, John," Gordon said. "Quite happy with the performance."

"Indeed," Franz said as he plowed the rock of a limo through the streets of Edingburg. A lonely saxophone played through the speakers.

"Wasn't expecting the fireworks bit though, Gordon said. "How ever did you pull that off?"

"Ah yes, quite a nice touch, the fireworks," Franz said. "That'll surely be having the City Guards' attention for a beat while we'r e out and about fulfilling our job descriptions for the IRA. Gosh, never thought I'd say such a thing."

"Well it's not like we're sipping tea with the Queen any more, Gordon. But yes, could have done with a name change. So unoriginal."

"J'es quite."

Johnny rubbed at the black leather seat next to him. "I didn't blow up anything," he said. "I'd never do something so brash. Cottard shot at some Xs on the wall. Next thing I knew I was pinned under a door and fighting off some guardsmen with a damn oar."

Johnny kicked a large crate on the floorboards that he was straddling with his legs, pushing it back toward the middle seats in the cabin.

"Careful!" Gordon said.

"No horseplay," Franz said. "It's not the best of ideas to be kicking that."

"What's in it?" Johnny asked.

"Nothing you want to be kicking."

"Quite right," Gordon agreed.

Johnny looked at the clock on the limo's dashboard. Three A.M. He flinched as a wooden plank smacked into the window next to him. Whirls of sand were beating at the thick glass. Any regular vehicle would have been swerving and swaying all over the r oad, the wind threatening to rip it off the road and add it to the twisting inferno.

"Eight tons of steel in this beast!" Franz said.

"One of the General's chariots! Oh, and she's a beaut!"

"How in the hell did y'all steal this?" Johnny asked. "I've held office and I've never seen the insides of this monster."

Franz smirked. "Oh, we have our ways, John."

Johnny brushed at his stolen uniform.

"Where are y'all going, and why?"

Gordon fuddled with the door lever.

"No need for such a direct approach, John. We have a couple hours to dawdle before sunrise."

"Jes," Franz said. "And we haven't a need for that unfortunate attempt at a southern accent. Leave that show for the masses on the ground."

Johnny glared. "I already dealt with that psycho Cottard kid. In the span of thirty minutes, he blew up a pier and nearly my entire damn face—" he touched the bandage wrapped around his head— "all because some cards in a deck told him to. And so in the interest of extending my lifespan, I'm going to have to require an answer."

"Oh, we're not doing anything worth getting your head wrappings all in a twist, John!" Franz said. "We'll spill the beans. We have gotten word from a raven that the central communication tower that sends and receives all communications, both private and public signals, is located somewhere in the neighborhood. We've been told that even Mr. Line's news footage is sometimes taped around Edingburg in order to get a more 'on the scene' feel if anything begins getting newsworthy."

"And there's most certainly news to be had," Gordon said.

"Then the show's footage gets transmitted to the central station located somewhere around here, edited, and then transmitted out to the rest of the city."

Johnny looked at them, surprised. "I figured it was handled from a single location, but how the hell do you two know any of this? That stuff's top secret. I've never even been leaked that info."

Gordon looked at his watch. "No, you haven't told us a thing yet."

Johnny watched a loose trashcan outside slam into a bent lamppost. The trash flew onto the windshields of the limo, then funneled up into the sky.

"Hell, I don't even know where it's broadcast," Johnny said. "Way above my clearance level."

"We may have been locked away for a few decades, but the radios still work quite fine at Alcatraz," Franz said. "Hearing all their mess got rather indigestible over the years and so Cottard, being the radio whiz that he is, found a way to gauge the signal strength. So finding it has become a rather simple matter of finding where the signal is strongest."

Gordon pulled out a small box with a decibel meter on it. The needle shook far to the right of the scale. "See, we're rather close to it now." He pointed to a light at the bottom right of the scale. "If that light flashes, that means the signal strength is way off this scale, meaning you've got to be pointing right at it." He pointed to the six-inch long antenna at the top of the box. "It detects the signal directionally with this antennaye. So finding the right spot is rather point and shoot."

Franz spritzed the window cleaner to clear off the caking of ash icing itself onto the front windshield. "Listening to silence will be quite therapeutic after all their hullabaloo and rampant chest beating," he said.

"Jes, quite," Gordon said. "All those TV reporters, Inner Circle personalities, and radio DJs are getting rather taxing, aren't they?"

"Quite taxing," Franz agreed. "Silencing all that noise will cause quite the ruckus amongst those trendy status-making juggernauts. The City Guard will have to take more time and manpower away from boxing off Edingburg to protect all their other media wizbangs."

"Jes," Gordon said. "After your show at the pier, John, they'll have to assume we can strike anywhere. So the guard will have to be spreading itself out a bit everywhere to compensate."

"Thin them out," Franz said, "and we keep time on our side."

"Okay, but why?" Johnny asked. "What's the endgame?"

"Mass exodus," Gordon said.

"What?" Johnny asked.

"Indeed," Franz replied.

"We'd like for all the children to have a chance to make a run for it when their applications go south on them," Gordon said.

"Jes," Franz said. "Whether we're totally successful or not with what we're doing, there's one major flaw with the application process, especially when there's a rebellion afoot right when the children apply to the City Guard." Franz crossed his throat with a finger. "It's just too much at once. No buffer during the transition from fake to reality."

"After a few days in, the children's eyes will have adjusted. They'll have had a chance to see what it's really like to be in the City Guard and many will become disenchanted with the show they've been convinced to personally cast. So we will go ahead and pick them up!"

"Allowing our cause to gain potentially loads of support," Franz said.

"Those children who desert will be hunted, John. Best we give them a new shelter and purpose, no?"

Johnny nodded.

"But the children can't get out if there's vetted City Guardsmen lining the exits," Gordon continued. "So we need to spread them thin and make the children a few more exits the guard isn't aware of. And by taking down the central communications tower, it'll be far more difficult for the City Guard to communicate and coordinate a counter if there's a mass desertion."

"Chaos!" Franz said. "Not to mention that Edingburg will be less drugged up on orchestrated propaganda, so the population might be more willing to support the movement and shelter any of the children we can't find or house ourselves right off the willow wood."

"Well when do we know we'll be able to strike?" Johnny asked. "And with what people?"

"'When' remains the question," Franz said, "but Mum will know." He held up an old portable radio. "An RCA Victor B-411."

"Ah, quite nice, Franz," Gordon said.

"Indeed. Cottard rigged it up. He made some additions as well, splendid signal."

Johnny crept to the front of the limo and took the radio from Franz.

"Ah, mahogany finish," Gordon said. Quite classy."

"Very," Franz agreed.

Johnny looked at the radio. It had a large dial in the middle of its face with radio frequencies edged along its circumference. The mahogany shone with a rich bourbon glow in the storm.

"We shall have to find a vantage point to get a sufficient signal from these gadgets. And we'll have to let the storm pass. Driving too far in this muck will surely end in quite the fender bender." Franz pulled up to a lone concrete building and peered up through the sky roof. "Twelve stories. That'll do." He turned around and looked at Johnny. "Up you go!"

"What? Me?"

"If you haven't noticed, John, we're bloody ancient!" Franz said. "We can't be popping up and down stairs all willy-nilly."

"We shall guard the limo," Gordon said. "Not the best of areas, after all. Wouldn't want the hubcaps stolen. Let us know what she says and point the antennaye around a bit. See if you can't find the jackpot!"

Johnny groaned, then opened the car door and ran through the storm to the building. He tore the door open and climbed the stairs, which ended in a small shed on the roof. He sat down, his legs shaking after his climb, and rested his forehead on his knees.

One, maybe two hours passed, then the storm came to an abrupt end. Johnny opened the shed door. Streaks of sunlight shone down on him as the yellow wall of debris roiled in a vast circle surrounding him. He was in the eye of the storm. Only the faint bangs and pings of clashing debris in the distance made any reverberation.

Johnny looked down at the radio in his hands, then up at the small patch of open sky above him. "Worth a shot," he muttered.

He flicked the power switch on. Fizz leaked out and then the sound of two pianos playing a soft melody came through. Johnny walked to the edge of the building, listening to their notes intertwining. He could see for nearly a mile in each direction. His mayor's office stood in front of him, with its four white pillars in the front and the copper dome with a long steeple jutting out the top. The New San Francisco flag, the seasonal cycle flag, and the 16-starred Colony flag hung down, wrapped around their poles in front of the building. He watched for any VIPs still filing into the panic rooms indoors.

"How does it feel?" Mom asked through the radio.

"Peaceful," he said, gazing out over his small pocket of silence.

"Tell me more. I haven't been out in so long."

"I'm in the eye of the storm. The winds have stopped and the walls of the storm surrounding us are thick, but there's still this … rising feeling."

"Coming from the ground or from within you?"

Johnny smiled. It was the barometric pressure, but thanks to Mom's praise, it was starting to be both.

"Why is it peaceful?" she asked.

"It's quiet."

"Hmm. Why else?"

Johnny looked up at the circling clouds. "Because when I look up and I see all the hell breaking loose just outside of my own realm, I can know."

"Know what?"

"That the bad is far too busy somewhere else to be bothering me." He leaned on the railing of the building. "And that whatever good that might be next to me is safe, if only for the moment. And in that moment, we don't have to worry."

"I like that, Johnny. I do so enjoy being in the eye of a storm myself. What I wouldn't give to be there now."

"You enjoy the eye as well? Most find it eerie."

"Yes."

"Then I guess it's my turn to ask why."

Mom laughed. "I … I guess it because there's nothing outside of it. In a way, the world is simplified to a single little space. A place where, for if only a few moments, people really have the opportunity to do as they wish if they liked. No outside power coming to destroy something pure. The last time I was in the pocket I used it to protest. Not my situation in life, but my frustration that everyone else thought it was so. I used my pocket time atop that podium. The podium the girls must apply on. I brought a man with me and we made love atop of it. We made love atop a podium many used to glorify and solidify lust as the one true power. We did it not only to vent, but to prove that the podium and the ideals it symbolized were not an inherent force; it wasn't gravity. It didn't hold us down for doing the opposite. The energy people feel from the podium can't be stored within it.

"Because the power that comes from the podium can only be created in the moment, when thousands of people all come together and agree that only lust can exist. But when the city left, there is still an us. And with us, only love emanated from that podium."

Johnny looked at the mayor's building, trying his best not to become jealous. Perhaps it was loneliness and the lack of things to hold onto, but parts of him couldn't resist attaching to the voice coming from the box. He did his best to remain coy.

"I've never seen my office from above. Especially during a storm. It's strange, seeing it huddled among the rest of Edingburg. I can't remember how many speeches I've given on those front steps, looking out on the crowds speaking through my mask. But to see it from the outside … changes it so. I've always tried to do big things for Edinburg, so to see it so small makes me wonder how big of an impact I could have ever made."

"Everything starts small, Johnny. I started as just a voice. Like you."

Johnny smirked. "So, are you going to tell me more about who you really are? Maybe not just your exploits."

"Hmm. I think the better question is who are you?"

"Hey I asked first. And we're in the pocket. It's safe here, like you said."

"You're in the pocket, Johnny."

"Well, you're in here talking to me." Johnny smiled. "Come on."

Mom's breath frizzed through the speaker. "Out there, I am Mom. But in here, you can call me the Missus."

Johnny raised his eyebrows. "Oh."

"I'm madly in love, Johnny. I am. And I know you still are too. In a man's sort of way."

"What's that supposed to mean?"

"Helena was her name?"

Johnny's knee buckled. "Hey," he huffed, "this is the pocket."

"I know, and that's why I bring it up. You need to be at peace with what happened to her."

"It was— it was only a few days ago. Get real."

Static oozed out of the speaker in a haze.

"I'm sorry, Johnny. I only bring it up because if you can start thinking of her anywhere, it'd be here, in a place locked away from the outside world where you don't have to think of anything outside of you and her. Everything that you two fought against or struggled with can be washed over with the rest of the storm."

Johnny exhaled. "You're ruining my pocket time," he said half-jokingly.

"Oh, Johnny. Trust me. The sooner, the better. And that doesn't mean you'll be discounting her, either. At least I do so hope it wouldn't. Keep her in your mind always, but let that stinging pain of her memory dull. That way you can think of her and what you had with her more freely, more fully, and sleep more soundly. She'd like that."

"You don't even know her."

"No, maybe I don't know what exactly what she means to you, but when the dust around us has settled, maybe we can have a sit down and find out. And maybe I will share a little bit more about my own man with you too."

"You speak as if … is he still alive?"

"I like to think some part of him still is," Mom said. "And so long as there's a part of him, I feel we can grow the rest of him back. At least in some way."

Johnny looked at the City Hall building.

"What will grow back from what's left," Mom said, "I don't know. But I believe that when we rearrange its roots it could bloom from the kernels of what remains. It can still be truly beautiful."

Johnny pulled the receiver from his pocket. He looked at the signal strength. It had gotten higher in the clear weather. "The central transmitter must be in this pocket." He pointed the receiver over the ledge of the building. The decibel meter whizzed up and down.

"In that case, I think you know where you have to point it," Mom said.

Johnny pointed the receiver at the City Hall building. The device beeped wildly, and the light flashed hot blue. The alarm echoed off the walls of adjacent buildings, filling the pocket with blaring bleeps.

"Shit," he muttered. He backed away from the balcony. "The steeple. It's a radio tower! It was right over my fucking head. How the hell couldn't I have known!"

"It's okay," Mom said. "At least you know now. That's the important part. Now you can do something about it."

"Like what? My ID card's got to have been tagged by now. And I'm sure it's filled with guardsmen now that we've filled the place with VIPs."

"Jonathan. Don't think of what you can do for Edingburg as mayor. Instead, just think of what can be done as *Edingburg*, then do it."

"I don't know what—"

The door to the shed burst open. Franz trotted forward with a bazooka over his shoulder. His cheeks were full of color. "We heard the bloody beeps! Where is it!"

Johnny glanced over at City Hall, then back to Franz's bazooka.

"Ah, I see!" As Franz turned, Johnny ducked under the barrel of the bazooka on Franz's shoulder. "Gordon! Must you be so sluggish?"

"Coming right up!" Gordon wobbled onto the roof with a black and white missile clutched in his arms.

Franz pointed at the City Hall building. "There."

The two walked to the edge of the roof. Gordon heaved the missile into the bazooka.

"No! Wait! What are you doing?!" Johnny shouted. "I know some of those people, for Christ's sake!"

"The eye's moving," Gordon said. "We've but only a moment to snip this bit in."

Franz aimed the bazooka at the dome of the City Hall. The flags in front of the building began to flutter.

"The winds are about to hit us," Gordon shouted over the rising woosh of the coming storm.

"What the fuck are you doing?!" Johnny shouted.

"Carpe diem, John," Franz said. He pulled the trigger. The missile shot out the tube, and a smoke trail zoomed up and over the City Hall. The missile punched through the dome and detonated inside the building. The walls quaked. Glass shattered. The pressure wave exploded through every exit.

Johnny held out his hands like a parent who's lost a child. He fell to his knees. Guardsmen began popping out of the City Hall building's perimeter.

Franz looked up at the smoke trail left by the missile. "Pretty whipped already, winds should have covered our position."

"Trails or no, enough standing about," Gordon said nervously as he looked up at a brown whirling wall of hell stampeding toward them.

"Oh, my," Franz said, looking at the storm. The two scuttled toward the stairs, then noticed the prostrate Johnny.

"He's having another one of his moments," Franz said.

"No. No. No, Johnny," Gordon said. "Can't be having any of this sort right now. This is the bloody edge of the eye we're talking about! No comin' back from this!"

"I'm so sorry, Jonathan," Mom said through the radio. The reception cut out as a bolt of lightning blasted a tin roof across the street. The radio began fizzling.

"Run, John!" Gordon shouted. Johnny rose to his feet, grabbed the radio, and followed them down the stairs to the street. Franz and Gordon piled into the front of the limo, and Johnny jumped into the back. The tires skidded into the storm.

An Imperially Civil War

Johnny lay face down on the long bench seat in the back of the limo. He paid no attention to the two old men bickering over who had a better understanding of the directions.

The City Hall of Edingburg was destroyed. Johnny couldn't stop counting, guessing the exact number of how many of his colleagues may have just been blown up.

Gordon peered back into the passenger cabin. "John? I'm sure that came off as a bit rash, but it had to be done. We needed to take out that station. Otherwise a whole lot of children are going to get mowed down when we try to break them out."

"Who cleared you to do that? Who said it was okay to blow up my fucking City Hall building! Was it her?"

"We made that decision," Gordon said. "When we heard the receiver beep. We knew what we had to do. Yes, Mum pulls the strings, but we decide whether our fingers are moving."

Johnny glared at Gordon. He wanted to rip off that innocent face of a weak old man and see the devil underneath.

"What the hell makes you think you can just blow people up like that! You heard some beeps so you blow up a building! What the hell is that?!"

"Because we understand, John," Franz said. "We are the guardians of this city. We understand this city better than almost anyone, even if we have been locked away. We know its forms, its structure, its reason. Because we know all this, we are able to know what's just and as guardians we must be and do exactly that—what is just."

"You two, you two are …" Johnny looked out at the whirlwind, then back at Gordon's concerned face. "You two are nuts. You're psychos. I'll bet you two were locked away for a good fucking reason, weren't you?"

Gordon shook his head. "John."

"No! What the hell makes you think you're so much better informed than—"

"Because we designed it," Gordon said. "The city, I mean. Everything from the sections and who they're for all the way to the sole purpose of the city's existence."

"The General locked us away instead of killing us because he relies on our knowledge," Franz said.

"And we'd tell him so long as we got something for the city in return," Gordon said. "It's through our negotiating and careful explanations of the workings of the city that there was even a mayor of Edingburg. "

"And mayor's office," Franz added.

"You … you killed them; you can't—"

"We are in a civil war, John," Franz said. "Whether you like it or not. And we are firm believers in justice and wisdom. You do not get that through nonviolence, nor is nonviolence even a virtue but simply a tactic. As you saw, it's not a very useful one against the General."

"No!" Johnny said. "You shot a rocket into a building! You can't know if everyone in there was guilty—" He lunged forward. Gordon batted him away and raised the driver window, sealing Johnny in the back.

"That City Hall had turned into a farce and you know it," Gordon said over the intercom. "It began working against the people, not for it. It represented an idea of obtaining freedom in a way the General knew he could combat. Destroying it destroyed that misconception.

"We will not turn into them, John. The big difference is that we are fighting a civil war while they are fighting a war. They see people from their colonies as invaders whenever they stop liking them. So for them, there is no limit, no boundary to cross. They look at us as if we're foreign. But we will look on them like a lost brother.

"They fight for the sake of power and material gain while we will be fighting for self sustenance and preservation. They want the opportunity to grow their coffers while we want the opportunity to grow ourselves.

"This city is made up of three parts. Each part is made to satisfy a separate part of the human soul. The inhabitants within each sector live there because that part of their soul is the strongest. The Inner Circle is supposed to house the most rational people, meaning those who are most inclined to seek wisdom and who are most in control of their daily urges, and it is they who oversee the entire city. The City Guard is the spirited part of a person, the part that believes in honor and duty. They are the ones who enforce the will of the rational part of the city. Edingburg is the appetitive. These people are most inclined to seek out fortune, material wealth, and who insist upon the need to satisfy any other urges they have.

"But the General warped what everything was intended to be. He made its rational part into a sophisticated appetitive. He's made it honorable to be appetitive. He's made succeeding in the realm of the appetitive the ultimate good instead of pursuing wisdom and virtue. He's distorted honor and duty into a means to obtain, instead of the reason for being. He's mangled every part of the human soul and rerouted all of its energy to satisfy the unquenchable thirst of his desires."

The limo passed an open gate topped with barbed wire and drove into a warehouse. "I hope that helps you understand," Gordon said.

Franz drove the limo into a large storage crate. Gordon unbuckled his seatbelt. "Our stop."

Johnny opened the door and walked out of the crate. A mechanical crane moving along the ceiling stopped and hung over the crate.

Franz and Gordon shut the door to the crate, sealing the limo inside. "No fancy floating crates here!" said Franz.

"Old school!" Gordon said. "No computers, no GPS, no central command or electronic log of the crate's locations or contents. Edingburg companies couldn't afford such a high-end operation. And thanks to you, Mr. Mayor, there weren't any subsidies to modernize it."

The crane's hooks latched down, lifted the crate, and floated it far down the warehouse.

"You knew the Capitol transmitted the signal," Johnny said. "That's why you put VIPs in there. So you could kill two birds with one stone."

"Firstly, we didn't place anyone anywhere," Gordon said. "Second, we only know what you know in that regard."

"I was misled," Johnny said.

"Really, and who did that?" Franz asked.

"Mom," Johnny said.

"Ah, then I guess you two need to be having tea together!" Gordon said.

"Come on, off we go!" Franz said. The lights in the warehouse snapped off. Gusts from the storm outside shook the warehouse.

Johnny called out for Franz, then Gordon. Nothing. He stepped on a loose pipe and fell onto his back when it rolled out from under his foot. He sat up on his hip, face to face with a glowing paw print that flashed blue on a crate, then faded away.

Glowing blue letters began writing over the crate.

"Hello again, Johnny."

"Glad to know you're still here."

It paused.

"For longer than I can."

"I've been keeping her safe."

"From a horrible man."

"But now you are here."

"So I must know."

"Are you here to stay?"

"Yes?"

"No?"

"Next time I see you."

"You will have told me."

"Just know that moving forward, there's no going back."

"Unless we already have."

The writing faded for good, and Johnny found a crowbar and cranked open the crate. Large work lights chomped on, and Johnny squinted. When his eyes adjusted, he saw it. A rusting tube.

"Quite the antique," Gordon said. The two old men were flanking him from a few steps behind.

"Jes, first of its kind," Franz said.

"They weren't always for simple fantasies," Gordon said.

"Yes, you kids really messed with something beautiful," Franz said.

"They were built to focus, to give one time to build and discover themselves while one slept," Gordon said.

"Amazing machine," Franz said.

"People became so developed with the machine," Gordon said, "discovering themselves, discovering their world, and then building with all the tools and materials they discovered they had within them. Now people just throw themselves into these tubes like throwing trash into a bin! Use it to numb their pain instead of treat it. Make them build and discover fake worlds and have them share their fake prizes with each other instead of their real selves! Fake, Fake, Fake!"

"Calm down, Franz," Gordon said. "It's not all his fault."

"Well, what kind of mayor just lets that happen!"

"He did not just let it happen. I'm sure he fought it."

"Well, he didn't fight it enough."

"Franz, need I remind you he's not the only human being in the world. We're all responsible somewhat, especially us, aren't we?"

"He still needs to get his act together," Franz pouted.

"Well we're working on it, aren't we!"

"I'm right here!" Johnny shouted. "I can hear you!"

"Hmm, quite," Gordon agreed.

"Didn't think you were listening," Franz added.

"Moving right along!" Gordon said, swirling a glass jar filled with a yellow liquid. "A bit dusty, but should still be able to put you in the mix."

Gordon opened a crate to Johnny's right. "Generator," he said. "Wi-Fi."

"Wi-Fi for this thing?" Johnny asked, pointing at the old tube.

"Sort of," Franz said.

"Sort of?" Johnny asked.

"Sort of," Franz replied.

Gordon connected the generator to the antique tube, and Franz did the same with his Wi-Fi. Gordon turned the latch on the tube. Its door creaked open, revealing the strained and cracked leather gurney inside.

"In you go," Gordon said. Gordon turned on the tube, which flexed its needles, ready for injection.

"What is this for?" Johnny asked.

"To meet her," Gordon replied.

"Mom?"

"Sort of," Franz answered.

What Are You Doing!

"What the fuck are you doing!" a guardsman shouted.

Steve looked up from the rifle that'd been slapped into his hands.

"It's not a fucking puppy, pledge! It's a ticket! A ticket to your salvation! Do you know what you do with a ticket? You use it before it ain't worth shit!"

Steve stared up at the huge man, his hands trembling under the gun barrel.

"So you tell me—do you wanna cash in that ticket before or after you get shot!" The guardsman slapped Johnny down the line of guardsmen. Rows of new pledges were being smacked and weighed down with ammunition, helmets, axes, grenades, basically anything that either made a hole or stopped a hole from being made was piled onto them.

"The answer is before!" the guardsman shouted after Steve.

Steve came to the end of the line. A huge bald man looked down at him. He was smiling something furious. "I got something for you. Little extra than the others. Give ya an edge." He nudged a guard next to him and showed him the syringe in his hand. Then he rammed it into Steve's stomach. He lifted Steve with his massive tattooed arms and brought him to his eye level.

"Yeah, feels good, don't it, boy?"

Steve's stomach felt like it'd been coated in napalm.

"Just gave you 'the Fallen's Kiss.' Keeps you focused and your thoughts pure, but man it burns like hell. Burns so hot, nothing else matters, that's how it keeps you so damn focused, no escape, haha! No other choice but to handle your shit! Enjoy your 20 minutes of clarity."

Steve gripped his rifle, his pupils dilated. Concern for social convention or manners left him. He slammed the gun into the man's chin.

The bald man dropped Johnny and stumbled back. He smiled blood. "There it is!"

The other guard pushed Steve down the line. "Move forward!"

Steve walked into an open brick-walled room filled with long tables. Another group, likely the opposing team, sat down.

A guard pointed Steve to a table. "Eat some shit and get moving to the training facility! Five minutes!"

Steve sat down to a tray with a spork. It seemed both teams were mixing together for lunch, with cyclers wearing both red and blue colors sitting together at the tables. Red for Hell on Wheels. Blue for Ghost Fox. Steve's stomach was screaming.

A kid nudged him. "Where do we get the food?" Steve turned away. "What are we supposed to be eating?" the kid asked the others as they sat down. Steve was grinding his teeth. "The fuck is the food?" the kid asked again.

"Shut up you fat fuck," said a familiar voice. Steve glanced up. It was Ryan, with a blue band tied around his head. "You just killed a man and all you can think about is stuffing your mouth." Ryan smirked. "Knowing you, you ate him, didn't ya?"

"Shut up!" the kid said. "I didn't mean to do it!"

"Didn't mean to do it?" Ryan smiled. "What, the kid just volunteered to get mauled by a that wolf-dog? Don't bullshit, Tinter, you killed him. The only question I have is how your fat ass fit in that cramped little coffin."

"Piss off!" Tinter said.

Ryan nodded at the bandanna on Tinter's head. "Red team. Good." He pointed at the minus sign branded on Tinter's throat. "Ha! The only time you aren't plus-sized!"

Ryan turned to Steve, who was pulling at his shirt, trying to rip the seams of its lining.

"Steve!" Ryan said. "Holy shit! You applied! He leaned back in his chair. "Thought you had a vagina between your legs." Ryan peeked under the table. Then he sat back up, his eyes filled with concern. "Did they forget to check?"

Steve gestured with his spork. "Keep talkin' and you're about to find yourself underqualified."

"Whoa! Mouthy!" Ryan said. "Nothing like that night at Kleiner's! Bitching about your bitch on that barstool and all."

Steve stood up and grabbed his metal tray. "Finding a new place to sit?" Ryan asked. Steve looked left then right, then slammed his metal tray across Ryan's face.

"Shit!" Ryan said, falling back.

"Lunch is over!" a guard shouted.

"We never ate anything," Tinter said.

"Food is for guardsman not pledges, you fat piece of shit!" the guardsman shouted. "Now move your ass to your training room! No more fraternizing with the fucking enemy! You should be *fighting* them, like that kid's been doing." He pointed at Steve. "That's a model fucking guardsman!"

Steve looked back at the lines of pledges still filing in from the hallway, all waddling under the weight of their new equipment. "Eat some shit and get moving to the training facility! Five minutes!" the guard by the entrance shouted.

The training facility room was a vast space held up by granite columns. A guard walked by, slapping potatoes into the pledges' hands. "What you have in your hand is a grenade! It's very dangerous. So you will only pull the pin when you are absolutely SURE you can throw it in time and far enough away to not blow your own ass off!"

Johnny looked across a waist-high barricade made of metal and hay. There were groups of straw men wearing bullet-scored helmets covered in splashes of blue.

"Now throw it at the targets!"

A volley of potatoes bounced off the straw men.

"No, you stupid shit!" a guardsman shouted. A pledge had thrown a potato at a lone straw man. "Throw it at the cluster of Ghost Fox! There's tons of them! So you need to get your kills in!"

The guard walked over to a heap of potatoes next to a knocked-over straw man and picked up a potato. "Congratulations! You've all graduated. Turn and be recognized!"

Guardsmen walked up from behind the line of pledges and slapped their shirts with a clot of red paint. "You are with Hell on Wheels! Company color is Red!" a guard shouted. "Your job is to kill Blues! You shoot them, you beat them—" he held up the potato— "you choke them with a fucking spud if you have to! It's the only damn way you're getting a promotion! Is that understood!"

"Yes, sir!" the pledges shouted.

Steve shoved his potato into his pocket. He looked at his hand. It wouldn't stop quivering. He looked up to the smile of the guard who'd injected him moments ago.

"Exit to the armory! Twenty minutes to showtime, boys!"

The pledges began filing through the doorway. A guard raised his arm, stopping Steve from entering the armory. A long streak of smoke rose from his fat cigarette.

"I bet you think you're pretty fucking cute, don't you, boy?" The guard puffed his cigarette. Steve noticed the guard had a black eye. "I give you a choice between two things and you go and take both." The guard slid his ax from its holster. "Can't blame you, really. Good fucking move, but a bad one to try on me."

The guard flicked his cigarette into Steve's face and grabbed him by the throat. Hatred poured into Steve to the point his vision shook. But the man had at least 150 pounds on him, and Steve's punches and kicks had no more effect than a toddler's.

"Next time hit something you can see, boy. Hitting a fucking monster in pitch black only pisses it off." The guard brought up his ax. "Time for payback."

There was a gunshot, and the ax stopped in midair. A trickle of blood rolled down from one of the guard's eyes. He dropped to the floor. Steve turned and saw Colonel Bradshaw holding a smoking pistol.

"If you're going to get killed, it'll be when you've got an ax yourself to swing back at the bastard. Not before."

Bradshaw walked over and looked down at the guard. "Piece of shit. No honor. No respect for battle." He took a deep whiff, then gagged. "Man's already so damn rotten I can't even enjoy the smell of a fresh kill!" He holstered his gun. Steve looked at the gun's pearl white ivory handle. He gave Steve a toothy grin. "I ever tell you about the time I killed 220 Peruvians? Bastards were trying to drive us out into the sea. Happened here back in … 1879. Didn't work for 'em. Peruvians scare easy. Hell, they're better at shitting themselves than charging the field."

Bradshaw looked over the confused Steve. "What? A man can't be reincarnated? The General may not like the idea, but fuck it if it's not true. He looked around and nodded. "Yeah, I was here before. I can feel it."

Bradshaw studied Steve. "Look at that. A newbie. Shaking over a dead body."

Steve didn't answer. Bradshaw leaned in, looking into Steve's eyes and noting the absence of pupil dilation. Then he looked down at the syringe that had fallen out of the guard's pocket. "How about this. You like questions. You answer me this question and if I like the answer, I won't immediately put your ass on the front line. What do you want to do next?"

"I want to take that pistol," Steve said.

"Hmm. And where will the barrel be pointing?"

"Your throat."

Bradshaw stroked the scar on his throat. "Why?"

Steve looked around the now vacant room. "Because I want to."

"Perfect." Bradshaw smiled. "You're doing much better this time round, boy." He slapped Steve on the shoulder. "Come with me."

They walked through the armory, passing hundreds of pledges all suiting up for the coming battle.

Two guards opened a pair of large double doors. Colonel Bradshaw walked through, Steve following. They climbed five flights of stairs and came to a large open room with blown-out walls and only half a ceiling. The view of the city stretched for miles. Guardsmen scrambled throughout the room, setting up comms, posts, maps, piling equipment on toppled-over tubes. Bradshaw tore open one of the doors of the tubes, exposing a trembling man. Bradshaw leaned in as he studied the Tuber, whose vacant milky eyes ticked around the room. Wires hung all over his body.

"Look at you," Bradshaw hissed. "Not even aware of what's happening right in front of you." He brought up his pistol and stroked the barrel against the man's face. "You see that, kid?" he asked, looking back at Steve. "This is what it's like when you're not paying attention!" He breathed on the Tuber. "And this is what it's like for the man who sees." He slowly cocked back the hammer of his pistol.

"Stop," Steve whispered.

"Do you know how this happened?" Bradshaw asked. "How this man eventually came to the point of being petted by my gun?"

"He was ripped down by people like you," Steve said. "People like you did this."

"You're right. But you're looking at me like I'm the only one who was attacking. This man and all those like him attacked people like me too. And you know what happens when they do that? They lose."

"It's a rigged game," Steve said. He felt nothing but hate, perhaps not because of the drugs. "You stick us in hell! And kick us when we're down so you can make a buck! Then if anyone rises up you have guns, grenades, goddamn tanks!"

Bradshaw pushed the Tuber's head to the right with his pistol. "No … It's life. And life is a war between men. And to win a war you must win battles. And to win battles you need not beat the enemy's weapons. You have to beat his soul. To truly beat a man, all you gotta do is understand him. Do that and you'll find that war's pretty simple, kid. All you have to do is decide what will hurt the enemy most within the limits of your capabilities to harm him … and then do it."

Bradshaw holstered his gun. "See, I don't need this." He pulled the suction cups off the Tuber's head. The man convulsed. His eyes whirled until the images they projected showed his reality: a smile made of browning teeth from Colonel Bradshaw, inches from his face. The man screamed. Bradshaw slammed the tube door shut and kicked the handle off. Screams continued to wail from within.

"But to do any of that, to have the will, I bring you to my point: you need character and ambition. That yellow bastard in there has neither. But I have a sneaking suspicion you might just have both. The real issue here is you're a little douchebag, kid. So we've gotta blow that outta your ass before we start making some money."

Bradshaw grabbed Steve's arm and dragged him over to a huge map on a plank of wood that balanced on top of eight toppled-over tubes. Guardsmen were arranging red and blue plastic soldiers all over the map.

"So here's our situation," Bradshaw said. "Alpha Group's got 1200 of my employees, mostly pledges. Bravo Group's got 800, Charlie 500, Delta 200. Equipment tally!"

"Fourteen hundred mini clubs," a guardsman answered. "Three hundred med-kits, 1,400 canteens, 700 gallons of water, 2,000 assault rifles, 900 thousand rounds of ammunition, 30 mortars with 500 antipersonnel rounds, 16 comms, and—" his finger ran down a list— "well now, 2,000 grub bags. A Ghost Fox hit squad came in and blew out a storage bin we had. Also, another 3,000 bags we bought from the Inner Circle went bad a year before the expiration date."

"Two thousand!" Bradshaw shouted. "That son of a bastard! Our kids are going to be starving come sun up!" The colonel snapped to another guardsman. "How many did they get?"

"Well, according to our recon team, they probably have around … 8,000."

"Fuck! All they gotta do is dig in and starve us out! How'd this happen?"

"Big shipment from the Inner Circle came in this morning."

"Yorker, that subsidized prick! He's got some shitty Inner Circle pricks on his side trying to ramrod us out of the industry! Stupid! This is exactly what they did to Scots!"

"We bought the bags to gain favor with other Inner Circlers and get this Edingburg stabilization contract sir," said a guard.

"Well that's the last time I pay to play," said Bradshaw. "From now on, our growth model is based off killing those Ghost Fox thugs. Not by greasing already dirty hands. Just ship food in from as many outside vendors as you can. I don't give a shit if you have to order takeout from City Wok!"

"Tried that. There's no new food being distributed to small third-party vendors, sir. The Great Greenhouse is reported of having packaging issues this morning. Only Inner Circle–run facilities are getting anything."

Bradshaw brought his hand to his face. "Inner Circle is really trying to shut us down this time."

"There's one more thing, sir."

"What?" Bradshaw growled.

"We got it in at dusk yesterday, right as the storm was rolling in. There's reports of entire buildings being leveled, sir."

Colonel Bradshaw waved him off. "Always happens. The General's blowing out people's homes who aren't playing nice in the sandbox. He'll write it off as happening during the stabilization period."

"But sir," the guard said, "there were no sounds or signs of explosives being used. No projectiles were spotted either. The recon team shot a drone at one of the buildings before the storm winds hit 30 knots."

"And?"

"And nothing, sir. There weren't any men fleeing the scene, shrapnel, or any signs of what caused it. Thermals got nothing either. When the storm starts rolling in, buildings are just falling down one by one, sir."

"Hmm. Colonel Yorker is too damn thick for crap like this. No way IRA could pull it off. Definitely the General's doing. Besides, with his rations, his ass is just gonna sit on his side of Edingburg and hunker down till our front lines starve out then he'll come over the line and finish us off."

Bradshaw leaned over the table, looking over the sprawling map. "Alright, fuck the damn buildings for now."

Bradshaw snapped his fingers. "Files!" A team of guardsmen waddled over with a safe and set it down beside the map. Bradshaw spun the dial and opened the safe with a key that hung from his neck. He looked up at his audience. "Turn the fuck around!" All eyes turned away. Bradshaw closed the safe and slapped a book onto the map. It was entitled *The Rommel Papers*.

"Luckily I'm one hell of a colonel. Already planned for every bullshit situation the bastards might put me into."

Bradshaw opened his book. It was littered with notes and stapled-in pictures. "Back when America was more than a city-state, men had wars. It wasn't a damn corporate game then. They were great wars. Some lasting decades, even. Millions upon millions of soldiers on either side. All of them armed with a sense of duty that it was their moral obligation to make the poor bastards on the other side of the line die for their country."

"One hour to showtime, sir," the captain said, checking his watch.

"It wasn't just a damn show then." Bradshaw tapped a page in his book. "Here's what I did in the Second World War. Hammered those Nazi bastards! We've just gotta do it again. Blitzkrieg, boys. Give our enemy no time to think. Confuse them. Make the godless ones in those foxholes pray. Follow that plan I've got in there and the cowards will be thinking with their feet in no time. And we'll pick up whatever rations those Fox bastards leave behind."

Bradshaw's staff looked it over and began moving plastic soldiers around the map. The colonel turned to Steve. "We may not have any panzers, but some amped-up teenagers should be able to swoop around just as fast." He brought out a golden ten-sided die that had different shapes on each one of its faces. "You are now with the 94th Infantry Division. It's a small squad of maybe four kids I've handpicked for the job."

"And what am I in all this?" Steve asked.

"You're going to be a train robber." Bradshaw stroked the map. "The Inner Circle's train comes right through this sector before it gets to Central Station. They're doing a final shipment before this Edingburg fiasco goes full swing. Bet you it's got another damn shipment for Ghost Fox on there. But you and your team will be making that *my* shipment. I've already had another team ensure that there won't be any security around the train, so she's all mine."

"I don't think I—"

"According to your gig profile, you've worked for years handling crates. Isn't that right?"

"Yes, but—"

"And so you know how to short-circuit them, don't you?"

"Yes, but—"

"And each damn train car is really just a bunch of boxes stacked together by the electromagnets in each crate, yeah?"

"Yes, but the crates are already loaded," Steve said. "I can only get to the outside ones."

"Great! So disconnect the outside crates, throw them off the train, and then disconnect the next layer! It's just a big cube-shaped onion, boy! Keep peeling the layers off the train until you get to the good crate. *My* special delivery."

"Well, what crate is that?"

"Oh, I don't know, kid. You'll know it when you see it."

"What the hell kind of answer is that?!" Steve shouted.

Bradshaw backhanded him in the teeth. "You may be drugged up, kid, but you will respect high command. You are a soldier now. Your job is to fight where you are told!" He grabbed Steve by the throat. "And win."

Steve's hand turned to a fist. Bradshaw drew his pistol and raised it to Steve's chin. "I'd consider saluting me instead, kid," Bradshaw whispered.

Steve's fist unclenched.

"Good," Bradshaw said. "Private Mendez here will take you to the 94th now. You'll be relieving the 6th of their pre-wartime activities. Now listen, kid. When you get to the train, hit the fifth train car from the engine. You fuck this up you might as well just stay on that train until you get blown up."

Mendez ushered Steve outdoors and with a slam of a door Steve was standing alone by a half-mangled building. Nothing moved. A gurgling sound came from down the road.

A rusting purple van with tinted windows pulled up next to Steve. The side door slid open. It was Ramfort, immersed in a jungle of bright flowers. "Mount up!"

"What? No!" Steve said. "How are you here? The 94th is picking me up!"

"Is that who they were? Kinda took their vans and stuff, but the 94th should be around somewhere." Ramfort leaned out of the van and looked left and right. "Don't worry about it. I'll be your 94th, baybay."

"I've been ordered to rob a train."

"Ah, no way! That's dope! And explains this equipment here!" Ramfort hopped out holding an electromagnet gun, walked around the front of the van, and hopped in the passenger side. "You're driving."

Steve stood where he was.

"Let's go, spy boy!" Ramfort shouted. "You did it! You got the orders and intel we needed. Jombo, we're the 94th! Robbin' trains! 94th! We got orders!"

Ramfort waved at the van pulling up behind them to follow. "Perfect, now we've all got orders. 94th! Trains!"

Steve slowly got in the driver's side. He looked down at the wheel. "I threw away my life just to intercept some orders? There was no other way?"

"Steve," Ramfort said. "You're a train robber now. When have you ever been so free?"

Precious Cargo

Steve looked down at the crate beneath his feet. Wind shot through his hair. Puffs of smoke fell back onto him from the train's engine.

He calibrated his electromagnet to the pulse requirements labeled on the crate. He held it to the crate and shocked it. The crate dropped, now magnetically disconnected from the rest of the block. He pulled up on the handle, his shoulders quaking as the crate slowly slid up. He looked over at Ramfort, whose rusting purple van was flanking the moving train. Ramfort shook his head.

Steve heaved the crate to the side of the train and threw it over. Ramfort swerved away from the tumbling crate, as did the trailing van. Steve had left a long line of crates in their wake at this point.

Steve disconnected the next crate and heaved it up to the wall of crates surrounding the open square he'd made. When he pulled it out, the crate gave a stark blue contrast compared to walls of gray around him.

"That's it!" Ramfort shouted in Steve's earpiece. "Robbin' trains!"

Infected Stuffing/The Seeds We Sow

Whirling blades sliced through the pixelated sky. Battle cries and and howls sounded into the ears of the hundreds of Tubers' earbuds, all experiencing the same simulation.

"Go! Go! Go!" Sergeant Kesey shouted.

Johnny's legless body and materializing hands were being dragged double-quick across a pavilion via two camouflaged soldiers. They were booking it toward a Huey whose chopper blades were only spinning faster with each rotation.

"Five seconds! Let's go!" the pilot shouted through the cockpit window.

The soldiers threw Johnny into the open side of the Huey and onto the metal floor. Johnny screamed, writhing in agony from his severed legs.

"Shit!" shouted Leary, a specialist wearing a rainbow-colored medic's helmet. "They turned on the pain! They fucking flagged the whole sector because of this guy!"

"Game's feelin' real now, boys!" the pilot shouted.

"It's what we signed up for!" shouted a soldier with a yellow peace badge stitched onto his uniform. A third soldier sporting big purple sunglasses cranked back the bolt of the M-60 machine gun on the Huey and started firing rounds into the wave of raging figures charging toward them.

"Get us the fuck out of E-Burg!" Kesey shouted.

The pilot gave a thumbs-up and brought the rotors to takeoff speed. At about ten feet off the ground he stabilized the rudders, adjusted the pitch, and was halfway through turning over the comms when he took a bullet to the face.

The Huey crashed back down to the pavilion.

Johnny's head slammed into the Huey floor, and his body went into convulsions.

"Fuck! We're losing him!" Kesey yelled. "Hit him with the needle!"

"No," Johnny moaned. Leary plunged a syringe into his arm.

Crazed men and women charged the fallen copter. Some in suits of armor, others near naked. All of them digital characterizations of people hooked into online cloud. The soldier on the M-60 realigned the gun's belt feeder and fired again into the digitized fray.

Sergeant Kesey grabbed Specialist Leary. "Get on those controls!"

"What?! I can't fucking do that, man!"

"Well, we can't *do* here, either! Just get us up!"

Leary scrambled to the controls and cranked up the lever controlling the blades. The chopper zoomed upward, the side gunner firing wildly as he lost his balance, then stabilized and hung still in the sky, 1,000feet above the ground.

Sergeant Kesey hoisted himself up, grabbed the M-14 next to the side gunner and fired down on the few stragglers who'd managed to grab and hold onto the Huey's landing gear.

"Fucker's got ridiculous grip upgrades," he said, firing his rifle into the last straggler.

Kesey watched the straggler's body plummet into the concrete pavilion, then turned back to Johnny.

"What the hell do I do now, man?" Leary asked.

"Just split," Kesey said. "Nobody's going to be shooting at us now. If they blow us all up at once they can't grab the IP address attached to this dude. That'll forfeit the Department of Smoke's bounty. Hell, they'd probably earn themselves a bounty in the process if they lose this guy's IP."

"He fully loaded yet?" Leary asked, his hands hovering over the chopper's controls.

Kesey examined Johnny's hands, watching his blocky fingertips hem into a detailed quilt of skin. "Just about," he said.

Johnny gritted his teeth and pushed his back onto the rear wall. Kesey slid open the right side door of the Huey, and Johnny saw all of Edingburg below—the online version, at least. A row of street blocks leading to the pavilion they'd just escaped was in fiery shambles. Lines of bodies dotted the street Johnny had been dragged through.

"Those damn pigs at the Department of Smoke started squealing the second we saw your avatar loading up in the dock," Kesey said.

"They flashed a stack of E-cash on your head so big
the whole damn city wanted a taste. Shit got so wild we had to pull you
out the dock before you even fully loaded."

He pointed to Johnny's missing legs.
"Those won't be coming back until you restart. They got blown off
halfway through the fucking alley. Luckily you weren't uploaded enough
to feel that shit. Fucking department saw there were other users
covering you so they turned on the pain to the whole sector. Those
monkey fucks are too damn stupid to crack our codes to identify us, so
they turned on the pain to break us up. Those bullets got the same bite in
here as they do on the outside."

Kesey dragged the dead pilot to the back of the Huey and set the
corpse down next to Johnny.

"You think those pigs got him?" Leary asked.
"Coding's your thing, man. Just fucking lay it on me. Flyboy
fried or not?"

"Good chance," Kesey said. "They were already monitoring this
sector when one of those dead heads killed him.
All they have to do is isolate the only dead/respawn
transmission that they don't immediately recognize. His mind's
probably wired so deep in limbo that he can't log his ass out.
Only a matter of time until they locate his tube."

"Fucking unreal," Leary said, sulking over the controls.

"They've got the cloud going 30 times unplug speed now," Kesey said. "Probably five hours in real time until they nab him; that's like a week in limbo."

"Can we bust him out long enough so he can log out?" Leary asked.

"Impossible."

"You just gonna give up on him!"

"Get real, man! I got love for the flyboy, but the code for limbo is way too fucking far out. He's fucking fried! Game over, man! Kid's done."

Kesey slid back down to the floor. He raised his hand, flicking his fingers into different positions to summon and banish different objects. He settled on a lit cigarette and brought it up to his mouth. He took a drag and exhaled. "So who are you? What's going on out there, man?"

Johnny looked down at his digital body. "Johnny McHenry. I am —was—the mayor of Edingburg. We just blew up part of the pier and Edingburg's City Hall building."

Kesey nearly dropped his cigarette. "Far out ... You're Joe. Hey, we got GI Joe on deck!"

"No way," Leary said. "It's Joe!" He swung around from the controls. "Shit, then we're really doing it? The revolution's gone hot!"

Kesey cycled his hands again and came to two cans. He smiled. "The purple bombers are unlocked!"

"No way, man. It really is real!" Leary shouted.

Kesey banged the bottoms of the cans onto the floor, popped the tops, and rolled them down the sides of the Huey cabin. They stopped on either side of Johnny, poofed open, and let out a huge purple haze. The vacant cabin quickly filled with purple smoke that poured out in two thick trails from the open side doors.

The soldier wearing purple sunglasses leaned in close to Johnny's face. "Johnny?" he whispered. His head turned to a high tilt.

"Yes?" said Johnny nervously.

"Johnny!" the soldier shouted. He began pacing manically from side to side, making the chopper sway.

"Hey, what the fuck!" Leary shouted. "I can barely keep this damn thing going straight as it is, man! Patch or no patch!" The soldier kept pacing. Between the purple clouds, Johnny could make out the man ripping at his hair.

"Ramfort, cut the shit!" Kesey said.

A pistol appeared in Ramfort's hand. He unloaded a whole clip at Johnny, who shrieked and thrashed wildly. When he opened his eyes, Kesey had pinned Ramfort to the ground.

"You're fine," Kesey said, letting Ramfort up. "He's just a bot based off the real Ramfort. Can't cause friendly fire."

"They can still scare the shit outta ya though," Leary shouted.

Ramfort crept to the edge of the chopper and turned back to Johnny, face devoid of expression. He hung his body out of the chopper, his fingers gripping at the edges. Aside from his purple sunglasses, everything on Ramfort began flapping wildly in the wind. Ramfort glanced back to Kesey again. Kesey glared back. Ramfort grumbled. Ramfort's feet stepped onto the Huey's landing gear and shimmied to the back of the chopper's exterior. He began spray painting a bright yellow peace sign on the side of the Huey.

"I don't think he likes you, Joe!" shouted Leary. He pushed an old cassette into the Huey's cassette player. "I Can Feel Him in the Morning" by Grand Funk Railroad began to play.

The Huey passed over the walls of E-Burg. Every single person in the virtual city looked up at them, backs arched and necks craned. The only thing that interested them more than the bounty flying over their heads was the purple smoke trailing from the Huey. Everyone in E-burg knew what that meant—Mom was coming.

One Love

Bit by bit the world turned green. A jungle of thick leaves, heavy underbrush, and sturdy branches permeated the landscape. The 20 or so songs on Leary's cassette had all played through.

Kesey stared out the side of the Huey, his legs dangling off the side.

Ramfort sat cross-legged, glaring at Johnny from less than a foot away.

"So what the hell is a bot?" Johnny asked, peering around Ramfort.

"You don't plug in, huh?" Kesey asked.

"When Ramfort's plugged in the system, the system logs his behavior. Then when he's logged off, his bot mimics his past behaviors.

Really just a fancy way for the

Man to get more fucking info on us, but it's got its perks.

Now we've got him always plugged in one way or another.

Ramfort's a weird cat, but shit, never thought he'd go all Rambo on you like that."

"So what's stopping this bot from being hacked by the department and killing me?"

"Pretty much the anonymity coding I've got attached to him.
They don't know which bot to convert—
or even if there's a bot with us, come to think of it."

"What if they just tell all the bots to kill me?"

"Well, then you'd be pretty fucked," Kesey said.

Johnny's eyes dropped back down to Ramfort, whose face had a smirk growing across it.

"Soon," Ramfort whispered.

The Huey began descending toward a rice field.
"This is the stop!" Leary shouted. Rice stems and roots knotted around the landing skids as the Huey touched down.

"Let's do it!" Kesey said. "Leary, help me get Joe outta here!"

Ramfort raised an eyebrow, his eyes still staring at Johnny.
"I can help," Ramfort said innocently.

"Piss off," Kesey said.

Ramfort looked up at Kesey.
"We've got quite the load of gear to move. And through the mud, no less. I'm a bot, so I can carry the big gun and Johnny,
whereas neither of you could do either on your own. Trip's like an hour as it is."

Kesey looked uncertain.

"Ah, just let him do it," Leary said, shaking his head at the huge pond of mud surrounding them. "It's gonna suck enough already."

"Fine," Kesey said.

"Don't I get a say here?" Johnny asked. Ramfort turned back to Johnny, his smile fully bloomed. He picked Johnny up and slung him over his shoulder, then
grabbed the M-60 machine gun with his other hand.

"What the hell!" Johnny said.

"Screw you, ya freakin' brat!" Ramfort yelled.

Kesey and Leary jumped down into the muddy field.

"I prescribe getting used to it," Leary said. "He's always like this."

"Kesey, aren't you in fucking command here?!" Johnny shouted.

"I'm no master commander, man. I just feel it." Kesey grabbed a pack from the Huey and heaved it onto his back. "And if people are vibing, then they fall in line."

"Make him put me down, dammit! This is ridiculous!"

"Time to walk the yellow brick road," Ramfort said as he started plowing through the rice field. "Ah, smell that fresh jungle pine. It's. So. Relaxing!"

"Put me down!" Johnny shouted. "I'm—"

"We should hang some of it from the Huey's rear view mirror," Ramfort said. His boots began slurping through the field. "Do you have a rear-view mirror?"

"Get off of me," Johnny said.

"Whoa now, you're on me, ya legless idiot," Ramfort said. His boots kept pushing forward. "Yeah, you probably don't have a rear-view mirror. Explains why you're such a douchebag."

"Put me down!" Johnny shouted. "I'm—"

"I know who you are, ya douchebag," Ramfort said.

"Look kid—bot—whatever the hell you are, I think you got me mixed up with someone."

Ramfort stopped dead. "Oh, I know who you are, Johnny."

"Yeah? And who's Johnny to you? Everyone seems to have a name for me I'd love to know yours."

"Douchebag," Ramfort said.

Johnny rolled his eyes. "Fine. Let's just drop it."

"Dropped," Ramfort said releasing his grip, and Johnny splashed into the rice field. He thrashed frantically, unable to get himself above the waterline without his legs.

"Fuck you, Ramfort!" Kesey yelled as he and Leary pulled Johnny out of the slop.

"We need him alive! You try and kill him again and I'm fucking deactivating you!"

Ramfort looked shocked. "He told me to drop him! You heard him! He loves orders. He gave some orders for me to drop him, so I did! It's not my fault the water decided to go and drown him."

"Fuck you, Ramfort. Don't bullshit me with loopholes! Leary, give me a hand with this dude."

Kesey and Leary carried Johnny out of the rice field and trudged into the jungle. A few hours later, Leary pulled out a map and pointed. "We've made it. Hamburger Hill. The summit's a good thousand meters up, so get ready to start sucking wind."

"Goddammit," Leary grumbled.

When they had made it halfway up the hill, panting and covered in mud, Kesey gestured for Leary to put Johnny down.

"Hey!" Kesey yelled. "You hear me? Help us out!"

A group of 40 or so people descended on them. They wore loose-fitting hemp clothing and flowers in their hair. Smiles of nirvana on every face.

"Joe, meet my merry band of pranksters."

They picked up Johnny and lifted him over their shoulders. Johnny panted, exhaustion aching in him. Hands waved under him. Johnny floated upstream, carried by a river of palms and fingertips. Others flurried around, lighting bamboo torches or stacking columns of smooth river rocks on top of one another. They brought Johnny to a small clearing in the jungle where a 20-foot-tall orange teddy bear sat up against a large tree, and laid him down between the bear's legs.

Johnny felt nervous. He hadn't forgotten the last time he'd seen an orange teddy bear.

"Hey, is this thing … is this a bomb?" he stammered.

"Yeah, man, it's the bomb!" one of the pranksters said, smiling.

The pranksters lit a large bonfire in front of the teddy bear. The flames flew upward into the jungle's canopy.

Kesey walked over and sat, leaning his back against the leg opposite of Johnny. He pulled out a pair of purple sunglasses with circular lenses and looked into the fire.

"Where is she?" Johnny asked.

"You're eager," Kesey said. He began puffing on another rolled cigarette. "You into her, man?"

Johnny lowered his face. "The General just killed my wife. And *she* just tricked me into wiping out dozens of my peers."

Kesey took a long drag from his cigarette and then held it out to Johnny, who waved it off.

"Ah, I see. She's helping you get up when you're real low. Sounds like Mom to me. But that don't mean you're not into her."

Johnny wanted to kick him, then remembered he had no legs.

"I get it, man," Kesey said. "Lost a lot of love myself. But that's love, man. It comes and it goes. Gotta let it be free, otherwise it ain't love, man."

"Do you know who she is? Mom?"

"Man, you need to start asking the right questions. It's not about who, it's about *what*, man. You need to expand your consciousness before you can even fathom this woman."

"Then enlighten me," Johnny said.

Kesey watched the embers on the end of the cigarette gray and flake away.

"She's ain't human."

"She's a bot?"

"Now hold on," Kesey said. "You see that cat?" He pointed his cigarette at Ramfort. "He's a reflection of something. Of the real Ramfort. At the end of the day he's about as three-dimensional as an Inner Circle girl. But Mom, she ain't that kind of bot. She's gone viral, man. She's spread all over the network. She's gotten inside everyone who's ever plugged in, man, and you know what she planted in us? A piece of herself. Cuz she's a real woman. She's alive, but in all of us. She took a kernel, a seed, flake, the smallest bit of herself and put it into all of us and let it grow free. It grew off our experiences and so that small little bit of her became a bit of us. And now all those little bits are finally coming together, man."

"Wait," Johnny said. "So the real her is dead?"

"You mean her body? You asking if her skeleton is still housing her soul? I don't know that, man. No one does. The main rumor going round says she's trapped, but where, man, we've got no idea. But that ain't the point. The point is Mom's alive in all of us. And I'm not even playin' metaphors with ya. She's in all of us cuz she's given us the seed we all needed to love each other, free of apprehension or predisposition. Free of the masks we wear all day."

Kesey looked over at the pranksters, the flames from the fire reflecting on his sunglasses.

"Purple smoke," Kesey exhaled. "Purple smoke's the calling card, man. Shit's not possible to download. They outlawed it for who the hell knows what reason way back. It's prophecy, man. It's prophecy. She's something from the past. And with her she brings the truth. We don't even know what way is up anymore The Department of Smoke's got us all upside down man, blaming all the wrong things, thinking all the wrong thoughts. Like that damn asteroid man. The one and fucked all this world up? Yeah, there was an asteroid that hit us, but you know what else? The asteroid wasn't that big, man. It gave us a good bang, but we're the reason why things didn't get better. All that pollution we made, it was like, killing Mother Earth's immune system. So when that asteroid came in, it just took her straight down. And instead of helping her, what happens? We decide to make it worse and blow each other up with some nasty nukes, man. Mother Earth isn't killing us. We've been killing her. And that just ain't right."

The fire grew stronger as the pranksters continued to fling whatever gave the slightest hint at being combustible into the inferno.

"They're going to blow our cover," Johnny said. "Everyone's going to see that!"

"Yep," Kesey said, leaning back against the teddy bear's leg.

The pranksters began chanting as they threw red-, blue-, and yellow-colored chalk into the sky and at each other. Another purple can appeared in Kesey's hand. He held it up, tinging it with the fork attachment of his multi-tool like a wedding glass. Everyone stopped and stared.

"They'll flag her signal the second it goes live." Kesey said. "We've got maybe 15 seconds before this whole damn jungle goes up. Don't forget why we're here. Show them that no matter how much hate or dread they drop on us, they will never extinguish the love. We hold for two minutes, grab him, get him out, and we go full knock!"

AK-47s flicked into every prankster's hands. Muscles flexed. Tie-dyed armor and mismatched army boots covered their bodies for the coming blows.

"Hold for what?" Johnny asked.

"Your conversation with Mom," Kesey said. "You're about to speak to the most wanted bird ever to exist. The General wants her so bad, her very existence is legend, man. Now it's you who's gonna make her fables real."

Kesey stood up. He took a final puff from his cigarette and threw it away. "Let's go, children. Stations." He glanced down at Johnny. "Do it." Pranksters flung ropes over and under the teddy bear's leg and strapped Johnny against it.

"What the fu—"

Someone pressed a mask over Johnny's mouth and nose, and it began pumping gas into his lungs.

Kesey popped the can in his hand. Purple lava leaked from the nozzle and spread across the ground. "Ten seconds till they hit us! Hold the guard back as long as possible! This is it, children! Our rebellion has truly begun! Love isn't free; time to pay for it!"

MiG jets zoomed over the treeline, dropping bombs in rows behind them. Johnny watched bursts of fiery lava burst over the canopy. Pranksters ran back and forth, shouting.

Johnny looked up and watched the giant bear's torso begin to fall forward, covering Johnny from a falling world. The gas coming from the mask began to take on a whiff of cinnamon. The darkness under the bear turned to hues of grayish blue. The wood and garbage on the fire began to fly away piece by piece.

A figure appeared. It glided toward Johnny, its legs moving slowly, but it closed the distance in only a moment. She illuminated in parts. Sometimes her bare torso and feet, other times with her partially covered face and robe-covered breasts. She stopped atop where the bonfire had burned.

"Jonathan," she said. "It's me. You can come out now. It's safe."

Johnny looked down at himself. The mask was gone, as were the ropes. But his legs had reappeared. He crawled out from under the bear. He glanced back to see that its back had burned.

"It's been a good bear to you," she said.

Johnny looked at her. She filled him with her quiet gaze. Even with just pieces of her flashing and fading, Johnny knew that he was seeing the most beautiful woman in existence.

"Jonathan, I have waited so long for this moment."

"I don't understand why. Why did you trick me? You got tons of important people killed at City Hall. And now people are dying so we can have this conversation?"

She made the slightest frown, and Johnny's anger relaxed.

"Jonathan, I know. I know everything you've been going through. It's as Kesey said, but those seedlings I planted aren't my own any more. When you arrived at Alcatraz, and Cottard did a memory recall on you, the flash on you was so strong, it tripped into the cloud and made aware, to some extent, every single seedling. And ever since then, they've been communicating with each other. Helping every mind not only think more freely, but to feel more freely as well. What it's turning into, I do not know. I am not whatever it is any more. I am only its mother."

She closed her eyes and took a long breath.

"My entire consciousness is in your mind and in your mind only."

Johnny stumbled backward and leaned on the bear.

"You feel drawn to me, Jonathan. I can feel it. And I'm so very drawn to you, because to you, I am not Mom." Tears brightened her eyes. "You are the man I made love to atop the platform, when the rest of the world was hiding away. I am your lover. Your wife, from long, long ago."

Johnny leaned against the teddy bear, his legs too rubbery to support him.

"The woman in the fire, Jonathan. That woman is me. What you think the General did at the protest, he actually did many years ago. But to you it's always like yesterday. The General toyed with you at the protest. He's aware of your condition and plays with your relapses.

"He told you at the protest he's kept you alive because you're useful. And sadly, that's true, Jonathan. He finds you useful because you are so incredible, and so incredibly broken. Part of your mind cracked on the day he did that to me. You couldn't face a world without me, but at the same time your mind knew so painfully well that I had gone. So total denial was impossible for you—your mind plays on repeat, completely unwilling to move on to a life truly without me and so utterly unable to face the guilt you feel for my loss. You live in a self-imposed purgatory, stuck between heaven and hell."

She pointed to his forehead. "In there you see me burning over and over again. I can't tell you how much it distresses me to see you this way."

Johnny looked down at his hands. Guilt, embarrassment, and grief began to fill him. "You can see them? My thoughts?"

"Yes, Jonathan. You've continued to evolve and were aware only of the new world, the world after what happened to me. But every few weeks your mind kills me again, and so you are held by a constant grief, always believing that I have just died. I wish you could have somehow known what happened in the tubes in the days before I died.

"Do you remember what Franz and Gordon said about the tubes? That they used to be more for human growth than human consumption? In those tubes our consciousness could combine and be with one another.

"I have to tell you a secret that I've held from you for so long." She looked down. "I knew what the General would do to me. So I prepared. I found a way. To download me into you while we were in the tubes together. So that at least part of me would be safe from him and I'd still be with you. I couldn't tell you because I knew you'd try to reason with the General. But that would have only jeopardized us both. I know I should have told you, but I had to make the decision we both know was the best for us. I've had to make so many hard decisions without you knowing the full extent. I'm sorry, but I had to break your trust in order to save what we value most."

"So you ... are *in* me?" Johnny asked.

"Yes. I've been with you the moment my body left this world."

"Why couldn't you just tell me after, in my head?"

"The General's too good. If he saw any change in you whatsoever he'd trigger a full investigation. He'd find out what I'd done. And then he'd find her."

"Her?"

"I did one other thing, Johnny. I made a clone of myself. Completely unconscious and unaware, with nothing in its brain, but completely habitable. We can bring me back, Johnny. We can be together again. But if he finds her first, it can never be."

Johnny looked back at the teddy bear. Small fires had reignited on its fur.

"Now I need you to be the man that not only I need, but the people of Edingburg need as well. The General has done everything in his power to isolate people from themselves, be it through hate, alienation, or distraction. He has shown the only thing he wishes to do is make humanity as animalistic and dreadful as possible.

"I've watched you through the years and you've never stopped being the man I fell in love with. So please, Jonathan, lead the people of Edingburg. Let this new energy bloom among our children; don't allow the General to smother or derange it. Let it be, for better or worse, as pure as you. Revolt."

"But why?" Johnny asked. "Why does he want you dead so badly?"

"We don't have the time, Jonathan. You must log out of the cloud before it's too late. It's time to let the record play through. Help our boys play the tape from the protest, so the whole city can hear it. They are already on their way. Goodness needs a voice. Let our message spread."

Johnny struggled to stand. He bent down to crawl back into the bear shelter. He looked back at her. Her face was wet with tears. He stood up straight. Though he still couldn't remember or validate a thing, his soul felt it was all true, wholly and completely. He walked over to her and held her hands.

"I love you," she said. From her body flashes of blue streaked outward, and she exploded into a burst of blue lights. Johnny flew back and was sucked into the teddy bear.

Screams reentered his world. Napalm dropped. Johnny shrieked as he was welded back into his virtual body.

Kesey was on his belly, staring at him through his purple sunglasses. He crawled over and raised his hand to Johnny's head, then made a yanking motion. Johnny fell from the cloud and back into the tube.

Joy Ride

"Where is it?" Ramfort shouted over the van's gurgling engine.

"Colonel Bradshaw said it'd be here!" Steve shouted back.

"Well it isn't here, Stevie Wonder!"

"Well shit, I don't know! Figure it out!"

"What?!" Ramfort shouted, raising himself from his seat with his hands. "Use your eyes! It's huge!"

The revolutionaries were driving down the Bayshore Freeway. Steve was doing his best to emulate a person who had ever driven a car before, keeping one foot on each petal.

"I can't see!" Steve shouted. "The sun's setting!"

"Jombo, can you keep an eye out back there?" Ramfort asked.

"How the hell do you expect him to see anything with all those flowers?" Steve shouted. I can't even see him! It's a jungle back there!"

"Would you just shut up and do something!" Ramfort yelled.

"I am!" Steve yelled back.

"You're just sitting there!"

"I'm driving! You're the one just sitting there!"

"That doesn't change the fact that you're sitting on your butt! You're a terrible driver!"

"Well, why am I even the one driving?!" Steve asked.

"It's over there," Jombo interjected in his deep yet gentle voice.

"Where?" Ramfort shrieked.

"Behind those buildings," Jombo said.

Ramfort jumped forward, pressing his forehead against the windshield. Silence filled the van. Only the nervous hum of the motor was audible. They all stared expectantly.

A sudden gap emerged between the buildings, exposing a large building standing alone in a sea of paved concrete. A long in front of the entrance stood nearly 80 feet high, with multiple squads of City Guardsmen surrounding it.

"That's gotta be it, the mobile radio station. Some jerk blew up the main station." Ramfort said, his voice solemn. He slunk back down into the bench seat and stared forlornly at the dashboard.

"Are …" Steve swallowed. His eyes were jumping from the road to Ramfort. "Are we seriously going to—"

The sudden screeching sound of flowerpots skidding over the van's aluminum floor interrupted Steve's question. Jombo was rearranging the flowerpots in the back.

Ramfort pressed the on button of the van's radio. "You still have the cassette, right?"

"Yes," Steve held it up with a shaking hand.

"Good. I'll bet anything Line is in that station. Doing his stupid show. He's got no idea that we're about to be his celebrity guests tonight." Ramfort dug into his own pocket and brought out his own cassette. He popped it into the van's tape player. "It Ain't Me" by CCR began to play.

Steve took a deep breath, trying not to panic as they sped toward the guards. How the hell did he get himself into fighting with these loons?

HQ HQ HQ HQ HQ

The tube door creaked open on its ancient hinges. Light filled Johnny's tube, and two shadows stood over him. In a minute he saw that they were Franz and Gordon.

"You all right, John?" Gordon said.

Johnny shivered in the corroded tube.

"Let's get you out of there, shall we?" Franz said.

They lifted Johnny by the shoulders and guided him to a small metal chair. With a jolt of panic, Johnny kicked it over. The clatter sent an echo through the large space.

Gordon unfolded a blanket and draped it over Johnny's shoulders.

Panting, Johnny looked around the room. Multiple projectors were all pointing toward a screen. On the screen were images of maps, code, people's profiles, emergency situations, everything.

"Where am I?" Johnny asked.

Gordon handed Johnny a cup of Earl Grey. "There you go."

"They've actually got decent tea here," Franz said. "Quite the godsend."

"Jes, a hint of the holy 'round here," Gordon agreed.

"Where the hell am I?" Johnny repeated.

"Oh, right," Gordon said.

"Well, seeing as you were in a shipping container anyway," Franz said, "we thought we'd take the liberty of moving ourselves to headquarters whilst you—"

"Met Mum!" Gordon interrupted. "How did it all go, John?"

"I guess … I'm the leader of this—" Johnny looked around at the blue rock walls surrounding them— "thing now."

"Oh, my," Gordon said.

"Not surprised," Franz said. "She always did like keeping affairs within the family."

"What? You knew?"

"Oh yes, John," Gordon said. "We've been quite close with the family for ages. You don't seem to remember due to the, hmm, severe bonk on the head you'd received."

"We felt it Mum's right to tell you," Franz said.

"Jes. We respect Mum far too much to overstep such a boundary."

Johnny walked over to the screen and studied the images. He saw what appeared to be a live map of Edingburg. It showed the locations of the two C-Corps surrounding and operating within Edingburg, and other supply depots. He found one spot on the map far more intriguing, however: the replacement radio station that had been set up after City Hall was destroyed. He traced lines connecting to the replacement station. They led to three small circles.

"What are these things?" Johnny asked.

"Well, they don't have truly powerful radio stations that they can just pop up on a moment's notice," Franz said. "So I'd suspect they're to catch the signal from the mobile station and boost it to the rest of the city."

There was a buzz, and the map blinked. A building on the map turned yellow.

A report shot up from one of the projectors onto the screen: "Meeting requested by high-value asset. Quote from asset: 'I've got 80 good kids that will fight, but they can only do that if they're not dead. We've got maybe an hour until that happens. Extraction requested.' —Agent #465."

"What was that, then?! Nikolai, we've got ourselves a message!" Kleiner rounded the corner, saw Johnny, and clutched his chest. "Sweet Florian!"

Nikolai looked at Kleiner. "Iz fine. Iz the mayor of Edingburg, Johnny McHenry. He iz vith us. Mother sent out a signal a moment ago saying he iz the new leader of the movement."

"*That's* what the decryption said?" Kleiner asked.

Nikolai nodded. "Positive. Mayor of Edingburg, Mr. McHenry is the new leader of the IRA. He is fighting against the General."

"He's been the mayor then! The one under the mask! All this toime!"

"Yez. Now we move forward."

Kleiner shifted his weight back onto his toes. He scratched his beard. "Right. Well. Okay then." With nervous steps Kleiner walked toward Johnny with his hand extended. "Pleased to have ye in me, uh …" He looked around. "Me private quarters, Mr., uh, McHenry."

The two men shook hands. Even though Kleiner stood at least a foot higher than Johnny, he seemed smaller.

The map beeped.

"Right!" Kleiner said, turning to the screen. He read the report. "We've got ourselves quite the opportunity here, lads. Got a chance to save some young kin and gain us some much needed support at tha same time."

"It's in the war zone," Johnny said. "Can we really get in and out of there?"

"Positive," Nikolai said. "You've been a great distraction. They've been moving slow."

"We're already in," Kleiner said. "We've mapped all the tunnels and sewer systems big 'nough to fit anythin' from a mouse to a truck. Took a good bit. This city was built on hoondreds a years ah sewers being built and fergot about. We've added a good number of secret openings as well to help get around without bein' detected by the guard."

Johnny turned to Franz and Gordon. "We had your tube shoved through a hole," Franz said.

"It was a spacious hole," Gordon assured him.

"Well then, why don't they just go into the tunnels?" Johnny asked Kleiner.

"We keep knowledge of the tunnels pretty close to tha chest. It's our loifeline, after all. So they don't know there's a hatch roight next to 'em. And we can't be givin' such info to a field agent who may very well be captured or even ah spy." He pointed at a hatch. "Someone with the clearance has gotta go oop and tell 'em."

Another report buzzed onto the screen.

"Amendment: 'The new leader of the IRA must be present and alone before I hand my employees over.' —Agent #465."

Johnny let the blanket slide off his back. "How do I get there?"

"Wut, now? That there looks like a trap, pure'n simple. I mean Mum just made her first transmission ever declarin' a new leader in her absence. An' five minutes lata here we are with a big ole pot a possible members that'r willing to help fight right when we need 'em most. Don't take genius to be seein' the horseshit in that."

Another report: "Source is insisting this isn't 'horseshit.' Source also strongly insisting on his identity being revealed, due to 'No chance in hell I make it out anyway.' The source is 'Colonel Bradshaw, CEO of the Completely and Utterly Fucked "Hell on Wheels' Inc.' —Agent #465."

Kleiner scratched his beard. "Hmmm. Mighty fishy, all dis."

Johnny looked at the member status on the screen. "Look, we don't even have a 100 trusted and active members now. *But*—" he moved his finger to another line of info— "we've got about 2,500 recorded sympathizers that have helped the IRA at some point. We got crushed at the protest. Lost hundreds of good members and since then we haven't done a thing to keep the people believing in the cause." He looked at Kleiner. "They don't even know if the IRA is operating."

Johnny pointed at the sympathizer reports. "We need to convert those people to the cause full time. And no one's going to convert to something they're not even sure exists any more. So we're going to need to prove we're still here. We need to show them we can win. And to win we'll need manpower. You see this?" Johnny pointed to the radio station on the screen. "They set that up right after I had the City Hall building blown up."

Kleiner's eyes widened. "Blimey, that was you, was it?!"

"Yes, I did it." Johnny heard Franz clearing his throat, but he ignored him. "So now we need to take this replacement station. It's not nearly as entrenched or secure as the one at the City Hall, and from there we can relay a message to the whole city—from inside Edingburg. Letting them know we're still active and can win. So how do I get to them? The kids?"

Kleiner massaged his beard, taking in the situation. "Uh, through the tunnels, o' course. The tunnels are roit over here. Roit this way."

Church

Johnny opened the hatch closest to Colonel Bradshaw and his team. He was in a small graveyard, about two hundred feet from the church Cottard had told him about. The church stood on the south corner of Capp and 22nd and was set back from what used to be 23rd Street's curb. Victorian-style townhouses stood along both ends of the street and wrapped the corner. The hatch shut behind him. The top of the hatch was a long flat tombstone.

A convoy of mangled trucks appeared down the road. Armed Phoenix pledges hung from the sides of commandeered trucks, which had been spray-painted blue, signifying they were now employed by Ghost Fox Inc. Johnny gasped and ran for the church.

A lone and immaculate silver APC with the Department of Smoke Emblem on its side rolled slowly through an abandoned block nearby. No one dared shoot at it, instead people did their best to ignore the huge megaphones fastened to its sides and top pointed in all directions. "You have come here to fight, not to fear! You have come here to become men, not to sit around crying beneath a windowsill! Stand up! Fire your weapons! Earn your promotions! Become the man that's always been within you. Let him out! Or stay down and wait for the real men to come and take you down for good!"

Johnny peered around the silent graves, feeling the wet moisture of the low-lying fog. A squad of rifles banged over his head from the apartments behind him toward the convoy of blues. Johnny threw himself to the ground. A rocket fired back from the convoy and shattered the front of the apartment complex behind him. More rifles fired from the building. Johnny thought it was the IRA, but he only saw red rifles. It was Hell on Wheels Inc. firing at Ghost Fox Inc. Pledges from Ghost Fox jumped off the trucks, ran into the nearby buildings, and fired over the open graveyard at Hell on Wheels. Bullets snapped over Johnny's head. He crawled back and tried to pry open the tombstone, but he couldn't lift it. He took cover behind a particularly large tombstone as more rockets slammed into the buildings behind him. One collapsed, sagging with an avalanche of concrete and pulverized wood as Johnny pressed his face into the dirt.

A mortar shell slammed into the apartment building across from the church. White smoke poured from the building, quilting the graveyard in a gaseous spray. Johnny crawled in the direction of the church. He saw a haze of red and angled toward that. He came to the church's raised porch with an open door hanging crooked from one hinge. He bolted through the doorway and slammed the door shut.

Bullets rained through the lines of long windows that spanned both sides of the church. Shards of stained glass rained down onto the stone floor. Johnny dropped down and crawled toward the back of the church, away from the door. He tilted his head as he crawled. Row after row of men with red spattered on their uniforms were hunkering down beneath the lines of pews, all too terrified to notice him. In contrast, one uniformed man stood on a pew in contrast with his arms raised. "You bring your hellfire into this house! A house of the lord! Here you bring your rage! When the fifth coming is upon us, may you be dead! For in this moment you shalt only know rage and not the hot dread of torment!"

A huge explosion rocked the church. The gunfire stopped. The man continued ranting. Johnny saw a man kneeling in front of the altar. Two ivory pistols were holstered on either side of his hips. It was Colonel Bradshaw, CEO of Hell on Wheels Inc. Johnny crawled to the colonel and tugged at his pant leg.

"Kneel." Bradshaw waved at a spot next to him. Johnny glanced at the windows, took a breath, and brought himself up to the altar.

"Have you ever seen a mirage?" Bradshaw asked.

Johnny kept glancing at the shattered windows, anticipating the next wave of munitions bursting through the tinted glass.

"A mirage," the CEO continued. "Something that looks so real, but is always out of reach."

The maniacal man on the pew threw his club. "May she damn you all!"

Bradshaw stared blankly at the statue of a woman in front of the altar. His fingers scratched through layer after flaking layer of polish on the altar until his nails dug into the wood. Then he looked at Johnny for the first time, starting with the General's uniform and then up to Johnny's innocent face. The colonel chuckled until he coughed blood. He quickly wiped it away with a handkerchief.

"You think the guard's bad?" Bradshaw asked. "Don't like big militarized corporations? You want to know what's worse? A life without honor and courage. That's the real hell. A world where the biggest and best things you do come from the end of a bottle or while crammed into some damn tube. That's hell.

"Because what can a man become when he is given everything? When there's no struggle nor great conflict to overcome? You can give a man the world, but when you do, you rob him of the supreme accomplishment that any man could ever stand to gain—his story. And that's all anyone really needs. Doesn't matter if you're a man or a lady. No one wants a life they can't look back on with some pride. Because if you're going to go and rob some poor bastard of their story, well, you're also robbing him of his character.

"When you do that you take away everything. Every scrap of evidence that ever proved you were even alive. And that's why the guard exists. To save us from the hell that is perpetually singing kumbaya. Without us, what would we be talking about? What would we even be doing? Is sitting around, getting fat, and laughing at yourself because your whole damn existence is a joke really the fucking way to go?!"

He coughed up more blood. "Count yourself lucky, not knowing what it is to get older. It's a bastard." Bradshaw made the outline of the cross with his hand. He looked up at the enormous statue of a woman in front of him. She stood over them, looking down with one hand stretched toward them.

"I like to think myself a Baptist, not that she cares, but she wouldn't be too pleased with the language."

"The Virgin Mary?" Johnny asked, looking up at the statue.

"Oh, no. There's no place for innocence here, boy. The General saw to that. Everyone chose to be here—there are no chains, none for restricting anyway. Everyone knows what they've done, why they did it … even if they've convinced themselves they don't."

Bradshaw looked up at the statue. "That's Mom. She's our—your—only chance. When I heard her in my head the other day, it was incredible." He reached into his front pocket and handed Johnny a locket of hair in an airtight tube. "Give that to Cottard. He'll know what to do with it."

Something exploded near the entrance to the church. The ranting soldier broke down and sobbed from his pew.

"What color was the door painted?"

"Red."

Bradshaw sighed. "Nothing is sacred any more. Everything's got a price. You've got two hours before sunset. And I've got all that's left of Hell on Wheels ordered to hit them with everything come sunrise. That should help keep Ghost Fox busy during your little broadcast, but only for a bit. I trained half those bastards on Ghost Fox myself before they went and switched companies on me for sign-up bonuses. They're gonna slice through my new recruits. My company is losing this battle with Ghost Fox in a big way. Inner Circle subsidized my competitor too much. Got weapons coming out their ass! Guess I didn't lobby and kiss around enough. Just built a darn good company. But at this level, I guess that's not what it's about. Anyway, I'll be CEO of nothin' in a few hours. I can't survive this corporate battle much longer, so we're gonna have to do a merger."

"What? You can't merge with Ghost Fox!"

"As if I'd give DipDaw the pleasure of licking his boot! Not happening. Besides, the low-level kids almost always get the ax with that kind of merger. So I'm a merging with the IRA."

Bradshaw marched down the center aisle, pushing a soldier sitting at the edge of the pew. The soldier slumped over, dead. The few remaining men who still breathed were glued to the floor beneath the pews. "You want to die and have no one notice like this poor bastard?!" Bradshaw yelled.

"We don't want to die!" the hysterical man shouted.

"Good, pledge! Then follow him!" Bradshaw turned and pointed at Johnny.

Every head rose from the lines of pews.

"Who the fuck is that?!" a pledge shouted.

Bradshaw drew his pistol and fired into the ceiling.

"That's enough from you! Did you sign up for pussy or to be one! I gave you a direct order, boy! You wanted to join the City Guard?" He glared at the boys. "Then get in line like a good altar boy! This is the *real* guard! This is Mom's Guard!" He pointed at the statue.

Johnny and the men stared at each other as Bradshaw walked back to the altar.

"They know?" Johnny hissed.

Bradshaw smiled. "Well, they know you. Picked them because they'd gone to the medics asking about their heads. Were hearing voices all day, except when the medics asked what they were saying they had no idea. They were nervous, but damn excited nonetheless and they couldn't explain why. Figured since I'm having the same batshit crazy stuff happening, I'd round 'em up. It's your job to tell them the rest." Bradshaw glanced down at Johnny's muddied uniform. "I assume someone's been busy tunneling." He grabbed a large comm phone from one of the pews and threw it to Johnny. "Get these boys to your HQ. I've got a feeling they're exactly what Mom's looking for."

Johnny looked at the comm phone in his hand. "Why do you—"

"You'll need them. A few more hands on deck might just save the whole ship from sinking. Radio'd some other divisions about our merger too. They'll be looking out for you." Bradshaw tapped the metal stars on Johnny's chest with the barrel of his pistol. "Commander."

The earth shook. Between the pews, psalm books rattled in their wooden cradles.

From behind the statue, a huge gun barrel banged through the layers of stacked rock. A wave of debris blew into the sanctuary.

Johnny spun around. A tank was barreling through this House of Mom. The pledges scrambled toward the church entrance. The tank knocked over the statue and crushed her under its tread. Bradshaw grabbed Johnny by the shoulder and slung him toward the door. "Tell her I accept my regrets!" he shouted.

As Johnny stumbled toward the door, the tank's front jutted down from the altar and fired. The solid shot eliminated Bradshaw and the shockwave hurled Johnny out the building.

A pledge grabbed Johnny's arm. "Where?! Where do we go?!"

Johnny ran in a daze, pointing toward the gravestone. The boys opened it and piled in.

Das Kapital

A rag hung from the end of Nikolai's finger. Johnny took it and rubbed the gunk off his face. They'd made it.

"Well, here's a spot o' good luck," Kleiner said, looking over all the lads standing in his subterranean headquarters. Carrie and her team were walking between them, offering water and towels.

Johnny looked at the comm phone that Colonel Bradshaw had given him. He clicked it on and spoke into it. "Hello?" No response.

"Best to be keepin' dat," Kleiner said. "Mr. Bradshaw's always had his ways."

Cottard walked among the pledges. "Seventy-nine … 80 kids." He jotted the number down onto a clipboard. He started grabbing the bags off the boys' shoulders and taking inventory of their equipment, devoid of expression or eye contact as he did so.

"Where the hell have y'all been?" Johnny asked Cottard.

"Where y'all been? Tarnation!" Cottard mimicked. He flicked some mud off Johnny's ear, then jotted down a number.

Johnny reddened. He grabbed Cottard by the arm and walked him away from the group. "The hell is wrong with you? I'm running this show now. Show some damn respect in front of these kids."

Cottard looked past Johnny to a group of pledges who were slowly starting to notice their conversation.

"Kids, huh? And what are you planning on using these kids for?"

"I'm not using them. I'm going to tell them what is actually going on and then give them a choice to join."

"Oh, because you know what the hell is actually going on?"

"Like it or not, they're adults now. We'll let them be responsible for themselves."

"Sure. Fine. Whatever. Knock 'em dead with that southern charm of yours," Cottard said. He walked over to a nervous pledge and yanked the kid's bag off his shoulder. "Inventory," he said blankly.

Johnny turned to the boys, who looked back at him with a mixture of awe and confusion. "I am the leader of the IRA." Some gasped, others exchanged glances. Cottard held up a finger, shushing them from anything they might say.

"It's our mission to cure the sickness that's overtaken this city," Johnny said. "A sickness that's held us down for too long! And it's lookin' like it's the everyday people of New San Francisco who caught the bug! At first it was just them, rippin' us down. The guard and the Inner Circle schemin', just seein' what the heck else they could make a profit on. Now that they've taken everythin' they're comin' to cash our very souls! They're trying to make us hate ourselves so much, we just roll up into a ball and shut up!"

He paused, letting his words sink in. "Now look. You've all got a choice. You can assume the futile position like they want, or you can stand and fight 'em instead. One way or the other, y'all be livin' in this city for the rest of your lives. It is up to you how you want to live in this city and what your place here'll be. So if you do go and decide to join us, then it's gonna get rough but at least you'll get to know what it is to be a real man. Now keep in mind a real man isn't just someone who can fight for profit, but who is someone who can fight for values. When you know you're not just goin' and doing the bidding of some rich old ass, but fighting fuh your own people. If you don't join, well … then life's still gonna be hard, but there's a good chance you'll never get anotha opportunity to gain some real pride in yourself." Johnny paused. "And eventually you'll die with no story to tell about your life, because all you did is what the others did—give up and be nothin'."

Johnny stared over the groups of boys. They looked back at him in silence.

"Whoever isn't with us, line up in front of me. You can go back to Edingburg and go do whatever it is you're gonna do with the rest of your life."

Not a single boy moved. Johnny looked around, trying his best not to show his surprise. Every pledge simply stood straight with hands by their sides and wide eyes.

Johnny turned to Kleiner. "We're going to need everything around here that pops real loud'n bright."

"Well, we're pretty short on the militarized stuff. But we've got us some flares, some flash bangs, smoke bombs, even some firecrackers we'd, uh, smuggled in fer tha holidays."

"Perfect, we'll take all that."

A moment later Kleiner, Carrie, and a few others walked back into the large room with rows of gurneys stacked with nonlethal ordnance. Johnny picked up a flare gun and turned to the boys.

"All right then, load up on these," Johnny said, pointing to the heaps of firecrackers and other assorted noisemakers. The boys ran toward the gurneys and began stuffing them into their pockets and hanging them over their necks.

Johnny began pacing around the boys. "We're going to raise one big, loud, and convincingly enormous invasion upon the wall these corporations put up around Edingburg's perimeter. We'll make the guard think we're big enough to blow a hole into the walls and create all kinds of havoc for them. The City Guard will have to redeploy many of their men to stop us. That'll get our boys inside Edingburg a window of opportunity to claim our real target. The mobile radio station."

"These kids are screwed." Cottard muttered.

Johnny walked over to Cottard. "Well, it's their choice, isn't it?" Johnny asked.

"Choice," Cottard snorted. "I've come to the conclusion that life is worth living. That's why I'm here. Not because someone gave me some bullshit choice."

Day Break Radio

Broadcast #7210

Good evening, Edingburg. Line, here to give you the latest and last update on Edingburg, a city under IRA occupation! I am joining you LIVE from INSIDE the occupation zone! That's right. We are in the fray for the first time, because we want YOU to get the inside scoop.

Let's begin.

We're only a couple hours in, but it seems Colonel Bradshaw, commander and CEO of Hell on Wheels Inc., has gone for an all-out blitz on the IRA! The death toll is already over the 1,000 mark! We've never hit that number so fast in an uprising. Not by a mile! Third party City Guard contractors are reporting that it's a struggle just to keep up with tagging the bodies and reporting them to the Inner Circle.

I know this all sounds intense, but hey, at least the uprising will be over sooner, which if you ask me is the real win here. Let's just get it done.

And Colonel Bradshaw's rather extreme tactics do seem to be working. He has gained ground in strategic locations. But word on the street says he's gotten the bad end of the stick when it comes to supplies, so I wouldn't be surprised if he runs out of steam—this means Ghost Fox may end up taking the biggest payday. But hey, that's what I'm talking about. The beauty of privatization. Competition keeps our city chugging even the darkest of times. Instead of one big fat army getting tired, allowing the IRA to regroup and strike back, New San Francisco has hundreds of small businesses ready to prove themselves and earn Inner Circle contracts at any moment. Because of the privatization of our armed forces, we have a military that never sleeps! So sleep tight, IRA, it's gonna be a long night!

Hanging by a Wire

A raven perched between the blades of the razor wire. Two rows of chain-link fencing ran for miles in either direction. Small pillboxes stood in the no-man zone between the fences. Lonely gusts of wind brought over whispers of mortar and gunfire from Edingburg. Small groups of figures rushed between apartment buildings on the outside of the walled perimeter. The raven cawed, flapped upward, and began to circle.

Johnny walked through the blown-out sheetrock walls of the apartment complex. Through the gaping holes he passed from living room, to kitchen, to bedroom, to living room, to kitchen, to bedroom, to living room again. He watched his cyclers unload their nonlethals in groups of two or three, making sure to keep their heads bowed beneath the windowsill.

"Keep it spread out, boys," Johnny murmured. "Throw the smoke bombs first. Let the smoke grow, then start throwing flash bangs and firecrackers. Start it strong at first, but make sure we've got enough to keep this going for at least 20 minutes." He stood up and walked through a hole in the wall to check on another unit. "Space out your ordnance as best you can! We gotta give them as much time as possible."

Johnny came to the end of the apartment complex, where he found Carrie leaning against a wall with her arms crossed, an AK-47 propped up next to her. Cottard was aiming his ungodly .50-caliber sniper rifle out the window.

Johnny looked at the AK-47 leaning on the wall next to Carrie. "A machine gun? Really? We're just keeping them back for a while."

"Hopin' the best for ya little plan, Mr. McHenry. Just prepared' fo' tha worst is all."

"Only shoot if I order it," Johnny said to Cottard. "We don't want our boys being part of an unnecessary murder. It's not good for them or our cause."

Cottard grunted.

Johnny turned and hurried back through the guts of the eviscerated building, peering between rooms, making sure all the boys were ready. They looked back at him crouched beneath or beside the windows facing the razor-wired fences and pillboxes outside.

Johnny watched one of the boys' hands tremble. The clump of fireworks in his hand clattered like shivering teeth.

Johnny took a breath. He brought a whistle to his lips and closed his eyes. He heard a raven caw in the sky. He blew the whistle. The cyclers threw smoke; many began yelling, cursing, shouting at the guards in the posts. Smoke clouds banged upward.

Long barrels slid out from the pillbox slits. Bullets slammed into the brick walls of the apartment complex. Ramfort's rifle boomed, sending up small explosions of pulverized concrete as he fired on the pillboxes.

Johnny picked up the comm phone he'd gotten from Colonel Bradshaw and tried again for an answer.

Before the Radio Station Attack

The old van rattled down the highway. Jombo poked his head out between a pair of sunflowers in the back. The three of them watched the exit onto 24th as it slowly drew closer. Steve glanced down at his arms, waiting for them to move the wheel. He looked over at Ramfort, who nodded. The sign was growing taller over them; they were close. It was time.

"Fudge it," Ramfort said. "Let's just get in there, play your damn cassette, and get the fudge outta there before you get me shot or crash my little beauty." Ramfort lovingly rubbed the van's melted plastic dashboard. He closed his eyes and took a breath. Then he started beating his chest and humming a tune. "Let's dooooo iiiitttttt!"

Ramfort rolled down the crusted passenger-side window and slapped a big purple transport sticker on the windshield. "Wooooooo! We're going to do it! Steve might get us all killed, but we're doing iiiiiitt!"

With a jolt of panic, Steve looked down to see his arms turning the van onto the exit.

A salvo of mortars detonated, tearing at a row of brick mid-rises. A rush of Reds emerged from the crumbling buildings and scattered for better cover.

The purple van slammed to a halt in the middle of an intersection. Brick rubble tumbled all around them.

"Who the hell are you?!" an officer in red shouted at Steve.

Ramfort jammed his face past Steve's. "The fighting 92nd!

Mounted convoy! We've got orders to take that radio station!"

"Radio station?" A spray of bullets ricocheted over the pavement. The officer took cover by pressing himself against the van. He looked over at Ramfort, whose head was sticking out the driver's side window.

"Hey, you're definitely not 21!" the officer shouted. "Who the fuck are you?!"

"Well neither are you, ya old fart! Who are you?!"

They glared at each other.

"I'm Major Jetter! Part of Bradshaw's Hell on Wheels! Officially we're guardsmen on assignment to lead a bunch of Red Phoenix Cyclers to victory!" He knocked on his helmet. "So that makes me the commander of a platoon of stupid little bastards! Now who the fuck are you?!"

A townhouse erupted, sending out clouds of bricks that thumped down onto the van's roof.

"Well, I'm the tank commander," Ramfort shouted. "Here's my Sherman!" He slapped the outside of the door, then pointed forward. "We've got orders to take that radio station!"

Jetter looked through a small alleyway between the rows of five-story buildings. "No fucking way! That's protected by the Department of Smoke! It's off limits!"

"Colonel Bradshaw's orders!"

"Bradshaw's orders, huh? He making a play?"

Jetter waved over a cycler who was lying beneath a car. As the boy ran over, he and Steve locked eyes. It was Yoden, from Kleiner's bar.

"So you're a Red too, huh?"

"Looks like it," Steve said.

"Pledge! Take a look in the back," Jetter barked.

Ramfort jumped out of the van. "The hell you mean take a look in the back? I am the commander of this here division." Ramfort pointed at the van that had pulled up behind them.

"You wanna go and get the Department of Smoke's muscle blowing up our asses too? They only hire the best in the business!" Jetter yelled. "You're answering to me! I don't give a shit what half-cooked idea Bradshaw's got! It's his fucking fault I'm even here!"

Jetter swung open the side door of the van. The inside was packed so tightly that large branches of flowers plumed out of the opening, their leaves gasping for breath.

"We are attacking that station!" Ramfort yelled. Jetter rammed the butt of his rifle into Ramfort's face, and stood over the fallen man.

"We've got a division of Blue Ghost Fox's almost twice our size heading right fucking for us. Let alone whatever the IRA's doing! We've already got more shit coming our way than we can handle! Now I am commandeering whatever the fuck you've got in these vans to help kill these fucking Blues!"

"Gah, fine," Ramfort said, speaking into Jetter's barrel. "Come on out, Dave."

The Samoan emerged from the thicket of flowers and stepped out of the van. The Samoan towered over the major and was easily twice as wide. His muscles bulged out from his white wife beater.

"What the hell is this!" Jetter shouted.

"This is Dave," Ramfort answered.

"Dave, huh." Jetter tilted his head up. "You got ID, Dave?"

Jombo took out an ID badge from the left pocket of his jeans and handed it to the major. Jetter studied the ID.

"Get in that van, pledge," Jetter said. "Check those pots. Find me something we need."

Yoden looked into the open side door. He took out a long knife and began stabbing the soil in the flowerpots. He twirled the dirt around and unearthed roots from the flowers.

Ramfort saw the look at Jombo's face and panicked. "Hey, that'll kill the plants if you chop them up at the root like that!"

"Why the fuck would we care," Jetter muttered, still studying the ID.

Yoden pushed himself into the van, then cursed as branches pressed against his face and thorns pricked his skin. He started stabbing wildly as he thrashed around the van.

"Just a bunch of flowers sir," Yoden said. He wiped his blade onto his pant leg, cleaning off the green blood of the plants. Yoden looked out at the Samoan, whose face had contorted into a look of sheer pain.

"What?" Major Jetter asked. He looked down at Ramfort, whose hands were sandwiching his head.

Jombo reached into the van and picked up a particularly mangled rosebush. The pot that held it was enormous; it must have weighed around 200 pounds. Jombo sat down on the pavement and cradled the flowerpot like an injured loved one.

"You're just a caravan of loons!" Jetter pointed at Yoden with "Dave's" ID. "Check the second van."

"Hold on, new idea!" Ramfort said.

Jetter pushed the muzzle of his gun against Ramfort's forehead. "Please, tell me your new idea."

"Um, we should totally … attack the radio station?"

"Goddamn it, I'm relieving you of command," Major Jetter said, cocking his rifle.

The building behind them erupted with another volley of mortars. Ramfort grabbed the barrel of Jetter's rifle and yanked it to the side as the major fired into the pavement. Ramfort sprang upward, slammed a metal button at the bottom of his palm into the major's temple, and watched him drop to the ground. "My caravan!" he shouted.

Yoden raised his rifle toward Ramfort. Jombo grabbed the end of Yoden's gun and slung Yoden across the intersection.

Ramfort looked up at the groups of cyclers staring at him through windows and doorsills. "I am Commander Ramfort of the fightin' 94th! You are all now part of my platoon!" He held up Major Jetter's rifle and emptied a magazine of bullets into the sky. "My platoon!"

Ramfort looked around for a reaction. Not a single rifle raised from Red Team in disagreement. "Good," he said. "I'm gonna make a speech." He smiled at Steve. "Check this out."

He sauntered to the middle of the intersection. "Wake and listen, you who are lonely! From the future come quiet winds that can only be heard with delicate ears! Good tidings are to come! You who are lonely today, you who are withdrawing, you who are … crapping your pants. You shall one day be the people of this city; out of you and out of your children to come, there shall grow a chosen people, and out of them, the over-man.

"Soon the earth shall become a site of recovery. And even now a new fragrance surrounds it, bringing salvation—and a new hope! From sunrise we have waited and planned, we have remained silent and counted the years of toil and wait with the lines on our foreheads.

"We have not given up on our virtue! We cannot. Or else we will truly lose the light whose warmth we've never had the opportunity to feel. But today, on this day, we finally have the chance to move closer to that light. And we must seize it. And so today our nightmare finally begins! We will not falter—we will fight! We will slay the devil that has suppressed us within the flames of his own hell!" Ramfort gazed over the ravaged buildings. "From the ashes, our dream begins."

The wind stilled. The pledges stared with soft, self-reflective eyes.

Then a pair of footsteps.

From down the street a lone Red cycler ran toward Ramfort. "Sir —" the cycler panted for breath— "are you in charge of fifth platoon?"

Ramfort looked around at the cyclers in the windows. A slight nod came from a few heads.

"Yep," Ramfort said.

"Oh, thank Anthony!" The pledge dropped his rucksack to the

ground and rummaged through it. He took out a large comm phone. "For you, sir. From Colonel Bradshaw."

"Bradshaw?" Ramfort asked. "What's he want?"

The boy slung his rucksack back on. "No idea." He turned on the comm phone; it gave a wail so sharp it chipped at the bricks of the buildings as the soundwave bounced off and around. He gave it to Ramfort and started running back the direction from which he'd come.

"Hello?" came a voice from the comm phone in Ramfort's hand.

Ramfort held the phone up to his face. "*Hello?* What kind of colonel says hello over a comm? Who's this?"

"Is this the commander of fifth platoon?"

"Yeah," Ramfort said. "What do you want, guy?"

"I need your confirmation code first."

Ramfort rolled his eyes. He bent down and rummaged through Major Jetter's pockets. "Yeah, totally, it's 289-347."

"Great. Have you received Colonel Bradshaw's orders regarding the merger?"

"Indeed I have," Ramfort said, glancing back at Steve in the van.

"And are you going to carry out the orders regarding the radio station?"

"Oh, yeah. I'm totally in, all the way, guy."

"All right, good. We have begun attacking the perimeter wall. That should be diverting at least part of the guard from that position. Colonel Bradshaw has also reinforced your flank a mile north, which should slow Ghost Fox down."

"Hmm." Ramfort lifted Major Jetter's head and pulled the pair of binoculars off his neck. He peered through the lenses toward the radio station. Some of the Department of Smoke's silver APCs were indeed leaving.

"Cool. So. Who are you?" Ramfort asked.

There was a pause on the other end. "Are you with us? Are you with the IRA?"

"Pffft, I put the RA in IRA," Ramfort said.

"Good. I am the new leader of the IRA. Johnny McHenry."

"What?!" Ramfort shouted. "Johnny!" Ramfort threw the comm phone; the strand attaching the phone to his arm swung it back at him. Ramfort grabbed at the dangling phone. "You? Why you? You suck! No, this is a stupid idea. I've told you for the last time, we can't go through with this insane radio station plan. So you've bamboozled a few city guards, so what? We've still got a division of Blue Ghost Fox twice our size coming right for us, you twat! We can't do it! How many times do I have to tell you that!"

The comm phone went silent. Steve honked the horn. "Let's go, pussy!"

Ramfort stood awestruck. "Pussy?" Ramfort marched over to the van. "Didn't you hear? He held up the phone. "Johnny. JOHNNY is running the IRA."

"I don't give a shit." Steve pointed at the radio station. "I care about that."

Ramfort's cheeks twitched. He looked back at the radio station.

Another volley of bullets sprayed over the streets. He walked a few paces toward the station, then held up the comm phone. "Hey, douchebag."

"Yeah?" Johnny grunted.

"We're doing it."

"Good."

"You'd better do your best to fudge this up as little as possible, douchebag."

The side door of the second van quietly slid open. Steve turned and watched in shock as Melody delicately stepped out of the van. She met Steve's eyes and stopped.

"Damn, bro," Yoden said, gripping his rifle. "There's a real hot chick in here!"

Steve got out of the van and walked back to her. She was wearing high-cut, form-fitting, and vibrantly blue dress. She stared up at him for a moment, then her head shot down. She turned toward a front door with a bricked stepped stoop and gently pushed the front door open. She looked back at him, her eyes beckoning for him to follow.

In a rather Victorian and slightly bullet-ridden living room, Melody and Steve sat on a couch with ornate floral upholstery. Beyond the balcony they had a perfect view of the radio station and the teams of City Guardsmen fortifying it.

The radio station was essentially a robotic transformer that'd clearly been hauled in by the 18-wheeler parked next to it. It had unfolded into a two-story structure that looked like a flat-topped pyramid standing on top of a bigger flat-topped pyramid. A 40-foot antenna rose from the top. Long narrow windows on the second floor reflected the sunlight. Silver guards huddled in front of the station's large metal double doors, standing behind their APCs and gun turrets. They unknowingly faced toward Steve and Melody, who sat in their well-shaded living room. Around the rest of the structure was a perimeter of stacked and demagnetized supply crates that were being used as a makeshift rampart.

"Why are you here?" Steve asked.

Melody pointed at the radio station. "You have the cassette, yes?"

Steve nodded. "Is this really going to work?" he asked. "People hear a thousand different messages a day. How is this one really going to make a difference?"

"Because it's better and it won't be alone. Everything we heard before is improvised on the spot. There's no depth or greatness to those messages. The state just bombards people on the same principle of cheap mass production. An unending narrative of self-interest that nearly no single individual can break from and be able to create their own. And if he did it'd fall on deaf or lost ears."

Melody glanced down at Steve's blood band. "The General's media goons write a narrative that keeps anyone from coming together. So even if people do despise the world his narrative creates, no one can generate the collective will needed to break free of this world. We're all trained in some capacity to follow these self-poisoning norms. Without using any of them, people wouldn't know what to do. What's on that cassette will create a new narrative, about a new life with different norms of thinking. And like all great works it will be replicated and adopted no matter how many cheap status updates they shoot at us.

"But know that this is only our first public move. The first of many. To create a new world we to take our seedling at let it seize its chance. Even a hundred seeds in the jungle can't grow if there's no light hitting the ground. Today we can finally plant it. Today, we will burn a hole in their media and do it at a time of great turmoil for many. From there, our seedling can grow."

Steve stared through the window at the ominous guns, turrets, and men standing guard a few hundred yards away. "We could die," he said.

Melody touched his shoulder. "I remember my first time," she said. "The person I loved most in the world was there with me. So it wasn't so bad. When you're pursuing the lives you've always wanted, how long you have left isn't what matters. All that matters is that you don't stop."

Fighting for Show

Johnny stared at his comm phone. He heard the click of the signal being turned off on the other end. The apartment complex shook under another explosion. The City Guard was getting more aggressive. They had turned on floodlights as dusk began to approach.

A cycler ran up to Johnny. "Sir, there's some Reds are on the other side of the fence!" Another cycler was waving at them while holding up a flag that had the Irish and Scottish flags stitched together.

Johnny crept to the wall and peered over the windowsill. He saw about 30 Red cyclers creeping up behind the guard's outposts on the other side of the fence. One of them was waving back at Johnny. Holding a company flag of Hell on Wheels with a large X painted over it.

"They must've gotten Bradshaw's message," Carrie said. "They want in."

Three Red cyclers popped up behind the guard towers wielding RPG launchers.

"Shit," Johnny said. "Get down!"

Three RPGs fired as one. A trail of smoke followed the wild paths of the rockets. Two of the guard's watchtowers exploded. The third rocket cut through the first wire fence, slumping down the chain link and contorting the razor wire into a mangled slinky.

"They're calling to us!" a cycler shouted. "I think they want us to cover them!"

Multiple City Guard contractor convoys zoomed toward the downed section of the fence. The diversion had worked, waves of smaller contractor groups all sporting their own color combinations had come to reinforce the perimeter wall. Nearly none were from corporate.

"Shit," Johnny said. "Throw everything but the flash bangs! Use up the bullets! Just cover those kids!"

Hundreds of firecrackers and dozens of smoke bombs flew out of windows, sending up a smokescreen so thick it seemed near solid. The Red cyclers below threw bed sheets over the razor wire and started crawling over the undamaged fencing. Cottard's rifle boomed, exploding the engines of the contractor's vehicles one by one. The guards responded with an overpowering surge of lead on the apartment complex. Cyclers screamed as the hails of bullets flew through the windows and chipped away at the layers of brick separating them from a hole-ridden death.

"I don't think the firecrackers are scaring them, sir!" a cycler shouted.

Johnny crawled to a bullet hole in the wall and looked through it with a small eyepiece. A pure silver APC pulled up behind the group of escaping Red cyclers. He watched the gunner on top of the truck open fire with his machine gun. There were screams, then silence.

The smokescreen parted. The man on top of the APC turret was looking directly at Johnny. It was the General. He grinned and waved.

Cottard ran into the room. "We're falling back!" he shouted. "Now! We've got three minutes before they come in here and maybe five before the storm hits!" The cyclers started running for the exits. He glared down at Johnny. "Was this part of the plan too? Whose side are you on?"

Outside, the raven swooped into the cloud of smoke and landed on the blood-soaked wire.

What Was Done

Journal Entry #125

When I was eight I had a friend named Jeffrey. I wanted so badly to help him realize his boyhood dream of climbing the biggest tree in the forest. It was hard for him though, seeing as he was blind.

So I did what any eight-year-old would do. I guided him up. With my voice and instruction he pushed himself higher and higher up the branches. We climbed so incredibly high that we entered a low fog. In the fog I could no longer see him, but I did my best to lead him higher. I was so proud of him and of me.

Which makes the moment when I heard the thump of his body hitting the ground so devastating.

He'd never climb again. Many said he was lucky to survive such a fall, though deafness, and then muteness, were added to his disabilities.

To this day I don't know if he was ever mad at me. He would just sit there, completely unaware of me sitting across from him at lunch every day in the cafeteria.

I never left his side, but I never could reach him either. The thought of abandoning him sickened me. But the idea of jolting him from his thoughts always paralyzed me with guilt.

So I hovered. Never so far that I'd lose him, but never too close, so he wouldn't know I was there. I'd turned myself into some form of guilt-ridden guardian. But I couldn't protect him from the cough. Less than a year later, it got him. We buried him in a field.

Ten years later I took an ax and cut that fucking tree down to the root.

Between a Rock and a Radio Station

Ramfort peered through his binoculars toward the east. The nightly storm was spreading over the sky. He lowered the binoculars and looked over the cyclers hugging the brick buildings for cover. Few could muster the strength to look back at him. Ramfort walked over to the van, opened the door, and yanked Steve out.

"Hey what the hell!" Steve said.

"I'm driving, you're staying with these pussies."

"What? No, I'm coming!"

"You'd better come! But you'll need to bring these kids with you!"

Ramfort looked through the alley between the row of buildings at the 300 yards of no-man's land that stretched before the station. "I'm going to ram those buttheads if I have to. That'll at least help get these pussies moving. We'll hit 'em seconds before the main clouds come so we've got some cover."

"But we don't have gas masks," Steve said. "If we don't make it in the station we're screwed! We can't breathe in this crap all night!"

"Well, then I guess you've all got some extra incentive to make it to the station, huh?"

Ramfort looked at Yoden. "Can you drive?"

"No, bro," Yoden replied.

"Broooo," Ramfort grumbled. "Hmm." Ramfort pointed. "You! Kid with the gun." All the cyclers turned their heads. "You! Yeah, you," Ramfort said, pointing a finger as he walked toward his intended target.

"The one in the red. Can you drive?"

"Um, I have once or twice."

"Good," Ramfort said. "Perfect credentials! You're hired." He grabbed the cycler by the back of the collar and brought him to the van. "In," Ramfort said. The cycler climbed in behind the wheel while Ramfort got in the passenger side.

"What's your name?"

"Mike," the boy responded.

Ramfort winced slightly. "Great name."

The cycler looked at him blankly. "Thank you, sir."

Ramfort turned to the back of the van. "You set back there?" he asked Jombo, who responded with a single grunt.

"He's good," Ramfort assured Mike. Ramfort reached under the seat and brought out a duffel bag. He unzipped the bag and took out a welder's mask. He put it on his head, leveling the shield above his face. "Alrighty then, Mike." He pointed to the radio station. "That way."

Mike's eyes widened. "Really?"

"Yes, Mike, really. Now pull up through the alley."

Ramfort lowered the windows as the van lurched toward the alley. "We will draw their fire," he shouted at the lines of cyclers to either side of him. "The second they start shooting at us, you must all charge as one and take the radio station! And whoever's driving my second van, you will follow them! That cargo you've got in the back is super vital! It needs to get to the station! It's like life or death or something."

The cyclers stared blankly at Ramfort, who looked them over and nodded. "Good. Everyone's on board." He leaned back in his seat and pushed in a cassette. "Surfin' Bird" by the Trashmen began to play. He wafted his hand. "Go."

Mike squinted into the setting sun as the van rumbled through the alleyway. They quaked in their seats as the van began to pick up speed, bumping wildly over every little imperfection in the asphalt. The City Guard began to take notice of a poorly maintained van on the horizon with a light spray of colored debris trailing from its back. Guns immediately jolted over their jeeps.

"Shit," Ramfort decreed. "Uh, keep going!"

"Do we really have to do this?" Mike screeched, his knuckles as white as a surrender flag.

"Shit, just keep going. Ah, shit. Shit, shit, shit! Keep going!"

Ramfort slammed down the welding mask to cover his face and sunk into his seat beneath the dashboard. "You should lean down," Ramfort advised, his voice muffled by the mask.

"Oh my god!" Mike bellowed. "I can't see! The sun's in my eyes!"

"Just chill out and get low!"

In that moment the sun dropped beneath the skyline. The blinding veil of light lifted. Mike could see. He shut his eyes for the upcoming revelation.

A barrage of bullets pummeled through the front window, lighting up the van in sparks and electrical shorts. Mike jolted in sporadic shocks as arrows of lead tore into his body.

The van hit a pothole and Mike's lifeless body fell onto the driver's side door, turning the wheel. The van veered left, spinning the van wildly like a dying beast. Black smoke poured out from its hood and through the shattered windshield. The van struck a lone lamppost and went still, its horn feebly whimpering.

Steve stood in front a phalanx of some 200 cyclers pressed into the alleyway. "Let's go, dammit!" he shouted. "This is our only chance!"

No one budged. "Bro, they shot him down just like that," Yoden said. "You saw that shit. We don't have a chance out there."

"We don't have a chance out here!" Steve said. "The storm's coming! We need a sealed building; the station's the only spot."

"I've made it through a night without a sealed building!" a cycler shouted.

"Yeah, bro, I'll take my chances," Yoden said.

Steve looked over at the smoldering van. Four silver jeeps were rolling toward it to ensure they'd successfully put it down.

Ramfort came to staring at the ceiling of the van. Smoke was pouring in from the pulverized engine. The screams from the horn died away as it ran out of breath. The entire front end of the van was blanketed in shards of glass. Ramfort's welding mask was riddled with dents from the barrage of bullets; the thick steel had saved him.

Ramfort looked down. Half his body was jammed under the dashboard. He scrambled to free himself, the glass cracking and popping under his frantic hands. His hand grabbed up at the rearview mirror, gave one last push, and with a long defiant scream he surged backward onto his seat. He lurched over the passenger windowsill to escape the smoke's chokehold. As he wheezed, he saw the silver jeeps moving in on him.

"Jombo, you alive back there?!" he asked.

The jeeps stopped, and soldiers poured out from every opening. They formed up and made a line with their shields. A man in a spotless officer's uniform walked forward wielding a silver megaphone. The officer slowly raised the megaphone to his face. "It appears you have run off course," he announced in his familiar irritatingly proper voice. "We did not order any flowers, but I thank you for thinking of me on my big promotion day."

Officer Crause looked over the smoldering van. No response. "You are clearly quite desperate. Othervise, you wouldn't be anyvhere near here."

Ramfort sat hunched over the passenger side door, looking at the officer through the cloud of smoke. "Ugh, this guy again," he grunted. It was Officer Crause, in his brand new silver-encrusted uniform.

"Sellout!" Ramfort shouted.

"Ahhh! It's you! Nothing wrong with a merger, Mr. Lustig. Good way to grow the business. I'm a Smoker now! He tapped the Department of Smoke emblem on his uniform and brought a fat cigarette to his lips. "And you? You seem rather bankrupt! Too weak to accept the fate you yourself have chosen! You are not strong enough to survive your own choices, so now you will burn in zem."

Jombo growled in a frustrated rage. The van began to shake as he threw flowerpots about.

"Merger, huh? I'll give you a merger!" Ramfort shouted.

"You will come out slowly and drop to your knees! Do this, oont we will help you realize the outcome of your actions in a clean and dignified manner!"

The van quaked as he sound of screeching pots reached a climax.

Crause watched the van shake. "In the name of God Almighty you will come out of that damn van! Or you can just stay in there and burn! Accept your fate and pay for the sins you chose to commit!"

A long sustained dissent bellowed from the back of the van.

Crause's silver megaphone clicked and went silent. Dusk had come. He signaled the jeeps to shine their spotlights on the van. Ramfort squinted in the glare of the bright lights. The whine of a spinning metal crept into Ramfort's ears from the back of the van.

The sliding side door of the van cranked open; smoke spilled out and pooled into a low-lying fog. Jombo's enormous frame materialized from the darkness wielding a M134 Gatling gun. The gun barrels spiraled, accelerating themselves into a whirlwind. A frenzy of bullets engulfed the patrol in lead. The jeeps were chewed up in seconds. Officer Crause's balance sheet was wiped clean.

Jombo stepped forward into full view of the spotlights. He was armored from head to toe in what seemed to be parts of beige ceramic flowerpots. The remainder of the patrol plugged round after round into his armor. The ceramic cracked and splintered, revealing a plate of iron beneath them. The guard's magazines emptied as Jombo continued his merciless spray of lead. Waves of heat from the Gatling gun wavered under the intense brightness of the spotlights; the smell of gasoline from its turbine filled the air. Jombo passed the small troop of guards and marched toward the radio station.

A volley of gunfire cracked from the main company of the Silvers. The cyclers watched Jombo recoil under the pounding of bullets. The M134 continued to whirl. The first winds from the coming storm began throwing dirt and ash into the air. Shouts from the City Guard's main company rose again as three RPG teams emerged.

A distinct order of "Fire!" rang from the company. Jombo roared. The storm shook the earth. Dust shot into the air as if an entire mine field had been triggered.

Three missiles launched forward. The vortex of barrels unleashed a hail of lead at the incoming rockets while the storm engulfed Jombo in a veil of ash and dust. Three explosions.

The cyclers watched in bewildered awe as Jombo's enlarged shadow become a projection onto a canvas of ash lit by the guard's enormous fog lights. Traces of red light followed every round from the M134.

"Fire!"

A fourth RPG swooped in and exploded. The red beam of light vanished; the gunfire ceased. The screen of ash went blank. Steve and the cyclers watched in silence.

Then movement. The shadow of a struggling figure came onto the screen, its image flickering in and out of existence as the floodlights illuminated the swirling ash. Jombo's shadow hunched over as he tried to regain his strength. Then he shrieked in pain and dropped back down off the screen. The men could still hear his struggled panting.

"I … I … I," Jombo panted. He seemed to be holding back tears. Then he gasped. "I can't." His panting accelerated. "I can't!" he bellowed. The long black line cast by the M-134 slowly rose upward. "I can't." His panting became faster, maniacal.

"I … CAN'T … STOP!"

Steve's jaw dropped. Jombo's shadow gripped the black line and jerked himself back onto the screen of illuminated ash. He screamed as he pulled himself up. The barrels of Jombo's gun began to spin and again a stream of whirling lead fired toward the guard.

A gust of wind revealed a man standing on top of a mangled purple van. A battered welder's mask covered his face. The cyclers stared at the masked man. "Charge the damn station, you pussies!" the man's muffled voice shouted.

Steve sprinted forward. Two hundred cyclers charged after him. The coming tsunami of the main storm clipped at their heels as it engulfed the world at their backs in blackness as they charged screaming into the oblivion ahead.

Killed via Kindness

"They all died because of you," Cottard said. He stood over Johnny, who sat against a blue wall. "That's what happens when *you* make them choose."

Johnny stared at the floor. They were back in Kleiner's subterranean headquarters. The surviving cyclers sat or lay on the floor, their eyes lost in the horrors that had begun burrowing into their long-term memory.

Nikolai walked up to Johnny and Cottard. "Reports say Red Team has taken ze radio station."

Johnny looked up. "Can we reach them?"

"No. The station hardvare is not strong enough to penetrate ze cloud. Ze storm must pass first."

Johnny stood up. "Are the receivers for the radio station still online?"

"Two of zem are. One is now down, but zat may be due to storm and fixable by morning. I don't think Inner Circle knows the station is taken. Ramfort take station right when ze clouds come in, so no one could radio out and send out distressful beacon to rest of ze guard. Ramfort perform good timing on zat."

"Ramfort? That was Ramfort who did that?" Johnny asked.

"Yes, he led the charge on the guard. Agents say they fight against Department of Smoke's special forces. So heavy losses. But ze station's still standing. So when ze storm clears and they turn on radio for compulsory radio spot vith Mr. Line, IRA will instead be filling the time slot."

"Good." Johnny glanced over at Cottard. "So with two receivers the signal will still get out to everyone?"

"Should be fine," Nikolai said. "If heard by most people, zen ze message should still spread and have much effect, but if vee lose more receiver, then that'd be not so good."

"When they find out it's not Line talking, the Smoker's Guard could shut off the receivers halfway through the show," Cottard said.

"Then we need to secure two of those receivers come sunrise," Johnny said. "But these kids need a break."

Cottard looked over the traumatized cyclers. "Yeah."

"We have many operatives in ze war zone. Could be possible for them to take ze receivers. We have given zem good gas mask so they can keep mobile in ze storm."

"What? Well how many do we have?" Johnny asked.

"Dozen, maybe."

"Storm or not, the Department of Smoke's guys will be out there. So no way a dozen guys can go out there, take over, and hold even one receiver by sunrise!"

Cottard begrudgingly nodded.

"Could we … can we just have a team of four to six set up around each receiver by sunrise?"

"Yes, we have comm room higher up and avay from here," Nikolai said. "Will only work for short range during storm. "Had to keep away from this secure place in case of signal trackings. Can communicate vith some up there."

"Alright, Cottard, that's where we need to go. Right when the radio station clicks on for the morning announcements, our guys start shooting. Tell them to keep the Smokers too busy to be answering any calls they might get."

"Good. More distractions," Cottard said. "Those clearly don't have any side effects."

"Just keep them pinned down," Johnny said. "Just distract them for a bit. No need to take chances by actually hitting any of them."

Cottard rolled his eyes. "I'll be sure to make it perfectly clear that it is advisable to miss the enemy."

A Muddy Mask

A banging echoed through the tunnels leading up to the comm room.

Men shouted; the clamor of feet followed. Johnny glanced over at Cottard, who was manning the radio in the gloom. Cottard's fingers twisted and turned, searching for a signal to transmit on.

Johnny snapped at Cottard to get his attention and fixed his eyes on the hallway door. The shouts coming toward them became distinguishable.

"Don't move! Don't bloody try it!" Something battered the door, which stretched to near its breaking point and slung back. Johnny broke into a cold sweat. Cottard spun his chair around. A wallop collided with the door and beheaded the tops of the door's bolts. The door crashed down.

Franz and Gordon dragged in a City Guardsman who was covered in a thick plating of mud from his feet to his gas mask. Johnny wrinkled his nose at the shit-infused vapors the guard was carrying with him.

Franz grabbed a small metallic chair and slung it into the middle of the room. The chair gleamed under a pair of fluorescent tube lights that were being held up by a fraying power cord. The fluorescent bulbs were the only working source of light left. Gordon shoved the guard down onto the chair, which squeaked under the sudden pressure. Franz took a length of rope from his shoulder and strapped the guardsman to the chair.

"Who is that, and why the hell did you bring him here?!" Johnny asked.

Gordon wiped some muck off his face and smiled. "We were looking across the line and we saw a building collapse in the distance. So we investigated, hoping to come to a discovery that Mr. Bradshaw may enjoy."

"The colonel? Why the hell are you helping him? And he's dead!"

"Oh how offensive, John. Just because someone is dead doesn't mean he's gone?" Gordon said.

"Look at him!" Franz exclaimed. "We found him cramming himself halfway into a manhole before we pulled him out. He's found the tunnels. Who knows how long he's been slopping around in them! Who knows what he knows!"

Johnny glared at the guard. "Where—"

"Slow down on the questions, child," Gordon murmured into Johnny's ear. "We put him through quite the questionnaire before bringing him to you. Most stubborn Yank we've ever come across."

"Then what makes you think I can get him to talk?"

"I have a feeling he'll only talk to you. Take care, child. We really didn't want to do this but we're running out of options. That we found him mucking through God knows what makes me wonder how safe the children really are up at that radio station. The exit plan might have turned into a trap. You're getting stronger. Remember that, John. We'll just be on the other side of this door." The two old men exited the comm room, gingerly propping the door into its frame behind them.

Johnny rubbed his scalp. How long? What did this guard know? How the hell was he going to get him to talk? He noticed there weren't any identifying company colors or logos on the uniform. Just standard issue.

A cold voice came from the being. "The tunnel I was heading to is under the southwest corner of 18th and Irving. It opens up in the backroom. Not far from the radio station. But it's not the closest one to them, I'll bet. A good backup option nonetheless, seeing as it starts miles beyond the Edingburg perimeter. The only hang-up is that it's now filled with tripwire and claymores."

Johnny looked at the man, stunned. He leaned down next to Cottard, who'd resumed his manning of the radio. "We still can't contact anyone in the radio station, right?" he muttered.

"Yep," Cottard said dryly.

Johnny rubbed his chin. "All right. Send a demolition team to 18th and Irving. Fill that hole so they don't run themselves into a trap."

"Sure, why not. Let's have an agent blow up the tunnel and hope Ramfort just figures it out."

"Could you stop being you for one damn minute? This is important!"

Cottard stared at Johnny and put on his headphones.

Johnny grabbed Cottard by the collar. "You fucking brat!"

A throat cleared behind them. Johnny dropped Cottard and turned his attention to the guard, who faced him from underneath his shit-smeared gas mask. Johnny marched toward the guard, dragging a foldable chair across the rotting wooden floor. He spun the chair, slammed it down in front of the guard, and sat. The overhang of light from the fluorescent bulbs showered over them.

Although the guard was covered in mud, the circular glass eyehole in the middle of the mask was perfectly clear. The guard sat completely motionless. He seemed to be more of a mannequin than a real man. Johnny's leg trembled in time with the buzzing of the fluorescent light.

"How did you learn about the tunnel network?"

"I found it a long time ago."

Johnny leaned forward. "How did you find it?"

"I knew where to look."

"That tunnel network is our best card," Johnny said. "If the General knew, then he'd wait to blow it up until everyone ran in. It'd be over. Why give away the tunnel now?"

"Because I'm already here."

Johnny hopped to his feet in a jolt of panic. The chair squeaked. "You?" He took hold of the soldier's mask and tore it off.

It was the General.

Johnny reared back and landed half on the chair. "What the—!"

The General smiled. "What, no hug?"

Johnny tried to look away, but the veil of fluorescent light blinded him from the rest of the dark basement. He was sealed in.

The General shook his head. "You are so damn pathetic. I mean, really. Firecrackers? You almost make killing your little revolutionaries boring."

Johnny stood up, doing his best to stand tall over his adversary. "It's a little different since the last time. Now you're the one strapped to a chair."

The General leaned forward, the rope straining to hold him back. His marble-black eyes gleamed in the light. He breathed venom: "You're right, I'm getting really ... really ... close."

Johnny's knees buckled, bringing him back to a seated position.

"But before I deal with you, where is she?" the General asked. "I was hoping we could finally occupy the same place at the same time and catch up."

"You ... you've seen her? You've seen Mom in person?"

The General chuckled. "You're incredible. Really. She got you this time, without you even getting a good view of her?" The General looked up at the light and smiled. "Too bad, really ... great rack. Too bad you don't remember them, you ungrateful impotent! You know what your problem is? You are victim to so many principles, rules, structures." His words slowly coagulated with each syllable. "No room for passion. The kind of passion that injects itself into your veins and takes over your body. The kind that makes the moment you're breathing in the only one that exists. The kind of moment you don't pretty up with fucking pleasantries or false manners, but instead you just cram all the real shit in. Pack it so tight there's no more room for: manners, pleasantries, denial, self-loathing. Instead, you fucking choke on it."

The ropes creaked as the General's puffed out his chest. His boot stomped on the rotting wooden floor. "And you keep choking on it until all that pure unrated shit you've shoved into that moment withers … and fucking dies." The general's body riled in the ropes constraining it. "Until … climax.

"In that moment of transcendence, in that very last tick, in that very last moment where you're all that's left. Everything else lying asphyxiated. An entire world, an entire paradigm, choked to death by your own convictions." The General flexed his hands, knuckles popping. "In that moment you are everything, because you are all that's left in a crumbling existence. You are God."

The General exhaled. He went still, his breathing slowed. A moment passed. "I don't know about you, Johnny boy, but I could really go for a cigarette right now."

Johnny did his best to remain deadpan.

"You should really start appreciating the simple things, Johnny." The General heaved up his boot and crossed it over his other leg. "Have you even noticed her scent, the way she moves, how her smile grows, how her pupils dilate when you— Are you with me, Johnny?"

"What, what are you saying? You … you've …"

The General nodded slowly. "She's a real spitfire, that girl. But a little blind. Yep, I know all about that bitch in your head. What's wrong, Johnny? Thought you'd found a woman who could penetrate my organization without me penetrating her? Dead or not I remember that one like it was yesterday.

"Did you think she was too pure to have a little lust in her? Too angelic to be touched by some wretch like me? Well, if it helps, you're half right. I've only touched half of her. The lower half. You've got the rest. The heart. The mind. She's never shared that part of her with me. But that's all right, I still enjoyed that plump lower half of hers to the fullest."

"You raped her …"

"No. No. No. Johnny boy, afraid it's not that easy an out. I'm a big believer in freedom, remember? Far more so than her, in fact. I let her tie her own ropes. She likes both of us, Johnny boy, and she enjoyed different parts of us without restraint." The General winked. "She's been getting her fill. But I haven't had a problem with that. That's what makes her the perfect woman, after all. Over time, she gets what she wants."

Johnny gripped his chest. He could feel the soot in his lungs burrowing into him.

"She's an Inner Circle girl, you twat. What do you think she really is, because she's definitely not the Virgin Mary. Remember that tank? The one that's been killing everyone you care about?"

Johnny's boot slammed into the General, who fell over, still strapped to the chair. Johnny stood over his adversary, engorged in rage.

The General coughed. "Good! Finally some fucking progress! Tell me how that feels? The adrenaline. That hatred you're finally letting flow?"

Johnny's lungs convulsed, and he fell back onto the chair.

"So … the tank," the General sputtered from the floor. "I can alter it all I want. I could give it a new paint job, I could have it ride around and drop off children after school—shit, I could make it fire sparkles and cupcakes if I fucking wanted!

"But no matter what I do with it, it needs jet fuel, gas or diesel. You try and put something else in it and the damn thing rattles like your lungs. And if I were to keep filling it with some shit it wasn't designed to burn, it'd eventually die no matter how much I've convinced myself that it runs on rainbows and sunshine.

"Well guess what, Johnny boy. You and me are no different. We can change everything about ourselves but the fuel. You, my friend, are no alchemist of the soul. So the shit you're filling yourself with is killing you. Yeah, it may kill others. Yeah, we may be keeping this planet on a perpetual wheeze with our industrious activities, but nonetheless we … feel … great.

"Johnny, we spent what? Thirty years together? We built this fucking city, for Christ sake! I know exactly what fuel you were designed to burn. Just let me fill up that little tank of yours, Johnny boy. Fill it to the brim!"

Johnny started punching the General as he lay helpless on the floor. Then the world skipped for an instant, and his legs buckled. He fell back onto his own chair, coughing uncontrollably.

"How's that little condition of yours, Johnny boy?" The General spat blood, then his face suddenly went dark. "If I remember correctly, I told you to stay in your little fucking cell until I set you free. But here you are sitting in this shithole while some kids are shacking up in my damn radio station!" The General looked up into the fluorescent tubes. "I thought of blowing up half the pier with your new little friend would be enough to satisfy your appetites. But I guess not."

Johnny's eyes widened.

"Grab the gun, find the X, and fire, right? Those were the orders —right, you little cocksucker?! How'd you like MY fireworks at the end there, huh?!"

Still wearing his headphones, Cottard didn't respond.

"Why didn't you just—"

"Kill you? Johnny. Johnny, Johnny, Johnny BOY. I can always kill you. Whenever I want. I can be on the toilet and suddenly decide that I'm over your crap. You'd be dead before my shit plopped into the bowl."

Johnny slunk forward and put his hands on his head. "Why not just kill me or Cottard or the whole damn lot of us?" he asked. "Why are you fucking with us!" He wobbled back up to his feet.

"Us? There is no us. There's just you and me." The General's eyes hardened. "And those damn kids fooling with my radios!"

The General's boot slammed into Johnny's thigh, throwing him out of the veil of light, he plummeted into the darkness surrounding them.

The General rose from his chair; the ropes melted away. A pistol materialized in his hand. Bullets fired. Johnny fell to a fetal position, but felt nothing. Johnny's eyes opened. Smoke poured up from the General's gun. Johnny turned his head. Cottard.

Cottard writhed on the rotting floor. His arms and legs thumped, wrestling against gravity.

Johnny heard the wood creak under the footsteps knocking toward him. A boot stomped his head, then his chest, his pelvis, his eye socket.

"You're getting in the way again, Johnny boy," the General said. "So now I gotta do it again. I gotta take another piece … of you."

"Take what you want. I need nothing."

The General kneeled down to the floor. "I'll hand it to you. Your rules, principles, beliefs have all created a truly … ingenious orchestration. You've taken those screams, whimpers, and cries coming from the most primal parts of your body and made all their cacophonous sounds come together into a soothing melody of denial." The General brought the muzzle of his pistol to his own ear. "So when the cries from your body finally hit your ear, the pain and deprivation they bring with them have somehow … transcended into a hymn of beauty and grace, bringing with it words to do completely unnatural things."

The General looked over at Cottard as he lit a cigar. "You know what you really are, Johnny boy? Because it's not some Socratic Buddha. No. Through your complex twists of reason, through your restraint of what is natural, you have made *yourself* into one thing." He bent down and puffed smoke into Johnny's face. "A pervert."

"Everyone in this city bends to you in order to get something," Johnny said. "You feed on their submission. And you love it when they fight you to try and get something. It doesn't matter to you what they do so long as you're at the center."

Johnny coughed blood. "But I'm not trying to get what you can offer. Because I'm not trying to get anything from your city! And that's what you hate. That what I am fueled by can only come from within myself! An appreciation of my own moral virtue. Because of that you will never be able to take hold of me. You have no leverage. All I require is the commitment to my own duty. All you can offer is a sense of rank, a sense of class, and a good buzz. And that is what you fear because you know that if everyone wants nothing, then you can't find joy in anything."

The General swayed over Johnny's body. "Cute ideals in an ugly world can't last forever, Johnny boy."

The room shook, the fluorescent lights swung. Dirt trickled down. The final battle between the Reds and the Blues had begun. The General sniffed the air for blood. He looked back at Cottard, who'd made it halfway onto his seat and was dully grabbing for the microphone at the other end of the desk.

"There you go, boy! There you go! Rrrrrreach for it! Tell Mommy what I've done! Tell her I've shot her child! … And I'll inform the father."

The General's eyes trailed down to Johnny. "Johnny boy? Do you remember about, hmmm, 29 years ago, was it? You were seeing this one woman. Very nice … great rack. Turns out that little bitch got pregnant. A few times, actually. All yours, you fertile bastard. Pretty sure that one there's your oldest."

Cottard flicked on the emergency outbound radio signal. The General smiled. "Found us."

A long high-pitched whistle grew louder, then terminated in an enormous explosion above them. A gaping hole blew through the wall with a blast of superheated flame. Most of Cottard flew backward; part of him stayed, his hands remaining on the comm table. Clouds of smoke and dust filled the bunker.

The General breathed in the scene and exhaled with satisfaction. Dirt and muck caked his muddied guard uniform. "Stay in this moment, Johnny. For as long as you can. Let the dust and debris fill you. Enjoy it all because, no matter what, I'm going to make sure—" he looked down at Johnny— "you choke on it last."

He took in another ash-filled breath. "Now I'm going to go see about your little bastards shacked up in my damn radio station."

The General trudged up the newly formed exit leading to the surface. He turned around. "But I'll be taking my time with the rest of your little snots. I've already got your cute little City Hall in Edingburg all fixed up. So we'll be transmitting from there instead. Figured I'd rush it. That way I can really enjoy wiping out the last of your bloodline. I wonder if they've ever even met Daddy?" the General asked almost to himself. "Well, at least that one has." He walked through the blown-out exit and disappeared into a cloud of ash and dust.

Part IV

The Truth

If you want to understand our story, then you'll have to understand the us, that is me.

Journal Entry #286
Back to Front

It's almost funny how tragically similar opposites can be. Spending their entire lives heading in opposing directions. Walking so far that eventually, when they turn around they'll no longer see the back of the other.

When he finally disappeared, I figured I'd never see him again.

But to my surprise, one day, after decades of walking, and years without even seeing the outline of my opposite I saw him again, walking toward me.

We looked nothing alike, neither were our paths, but we had both arrived at the same destination. We were separate in our paths, but we share the same conclusion.

What Was Done
Journal Entry #125

When I was eight I had a friend named Jeffrey. I wanted so badly to help him realize his boyhood dream of climbing the biggest tree in the forest. It was hard for him though, seeing as he was blind.

So I did what any eight year old would do. I guided him up. With my voice and instruction he pushed himself higher and higher up the branches. We climbed so incredibly high that we entered a low fog. In the fog I could no longer see him, but I did my best to lead him higher. I was so proud of him and of me.

Which makes the moment when I heard the thump of his body hitting the ground so devastating. He'd never climb again. Many said he was lucky to survive such a fall, though deafness, and then muteness, were added to his disabilities.

To this day I don't know if he was ever mad at me. He would just sit there, completely unaware of me sitting across from him at lunch every day in the cafeteria.

I never left his side, but I never could reach him either. The thought of abandoning him sickened me. But the idea of jolting him from his thoughts always paralyzed me with guilt.

So I hovered. Never so far that I'd lose him, but never too close, so he wouldn't know I was there. I'd turned myself into some form of guilt-ridden guardian. But I couldn't protect him from the cough. Less than a year later, it got him. We buried him in a field.

Ten years later I took an ax and cut that fucking tree down to the root.

I guess I just can't let the things I feel guilty for taking part in. But, I'll be damned if I'm the only one to pay for our sins.

My Importance
Journal Entry #6

So….why me? Why do I have to be the one telling this story? Well it's simple. I'm the only one that knows it in its entirety. All of us were there, but I was the only one truly present and the only one who must endure the consequences of our actions. That makes me the omnipotent narrator, you see?

It's very difficult, remaining fully lucid. I can't even tell you it's worth it, because it doesn't necessarily enable you. Whether I like it or not, there are pros to drinking the Coolaid.

But here's the thing. I will never give up on my lucidity. Because true lucidity is my justice. Lucidity is my rebellion against this absurd universe that surrounds us with nothing. A world that gives us life but no inherent meaning. Instead of giving us direction it gives us the opportunity for self delusion and purpose; allowing us to justify anything in this vacuum of metaphysical nothing.

So I reject this world. I reject the nothing that surrounds me. That way I can see through the delusion. That way I can still find the hole in this nothing; so that when I finally find it, I can run through it. Like a madman, I'll charge through this universe's fatal wrinkle; until I collide into the something where all this nothing is housed.

That moment of impact will be my transcendence.

Campfire Stories
Journal Entry #126
I remember sitting next to a campfire once when I was very young. I thought it was so strange that the fire would sporadically crackle and pop from out of nowhere. It wasn't until much later in my life that I discovered the cause for this is due to these little

micro-pockets in the wood that are filled with sap. When the fire draws near the pocket, the sap begins to jump and bubble as its home turns into a frying pan. Then the sap explodes and the pocket sits in shambles, the walls covered in soot, the curtains singed. For a moment everything in the pocket lies still, until the flame slowly creeps into the doorway.

You Feel Me?
Journal Entry #825

I know I don't readily make sense sometimes. But that's okay. Sometimes being understood isn't all that important. I remember back in the days before the storms we were constantly told about the starving children on some side of the world.

We'd be lectured, in great detail about the disease, hunger, murder, and all other forms of hell that plagued them on the most daily of occasion. I remember taking a test on their plight in class. I got an A+. In fact, so did most the class. Even our parents knew.

But you know what's strange? While we all understood, so fully, these people's situations, nothing changed for them. Nothing got better for the people living in chronic plight. And now I know why.

The first people that came to hear my story, I spoke to them. I told them everything that happened; from point A, to point B. When I'd finally concluded my report, they understood it all perfectly. And based off the facts, they even pitied me.

But here I still am.

So this time, I have a new kind of story to report. One that has nothing to do with you quantifying the X amount of horrors I go through so that you must then give me Y amount of pity. Let's just skip such a non-consequential equation.

Instead just feel my story as if it were your own, and overtime, you will come to understand. Once you do, feel free to help.

Ripped Gold

Johnny and Nikolai looked down at Cottard. Machines worked to keep Cottard's heart pumping. His handless arms hung over the side of a metal gurney.

"Will—" Johnny cleared his throat. "Will he make it?"

"Not sure," Nikolai responded.

Gordon ran into the operating room. "Good Lord, no!" he cried. He caressed Cottard's face. Franz stood in the doorway, arms folded. "Our boy," Gordon said, his eyes welling.

"Why didn't you tell me he was my son?" Johnny asked.

"It wasn't our place," Franz said. "And we hadn't seen you in so long we'd begun to think of the whole family dynamic a bit differently."

"But he's my son."

"Ours too," Franz said, arms still crossed. "We love that boy. He was a glimmer of hope in that dark cell. He was our innocence."

"Is!" Gordon said. "Is!"

"What do we do now?" Johnny asked.

Nikolai's fingers activated and began cutting into Cottard's arms with a laser. "Operation begins."

Gordon looked down at Cottard with wet eyes. "We eliminate the man who has taken the harmony out of this city. This man must return to his rightful post. I can not stomach seeing another child on this gurney."

"I obtain info from agents," Nikolai said, not looking up from his surgery. "All receivers are now down. The radio station's signal will likely fail to break even Edingburg's perimeters."

Gordon and Franz's gaze drifted to Johnny.

"We must take City Hall," Johnny said. "The General has repaired the tower. That'll get them a signal."

"Yes, iz good. If info you say true. Zen City Hall tower will act as von big receiver. Will work."

"But what about the children at the station?" Gordon asked.

"Ramfort is still there," Franz said.

"And the Steven child!" Gordon said. "Doing all this will take focus away from getting them out safely!"

"We can't get into the station now even if we wanted to," Johnny said. "The General's compromised our tunnel system. And you know we don't have enough people to take on any guard outfit in a direct fight anyway. The General said he'd let their broadcast play first. Bastard wants to enjoy the show himself. So that means we've got time to rush over to the station with who've we got left and to rig the signal from the City Hall so it does get played everywhere. With any luck, who's left of Red Team will answer the call to rebel. From the sounds of it, they've run out of options. So we can be their way out. With enough of them we could make the Blues fall back long enough to get them out of the station."

"Let's do it," Franz said. "To the City Hall!"

"Department of Smoke's guys will be crawling all over City Hall now that it's back online," Johnny said. "And we've got 80 exhausted kids."

Franz and Gordon looked at one another.

Gordon pressed his circular bifocals up on his nose. "How about a more low profile option?" Gordon suggested. "We still have the officer's uniform you grabbed at the pier."

"And I've got a limo parked out front," Franz said. "With all that to show off, we'll glide right into the City Hall unchecked."

"Wear this." Gordon held up a small earpiece. "Nikolai will talk you through the signal redirect steps. With our prestige and some slight of hand, you should be in and out without a single guard throwing even the slightest tantrum."

Special Delivery

Franz sped through empty streets of Edingburg. The early hour's haze of low-grade toxins still hung in the morning air. Gordon sat next to Johnny in the back of the limo.

Johnny looked at his analog watch. 9:00. "We've got an hour to slip in and turn the station's signal over. Still no movement from the guard at the radio station?"

Gordon looked down at the code running down his green LED screen. "It seems the guard has just plopped themselves all around the radio station, but they aren't getting their hands dirty just yet."

"He said he'd be taking his time, the prick," Johnny said. "The second we're done with the station I want everyone at HQ over there ready to strike the guard from the rear. We'll just have to hope enough kids from Red Team defect to us and come to help."

"Franz, don't you think maybe we're still cutting it a wee bit close?" Gordon asked. "Shouldn't we make the children our first priority, then deal with the rest? Perhaps we could—"

"No," Franz said, glaring back at them. "We have to do it this way. And if Ramfort's anything like his father, he'll never leave that station until that tape gets played all over the city. This man has come to rot the harmony of the city."

"It's not like he'd always meant to," Gordon said.

"Are you defending him?! He's taken the people of this city down such a mangled and twisted road the quest for true knowledge will soon become an impossible one!"

"Franz, we must calm ourselves."

"No! What he did to our poor Cottard crossed the line! Oh, he most certainly crossed it! The children are off limits!"

"Cottard's an adult now, Franz," Gordon said.

"Not to us! Never to us!"

Gordon took off his glasses and rubbed his eye. He glanced at Johnny. "Fine. Fine. I understand, my boy. I understand."

"We must do it in this way," Franz said, his voice softer now. "It's still in line with Mum's instructions. It's just not the preferred version, but it'd be wrong if we let such an animal continue to thrash about where there are so many children's lives at stake."

"Agreed," Johnny said.

Franz looked at Johnny through the rear view mirror. "Glad you understand our position, John."

They came to a barricade with machine guns nested along the sides and top. "Blast, they have a checkpoint this far out from the City Hall!" Franz yelled.

"John, your papers!" Gordon said.

Johnny grabbed the stolen ID badge in his commandeered uniform and slung it at Franz. The limo slowed and stopped in front of a heavy metal checkpoint gate. A masked guard tapped on the glass. Franz only just broke the seal of the window screen. He threaded the ID badge through the crack.

The guard banged on the glass. "The hell! Roll down your damn window the whole fucking way! I don't give a shit if the storm fucks your interior!"

"Look at the fucking badge, you twat!" Franz shouted.

The guard looked at the badge, swallowed, and cleared his throat. "I— I will expedite the call. My apologies, sir. Can barely see through this mask."

"Goddamn right you will! Who the fuck in the Inner Circle gave you the gate contract!" Johnny barked from the back. "Hustle!" The guard nearly fell over as he sprinted away.

"No need to be so rude," Gordon said, shaking his head.

"One must act the part," Franz said.

The guard ran back and pushed the ID badge through the crack in the window. "I haven't received approval as of yet, but—" the long beam keeping the barricade closed rose upward— "please proceed."

"There you go, kid," Johnny growled. The guard snapped and saluted, his feet slapping together. The limo moved forward.

"Good show," Gordon said.

A red phone in the checkpoint booth began crying out for attention. The guard ran over to answer its call. Fury poured through the phone's earpiece. The guard turned to find the slowly disappearing limo. "Yes, sir!" He slammed the phone back onto its hook. With hyperventilating breaths, he ran into the middle of the street and with fumbling fingers cocked back the bolt of his rifle and fired at the limo. Other guards spun around in confusion. "Shoot!" the guard yelled, his finger pointing at the limo. "Fucking shoot!" They fired.

The limo's wheels screeched and zoomed forward; its taillights disappeared into the fog. The gate guard ran to the red phone. "Perimeter breach! Bring it out!" he cried into the mouthpiece. "Bring it out!"

"By the gods, that was close," Gordon said.

"Quite," Franz said.

"What the hell happened?" Johnny asked, peering through the bullet-cracked rear window.

"That ID you've got must be flagged," Franz said. "But it's going to take a lot more than a few rifle rounds to penetrate this baby." Franz patted the dashboard. "Do you see anything back there? This girl's got one hell of a blind spot."

"No," Johnny said.

Gordon unbuckled and peered out the side windows. "Nothing's come round quite yet. Perhaps we can steer clear of them and just drop John off 'round the corner."

Johnny's heart skipped a beat. "Well, hey, they're looking for us now," he said.

"No, they're looking for your badge," Franz said. "They never saw your face. Let them see you, flash the badge, and the low-level guards will snap to until an official alarm comes out."

The limo zoomed through Market Street. The streets were empty as they started up a steep hill.

"Bloody hell, it's like they evacuated this part of the town as well," Gordon said, his face pressing against the glass. "Not a soul to be seen."

The limo began driving up a small hill in the road. A block behind the limo, tracked wheels cranked to a halt. Ash and dust bounced off its armor. The turret churned round, and its 40-foot-long barrel swung and stopped between the limo's taillights.

Johnny looked back through the cracked rear window. He saw the tank's barrel staring at him, then a puff of smoke rise from its muzzle. He fell to the floor of the limo. "Get down!"

The missile hit just below the trunk. The limo flipped forward. Gordon flew into the wall between the cabin and the driver's cabin. The limo toppled over, skidding to a stop on the pavement.

The Abrams tank's treaded wheels twisted, aligned with the upended limo, and began pushing up the hill.

Johnny hung upside down from his seatbelt. He saw Gordon sandwiched between the wall and the huge crate they always insisted on bringing with them. Johnny frantically pushed at his seatbelt buckle. It clicked, and he fell to the ceiling.

Johnny pushed open the door and crawled out. He looked back and saw the tank slowly rumbling up the hill toward him. He grabbed Gordon, who lay partly outside of the broken window, and tried to drag him from the limo.

"Oh no, my boy," Gordon moaned as he rolled over. "There's no time to waste on an old dog like me." He brought out a lighter and held it out to Johnny, then patted the crate lying beside him. "It's time for that blasted machine to unwrap its present. When the tank comes up this hill, flick that open and give us a light. Just make sure that you're well clear."

Johnny looked at the lighter. It had a bird etched on its face.

"What? Were you always planning to … That's a bomb?!"

"Always be prepared, Johnny. For anything. But we don't have any bloody time left! So go, child!" Gordon coughed. "Please. Look after the children. Waste no more time on a couple old dogs like us."

Johnny rose to a crouch. A high-impact round boomed into the building beside them. The pressure wave of the blast threw Johnny off his feet. He rolled down a steep street.

Franz reached back through the window of the driver's cockpit into the cabin. Gordon grabbed it. "It was a good life, ya crazy old coot."

"Indeed it was," Gordon said, "indeed it was. Not a bad go 'round this time."

"Til next time."

The tank's front reared up as it came to the apex of the hilltop. The iron tread grabbed at the still-spinning wheels of the limo. The Abrams spanned ten feet upward until it hung over the entire limo. The tank fell, dropping its immense weight onto the wheels and reinforced steel cabin walls. The crunch echoed off the walls of the surrounding buildings.

As Johnny stumbled in a panic down the hill, the Abrams's turret churned again. Its barrel trained on Johnny, who was now frantically pushing up on the lighter's casing, trying to open it.

The tank fired. A nonexplosive round slammed into a mid-rise, knocking Johnny down with a hail of rubble.

Johnny's fingers found a cigar in his uniform. They took it out and put it in his mouth. Habit kicked in. His hands flicked open the lighter and spun the flint wheel.

The crate exploded. A flat wave of pressure plumed beneath the tank, disintegrating every window or door along its plane.

Johnny strolled toward the City Hall, his cheeks pulled in as he puffed on his cigar, fingers trembling.

Das Kapital

Johnny started up the long rows of the City Hall's front steps. No one stood in his way. His boots made the sole source of sound outside the ringing in his ears.

He stopped in front of the huge red doors at the top of the steps. He peered around. Emptiness. Absolutely no one. He gritted his teeth. "Shit. Just move. Keep moving."

He took some short quick breaths, trying to force his mind back into lucidity while at the same time not being overcome by the double homicide he'd just witnessed and arguably committed. He bit his cigar and straightened his posture.

"Those better really be my kids in that fucking station."

Johnny pushed open the large red front doors of the City Hall. The room echoed with the groan of their metal. There was a faint tinkle of music. Classical. A piano and horns. Johnny walked into the dim room. His boots clopped on the green granite floors, leaving footprints in the thin layer of dust. He could only make out the familiar granite pillars and the now-patched green copper dome above that'd apparently been harboring the radio beacon since before it even oxidized.

The front doors swung shut behind him. Its lock clamped. Lit candlesticks floated downward, lining the edges of the room. The needle of a record player jumped and skipped to another part of the song.

A huge flame burst to life at the other end of the room. Johnny stumbled back, his boots squeaking over the waxed floor. A large dark figure stood in front the fire, casting a shadow that enveloped Johnny.

Long looping horns rose from the figure's head. The figure stepped forward, its armor clanking, smoke puffing from its nostrils. As Johnny felt for his handgun, it pulled off the horned metal mask. It was the General. He stood smiling at Johnny, covered from head to toe in medieval armor. Johnny bent over as his wounded lungs turned to fire.

"Right on time," the General said. "We have a meeting with the board." He grabbed Johnny by the back of the neck and pushed him to the middle of the room.

A large circular oak table rose from the floor under the dome. A small fireball floated downward and found its place in a built-in metal dish at the center of the oak table.

The General pushed Johnny's face onto the table. "Put it on," he growled. "They'll be here soon."

In front of Johnny lay his iron mayor's mask. He tried rising from the table, but the General shoved him back down again. "We've been having a little too much fun lately, Johnny boy. Now the masks are demanding to meet. But don't worry, I'll get us out of this mess."

Johnny's lungs convulsed, and a spray of blood flicked over the table. He laughed. "You haven't told them that your puppet mayor cut his strings and is now the leader of the IRA. Can't wait to hear you explain that!"

The General slammed Johnny's face into the table. "You've gotten many hundreds of kids killed this week. Turned my hunt for rebels into a goddamn turkey shoot. I should be giving you a medal."

Johnny let out a phlegm-thickened chuckle. "You're losing favor with the other masks. Your body count's getting too high for the city to stomach. And now you've got someone close to you that's been busy blowing up parts of town. Give me a medal? I'll give you a nail for your coffin."

"Trust me, Johnny, the board doesn't fancy risking their necks to squeeze me out. They'd rather go with the easier, softer option." The General patted Johnny's head. "So … Dad, I suggest you hold back at the board meeting or that brand new family of yours is going to have some empty seats at this morning's breakfast table."

The table thrummed as the General slammed a fist into the back of Johnny's head. Everything went black. When Johnny came to, his metal mayor's mask had been placed over his face. He was seated in his place at the oak table. Six differently sculpted masked figures draped in red robes sat along the circumference of the table, all staring at him through their stoic metal masks.

The horned figure sat across from Johnny. His voice spoke in dismal undertones: "A meeting of the city's leaders shall be called to order. This meeting shall follow the conduct and rituals that were established at the inception of this board. This meeting shall be lead by I, the Oryx, the General and keeper of this city."

A leathered fist from every member banged atop the table twice in unison.

Johnny's mind screamed for a plan. He brushed his jacket, trying to find comfort in the slight impression of the Beretta handgun concealed in the front pocket. Johnny looked at the General through the small fireball in the center of the table.

"At this table sit the most powerful and patriotic," the General said. "All here keep their domains orderly and profitable for the greater good of the whole. Under penalty of death, we decree the anonymity of our persons. The roots of concerns and suggestions voiced at this table shall never become exposed to scrutiny. When consensus is reached, all thoughts and coming actions will be bundled and placed on our collective shoulders. Its weight shall be held up by nothing less than the unified will of those who sit here now."

The General raised his two armored hands. "Are we of one mind?"

All fists banged atop the table in three coordinated beats. The General's metal fist slammed down and shook the table. "By our unanimity this contract is sealed."

"We are witnesses," the masks spoke as one.

The General brought out a long double-edged knife and set it on the table. "And for those who come to break this seal, let their blood be freed from their veins."

"We hold the knife," the masks spoke as one.

"Then let us begin," the General said.

A mask turned to Johnny. "It is your zone causing this imbalance. Explain to us the nature of this rebellious movement."

Johnny felt every mask turn toward him. His face began to broil under the fireball's intense heat. He glanced around, watching the reflection of the fire flutter on the metal masks of his peers. He guessed at the number of bullets he'd get off before they stabbed him. The idea of becoming a martyr soured. No, he thought, I'm not dying here today.

"This rebellion is chipping away at every weakness, every hole, every unattended nook and cranny we have," Johnny said. "It targets citizens that our current system has foolishly designed to let rot. Whether it be the husk of a man in a tube machine, a forgotten child in the ghetto, or a cycler who found themselves on the losing end of the coin, the rebellion takes them. They convert them. They weaponize them. And so, bit by bit, piece by piece, they are successfully amassing, organizing, and militarizing the very people we have damned."

A puff of smoke exited the General's mask. "So propose your solution."

Johnny leaned forward. "Balance must be restored. The IRA has been at work for decades, and their capabilities have been woefully underestimated. Due to this horrid miscalculation, there is no way to know the number of crevices, back doors, and minds it has already crept into. No way to adjudge the solidarity of our own ranks. Members, groups, alliances have all fallen out of sync because of one man's lack of mental fortitude.

"We were not thrown into this position overnight. We were brought, slowly over the years, to what we're seeing now—the long-coming culmination of one man's shortcomings. One man's flawed system. One man's identity, an identity that tarnishes us all."

The masks turned toward the General. The General growled.

The masks looked at one another. "Make your suggestion," one hissed at Johnny.

"We're rapidly losing our ability to bend the aspirations of the common man to our will. But for now, in this small space of time, we still have the advantage. So we must seize it while we still can. And so —" Johnny looked around the table— "in order to save ourselves before this situation turns black, we must reorganize the board itself. Doing so will offset the IRA's message and weaken their ability to inspire plots against us, buying us the necessary time to find the source of this threat and cut it from the root before it grows strong enough to cut us from our own."

"Yes," the General said, "this is the right path. But not for us. We must force this same plan upon them—penetrate their network and coerce them into restructuring in ways advantageous to us."

"How would this be possible?" a mask growled.

"Because we have him." The General pointed at Johnny. "She is aligned with him. He is their new leader."

A gasp fell over the table.

"Through a series of maneuvers I have given him the proper breathing room to operate, allowing him to execute calculated atrocities against our city, including bombing this very building. These actions have enabled him to gain favor within the network, so much so that he now sits at the top of the IRA's food chain. But as you can see—" the General spread his arms across the perfectly mended room— "the damage he's dealt has not even left a scratch."

Johnny's lungs buckled. He'd been exposed, but was now being hidden by the very light the General now shown on him.

"We must continue this charade. Fighting battles that wound us. Allowing the IRA's dialog to spread to some measure. But with the right amount of control, the wounds they inflict upon us will only be skin deep. And in return for going along with this little game, we will possess a great enemy and be able to point them at anything. And they will happily destroy our rivals in the name of the IRA. When the dust clears from the IRA's increasingly heinous attacks, the people of Edingburg will come running to us as their savior."

"How can we be sure he will be able to coerce the IRA into such behavior?" a mask asked.

"Simple," the General said. "The IRA's strength is their ability to maintain their message and their unity, and they've just come together under one leader. So all we must do is take him out of the picture. Without him Mom loses the leader of her IRA and a new and very powerful seat opens up. And I'm willing to bet that the next man to fill it won't be so careful with maintaining their message."

"We will never bend!" Johnny shouted.

The masks turned slowly toward Johnny.

"Looks like he's gone native. No matter. Your work is done. During the IRA's restructuring," the General continued, "we will push them and their precious ideals to the breaking point. With time they will do what all men do when innocence is put under extreme stress. They will revert to their primal instincts and start biting at everything like a mad dog. And all we need it to do is bite the wrong thing, and why not make that thing the very entity we want bitten?"

The General looked over the table. "Are we of the same mind?"

"Aye," a lone mask agreed. The other masks glanced around.

"Aye! Aye! Aye! Aye! Aye! Aye!" shouted all the figures.

"Then it is settled," the General said.

The fire on the table flashed in Johnny's eyes. He gripped at the wooden arms of his chair. He knew he only had a moment left. This was his only chance to do something. He erupted from his seat and whipped out his handgun.

"I will no longer be your damn puppet! This is where we end!" Johnny fired a single round at the General. The bullet sunk into his chest. The General made no movement. Johnny looked at the General's entry wound. Then a trail of smoke began floating upward from his own chest.

Johnny clutched his chest and fell back into his seat.

"Fool" a mask hissed.

The General leaned forward, grabbing the knife off the table and pointing it at himself. His mask's black eye slits stared into Johnny's quivering soul.

"Do you know what you have done!" a mask said.

"You stab one, you stab us all!" said another.

The General drove the blade into the bullet wound. Johnny felt as if his chest were being sliced open. His damaged lungs wheezed as the General slowly and silently dug the knife deeper into the wound.

"Do you see!" a mask cried.

The General pulled the knife out. The bullet dropped onto the table. He drove the blade into the fire. When the metal glowed red, he pressed the knife against his chest. Flesh sizzled until the wound shut. Johnny screamed.

"Leave us," the General said.

"He is a liability. Restrict him," a mask said. Fists beat the table. The smoking and bloodied knife clanked from the vibrations.

"Leave us!" the General roared.

Johnny watched the masks turn to clouds of black. Their clouds spread upward, combined, and blew into the General.

Johnny emerged in a black dimension. He saw her.

"You're alive, Jonathan. You're intact. Nothing has changed. I'm still here. With you. I'm know what it is, Jonathan. What we awoke. It's more than shared consciousness now. I can feel it. It's becoming a conscience all its own. Protect it, Jonathan. Don't let him hurt another one of our children."

Johnny felt himself rising. A light emerged in front of him. It grew as the nothingness behind him pushed him forward, into the light.

"Jooooooohnny Boy? You still with me? Or am I finally talking to myself?"

Johnny groaned. He felt like he'd been dropped into his chair from the ceiling.

"Well, would you look at that? I still have an audience."

He felt the General taking the smoldering tip of the knife from the fireball in the center of the table.

"You know, I'll give it to you. You did something that took a pair. You went for it. Been trying to make you a man for who knows how long. But there's just one problem I have with that, Johnny."

Johnny could barely see through the slits in his mask, and his lungs struggled for oxygen.

"The problem, Johnny boy," the General said, "is you are the victim in this relationship. Understand?"

"Fuck you," Johnny grunted.

"How about you take that mask of yours off. But make sure to enjoy it! It's the last thing I'll ever let you do."

Johnny raised a hand to his face.

"That's right, come on."

Johnny unhooked the back, and let the metal mask slide off him and clank to the ground. He was sitting in front of a long mirror. And in its reflection he was a 62-year-old man with a bullet wound. A horned mask lay on the ground next to him.

"Seems you've put a few years on, Johnny boy," his reflection said with the General's voice.

Johnny tried to move his hand, but the reflection in the mirror showed it only quivering. The General waved his hand in front of the mirror. "Now it's mine." The General smiled, watching the quivering hand slowly go still.

"For too long, we've had to share. The board wasn't sure about giving me full control until now. But after that little stunt of yours, you're officially banned from sneaking out the back to go run errands for that bitch. Now I've got total control of this body." The General's hand turned to a fist. "Now *you're* just a voice in *my* head."

"What?!" Johnny's voice screamed out, but the reflection's face remained relaxed.

"The board? The masks? It's made up of us, Johnny boy. Just different aspects. You're the saint. I'm the sinner. The board's the rest of us. There were others behind those masks originally, but now I run the show."

"But I shot you!"

"Come on. You shot me? Impossible. You shot you. We shared this old sack of bones, Johnny boy! But I'm the one at the helm, remember? I'm the one wearing the horns. No, this is my body. Every time you thought you were talking to me, I was talking to you. It's why you found it difficult to shoot yourself back at the protest." The General chuckled. "A while back I started calling you Casper. But it let on too much. Screwed things up. Hilarious, though."

"Those were blanks!" Johnny shouted.

"Do I look like a guy who shoots blanks?" the General scoffed. "Look how big our family is."

Johnny fell silent. Our family ... *our* family?

The reflection in the mirror stood. "Yours, mine. All the same, Johnny boy. Now that I run it all happy to share. So let's talk about us. Remember Haadin? I'm the beast, remember. I'm that primal part. I'm that common ground that exists within every soul in New San Francisco."

The General started taking off his armor. "And you, you're the superego. You helped give the people a justification for my actions and their own. But now that there's really nothing worth doing any more, you're just the douche who makes up a bunch of rules telling us that what we want is bad. But maybe you're right, Johnny boy. We needed a regime change. Our city is failing. The game we've been playing have become … repetitive. Nothing new—right, MOM?!"

The General glared into the darkness as if trying to find her. His eyes clamped shut. "Still not coming out! You bitch!" His eyes closed. "Again and again and again we play this game." His face turned up to the ceiling. "It's so … boring now. This game must end." The General looked back down at the mirror. "But when it does, I'll be the last one left, during that last of last moments. Looking down on it all. Ready for the final asphyxiation. Angelic." His breath hissed through his teeth as he sucked in air. He took a moment. Johnny was all but gone now, silenced, not even an apprehension of conscience weighing on the General's thoughts.

"But to truly end this. We'll need a real big bang. Get the energy up. Tubers, guardsmen, sluts, that's not gonna do it."

The General looked up at the radio beacon above him. He grabbed a cigar and sat back in his chair. He flicked open his Zippo lighter and lit a cigar, waiting for the signal to come.

"Let's see if our boys can make us proud. If they do. I'll pay them a visit."

This Message Brought to You By

Jumbled static filled the radio station. Ramfort's hand incessantly wiggled the toppled-over radio station's main dial. His eyes had gone red due to his long unbroken glare at the dial. Cyclers lay about with red cloths stuffed into their ears, trying to block out the fizzled hisses and static sprays coming from Ramfort's radio room.

In the corner of the radio room sat a man tied to a metal chair. The man stared at Ramfort through a pair of sunglasses some would call fashionable.

It was Line.

"It's just not gonna happen, buddy," mocked the bound man. "They've shut down the whole damn network. Your little message just isn't gettin' through. Your poisonous little message has been put in quarantine. So enjoy decontamination. You lecherous, disgusting—"

Line was interrupted by Ramfort's tongue sticking out and spitting at him. Ramfort returned to the radio receiver he'd shoved into the middle of the floor.

Steve sat motionless on the floor, staring at the woman tied to the seat next to Line.

It was Leslie.

She stared back at him. Silently shaking. Like she was seeing a ghost.

Steve glanced down at the red dress Leslie was wearing. It'd been hemmed to be nothing more than a quarter-inch barrier from her naked body. It was a newly inducted Inner Circle girls uniform, tailored to perfectly fit and shape her every curve. She'd somehow already graduated from the Department of Ladyhood.

"What's with the chick anyway, Line?" Ramfort asked.

"Well, we *were* going to interview one of Edingburg's best new applicants. Show the Irish that even they can do things right."

"You left me," Steve said, staring at Leslie.

Leslie's shaking intensified. The ropes constraining her low cut dress line. The building began subtly shaking under the gusting rage of the storm outside. The metal casings of the radio equipment thrummed, the lighting shook.

Steve spoke in a daze: "You made me believe you'd stay with me. So I would stay with you until you did it. You used me for support, but not to grow us. You used me as an emotional stepstool to go elsewhere. You used me to give you the confidence to reach higher. And you left me in the hole, because I was no longer useful. I wasn't a lover to you; I was a tool."

"No," she whispered. Her eyes reddened, threatening tears.

"Don't," Steve said.

Leslie began sobbing. Tears flowed down her cheeks.

Ramfort looked up from his dial. "Nope." He walked over to Leslie, grabbed her chair, and dragged her out of the radio room as she screamed. Ramfort parked her chair in front of the second floor window over looking the parking lot of casualties and the city beyond.

Steve followed.

Ramfort turned away from her after giving her a quick "shoosh!"

He stepped back into the radio room, grabbed the door, and proclaimed, "You're not the only one getting around, girl! Steve's got bitches all over him now. Sniffer made out with him for like three minutes straight. There … was … tongue." Ramfort slammed the door, leaving Steve and Leslie alone in the small hallway and staircase leading down to the first floor of the radio station.

"Who," she looked down. "Who's Sniffer?"

Steve looked out the window. Between the gusts of smoke and wind he could see the outline of dozens of his peers, their faces down on the pavement. The static from the radio room still flicked and buzzed through the door. The storm seemed to be doing its best to be beat itself through the window.

"About 80 guys are dead out there," Steve said. "How many guys have you been with?"

"Stevey." She closed her eyes, trying to collect herself. "It's not what you think it's like."

"So what, like only six then?"

"Stop. You're better than this."

"Better than what? What I am now! You were part of me! We grew up together! I've only ever had you! As a friend, as family, as a lover, as anything! I wish it wasn't true but you're part of me! You're part of who I am! So now that I know you're rotten, maybe that piece of you that grew in me is rotten too!"

"Steve I had to! It's my life! There's nothing rotten about trying to become something." She looked down. "And you knew. You knew I would. We tricked each other. Neither of us wanted to end things, so we waited until the final possible moment. We held on as long as we could. This is my destiny. I chose to grasp it. Did you get that loan for your house? I got you qualified by trending so much and this broadcast. You could buy anything."

Steve stared out the window. His arms clutching the seals. His body shook. How could she talk to him like this? Like her sins of leaving him were absolved because of her ability to clear him of financial debt.

"You're going to get yourself killed obsessing over this cassette thing, Stevey. Please. Just leave."

Steve looked at her. His face had gone grim. "I didn't want a house. I wanted us. This—" his arms shot up, pointing at the dead and motioning toward the radio room— "this is my destiny. And you are no longer part of it."

His hand turned to a fist. Rage filled his veins. The blood pumped through his eyes so hard that his vision shook. He took a step toward her. Part of her tried to scream, but the other part froze her lungs. The static from the other room grew louder.

The window shattered. Steve dropped down beneath the windowsill, cutting his hand on the shards of glass on the floor. Bullets began firing through the window. Leslie screamed.

Steve watched her as she thrashed in the chair, trying to get out of the line of sight of the window. "Steve, help me!"

Another wave of bullets fired through the window. Steve found his arm reaching out to the chair; he reared it back. He looked at her, wondering if it was time to let nature take its path. Perhaps *this* was her destiny.

"Oh my god, please Stevey!"

Another hail of bullets. One skidded her shoulder before it buried itself into the metal wall behind her. She gasped, nearing shock.

Steve's foot rocketed out, slamming her chair into the back wall and away from the bullets. Steve looked down. Motionless, he listened to her frantic panting.

Suddenly the static stopped. A light went green in the hallway. A clear hum filled the room. Ramfort stared at the dial in the other room, holding his breath. He gently picked up the golden mic lying on the floor next to him and brought it to his face. He clicked the small button at the base. "Are we on?" he asked, his lips barely moving.

The hum continued to fill the room. Ramfort's eyes darted between speakers.

A crackle, then crystal clear connection. "You are on."

Ramfort jumped up, ran to Line, and smooshed his face. "We're on!" He opened the door and thumbs-upped Steve.

A voice came over the speakers: "Zis is Nikolai. I have dialed into your station. I give to you quick update. Signal reaching entire city. Colonel Bradshaw iz dead. Hell on Wheels Inc. losing badly despite very high losses for Ghost Fox. Will attempt to make rescue of you, but heavily outnumbered. You should run if possible."

Ramfort looked up from his face smooshing and checked his watch. 9:56.

"Oh! Four minutes till showtime, Steve!"

Steve peered through a crack at the base of the window. The fog was burning off, revealing their situation. "There's gotta be 200 Foxes out there. There's 25 of us."

Ramfort walked up to Steve. "Yeah … But we're on. Cassette, Steve. Come on." Ramfort wiggled his fingers. "Let's make all this count for something, baby."

Steve looked down at Melody, who now stood quietly at the base of the stairs. How long had she been there? He dug the cassette out of his pocket. He held it up and looked at it, scrutinizing the rolls of tape within. "This better be good," he said.

The pair walked into the radio room. Ramfort pointed Steve to the cassette player and began piling slews of gadgets onto his arms. He heaved them to the middle of the room, forcing the wires of the devices to sprawl and stretch to accommodate his new layout. Ramfort looked at his watch, 9:59.

Ramfort pointed at a button next to Steve. "Press that and we will go live to the entire city. I'll do an intro, then play that cassette, baby."

Steve reached out to press it. "No, wait!" Ramfort cried.

Ramfort closed his eyes and slid to a cross-legged seat on the floor. He began taking long meditative breaths. Then he clapped a pair of headphones onto his head, grabbed the mic, and pointed at Steve.

Steve turned to look at Melody who'd slipped into the room, then hit the button. The transmission beamed out all over the city. They finally had the ear of every citizen in Edingburg.

"Gooooooooooood Morrrrrrnnnnnnnniiiiiiiiiinnnnnnngg San Fraaaannnnnnsiscoooooo!" Ramfort's fingers flew over the controls. Gunshots and recorded explosions fired over the speakers. "I am your Jocker of Discs, RamFORT! Here to let YOU know about the coming shitstorm.

"So unless you're mildly deaf or a diligent Tuber making fake walls even taller, you've probably noticed there's been a couple explosions going on around the city—and not just in Edingburg. Nope! But the big boom was at the Edingburg City Hall building. And why? Because the IRA is alive and well, that's why. I should know; I'm part of the movement.

"Oh, I can feel your reaction through the wires right meow. There's a rebel in our midst? Say it ain't so.

"Hey now, hey now, hey now. Don't worry your pretty little heads. I'm not going to fart on your babies or anything. Oh, I can hear it now." His voice went super deep: "It's those godforsaken terrorists again." His voice went to a high-pitched old woman: "Emril! I'm scaaaared. If they blow up the world then I can't update my status online." His voice went low again: "Little terrorist whippersnappers need to quit hee-hawin' around. Go get a goddern job like me and my pappy did." His voice went high: "Oh, so cute, you're whole family never came up with the balls to apply for the City Guard." Voice low: "Now that's enough neighin' from you, Margret. Pffftt. Woman couldn't even get in the Inner Circle and she gives me this sass."

Ramfort's voice went back to normal: "No, no, no, no, no, no.

Look, Emril … Margaret, just take a breath. I've gotta talk to the Phoenix Cyclers now.

"Hey, guys. Yeah, you, the 21-year-old with the gun and the crap in your pants. Is that rag on you red? Because if it is, you're totally screwed. Got some updates for ya. Colonel Bradshaw's dead. Confirmation numbers on that is 29473-39. So be looking at your sergeants. And when your sergeant's eyes grow big, you'll know it's the truth. And if you're a pledge or private I hear you transferring to another corporation isn't really possible. And if you're stationed within those brand new walls surrounding Edingburg, you know exactly how you're about to get fired.

"But I don't want to simply be the bearer of bad news guys; I want to give you a solution. The solution is to join the BEAUTIFUL IRA. But who are we? Are we really terrorists?

"I don't blame you for asking. We've been painted as the boogeyman for a long time meow. So what we've got here today is something special. Something that we can show that proves we are indeed more than a bunch of fanatics."

Ramfort closed his eyes. "Please. Listen to this message. It's from a person who has been the voice of our cause many times. He's about to explain why we go to such great lengths to do such peculiar things. People of Edingburg, this is our message unto you. We hope you dig it."

He pointed at Steve, who looked at Melody. She gave him a faint nod. Steve slid in the cassette, closed it shut, and pushed the white casing closed with a blood-stained fingerprint. The cassette's teeth began to turn.

A crackle. Melody brushed Steve's hand, and he took hers in his own. Then a voice spoke out over the whole of the city:[1]

"We don't want to become your emperor. That's not our business. We don't want to rule or conquer anyone. We should like to help everyone, if possible. Edingburg, guardsmen … the Inner Circle … Tubers.

"We all want to help one another. Human beings are like that. We want to live by each other's happiness—not by each other's misery. We don't want to hate and despise one another. In this world there is room for everyone. And the good earth is rich and can provide for everyone. Life can be free and beautiful, but we have lost the way.

"Greed has poisoned men's souls, has barricaded the world with hate, has goose-stepped us into misery and bloodshed. Machinery that gives abundance has left us in want. Our knowledge has made us cynical. Our cleverness, hard and unkind. We think too much and feel too little. More than machinery we need humanity. More than cleverness we need kindness and gentleness. Without these qualities, life will be violent and all will be lost …

"The cloud and the radio have brought us closer together. The very nature of these inventions cries out for the goodness in men, cries out for universal brotherhood, for the unity of us all. Even now my voice is reaching millions throughout the city—millions of despairing men, women, and little children—victims of a system that makes men torture

---

[1] This speech is adapted from Charlie Chaplin's speech in *The Great Dictator*. *The Great Dictator*, directed by Charlie Chaplin. Charles Chaplin Productions, 1940. Adapted with the permission of his estate.

and imprison innocent people.

"To those who can hear me, I say: do not despair. The misery that is now upon us is but the passing of greed—the bitterness of men who fear the way of human progress. The hate of men will pass, and dictators die, and the power they took from the people will return to the people. And so long as men die, liberty will never perish …

"Cyclers! Don't give yourselves to brutes, men who despise you, enslave you, who regiment your lives, tell you what to do, what to think and what to feel! Who drill you, starve you, treat you like cattle, use you as cannon fodder. Don't give yourselves to these unnatural men, machine men with machine minds and machine hearts! You are not machines! You are not cattle! You are men! You have the love of humanity in your hearts! You don't hate! Only the unloved hate, the unloved and the unnatural! Cyclers! Don't fight for slavery! Fight for liberty!

"In the 17th Chapter of Saint Luke it is written: 'the Kingdom of God is within man.' Not one man nor a group of men, but in all men! In you! You the people have the power, the power to create a better world. The power to create happiness! You the people have the power to make this life free and beautiful, to make this life a wonderful adventure.

"So in the name of humanity, let us use that power. Let us all unite. Let us fight for a new world—a decent world that will give men a chance to work—that will give youth a future and old age a security. By the promise of these things, through mangling their very definitions, brutes have risen to power. But they lie! They do not fulfill that promise. They never will!

"Dictators free themselves, but they enslave the people! Now let us fight to fulfill that promise! Let us fight to free the world, to do away with these walls, to do away with greed, with hate and intolerance. Let us fight for a world of reason, a world where science and progress will lead to all humankind's happiness. San Francisco! In the name of humanity, let us all unite!"

The tape came to an end.

Ramfort clicked his mic on. "Cyclers. We've barricaded ourselves into the radio station on Portero Hill. We're surrounded by hundreds of the Ghost Foxes who've gotten it into their minds to eliminate us. Now is the time to for you to make your decision. We've already made ours. Join us. Come to the station. Liberate us and become part of something truly great."

Ramfort clicked off the golden mic and rubbed his head. He stood up; the devices slid off him and clanked onto the floor.

A megaphone clicked on outside the station. "It appears your 15 minutes of fame have come to an end. Now it's time to pay the bill."

Ramfort left the radio room and walked up to the broken window in the next room. Hundreds more Blue Cyclers had arrived. Standing at the front of this army was the General.

"If any of you in there fire even a single round from my station, the whole fucking building will immediately be wiped from existence!" the General shouted through his megaphone. "You got me?!"

"Shit," Yoden said.

"Ha! Yeah, right!" Ramfort shouted. "You shoot this place up and you lose your ability to broadcast your big war show!" He laughed. "I mean, man! The rumors alone that will come from complete radio silence after that doozy! Won't look good! Some people might think you're losing control, Private!"

A tooth-filled grin filled the General's face. "So you tricked some Reds to join you in there, huh? How many left?" The General looked around, counting the bodies of the Red cyclers who had charged the station. "You had a platoon, so. You've got 20–30 alive in there. Even less uninjured.

"I'll tell you what. Seeing how this Phoenix Cycle class is dropping dead at a higher than normal rate, I'll be needing a couple more privates to join my ranks. I'll accept the first four kids who walk out after everyone else in there is dead. And if I don't see anyone coming out in three minutes, you're *all* dead!"

The General turned to the crowd of Blues. "Who here's got some balls?!" The Blue cyclers roared. "Then fucking prove it! I want 40 volunteers. Forty hungry pledges who want to prove their mettle by charging this fucking station and killing every little terrorist bastard that's holed themselves up in my goddamn radio station! Now form up!"

A trickle of Blues ran forward and lined up in front of the General, rifles by their side. The General walked around the lines. He put down the megaphone, but his voice boomed just as loudly as it had before. "Good! You few are going to do very well in the City Guard. Drop your rifles to the ground!" The volunteers did so. "Now who here has a pistol!"

"Sir!" a guardsman shouted. "None of the pledges were fitted with pistols, sir!"

The General marched up to the guardsman and screamed in his face. "I did not fucking ask you what you did or did not give them! I asked them what they have!"

One of the volunteers held up a pistol. The General marched over. "How did you get this pistol, pledge!"

"Sir, I took it off a Hell on Wheels officer, sir!"

"Did you kill him?"

"Sir, I did, sir!"

"That's fucking beautiful, son! Do you have your ax!"

"Sir, yes sir!"

"Have you used it!"

"Sir, yes sir!"

"Goddamn it, son. You are stupendous. Most pledges don't have the stomach for such an honest tool!"

The General grabbed the cycler and brought him to the front of the ranks. Steve recognized him through his hole in the wall. It was Ryan.

"What's your name, son!"

"Sir, Ryan Flonders, sir!"

"This is your new squad leader!" the General yelled at the volunteers. "Guardsmen! Assure these volunteers have an ax and a pistol!"

Guardsmen rushed through the lines, loading them up.

"This is a siege, gentlemen!" the General shouted. "Not some bullshit ranged battle you look at through your gun-sights! This is the good shit! It's close quarters! It's personal! It's a fight won by passion and a strong will to survive!"

The General snapped at a guardsman and pointed to his M79, a stubby single-shot grenade launcher. The guardsman ran over, placed a single explosive round into the chamber, swung it shut, and handed it to the General. The General jammed the M79 into Ryan's chest. "Give our guests a welcoming present." Ryan looked over the gun's wide and short barrel, at its painted orange tiger-striped camo.

The General marched toward the station. "What's it gonna be? Are a few of you going to walk out of my radio station or are these kids going to have to run in?"

Steve watched a wide-eyed Yoden shivering in the corner of the radio room. Steve walked up and grabbed Yoden's rifle. Yoden surrendered it willingly. "I wasn't gonna," he said. "What are we gonna do, bro?"

A gun roared, Steve whirled around to find a cloud of smoke around the windowsill. Ramfort had blind fired out the window with an ancient eight-barreled pistol, a relic of the Napoleonic age.

"Any of those hit you, Private!" Ramfort shouted at the General.

"One minute left!" the General roared from down below.

Ramfort bent over and furiously began reloading lead balls into the muzzles, muttering under his breath. Melody slapped the gun out of Ramfort's hands. Ramfort looked up at her. "Oh, what the! Don't you get all antiviolence on me now!"

"The rest of the Reds are coming. We need to buy time until they get here." She paced out the radio room and started walking down the stairs.

"One in the noggin and we've got all the time in the world!" Ramfort said.

Steve kicked away Ramfort's ammunition and followed Melody. He found her standing at the end of the first floor's wide hallway, facing the double doors at the entrance.

"You're not going to—"

Melody raised her hand. "Steven," she said quietly. "I want you to know … what I want." She turned to face him. "I want a life where we can be us, fully." She took his hands. "And be proud enough to fully develop into what we can and should be."

Steve smiled at her. "Only if you give me a straight answer as to why you're so obsessed with me."

Her face made feints of amused and embarrassed twitches.

"Fine. Do you remember the memory I shared with you? The one with me sitting on a mountaintop, the one who kissed me and asked for me to be his?"

"Yes."

She shut her green eyes and took his hand. "That man was you. When we were older. From a long time ago. So you see?" Her eyes reopened. "It was you who was a little obsessed with me."

"I'm … what?"

"Steven." She touched his chest, where his Phoenix tattoo was inked under his shirt. "Have you ever wondered why it's a *Phoenix* Cycle? It's not just a name. It's part of a greater understanding that the founders understood but has since been forgotten. When a Phoenix dies, it comes back." She looked up at him. "From the ashes.

"So here I am, and here we are. With a chance to become better than before. And while we've only just met this time around, I know that within you there is the same man who is every bit as willing to seize the opportunity."

"Ten seconds!" echoed through the other side of the heavy metal double doors. Melody let go of his hands. They gazed into one another and shared, for their first time, the warmth that was themselves.

"Someday we will transcend, Steven. And maybe that day will come soon."

She turned, pushed open the doors, and walked into a decaying sunrise of yellow and blue.

Hello Again

Pebbles crunched under Melody's shoes. She walked toward the single black silhouette standing in front of a sea of blue-ragged uniforms and boots. She stopped, her eyes fixed on the five silver stars on each of his wide shoulder blades. She stood in the shadow of his far larger figure, her white skin glowing.

"Well, looky here. Looks like we're finally transitioning from the Ghost of Christmas Past and getting to play with the present one."

"Not transitioning. Adding this time."

"Mmm. The more girls the merrier." His stance became larger, his hands on hips.

"Yes."

"I love it when you just say yes. Nearly as much as that little winter wonderland you've always got snowing somewhere. Speaking of which, have you found my fabulous little gardener? Jombo?"

"Yes."

"Hmm, it must be quite the snow globe right about now." With a wrench like an old jeep transitioning to a nearly forgotten sixth gear, his words next came out sincere. "I would lie in it again."

Melody took a step closer. She removed her pearled pin, and her golden hair cascaded in his shadow. She wrapped her arms around him, pressing her body into his own.

Instinct instructed him to return her embrace. But then he felt his body leaving itself as nerves fired on for the first time in decades. His arms began to shake.

"I am here, Jonathan. I am here. It's okay, what you did to me. But it's not okay what you're doing to yourself. I love you the same and as fully as I always have. And now that I'm here again, there's no more excuse for you to hate yourself. In fact if you still do, you'll only be hurting me again."

The General's arms dropped and dangled at his sides. The wind picked up lightly and spread bits of debris across the potholed parking lot. Blue rags fluttered from the arms of hundreds of confused cyclers watching their soon-to-be leader. Steve watched through the long slit of light between the double doors. He glanced down at his blood band.

The General looked up from Melody hugging him into the clouds. He removed his sunglasses, exposing his closed eyes.

"I guess you win," the General said. "You can still make me feel something. But I'm not what I was when we last met."

Melody felt a pressure on the side of her head. The firing pin of the General's Beretta clicked back.

"I've evolved much past that. I'm not the same man."

He felt her maintain her hug, then take in a long breath.

"And I'm not the woman you proposed to on that beautiful red mountain. So if you want to get to know me, hold still."

Melody pushed her thumb into her pearled pin. The General felt a long prick of a needle slide into the back of his spine. It felt like he was being injected with lava. She stepped back and looked up into his quivering and strained eyes.

"Pain is what's kept you moving," she said. "It made you into you. The finality of her death perpetuated your own sense of the inherent evil within your soul. So over time you came to accept it by making it normal. Laughing at it and practicing it. Instead of becoming better you did the worst thing you could do. You accepted yourself for what you were not in order to numb the pain. And by doing so you settled for this.

"Piece by piece you've been ripping the good in you down. Dissociating it, wrecking it until you finally burned it to inert ash. That I can't forgive. So I have injected you with the very thing you've been poisoning yourself with. Except this—" she held up the pearled pin— "will only bring you pain when you act like this General you insist on being."

She placed the pin back in her hair, then took his nearly paralyzed face in her hands. "Instead of using pain to rip you down, we will use it to bring you back, Jonathan. If you can't do it for yourself, if you can't do it for me, do it for your sons."

She took a step back. They looked at one another. His eyes could hardly move but he could see the lace of her blue dress fluttering in the wind. He did his best not to remember how exactly the same she'd once looked.

A hail of bullets fired. His eyes jerked and focused. The Reds had come. Hundreds of them. The Blues and the City Guard returned fire. His eyes went back to hers.

"I've wired the radio station to blow," she said, then turned back toward the building.

A team of guardsman came running up to the General and

encircled him with their riot shields. "Orders, sir!" said a sergeant.

The General did his best to contain his shaking to within his uniform. His arm trembled upward to the station. "Nobody shoots her. The plan is extract and preserve. Bring your armored convoys up and be a bullet magnet. Keep the fire away from the station as much as possible. Send those volunteers in. Kill who they gotta and extract anyone in there looking important—including that girl! Then have that convoy fall back. Loop the Blues around this lot now and flank these fucking traitors."

"Yes, sir!"

"Double quick! Get the direction of fire off my fucking radio station!"

"Yes, sir!" The sergeant beckoned Ryan and his team. Ryan sprinted over, got his orders from the sergeant, and hurried to the General.

The General looked down at Ryan. "I want a DNA record of who you kill dead in there. For my personal records."

"Yes, sir!" Ryan shouted.

The General grabbed the tiger-striped M-79 with trembling hand and flicked it up. He coughed and wiped black onto his sleeve. "Give your first orders, son,"

Ryan's feet slapped together, his neck snapped straight. "Sir, yes sir!" He looked at his team of 40 cyclers. "Form up! On me!" he shouted. The cyclers bunched up around him in front of the radio station.

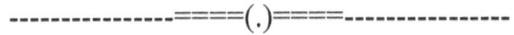

Yoden ran up the stairs to Steve and Ramfort. "What the hell are we going to do!" he cried.

Ramfort looked over at Line. "We've gotta get that crate up here, the one from the train."

They ran downstairs, where the Red cyclers stared at them with their backs pressed against the walls. Ramfort rushed to the crate and started heaving it. Steve and Yoden stopped under the communal stare of the cyclers. Jombo stood silent among them.

Ramfort looked up. "What?"

"What do we do with these?" Jombo asked, gesturing to the cyclers. "They are in danger."

"Well, what do you think?" Ramfort asked. "Collect explosives from the dead guardsmen and set up traps in the hallway."

"But there's too many of them!" a cycler cried.

Ramfort kept pushing at the crate. "Well, maybe with that attitude," he snickered. "Steve! Yoden! Team effort over here! Crate! Stairs! Go!"

"This is bullshit," a cycler yelled. "You brought us here! This is your fault!"

Ramfort turned to the cycler. "Well, yeah! You and I both know you don't have free will!"

Melody slipped through the double doors. Ramfort looked at her. "Oh, thank Mom. You're back. Could you deal with these schmucks?"

Steve hurried up to her. "What did you just do? Why? Why did you have to hug him?" His face went red. "Are you really on my side!"

"What the hell!" a cycler shouted. "You fucking nutjobs are

getting us all killed! Fucking fix this!"

Melody's gaze stayed on Steve. She raised a small detonator. She turned slowly to the cycler. "Leave." She pressed the detonator.

There was an explosion, and a wave of debris ripped in through the room. The cyclers hit the ground. The rear walls of the radio station had been blown apart.

"Out!" Jombo roared at the cyclers.

"Steve! Yoden! CRATE!" Ramfort shouted.

"I'm not an innocent," Melody said. She stepped to Steve and pressed her lips to his. She looked at him with a smile. "Timing."

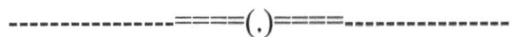

Ryan stood smirking in front of his squad. They were ready. Ryan took a few steps toward the front door of the radio station. He held up the M79, pointing it at the front door.

"Knock, knock!" he shouted. A grenade exploded out of the barrel, shattering the front door.

"Last one in gets a bullet in the back of the head!" Ryan shouted. His squad of volunteers charged forward toward the radio station, ax in one hand, pistol in the other.

Jombo stood in front, protecting the escape hole with a small band of cyclers watching the coming storm of troops flood toward them. "It's too late!" a cycler shouted.

Jombo gripped his axes. "It is through us that peace and tranquility will someday flow into the windows of our homes and be breathed in by the lungs of our people," he said. "And they will know what we are about to learn today."

The first wave of men crashed through the remains of the front door. Guns fired. Explosions rocked the hallway. Men fell, but even more pushed forward into the station.

----------------====(.)====----------------

Steve stood still in the middle of the second floor as thumps and screams rose from below. Ramfort fiddled with the large metal crate. Yoden gripped his rifle, staring at the door of the radio room they'd shut themselves into.

"Just give up!" Line shouted, struggling against the ropes securing him to his chair.

Ramfort unlocked the metal crate. Steam flowed out of the crate's edges as he opened it. He stuffed a red rag into the crate and jumped backward.

"You're going to get us all killed!" Line shouted.

Ramfort walked over to Line and began untying him.

"The hell are you doing!" Yoden yelled.

Ramfort threw rope from Line's chair at Yoden and Steve. "Tie yourselves up!" He dug in his coat and brought out blue rags. "Change your colors! We're hostages now!"

"What's in the crate!" Yoden cried. "A machine gun?"

"No, but it'll need one," Ramfort said. "Tie yourself up!"

Ramfort grabbed Line and shoved him into a locker. "This won't work, you fucking nut!" Line shouted. "You're all going to die! You're all branded! There's no getting out of this, you cowards!"

"Shit, bro," Yoden said, gripping his throat.

"Pffft. It's a plus and a minus sign," Ramfort said, hopping on one foot as he took off his shoe. "You've got a minus sign branded in ya, we'll just burn it into a plus."

Line smiled.

"Now put a sock in it," Ramfort said, shoving one of his socks into Line's mouth. "Steve, magic wand and potato. I know you're carrying."

Steve dug them out. Ramfort ran over to a table and quickly fastened two wires to the potato and one to the end of the wand. The table shook from the hell continuing beneath them. Ramfort attached the wires to a grounded metal stick he ripped out of a radio part. He shot volts through each end, the power making the metal sizzle. He took a pair of pliers and picked up the thin and short heated metal stick and raised it to Yoden's throat.

"Whoa, bro!" Yoden cried.

"Get a little sizzle now or a big gash in your chest later."

Banging and shouting shout through the door.

Yoden nodded.

"'Kay, great." Ramfort slammed Yoden's head into the wall and pushed the rod against his throat. Tears formed in Yoden's eyes as smoke rose from his burning skin.

Ramfort inspected the new plus sign branded into Yoden's throat. Then he walked over to Steve, who tore off the goo that Colonel Bradshaw had sprayed on it.

"Do it." Steve closed his eyes.

"You're good," Ramfort said.

Steve opened his eyes and saw Yoden staring at him.

"Whoa, bro. It's already a plus."

Ramfort held up a rope and began tying Steve up. "Down," he said. Steve sat on the floor. Ramfort then tied up Yoden. He took Yoden's rifle and laid it atop the open crate.

"All right, showtime." Ramfort put on Line's sunglasses, sat on the chair Line had been tied up in, and taped himself to the chair. "Everyone play hostage. Sell it!"

"What about your branding, bro!" Yoden shouted.

"Ha! No way am I branding myself! Are you nuts?"

"Why didn't we just leave?" Steve asked.

Ramfort looked at Steve through Line's sunglasses. "Steve! Don't you get it yet? Our entire job is to infiltrate and spread the message. That's *all* we've been doing. Now we've played the cassette. Cool. On to the next thing."

There was a clamor of boots on the stairs. They watched the doorknob wiggle. After a short pause, the knob dislodged and fell to the floor. The end of an ax blade rammed through the hole where the knob had been. The door ripped open.

"Don't shoot!" Yoden yelled.

"Hostages! Hostages!" Ramfort yelled. "We're hostages!"

"We're with Ghost Fox!" Yoden shouted.

A gang of Blues ran inside, axes drawn.

"Halt!" The Blue cyclers stepped aside. Ryan walked into the doorway.

"Thank fucking Christ you're here, kid," Ramfort said. "Pretty sure those little jobless bastards were just about to make sweet love to that weird kid over there," he added, his eyes shifting to Yoden.

"Identify yourself!" Ryan yelled.

"Who am I? The fudge? I'm Line, kid. The host of the obligatory morning announcements."

"You don't sound like Line."

"That's a voice I do, kid. It ain't me."

"Then do the voice!" Ryan yelled, yanking Ramfort's head back by his hair.

"The frack do I look like to you, huh?! Some fudgin' Edingburg rat?! Look at me! You think I got these fudging sunglasses in Edingburg?!"

Ryan stood straight. "And who the hell are these kids?" Ryan looked at Steve and Yoden and his eyes widened. "The hell! Yoden?! Steve?!"

"We're hostages, bro!" Yoden shouted.

Ramfort glared at Yoden. "Yeah, that's Yoden, I think. But I don't know who the fudge Steve is."

"That's fucking Steve."

"Nah, that's like Dave or something."

"Bro, I'm on Blue team, bro!" Yoden cried. "C'mon! I got branded, see!"

"We grabbed these little shiznits early in the liquidation phase of Edingburg," Ramfort said. "They were supposed to protect us from any crap that might go down. But look at how that went!" Ramfort glared at Yoden to shut up.

"Why wouldn't you just use real guardsmen?" Ryan asked, leaning down toward Ramfort again. "This place was under their direct control?"

Ramfort looked up at him over his sunglasses. "You caught me, kid. I wanted to do an interview of some kids—in the battle, you know. I mean, think about it. The ratings I'd get. Forget about it. Hell, I've got Steve's girlfriend right over there in the corner." A pledge dragged her chair into the room. "Ohhh shit," Ryan gasped. "Looking good, Leslie."

Ryan stood straight, looking down at Steve and Yoden. "Come on, bro," Yoden whimpered. "We're friends."

Ryan stared at Steve's angry face. "Makes sense. Scoop up a live exclusive that no other reporter could ever get. Little lost love angle. I like it. Cut 'em loose!"

Just then a person stood up from the open crate. Everyone froze, unsure of what the hell was going on. Steve stared at the young man dressed in rags looking back at the crowd with an unassuming gaze. But what was even stranger to Steve is that the man looked exactly like him.

The man in the box picked up the rifle that Ramfort had placed at the edge of the crate. Shouts erupted throughout the room. Ryan raised his arm and fired his pistol into the man's chest. Steve's doppelganger looked up in surprise, then fell back into the box.

"Holy shit!" Yoden yelled.

Ryan looked into the box. He turned to Steve, then back to the box. Then to Steve again. "The fuck," he murmured.

A guardsman ran up the stairs. "The fuck is taking so long?! Let's move!"

Ryan pointed to the crate. "We're taking this body with us. The General will want to see it."

Rifle fire cracked outside the station. "Shit! Looks like all those defecting Reds are showing up now!" a Blue cycler by the window shouted. "We're outnumbered out there!"

"That's it! This operation's over!" the guardsman yelled. "Extract and double back! NOW!" He cut Leslie free from the chair. "Burn this shithole down! We can't let this place fall to the reds again."

Ryan heaved the body out of the crate. "Let's go!" the guard shouted. "You—" he pointed at Steve— "drag out that body."

The Blues started running out of the building, chucking explosives into rooms as they went. Ramfort, Yoden, and Steve were rushed down the stairs. "Keep that one!" the guardsman yelled, pointing to a bloodied Jombo. "He's the General's gardener or some shit. He'll want to see him."

The guard and Ramfort were the last out. The guard looked over Ramfort, whose sunglasses had fallen off. "Wait, you're not fucking Line."

Ramfort raised his eyebrow. A blade slid out from beneath his sleeve.

-----------------====(.)====----------------

Steve and Yoden hauled the body into a City Guard APC. A guard ran by and shut the hatch behind them. Yoden crawled up to a side window and caught a glimpse of Ramfort sprinting across the parking lot. The radio station burst into flames.

"Holy shit, that was a close one!" Yoden said. His laughs turned to silent tears, and hushed sniffles. "We made it! We actually made it! We're in!"

Steve stared at his dead body on the floor.

Rebel Radio

FM #97.9

Gooooooood mooorrrnninnng, San Francisco! The new one ... I am your brother at arms, Ramfort. Back by popular demand!

I'd like to thank all you beautiful people out there who've set up antennas and even receivers around Edingburg, boosting our signal to nearly every part of the city. Thanks for sharing. We love you too.

Now to it. It's only been a day since we last spoke, but sweet Mary has a lot gone on.

Firstly, the Inner Circle's mission of making Edingburg their kinda pretty has come to a less than photogenic end. However, to the General's dismay, turns out not everyone decided to play for keeps. After hearing our little broadcast yesterday, many of the ostensibly doomed Red Team cyclers were inspired to join the IRA. Luckily, in their moment of supreme virtue our super-sexy secret agents were there to take our newest converts out the war zone's back door. They're now safely with us and will be ready to go for Act II.

They're a spirited crew. In fact, our newest boys have made a special request for me to repeat the following: "Hi, Mom!"

A special thanks goes out there to the boys who attacked the radio station during Edingburg's open revolt. Wouldn't be here without you. I'm raising a potato to ya now. You're the real MVPs!

Now for what's next ... pew pew pew buuuuooohhhmmm!

Catch my drift?

Here's the problem, my countrymen. We live in Edingburg. It stinks. It smells and someone else owns the poo. But hey, that's part of being poor. Not owning stuff. So the real raw deal here is what they *do* give us. Yes, I'm talking about those less than shiny tubes and less than organic tube juice we shoot up on so we can go build virtual poo in a world that smells less like poo.

And that kind of poo is the worst poo, my comradios. Because it turns us into poo. So stop it. Don't be poo. Turn it off. Tune out. Drop back into Edingburg and smell the poo.

When you're done taking it all in, please grab your trousers by the crotch and see if you've still got a pair between those legs of yours. Now if you're a lady don't worry about the absence, totally fine. And remember, ladies, Ramfort ain't about those Inner Circle hos, so don't be getting self-conscious on me. Remember, bitches are for petting, not comparing.

Here's the thing, boys and ladies, you don't need to be so self-conscious any more. Nope, you're done with that, because if you're listening to this, then you certainly have a pair. And ladies, you've gotta be a feisty one. Roarrrr, baby.

Well, my big-balled brethren, my classy ladies, this is RamFORT reminding you to keep on swinging until our invaders have finally been spayed and neutered.

Now enjoy an old classic.

A rock version of "Johnny Rebel" began to play.

Inauguration

Gray uniforms stood at attention. Pressed pant lines gleamed in every row under the strong noontime sun. The General stood at the center of the Inner Circle side of the great stadium where the Phoenix Cycle girls had been chosen days earlier. The General gazed over his newest divisions of admitted guardsmen. All of them with blue tags and small Ghost Fox insignia hemmed on their uniform's front.

Steve was standing to the left of Yoden, who stood to the left of Ryan. All three of them stood straight with their hands pressed behind their backs, in the very front row of the Phoenix Cycle graduating class.

The General's voice boomed over the sea of gray uniforms.

"These walls. Your walls. Are the city's lifeline. Without them, nature would have buried our people in ash and dust. But you don't know why." The General rested his arms atop the guardrail in front of him. "You don't know why these walls are so vital to our people's survival. To understand them you must understand nature itself and our relationship with her.

"Nature is our estranged mother. In the past she loved us. She nurtured us. She gave us life. But then she did what she does to all of her children. She set fire to us and pillaged our lives into ash. She tried to reduce us to fertilizer to feed her new beloved.

"And that is Mother Nature. Her love always changing with her cycles. She'll hold you close, then she will pull you away. She supports you and then cuts you down. She is beautiful, she is fickle, she is a loving monster.

"The only way to survive such a woman is to become independent of her love and stronger than her hatred. To stay firm between her bombardments of rage. To maintain your focus when she rips you lower than you ever thought possible. And most importantly, to remember your scars when she turns sweet.

"And that is why—" the General banged the side of the rock wall — "these walls are vital to our survival. They keep us contained and free us from distraction. They ensure our focus. Inside these walls we are given the space we need to listen to ourselves instead of her ill-fated suggestions. These walls allow us to grow to the full capacity of ourselves.

"And that is exactly what you are all doing. Growing. By uprooting the weeds and debris of your past lives, you've cleared the obstacles that blocked your own growth. Through chaos and bloodshed you have allowed yourselves a new life. A life that is now free to grow as nimbly and with as little false modesty as nature herself.

"It is because of these walls, gentlemen, that everything is within your grasp. All you must do now is protect these walls and grasp the opportunities that grow from them."

Lines of guardsmen marched down the rows of the new recruits, holding up long poles with a golden phoenix perched atop, their wings spread.

"To thrive within these walls requires strength," the General continued. "You must become as hard as the twenty feet of solid rock that separates our city from Mother Nature's grand graveyard. Do so and you will thrive."

The lines of guards halted. They jammed the Phoenix poles into holes drilled in the earth, standing them up.

"Form up!" Colonel Yorker shouted from behind the General. The lines of guards jerked right and faced the backs of each line of recruits.

"Our guard has no room for the weak or the complacent," the General said.

"Recruits!" Colonel Yorker shouted. "Abooout face!" Steve, Ryan, Yoden, and thousands of Phoenix Cyclers spun 180 degrees. Steve looked into the piercing blue eyes of the guard in front of him.

"The wealth these walls have created have made possible parasitic behavior, complacency, weakness," the General said. "But understand, the men inside these walls know that such a cancer cannot be allowed to exist. That it must be ripped out before the whole falls."

"Guardsmen, draw!" Yorker barked.

Steve watched the blue-eyed guard's hand snap up to his hip. He gripped his pistol. Its barrel flashed up and aimed between Steve's eyes.

Lines of arms now aimed down range, all pointing to a recruit's head. Their metal barrels shined in the noontime sun.

"Survival is no longer decided by the rage of Mother Nature," the General said. "She has lost her grip on us. So it must be us who carry out the sentencing of life or death."

Steve could feel the sun's warmth bleeding into the fibers of his uniform. Sweat beaded on his forehead.

"And it will be those who live without passion, who seek comfort instead of glory, who must be cut out."

A device drove into the stadium. A huge two-pronged switch protruded from the top with coiled conductors and batteries stacked around it.

Colonel Yorker pointed at the guard standing by the device. The guard cranked down the enormous switch. Electricity poured through its conductors and magnetized the air of the whole stadium.

Steve turned to the sounds of a pained Yoden, who was clutching the brand on his throat.

Yorker waved at the switch operator. The current stopped.

"Recruits! Abooout face!" Yorker shouted.

Steve, Ryan, and Yoden spun in place and looked up at the General, pistols now aiming at the backs of their skulls.

"Your sentencing begins today. Today you as a unit will finally be perfectly polarized. "

Yorker's arm fired up, then punched his chest.

Steve shut his eyes.

Gunshots fired as one, followed by a series of thumps. Steve opened his eyes. He watched Yoden drop to his knees, the back of his head smoking. Yoden's body fell forward, and his face smacked into the earth.

"Recruits, abooout face!" They spun again to face the guardsmen. Steve and Ryan glanced down at Yoden and then at one another.

"Retrieve!" Yorker shouted.

The guard standing behind Yoden holstered his still-smoking gun.

He grabbed Yoden's body by the ankles and dragged the corpse down the row of recruits, leaving a trail of blood after him.

"Fail to reach for greatness and you," the General said, "just like any coward who surrenders to the elements, will be buried under a mound of ash."

A pair of guards heaved up Yoden's body and began to swing it left and right. Steve winced at the blank thud of Yoden's body being dropped into one of the metal caskets they'd all been partially drowned in earlier.

"Hell on Wheels Inc. has gone bankrupt. The recruits it received on application day cannot be trusted due to their mass desertion. We will not allow bad blood in our ranks. So for now, Ghost Fox is the sole corporation who can handle the Inner Circle's and my contracts. Enjoy your monopoly while it lasts."

The guardsmen carted the casket away.

"Guardsmen. Honor!" Colonel Yorker shouted.

The guard in front of Steve grabbed him by the shoulder. As Steve stood frozen, the guard dug into his pocket and brought out a medal. It was shaped like a Phoenix, its talons gripping an ax. The guard pinned it onto Steve's uniform and stepped away.

"Guardsmen of the new Phoenix Cycle class. Turn and stand affront your new master commander and CEO!"

Steve turned around. An eruption of applause jolted him. Hundreds of Inner Circle women were now surrounding the General and Colonel Yorker. All of them wore long red dresses of different cuts and shapes. He recognized many of them as his eyes darted from face to face.

"But if you do REACH!" The General stretched out his gloved hand. "You will grasp the sweetest of fruits bared by these walls."

Rand hovered forward. She held out a cyclamen flower to each recruit in the front row. She stopped in front of Steve and squinted, inspecting his features. Steve's face went still; he did his best to look past her. She floated closer, smiled, and held out a golden cyclamen. "You may hand this to any woman you like. Enjoy, child. You've earned it."

Steve took the flower with stiff fingers. A glass thorn on the flower's stem pricked him.

Rand hovered to Ryan. "You may hand this to any lady you like. Enjoy, child. You've earned it." Ryan took the rose, then slowly turned to Steve.

"New inductees!" Colonel Yorker shouted. "Form twos!" The Phoenix class shuffled into lines of two. Steve and Ryan stood next to one another.

The needlelike column that had taken Steve's girlfriend away from him lit up and began to lower. Cheers broke out from the Inner Circle girls. Hundreds of newly inducted guardsmen roared. Drums and electronic hymns beat into the air. Artillery fire shot out from the Inner Circle and exploded over the enormous stadium, leaving shining clouds of golden smoke.

The needle dropped to Steve and Ryan's feet. A guardsman waved them forward. Rand smiled at Steve as he took his first step onto the needle leading to the Inner Circle.

Steve and Ryan marched forward side by side. Gold flakes fluttered down on them. The lights at the opening of the wall brightened with every step.

Steve looked up at the Inner Circle girls. There she was. Leslie. Her hands clapped wildly, but her face was far more somber. Steve looked over to see Ryan staring at Leslie as well. Ryan glanced over at Steve, who stared back.

All eyes in the stadium watched the boots of the guardsmen marching forward over the Inner Circle's walls until their soles were completely engulfed by a bright blinding light.

Wrapping Up

Lost Cargo:

The wind dissipated. Bullet-ridden buildings cast dotted shadows along the ground. The line of boxes left from Steve and Ramfort's train robbery sat alongside of the train tracks. Quiet beeps quietly pinged up into the air. The LED screens of the boxes flicked on. Their locks unclamped. Dozens of lids slowly slid open.

Wreckage:

The front of the tank's light flickered. The Abrams's insides rumbled. A fist banged upward, through the top escape hatch.

Mind Bend:

A humming Kesey sat cross-legged in a grassy field. Hundreds of longhaired men and women surrounded him, dressed in tie-dyed camouflage. They sat, eyes half closed, humming as one. Streams of gold floated up from them and pooled together into a ball of light above them.

New Leadership:

"Goddamn you, Ramfort! What took you?!" Carrie asked.

Ramfort stood in the middle of the rows of long bench tables that had been set up in HQ.

"Had to give a sermon on the radio."

"Two days it's been!" Carrie spread her arms and hugged Ramfort, whose whole being stiffened.

Kleiner came into the room. "Ah. Finally, child. It's been two days withoutcha now."

"Why does this matter so much," Ramfort asked, stretching his neck away from Carrie's prolonged hug.

"Well, we care about ya, child. An'—" Kleiner peered around the empty main room— "Cottard. The child'll make it, but he ain't fit fer nothin' heavy. An' it's seemin' we lost Johnny fer a bit. So—" Kleiner peered around, making sure no one else was present— "guessin' that leaves you to be runnin' things round here. Seeing as you're next in line in the family business."

Ramfort's eyes widened. He squeezed Carrie's face cheeks. "Johnny's gone!" Ramfort squeaked.

Blast doors slid open. Hundreds of escaped Phoenix Cyclers from Hell on Wheels Inc. started filing into the room, sacks of potatoes slung under their arms. They sat at the long tables and started on their lunch.

"Wooooooooo!" Ramfort shouted.

The Cyclers stopped piling potatoes out of their sacks and froze.

Ramfort raised his arms over his head. "IT'S TIME TO GET THIS THING GOING!"

This concludes Section C, Row 28, Column 15 of the Phoenix Cycle.

Journal Entry #248

We are all rays born from the same sun. We all shine bright, our energy derived from the same source. Our brightness is our unity, for it is our source of being, but it is also our tragedy.

The light within us illuminates what is in front of us. The light lets us see our world; it lets us see each other. It lets us see our fellow man. Our eyes open, not only to our brother's happiness, but also his hardships, and by seeing them we become aware of them.

From awareness we are given the chance to care for and even love one another. And by delving into love we become unified in a far more moving manner. But from this form of unification comes questions. Questions that bring pain to us all. Questions that make us want—need—to understand each other. But to understand our brothers requires answers ... answers to who we are ourselves.

The question of who we are must be asked and it must be answered in order for us to truly understand one another—because, remember, we are all from the same sun, and therefore we are all one from the same source. So it is impossible not to know your brother while at the same time not to know yourself.

To answer this question, we look inward. Though our light gives us the energy to ask, it also makes us powerless to find the answer. For when we look within us to see our true selves, we are blinded by the very light that makes us wonder. The same light that makes us who we are.

So we look up. We look up to our parent for the answer, the one who has sentenced us to our current condition. Wondering,

"Maybe if I understood where I come from, maybe if I knew why I was here, I could see—and understand." So we look up. But when we do, our questions are only answered with more bedazzling, shining, blinding, light.

But we still try to see. We still stare into the shining face of impossibility, gazing aimlessly for an answer. And in the end, we only find absurdity.

And that's okay.

Appendix

Speech from *The Great Dictator* by Charles Chaplin:

I'm sorry, but I don't want to be an emperor. That's not my business. I don't want to rule or conquer anyone. I should like to help everyone if possible—Jew, Gentile, black man, white.

We all want to help one another. Human beings are like that. We want to live by each other's happiness—not by each other's misery. We don't want to hate and despise one another. In this world there is room for everyone. And the good earth is rich and can provide for everyone. The way of life can be free and beautiful, but we have lost the way. Greed has poisoned men's souls, has barricaded the world with hate, has goose-stepped us into misery and bloodshed. We have developed speed, but we have shut ourselves in. Machinery that gives abundance has left us in want. Our knowledge has made us cynical. Our cleverness, hard and unkind. We think too much and feel too little. More than machinery we need humanity. More than cleverness we need kindness and gentleness. Without these qualities, life will be violent and all will be lost....

The aeroplane and the radio have brought us closer together. The very nature of these inventions cries out for the goodness in men—cries out for universal brotherhood—for the unity of us all. Even now my voice is reaching millions throughout the world—millions of despairing men, women, and little children—victims of a system that makes men torture and imprison innocent people. To those who can hear me, I say—do not despair. The misery that is now upon us is but the passing of greed—the bitterness of men who fear the way of human progress. The hate of men will pass, and dictators die, and the power they took from the people will return to the people. And so long as men die, liberty will never perish. ...

Soldiers! Don't give yourselves to brutes—men who despise you—enslave you—who regiment your lives—tell you what to do, what to think and what to feel! Who drill you, diet you, treat you like cattle, use you as cannon fodder. Don't give yourselves to these unnatural men—machine men with machine minds and machine hearts! You are not machines! You are not cattle! You are men! You have the love of humanity in your hearts! You don't hate! Only the unloved hate—the unloved and the unnatural!

Soldiers! Don't fight for slavery! Fight for liberty! In the 17th Chapter of St Luke it is written: "the Kingdom of God is within man"—not one man nor a group of men, but in all men! In you! You, the people have the power—the power to create machines. The power to create happiness! You, the people, have the power to make this life free and beautiful, to make this life a wonderful adventure. Then—in the name of democracy—let us use that power—let us all unite. Let us fight for a new world—a decent world that will give men a chance to work—that will give youth a future and old age a security. By the promise of these things, brutes have risen to power. But they lie! They do not fulfill that promise. They never will! Dictators free themselves but they enslave the people! Now let us fight to fulfill that promise! Let us fight to free the world—to do away with national barriers—to do away with greed, with hate and intolerance. Let us fight for a world of reason, a world where science and progress will lead to all men's happiness. Soldiers! in the name of democracy, let us all unite!

Hannah, can you hear me? Wherever you are, look up Hannah! The clouds are lifting, the sun is breaking through. We are coming out of the darkness into the light. We are coming into a new world, a kindlier world, where men will rise above their hate, their greed and brutality. Look up Hannah. The soul of man has been given wings and at last he is beginning to fly. He is flying into the rainbow, into the light of hope, into the future. The glorious future that belongs to you, to me, and to all of us!

Look up Hannah, look up!